LET ME SHOW YOU AN ENDLESS TRAIL OF SUNSETS

LET ME SAVE YOU.

JEFF SOMERS

THE ELECTRIC CHURCH

New York   London

Orbit
Hachette Book Group USA
237 Park Avenue, New York, NY 10017

Orbit is an imprint of Hachette Book Group USA.
The Orbit name and logo are trademarks of
Little, Brown Book Group, Ltd.

The characters and events in this book are fictitious. Any
similarity to real persons, living or dead, is coincidental and
not intended by the author.

ISBN: 978-0-7394-8975-8

Printed in the United States of America

THE ELECTRIC CHURCH

THE CIRCLE OF LIFE IN THE SYSTEM OF FEDERATED NATIONS

01001

"You screwed up, Mr. Cates."

I was on the East Side of Old New York, the original island. A dive, no roof, the worst gin I'd ever had too much of and no familiar faces around me. It was cold, and I felt feverish, sweaty—I felt like shit and I was getting worse with every cup of the dirty liquor I bought with my dwindling yen. I wasn't sure what they made it from—paint thinner was my best guess—but it was terrible.

Immediately, the man on my right and the grizzled, one-eyed woman on my left stood up with their cups and walked away. No one else at the table even looked at me. If I got murdered sitting here they'd just roll me onto the floor and forget about me. I had no people here. It wasn't my part of the city.

I knew the voice, though. I tightened my grip on my own cup and quickly scanned the place without turning my head. The

1

place was packed, just like every other illegal gin joint in New York. It was just the ground floor of a ruined building, all tattered gray concrete and broken rebar, ancient graffiti and bloodstains. Next week it would be abandoned again, dusty and shadowed, and the week after that it would be another bar, serving liquor made from rubber tires or ground glass or some other nightmare. The walls all around ended in a ragged tear, the entire second floor of the building gone, torn away by riots and time and several hundred hover displacements as System Cops hunted people like me through the streets. It was filled with scavenged tables and chairs, a crazy collection of mismatched furniture and unhappy people.

"You *fucked* up, Mr. Cates," the voice emphasized, and a hand fell on my shoulder.

I imagined I could feel the blade right behind me. I'd seen enough barroom executions to know the drill—guy walks up behind you, says something, one hand on your shoulder to get leverage and then a knife in the back, angled up, the victim half-paralyzed and very little blood. It wasn't a bad move, normally—except for the little speech, which was just a waste of advantage. My eyes jumped from a pile of rocks to a pack of slope-shouldered shitkickers milling about the edges of the place to a rusted steel table with two flat metal planks welded to the legs for seats set right against the far wall. It looked sturdy enough.

Heart pounding, I took a deep breath and glanced at the security I could see. I figured it would take them about twenty seconds to get to me. I'd killed people in less time.

The bullshit, it was endless. I hadn't had a very good night and was in no mood to watch it get worse. I didn't move right away—assholes twitched, assholes always thought it was harder to hit a moving target and they thrashed around constantly. I knew better. I wasn't the oldest person in the room for nothing. With his heavy hand on my shoulder, gripping tightly, trying to be intimidating, I took a few seconds to take in my surroundings.

I saw it all—every face, every position, every table, chair, or pile of rubble they were sitting on. I saw the twitchy augmented security—illegal muscles with its own alien IQ layered all over their bodies—making sure no one got crazy. I saw the red-eyed beggars eager to drain the dregs from an abandoned cup. I saw it all and fixed it in my mind, even the Monks. The Monks with their creepy plastic faces and mirrored glasses were always in these places. They were supposed to be immortal—humans who'd signed up to have their brains placed in advanced cyborg bodies, in order to pray for eternity or some such shit, and by the looks of them they believed it. Three of them were working the tables, scanning faces and talking to people about death and sin and forever.

I dismissed them; I'd heard of people messing with the Tin Men and finding out they were dangerous, vague stories of a guy who knew a guy who'd tried to rob a Monk in a dark alley and lost his arm for his trouble, or stories of people going to sleep after a bender and waking up Monked against their will the next morning—there was so much bullshit, you didn't know what to believe, and I didn't have time to figure it out now. I didn't know whether to believe their spiel about "salvation through eternity" either. I figured it was best to just give them a wide berth and hope they never scanned *my* face.

I had the layout fixed in a moment: thirteen tables, approximately three hundred people crowded into the space, one narrow, inconvenient exit guarded by security. Probably a hidden escape-hole for the proprietors, too. The security guys weren't much better than the customers, skillwise. One on one I wouldn't have much trouble with them, but with a crowd and narrow doorways, they'd be trouble enough.

This was why I was still alive. Most people in my line of business, they just blazed away—all muscle and ammo. No research. No patience—they lived and died by their reflexes. Especially if their reflexes were augmented with black-market gene splices.

Me, I was *tired*. I was old school. I liked to use my brain a little.

I shifted to the left just a tick, brought the cup up, and splashed gin into the big guy's eyes, and knew I'd hit the mark from the sudden squeak of surprise. I spun left and his knife flashed into the empty space in front of him. I slapped out my hand and took him by the wrist, firmly, and stood up, rolling his arm behind him as I moved, something popping loudly in his shoulder as he dropped the blade with a clatter onto the floor. I kicked at it and it disappeared, most likely plucked cleanly off the floor as it skidded by some enterprising criminal. From the look of his expensive clothes, my admirer either was rich, worked for someone rich, or was a System Security Force officer. But System Pigs didn't need to hire guys to arrange murders; they just showed up, pinched you, and shot you in the head in some deserted alleyway, usually after emptying your pockets. This guy, from what I remembered when he'd hired me a few days before, didn't talk rich. He was just a middleman who'd come up in the world.

Now *I* had leverage, and I used it to slam him face-first onto the table. No one else sitting around me had moved. I leaned down, smothering him, and chanced a look up. Security was just starting for me, a little slow. Fuckheads. You couldn't find good help these days. I thought, *I could kill this bastard six times before you made it to me, assholes.* Keeping my eyes on security, I put my mouth into his ear.

"You owe me fifteen thousand yen, motherfucker."

He was having a lot of trouble breathing, with my weight on top of him and his arm nearly broken. "You . . . fucked . . . *up* . . ." he gasped.

I twisted his arm a little more, and he finally made some real noise, a strangled cry that dissolved into a gurgling moan. "What was that?"

"They found her . . . hanging from a . . . fire escape . . . goddamn . . . goddammit . . ."

I felt pretty confident that I had this guy under control, so I looked up again. Security was still a few tables away, sauntering toward us, not hurrying. They were used to sodden lumps of shit causing a ruckus. I'd overestimated them, no doubt, and dismissed them from my worries.

"My employer . . ." he stuttered out, "will not . . . be happy . . ."

My sense of outrage turned my vision red for a moment. This asshole owed me fifteen thousand yen, had tried to shiv me in the goddamn *back,* and now he's *complaining* to me? I tightened my grip on his wrist and pushed with all my might, and the bastard finally screamed as a sharp cracking sound rewarded my efforts.

"You lied to me," I hissed. "Or you're incompetent. The subject was not alone. You said nothing about professional protection—moonlighting SSF, a fucking *cop* she looked like, and a lot of goddamn trouble." I twisted his arm again, savagely. "And there was a *child,* you shithead. *In the room.*"

I looked up. Security had split up, coming around the tables from either side, looking to flank me.

Amazingly, the big guy started to shudder, and I realized he was laughing, whether from reaction or shock or some bizarre sense of humor, I didn't know. My eyes swept the table, black and tan and white faces, all more interested in their gin than in my little drama—a drama they'd seen, a drama they'd acted in. Boring stuff.

The big guy had suddenly found his voice, slurry and close to unconscious as it was. "A child?" he gasped. "Who gives a shit, a child? You're hired to eliminate someone, you do it. A child? Fuck, you kill that piece of shit, too."

I wanted to hurt him more, I wanted to make him feel it. I trembled with the urge to do him violence. But I could see, in my peripheral vision, that security had arrived and were sneaking their way around the table, coming at me from the left and right. I let out an explosive breath, released the big guy, and in one practiced motion reached across my body into my coat and came up with a gun in each hand, each pointed at one twitchy musclebound asshole. Security paused, looking at each other across me. No one at the table moved, or even seemed to be paying attention. The big guy looked to have finally passed out.

"We don't give a shit," one of the security guys said with the mushy accent of oft-broken teeth. "Just take it outside."

I nodded. I was civilized. I didn't kill children and I did not shoot men whose only crime was doing their job. Not unless I had to. "I'm leaving. No trouble."

Even shitheads respected you if you played by the rules.

One of them swept an arm toward the door, inviting me to take my shit elsewhere. I was full of terrible gin eating away at my insides, and I was a sweating, unwashed mess. I'd killed someone just a few hours ago, the wrong person, worth exactly zero yen to me, and the mark I *had* been hired to kill, and the kid, would both likely be dead tomorrow when the contract went out to someone else, some other Gunner with less scruple. Some kid who had never known anything but the System, nothing but a unified world and the Joint Council that ran it. And the cops—the Crushers who walked the streets and kept order, more or less, and the officers, the System Pigs, who cracked heads and shook us all down, who'd grown rich off us like fucking bedbugs sucking for all they were worth. Someone who'd never known anything better was possible.

I took one step backward, slowly, bringing my arms in and holding both guns ready just in case. As if movement had triggered something, a sudden roar filled the air, and I froze.

"Hover displacement!" someone shouted.

"Pigs!" someone else added helpfully, and the whole place was chaos. Everyone leaped up and made for the exit, the fucking morons. I was forgotten. I found myself standing there with guns drawn while everyone in the place pushed past me. For a moment I was frozen in shock, but when the cops kicked on the floods and the whole space filled with harsh, white light, I found my legs. I moved against the current and rolled under one of the tables.

This sort of shit usually didn't happen—the illegal bars were so common, and the Crushers liked making a little extra money in bribes from what they saw as a victimless crime. When enough was enough and time came to shut things down, everyone knew it was happening and the cops ended up raiding an empty place, confiscating a lot of stale booze, and smashing up some burned-out still; meanwhile a new place opened up in some other toothless shell of a building. The circle of life in the System of Federated Nations.

A hover meant officers, real police. This was a step up, this meant someone in the place was wanted. The Crushers in their sloppy uniforms you knew by name, they cracked some heads but were generally all right, just doing their job—and maybe,

7

on good days, you could even admit they did a necessary job, keeping us jobless wonders from tearing each other apart. But the System Pigs, they were a step up, the elite. They were more dangerous, greedier, and they didn't crack heads. They put bullets in them.

I reholstered the automatics and drew my lucky gun, made by the Roon Corporation out in California, a modified model 87a (illegal because it was fully automatic, unregistered, and lacking DNA scan locks). Expensive, with action like silk. The exit, as expected, was blocked by the crush of assholes trying to escape. In the bright light of the hover, they were crisp, sharply defined, a mass of desperation. I racked a bullet into the chamber and ran a dry tongue along my lips, my stomach feeling like it was on fire, my head aching. I was *old*. I'd been old for years.

"Attention!" came the booming metallic voice of the hover's PA. "This is Captain Jack Hallier of the System Security Force! Stand still and submit to authorized scanning and identification procedure!"

That was formal bullshit. The SSF didn't give a shit if you submitted or not. They usually preferred you didn't. The Crushers you could reason with, strike a deal—they were human, even if they carried a badge. The Pigs, though—fuck, they *weren't* human.

On cue, I saw a dozen boots drop from above and hit the floor, swirling, headache-inducing patterns on them, Stormers in Obfuscation Kit. No proper SSF raid happened without Stormers in their ObFu, practically invisible when they stood still. From my temporary shelter I looked around, and did a double take: To my left, hiding under their own table, were three Monks. They each turned to look at me with their terrible mask faces, and then looked away. I blinked, twisted around, and began crawling away from the exit, toward the far wall, hands and knees, old-fashioned. Behind me, bullets started flying.

I just kept crawling. I'd killed twenty-six people. I wasn't going to allow myself to be picked up in some random grab. When I made it to the wall I didn't waste time: I jumped up, climbed up on the table I'd spied earlier, and threw myself over the wall, landing hard on the other side, my head bouncing on the broken pavement. Lying in the damp shadows, head ringing, I elected to just stay where I was for a moment. Above me, I could see the ass end of the SSF hover floating. In a way, it was beautiful, a rectangle of metal, blurred by displacement, lights blasting through the evening, Stormer tether lines snaking out of it like tentacles, all of it like some horrible, bloated insect.

A pulse of panic shot through me and I blinked, my head clearing. I forced myself up, checked my weapon, and limped for the deepest shadows a few steps away, a painful hitch in my back making me limp a little. Everything in this area of Old New York was a ruin, left over from the Unification Riots decades ago. It was all shadows and sharp edges.

Hidden for a moment, I caught my breath and thought.

The gunfire increased, and I watched more Stormers snake to the ground as a determined contingent of my fellow scum broke out of the bar and took cover behind more ruins. It was all lit up for me perfectly, fifty feet away, clear as day. There were always hardasses who thought they could blast their way out of anything—kids, youngsters who didn't know shit except how to pull a trigger and so thought they were all grown up, who thought that because they'd outrun some Crusher on his rounds they knew cops. You didn't know cops until a couple of System Pigs kicked your ass for fun.

I let my eyes adjust and scanned the street outside the bar, away from all the commotion. At first everything seemed still and empty—usually New York was a press of humanity sloughing this way and that in search of something to do, something to steal, anything, but an SSF hover cleared the streets admirably, and the area was deserted, and probably was for blocks around. But a second or third look revealed a glow of a cigarette here, the outline of a shoulder there—SSF officers, waiting, letting the Stormers soften the place up. These cops didn't fear the hardcases—they stood out there just waiting for someone like me to scamper right toward them, get gunned down or—worse—arrested, if they were bored and feeling cruel. There were a couple of Crushers I didn't mind, but there wasn't a single System Pig I'd hesitate to kill, if I thought it wouldn't bring the whole SSF down on me. Watching the faint movements of the Pigs hiding in the darkness across from me, I realized I was going to have to sit tight for a while. There was no way to get away from the area with them on the lookout.

The noise muffled by distance, I calmed myself. I'd heard a story, once, about Cainnic Orel, who'd been a legendary Gunner (he'd founded the Dúnmharú, his own personal Murder Incorporated), with more than fifty confirmed contract kills and not one arrest. I'd heard that he'd once hired a Techie to disconnect a target's security system, slipped in and hidden in a closet, and then had the Techie reconnect the security, complete with motion detectors, just so the subject wouldn't notice anything strange when he came home. So Orel had stood stock-still for forty-eight hours, waiting. And when the subject came home and deactivated the security system, Orel had stepped out, shot him in the head, and walked away like nothing had happened.

From what I heard, Orel had retired rich. Standing in the shadows, I knew I'd never be rich, because five minutes into my vigil I was aching all over and going batshit.

There was a small explosion somewhere nearby; the hardcases were putting up a good show, and it sounded like a few of them had some serious firepower, too. That would slow down the Pigs, but not for long. The Pigs were funded by the System, and had everything. I'd had to work long and hard to get a Roon, the best handgun in the world. The SSF issued them like candy.

I froze, stopping myself from leaning forward in the nick of time. Casually, as if nothing were happening, the three Monks emerged from the bar and walked past the Stormers. They didn't hurry. Bullets flying everywhere, and they didn't seem to care. I watched them in fascination as they moved blithely away from the chaos, and the cops didn't pay them any attention. They were a protected religion, of course, and from what I'd heard the Electric Church had a lot of pull these days, maybe enough to cause even the SSF trouble. So the Pigs were playing it safe.

I was about to look back across the way to see if the perimeter cops had shifted, when someone broke from the bar and made a mad dash behind the hardcases into the night. By sheer dumb luck, he made it — no one shot him, and as he sped out of the light, his path intersecting the Monks', it looked like none of the Stormers had picked him up. I thought he was just going to make it, an amazing escape, but as he ran near the Monks, I could have sworn the Monk nearest him moved — twitched, shrugged, *something* — and the runner suddenly crumpled to the ground. The Monks just kept walking, and were swallowed up by the night. He stayed where he was.

I shook my head. It was far away, and the glare of the floods hurt my vision. He'd probably been nailed by a random bullet, or a sniper. I scanned the black rooftops of the empty buildings. Snipers, too. Whoever they were here for was in for a world of trouble.

I thought of Canny Orel, and my feet ached even more.

"Got any flatfoots I can have?"

The voice was flat and monotone, and too loud; not someone hiding. I moved my eyes, imagining the noise they made, and there just a few feet away was SSF, a tall, blond officer, cigarette dangling from a thin-lipped, small mouth. He was dressed expensively, dark suit and heavy overcoat. A linkup bud shone in one ear.

I stared. Moving my eyes seemed like a bad idea. I had little doubt that if this cocksucker saw me, he'd shoot first and think about it much, much later, with a mild sort of curiosity about who he'd killed.

Moments later, two Crushers jogged over to him. They were older than him, and breathless, two beat cops with sidearms, in uniform, one tall and bald and unshaven, the other shorter and stockier, his white hair standing up in a shock on his head. They both looked sweaty and tired. I could see the officer's eyes as he stared at them. They danced, moving this way and that, unsteady, like fluttering wings. It was creepy as hell.

"Jones and Terrell, Captain," the tall one said as crisply as he could.

"Great," the System Pig drawled, cigarette wagging up and down. "You two look like fucking geniuses. Okay, geniuses, here's the deal: We got a fucking cop-killer in here somewhere. Earlier today Colonel Janet Hense, working undercover, was popped over in Harlem. Working Sec on a VIP." He paused to remove his cigarette. "We don't think the shithead knew he was popping a cop, but who gives a fuck? We're going to pull his arms off and beat him with them, okay?"

The two Crushers shifted their weight uneasily. "Absolutely, sir," the shorter one said.

"Don't talk, numbnuts," the captain said, his voice betraying no emotion at all. "We don't actually know who we're looking for. We don't have an ID, okay? We have a good tip that the shithead was in this bar. We have a description. Listen carefully, geniuses, because I will not repeat it."

The good captain went on to describe *me*. Pretty accurately, too. The woman flashed through my mind: Hanging upside down from the ancient fire escape, guns still clutched in her hands. I wanted to move so badly I thought about just shooting the three of them where they stood and rushing out into the night, screaming. It wouldn't make my situation any worse; if I got IDed as a cop-killer, I might as well shoot myself, because it would be less painful than what the SSF would have ready for me.

"Got that?" the captain said. "Now, the only reason we're using you assholes is because we got a crowd in there, and some of them are obviously unhappy that their liberty is being curtailed. Fuck 'em. But we need bodies to manage them, and I've got a temporary manpower shortage—every day there are more of these rats breeding in the streets. I know you guys who walk a beat have trouble with complex thoughts, so I'll make it simple for you: Get your ass into that space and practice some crowd control. Think you idiots can handle that?"

The Crushers looked glum, because this raid was costing them at least three or four more days of steady bribery. Plus it was always fun when the System Pigs showed up in their fancy clothes and their fucking hovers and kicked you in the balls for a few hours. They saluted and headed off, the night filled with noise, light, and the constant thick pressure of displacement. A second later there was a loud crash and a sudden flare of light as something exploded inside the still-crowded bar. The SSF officer just stood there, smoking, hands in pockets. There were a hundred people not far away who wouldn't mind putting one in his ear, but he didn't look worried. And why should he? The System Pigs were very good at what they did, carefully recruited and trained to an amazing level of skill. Everyone was afraid of the System Pigs — because it was damned hard to beat them, and if you did, you had the whole SSF on your ass. I glanced up at the hover, blurry and roaring, and then back at the captain. This was the hammer, coming down.

I was straining so hard to remain still my muscles were twitching. I was no Canny Orel; I wasn't going to retire rich and live to a ripe old age. I was twenty-six and I'd already lived too long and I couldn't stand still for half an hour much less two fucking days. When the SSF officer finally turned away, flicking his cigarette into the air in a glowing arc, I almost sagged with relief. I had to get moving. I couldn't hide forever, and soon enough they'd have the Crushers doing sweeps of the area on foot, and the hover's heat sweeps scanning the ground. I could handle a couple of Crushers; I didn't think I could handle an entire brigade of them, and I didn't know if I could handle an officer, much less the ten or twelve of them I counted in the area. I'd seen the System Pigs in action. They were smart, and they were fast, and they were armed to the goddamn teeth — and no one was going to come after *them* if they killed *me*.

I eyed the darkness around me. The System Pigs had an eye on the perimeter, obviously, and I didn't know of any Safe Rooms or friends in the area. To my right, there was the bright glow of the hover, which had shifted position to illuminate the patch of ruined street outside the bar, where an intensifying firefight between cops—Stormers in their ObFu and the poor Crushers in their ill-fitting uniforms, clearly thinking they didn't get paid enough for this shit—and the shrinking number of hardcases continued, the hardcases ensconced behind two ancient, rusting vehicles on their sides, internal combustion tech, useless except for emergency shelter. The Crushers might as well have been throwing stones at the steel barricades, but the Stormers had high-powered rifles, and were having more success.

I looked up, examining the low and ragged wall I'd just pulled myself over. I felt tired just looking at it, but it was my best shot at this point. The System Cops had almost certainly done a heat-signature scan on the interior of the bar and determined we were all on the run. Running out into the night wasn't going to get me anywhere. It was back over the wall for me.

I took one last look around, squinting into the blackness around me. There was no way to tell whether some pair of night-visioned eyes was watching the wall, so it was best to just choose my moment by instinct and make my leap. I would have to make it over quietly and smoothly. If I ended up hooked on top of the wall flopping about like a dead fish, I'd just be target practice. The cops were making a statement here: An SSF officer had been killed, and the person responsible was going to be killed in turn, and any place that had given him shelter during the day was going to be leveled to the ground. I either got away completely unnoticed, or I was a dead man—if not today, then tomorrow.

I eyed the top of the wall, took a deep breath, and launched myself at it. *Keep moving, keep moving.* I tore my hands up on the sharp stone and metal, pain slicing up my arms and lodging in my brain. I heaved with everything I had and pulled myself up, rolling over onto my back. For a second I stared up at the night sky over Old New York, a crisscross of light chains, hovers moving in complex patterns, freight and rich people.

Keep moving, keep moving . . .

I rolled off the wall and landed softly but awkwardly back inside, instantly crouching and touching the floor with my bloodied hands. I stayed there, trying not to breathe, and peered around the place, listening for any sign that I'd been noticed. There was no change in the cacophony outside, but I didn't relax, because strolling with her back to me was a Crusher.

Generally, you only feared the Crushers when they came in force; they weren't the officers, the System Pigs, they were just beat cops with peashooters. I thought of them as just like me, just citizens of the System of Federated Nations who hadn't had many choices and who'd made what seemed like the best of a bad lot. I only fucked with the Crushers if they fucked with me.

This one was obviously addicted to getting black market genetic augments. She had skinny, normal-looking legs and a skeletal face that hinted at someone who didn't eat well, or often. In between the two was a broad, fantastically muscled abdomen and chest and two arms that rippled with every gesture. You could get an awful lot done to you—emphasis on *awful*—by black market surgeons these days, like night-vision eyes or a complete nerve-burn that inured you to pain. The lab-grown muscles were big business. They weren't strong muscles, and they didn't last forever—just like all the black market augments, they were inferior tech performed by half-tight asshats—but for a while they looked good, and for some suckers that was all that mattered. Looking at her profile again I figured this one had been diverting her grocery budget to augments for a long time now.

I froze and watched from my shadowed position at the base of the wall. I scanned the room again. No one ever opened one of these illegal places without an exfiltration plan, so I was counting on there being a secret way out. The System Pigs were well-trained—we were all terrified of them for a reason—and well-equipped, but they were arrogant bastards, too. I didn't think it would have occurred to Blondie out there that one of us *rats* might actually have managed to slip down a hole and disappear. I studied the bar area, from which the owners had run the place. This was too obvious, of course, because even a dim Crusher like my Lady Hulk here would think to check it out for ratholes. Still, it would have to be a place you could easily get to from the bar, a spot you could roll into within seconds, before any System Pigs showed up with enough on the ball to take notice of such things. My eyes traced the shadows and cracks on the walls, on the floor, and I made out a curiously squared set of cracks in the floor near the makeshift bar.

I took a slow, deep breath, gritty and damp, and fixed the spot in my mind. My heart was pounding and my stomach was in revolt; I regretted every sip of the oily booze they'd been serving. I glanced at the Crusher, walking slowly around the room; it was surprising, sometimes, how long you could hide in plain sight if you kept your head. I was dressed for the shadows, of course—I was a Gunner, we spent half our lives standing in shadowed corners, waiting for someone to walk in through the door and be killed—and the Crusher was bored and obviously not too bright; I figured I could squat there in the dusty shadow of the wall until next week and not be noticed. But I doubted it would just be the Crusher and me for much longer. The Pigs were going to note they hadn't scooped up anyone that looked like me soon enough, and while perhaps not very surprised at this discovery they'd at least do a final sweep of the area before giving up. I had to get out in the next few minutes, while my dimwitted colleagues continued to provide distraction and sound cover.

I considered. I couldn't just toss a chunk of concrete and distract Lady Hulk; with the hollow punching noise of rounds denting metal, the angry shouts and the continuing roar of the hover, she probably wouldn't hear it. I squatted, listening for a second or two, chewing on it, and the bullets gave me a sudden inspiration. I tightened my grip on my Roon and considered Lady Hulk and the noise outside. I thought it very probable that no one outside would notice one more shot fired, and Lady Hulk offered a lot of nonlethal targets on her huge, rippling body. I didn't want to kill her; she was just doing her job. But she was standing between me and the rest of my miserable life, so she was going to have to take a bullet. I tracked her as subtly as I could as she paced, waited for a fresh volley of fire outside, and popped her in one shoulder. She went over like a wet sack and I launched myself at the rathole in the floor.

I hoped fervently that there wasn't a lever or catch that had to be manipulated before the hole would open for you. This was the life: one goddamn thing after another. I hadn't had a peaceful evening in fucking *years*; it was always this constant race from one emergency to another. Thinking that one more emergency might just kill me, I threw myself bodily at the floor just as two gunshots, sounding ridiculously small and harmless —*pop! pop!*— burped behind me.

I didn't have time to think about my bad luck—though bad wasn't even the right word, they'd have to invent a whole new fucking language to describe my luck. The floor split downward as I hit the spot, and I fell into empty space. A split second of panic free fall, and I hit the ground beneath hard, my teeth rattling in my head, my gun knocked from my hand.

My whole body vibrated, a humming sensation. One jittery heartbeat, two jittery heartbeats, I just lay staring up, my body made of stone and damn, it would be nice to just fall asleep, just fuck it all and close my eyes. Take a rest for the first time since I'd been five, the first time since *Unification*, when the world was separate nations instead of just the System.

A surging wave of panic swept it all away, and my body came back online screaming with pain and still vibrating. I sat up and spun around the dark space, searching with shaking hands for my Roon, my fingers closing around it just as the rathole above me flipped downward again, the weakened light of the hover's searchlights lighting me up. I didn't pause to think or aim, I just raised the gun and spat three shots upward. The rathole snapped closed again and I spun and forced myself into a staggering, unhappy sprint down a narrow man-made tunnel. I wasn't in the sewers, which had long been the underground highway for the criminals of Old New York. This was a tunnel built specifically as the escape route for this place. Good work, too, a tight fit but the air felt dry and sealed, the stone floor solid beneath my feet. I'd been in escape tunnels that had felt ready to come down on my head if I sneezed, so I appreciated a competent job.

I tried to pick up my pace. I figured I had an SSF officer on my trail, and the System Pigs weren't like the Crushers they commanded—they weren't easily scared and they weren't stupid. I wasn't going to have much of a lead. As I skidded around the first turn, I heard the rathole slap open again, and the heavy thud of someone dropping down onto the floor. The SSF officer, of course, would not have fallen like a sack of shit onto the floor and been stunned for a count of three. He'd undoubtedly landed gracefully on his feet, gun held firmly

19

in one hand. The System Pigs annoyed me with their smirking perfection: They pushed people like me around, shook us down—it would be okay if they were really trying to enforce the law, but the SSF officers were just as bad as us—worse; they had that badge, and a budget behind them, which meant no one short of Internal Affairs could slow them down.

I knew what was waiting for me if this one caught me: a bullet in the head. There was no due process with them, no rules of law. They could do whatever they liked, so they did. The only question was, would I get a ridiculous speech before the bullet in the head, or not?

I kept running.

The tunnel wasn't very long, of course. After about fifty feet more of twisting and turning, I stumbled to a halt just before a blank wall of earth. I looked up, and there, a few feet above me, was the ass end of a ladder bolted in place. Internally, I swore; there had probably been something nice and convenient to boost up on—an old stool, *something*—that the clever bastards who'd built the place had pulled up after them just in case they were pursued. For a second I stood there hating them with all I had, and then there was a bellow from behind me in the tunnel.

"You made me run!" the System Pig shouted. "I'm going to eat your fucking kidneys, asshole, for making me *run*."

Thinking that my day was improving at a record rate, I stuffed my gun into my pocket, gathered everything I had left, and leaped for the ladder, catching the bottom rung with the tips of one hand's fingers. Grunting through clenched teeth, I pulled until I could get my other hand onto the rung, and then reached for the next, legs dangling and breath whistling in and out of my nose. Arms trembling, I pulled one more time and managed to get one foot onto the bottom rung, pulling the rest of myself up just as two bullets smacked into the wall where I'd just been hanging.

"Mother*fucker*," I heard the SSF officer hiss. I didn't look back, I just kept pulling for my life. The only thing worse than being shot in the back by a System Pig would be getting shot in the *ass*.

I emerged, panting and sweating, into a damp-feeling space, a basement a block away, just outside the perimeter the cops had set up. It was dark, so dark I was blinded for a moment before dim shadows made themselves apparent. I didn't stop to enjoy the view, I crawled out of the hole and pushed myself up, spinning fast to get a look around. I had no idea where I was, but the cop was right behind me and I didn't have time to think up something brilliant. I oriented, squinting, and shot twice at the opening in the floor just to discourage him, and then spun around again, blinking dust and darkness out of my eyes. There were windows, high up and impossible to reach, and vaguely I discerned a stairway leading upward. Everything else was dark, mysterious. I started for the stairs, but at the bottom I paused—where was I running to? What was up there? I'd lived this long because I wasn't some asshole running around blazing away, being stupid. If I was going to live another day I had to hold on to that.

Sweating freely, I jumped on the first step and heard a satisfyingly loud creak. I mimed running up the stairs, bringing one foot and then another down onto the ancient wood. Then I took a step backward, gingerly, and crept slowly back into the shadows, until I felt a wall behind me, slimy and cold. My eyes had adjusted to the murk, and I could pick out the rathole exit in the center of the room. Just as I came to a dead stop, gun up but held close in toward my body, the System Pig's head appeared for a second, then dropped down again, trying to draw nervous fire. I stayed stock-still for a few endless seconds. I was a Gunner, I was a professional, and I was damned if this System Cop *prick* was going to fuck me.

His head reappeared. I felt exposed, and my heart leaped inside my chest. He stared right at me . . . but couldn't see me. He was blinded, just as I'd been. But I could see him. It was the blond Pig from the street, with the dancing eyes. A chill went through me.

He swept the room with his unseeing eyes and then was up and out of the hole, moving fast. Gun up, he whirled around, calm, but in a hurry. I had the drop on him, I *knew* it would be easy to pop him . . . but System Pigs were always tougher to kill than you thought. They always turned out to be luckier than they had right to be. And scraping your living off the streets of Old New York, you lived by one basic rule: Don't fuck with the System Pigs. The Crushers, sure. But the officers, no—too many hotheaded assholes had gone down in flames thinking they could just get the drop on a System Pig and walk away from it.

Wiser men, *older* men, like me, we bided our time. Besides . . . it seemed unfair, to be hiding in the dark, taking a sucker shot. Dishonorable.

He saw the stairs and went for them, dropping at the last second and coming up ready to fire. When nothing happened he didn't hesitate, he sprang up and pounded up the stairs.

Slowly, I let out my breath, and slowly, I drew gritty, moldy air in. The cop's pounding footsteps grew dimmer, and finally faded completely. I waited for a count of fifty, ready to cut the bastard down if he came back down the stairs, then slowly knelt, allowing myself to breathe in little shallow gasps, quiet. I felt the floor with my aching free hand and selected a good-sized hunk of rock, weighing in my hand before flicking it at the stairs. The rock struck the third step up and then thunked down onto the next step. It sounded like an explosion to my ears, but there was no response.

I took a deep breath, my chest shuddering with its force, and the spots in front of my eyes fading. I just breathed for a few seconds, filling my lungs, and then I sprang, rolling myself into a ball and throwing myself toward the rathole, ending up on my back, gun raised, sweeping it left to right. Nothing happened. It was just dust settling and my panting.

I stood up and took the stairs two by two, emerging into another empty shell of a building, nothing but rubble and load-bearing beams, plaster dust and the remnants of a million hasty camps. I could see the city beyond the walls, dark and empty, and a few blocks away the weak light of the slightly more populated downtown, familiar and, for what it was worth, home—a single room that I had all for myself. Not much but at least I didn't share it like most of us, fifteen people at a time, or a room shared in shifts of six or eight hours. It was *mine*.

I considered the possibility that my System Pig was waiting in his own shadows, waiting for me to emerge. I considered my luck up to that point, which had taken an unexpected upturn toward the end—the cop hadn't seen my face. I could pass him in the street tomorrow and he wouldn't know me, and the thought suddenly made me very optimistic. I crept to the shattered opening in the wall that led to the street beyond and poked my head out, looked around, and then stepped into the dim moonlight. I stood for a moment, a perfect target, and a thrill of insane risk whipped through me. I looked up at the jewel-like strings of hover lights far above, so far they were silent and almost static, moving gently, rich people zooming from place to place without ever having to come up against someone like me, a killer, covered in dust and hung over. A man already too old.

But the strange optimism stuck with me as I darted back into the shadows and headed for home, my streets where I knew people, where I knew the Safe Rooms and where I had allies—not many, but better than nothing. I felt lucky. I felt like maybe my fortunes were about to change, and maybe I wouldn't spend the rest of my life being chased by people who wanted to kill me.

I

NO ONE PAID FOR
GRIEVOUS INJURY

01110

—————

"First, they remove the brain."

I wasn't really listening to Nad. I *never* listened to Nad, actually. We were standing in a shadowy doorway on Bleecker—just a doorway, a rectangle of ancient brick melting away to dusty rubble on either side—watching the gray faces flow by, waiting for one in particular so we could kill him. Well, so *I* could kill him. Nad wasn't a Gunner. He wasn't even much of a criminal; he was possibly the worst pickpocket that had ever lived, and over the years had been pinched by the Pigs so often, with the mandatory accompanying beatings, that he'd started to go a little crazy in his middle age. He was all about conspiracy theories, always telling anyone who'd listen about the sinister forces that ruled the world. For me, it was a lot simpler: Hostile assholes with badges ruled the world, case closed.

Nad was pretty much useless, but I felt sorry for him. I paid him a pittance to work lookout for me on these shithole jobs I picked up, murdering small-fry criminals who'd overstepped their bounds or owed too much yen for too long. Of course, he was pretty useless as a lookout, too.

"You can't digitize the brain," he continued after a lazy pause, "I mean, you can, but it doesn't work. What you get on the other end is bullshit. It sounds okay at first, but when you get into it, the thought process is fried."

"Uh-huh." I'd spotted a cigarette butt on the street a few feet away, only half-smoked. I wondered what the odds were that in the five seconds it would take to claim it, my job would walk by and I'd spend the next five hours listening to Nad while tonight's dinner drifted away. I licked my lips and scanned the crowd.

"So the Monks, they remove the brain. They slice open your head like a fucking can, remove the brain, and put it in one of the Monk bodies. They hook it up, thousands of threads, so thin you can't see 'em. Some of 'em are data transfer lines, some of 'em are electrical, to stimulate the organ. Then they fill the head up with a nutrient solution, to preserve it.

"Fucking *bam!* You've got a Monk."

I sighed. "Nad, everyone knows this. It's on the fucking Vids." There were more and more "Special Reports" on the Electric Church showing up on the huge fifty-foot public video screens every day, reporters with perfect skin cheerfully telling us that the fucking Monks were everywhere, in case we hadn't noticed.

"Yeah, but Ave, think about it: Who's volunteering for this shit? Who's walking up to one of the Tin Men and saying, hell yeah, cut my head off and vacuum out my brains! Fuck that. The Monks are hunting people. I know a guy—"

I winced. Every bullshit story on the street started with *I know a guy*. It was the international *code* for *bullshit*.

"—Kitlar Muan—you know him, shylock outta the Bronx. Or knew him. He was telling me a few weeks ago how one of these Monks was like following him. Always around, always holding up walls or some shit wherever Kit went. Then, one day, Kit's gone, out of touch, and the next day, he's a fucking Monk. You know how the Monks go around and say hello to all their old friends, tell them how they converted? So there I was, and here comes this Tin Man, all vinyl smiles and brand-new black robes, and it walks right up to me and sez, 'Good morning, Nad, you used to know me as Kit Muan, now I'm Brother Muan of the Delta—"

I let Nad's chatter wash over me, bored. If Nad thought the Monks were shooting people in the back and cutting off their heads, it was a good reason to believe otherwise. I kept my eyes roaming over the good citizens of what was left of downtown Manhattan, angry, yellow faces, but I didn't see my mark. I stamped my feet in frustration, cold and tired. It was a low moment. Things had gone downhill at a furious pace since my near-death experience on the East Side; the Pigs were still circulating my description and going hammer and tongs at trying to track down who had murdered Colonel Janet Hense, and I'd exhausted my credit spreading the fog thick to keep my name out of it. Not only was I broke as a result, but being so blatantly connected with an ongoing cop-killing investigation made me a hot property, and business was not good. So Avery Cates the Gweat and Tewwible was reduced to pulling street work for low-rent dipshits. A man needed to pay his bills. If you didn't pay your bills, people like me stood in shadows waiting for you and slit your throat, and I had a lot of bills coming due. Street Work paid shit, but it *paid*.

There were, in fact, a trio of Monks across the street from us, and I wasted a moment staring at them. It was a typical scene for them: two standing on either side of a third who stood on a box, preaching. And preaching. And preaching. Walk by in the morning, and this freaky thing with corpse-white skin, dressed all in black and wearing mirrored sunglasses, would be making a speech about salvation. Come back at lunch, the same freak was making the same speech. At night, it was still there. At first we all thought they were fucking Droids. It was a joke: The same Droid that took your job last year was now putting God out of business.

As I stared, one of them turned its pasty white head and looked back at me. I fought the immediate urge to look away, get interested in the near distance suddenly. I just kept staring—you had to keep the act up. I was Avery Cates, toughest bastard in the System, and I would stare at creepy Monks if I wanted.

The Monks all looked alike. Their plastic faces were capable of expression, in weird, programmed contortions that never looked natural, but their faces were identical. At first you saw them here and there, heard rumor of them. Now they're everywhere. You see Monks in the street, on the trains. The Electric Church was a registered religion. It was all very legal—they claimed to have paperwork on every member, showing voluntary submission to the conversion into a Monk. So far the System Pigs bought it, and left them alone.

After a moment, with extreme casualness, I looked back for the cigarette butt and licked my lips. It was almost half a cigarette, and looked to be of good vintage: Pre-Unification. Stale as hell, but still better than the shit you got these days, even if you could afford them. Which I manifestly could not. I stared transfixed at it, and wondered if anyone I knew would see me kneel to get it. You had to keep up the rep all the time.

Nad nudged me gently with one elbow. "That's our man."

I looked up, flushing, angry at myself. Staring at a fucking cigarette butt while tonight's meal ticket strolled by, my ass saved by a dried-up burnout like Nad Fucking Muller. I made fists with both hands and resisted the sudden urge to punch Nad in the face.

I recognized my mark from the grainy files I'd seen: a short, heavyset guy in an ancient leather overcoat about a foot too long for him, worn like a half-rate royal robe, dragging along the street. He was flanked by two huge men who couldn't bend their arms, muscles on muscles twitching. I kept my eyes on the mark, who *bustled*, walking fast. The Little Prince. His name was Rudjer something; it didn't matter. He was low on the food chain and was trying to rise from the depths, and he was about to explode.

I studied the trio. Their eyes were straight ahead, faces set in the usual hardassed grimace—we all had it engraved on our faces—acting like the rest of the poor fucks on the street would just naturally get out of the way. Which they did, because even though the Little Prince was a nobody who didn't realize his button had been pushed, he still had more juice than most of the people around him. He had some yen, some muscle, and that snazzy overcoat.

He glided past me, one of the monsters on his payroll lifting a skinny kid off the ground and tossing him aside to clear a path. I didn't move. Nad started to twitch next to me, impatient, but I held up one hand without looking at him and he shut up. I'd quieted Nad down the hard way often enough; he was well-trained by now.

When they were past, I stepped out into the flow of bodies and matched their pace, keeping my hands in my pockets. My own coat wasn't as regal as the Little Prince's, but it was functional, and contained a number of useful items. It also had holes cut into the pockets so you could arrange your hands without being seen. Keeping my eyes on the three amigos, I felt around for the blade I'd secreted in an inner pocket and took it firmly in one hand. The Little Prince was small fry and barely paid enough to be worth it—a bad man, certainly, no better than me, but not exactly someone who'd enhance my reputation. Bullets were too expensive for shit like him.

I followed in their wake for a while, watching. I knew Nad had slipped into my gravity without having to look; Nad and I went back a long way, and he'd never liked being alone. It didn't take long to establish that the Little Prince's security wasn't worth whatever he was paying them: Like a lot of amateurs, they were one-dimensional, and thought all their troubles would be coming at them from the front, with plenty of warning and a lot of fanfare. Not once did they look back.

Turning my head a little to get an idea of the environmental factors, I almost missed a step, because three Monks were keeping pace with me. I couldn't be sure—the Tin Men all looked alike—but my immediate thought was that these were the same three who'd been preaching across the street from us. One was looking right at me, marching through the crowd like it didn't need eyes. I stared back at it in surprise for a few steps, then tore my eyes away, checking my meal ticket. They were still pushing through the crowd like they owned the streets. From the show they were putting on—all grim determination and regal pomp—the Little Prince was probably out on his collections, squeezing water from stones and performing other miracles on a par with getting money out of my fellow citizens. This all worked to my advantage, because tough guys didn't look over their shoulders to see who might be creeping up behind them, and tough guys didn't need to take basic precautions. More shitheads died being tough every day, when a little good old-fashioned paranoia and cowardice went a long way. It wasn't even cowardice. It was an aversion to death.

The Monks were still keeping pace, but were no longer looking at me. They just floated through the crowd. They were harmless, in my experience, but they creeped you out. Even people who made their living killing and maiming their fellow human beings shied away from those perfect rubber faces, that serene certainty. I didn't doubt the Monks could defend themselves, but every Monk I'd ever run across had been unfailingly polite and nonconfrontational. They still made my skin crawl, and having three of them following me like fucking albatrosses made me nervous.

The crowd thinned a little as we moved north, makeshift stalls sprouting up on the sidewalks, in the streets, little shacks built from scrap wood offering whatever people could scrounge to sell, generally stuff no one thought was worth stealing in the first place. The goods got better as you moved uptown, until you finally reached a point where the Crushers started eyeing you distrustfully and the stores had decent security in place, mainly to keep people like me out. I tensed up a little, resolved to ignore the Monks. If the Little Prince was going to put the squeeze on someone that owed him yen, it was going to be here. Much further uptown and the Little Prince would be outclassed.

Sure enough, he stopped in front of a flimsy stall that was staffed by a man about my age and two young kids with the hollow look of poverty. The place was selling meat pies, the meat not much of a mystery considering the pile of dead rats the boys were engaged in skinning right there in the street. Business was slow, because rats were everywhere, and if I wanted one, I could catch five without working up a sweat.

The proprietor stepped forward, wringing his hands. I didn't listen to what was said, I just watched: The Little Prince stuck out his chest and crossed his arms, listening to whatever plea the old man was shelling out with his chin thrust out, nodding importantly. The two goons just menaced the whole operation, making the boys flinch and knocking shit off the counter, being tough.

I moved fast. There was no talking. No speeches. I wasn't here to make an impression. I scanned the street quickly for Crushers or—worse—System Pigs, and saw nothing, not even the three Monks. Then I stepped up behind the Little Prince, and before anyone could react I just pulled my blade from my pocket, grabbed him around the shoulders, and dragged the knife across his neck, the blade sinking in deep. Then I dropped the knife, stepped back, and drew my automatic. I didn't point it at anyone in particular; that often got misinterpreted, and just encouraged gunplay. I was just discouraging intervention while I waited for the Little Prince to actually die. No one paid for *grievous injury*, after all. The two goons paused and stared, first down at the Little Prince where he lay gurgling, then at me, and finally at each other.

One muttered something under his breath and turned to the other, gesticulating forcefully and hissing something foreign—half the hired muscle in the damn city spoke gibberish.

The other swore—you didn't need to speak the language to recognize swearing—gesturing at the Little Prince, then threw up his hands and glared at me. *"Non mon problème, okay?"*

They knew the score: With the Little Prince dead, no one was going to pay them, so there was no longer a job to do, and they certainly didn't want to end up dead, too. *Non mon* fucking *problème* indeed. These were the bottom-of-the-barrel assholes; you couldn't trust them—they had no goddamn pride, no ethics. To illustrate the point, his fellow made a show of wiping his hands, and the two of them lumbered off, arguing loudly. I looked at their former employer, and he stared up at me with wide, dead eyes. The family was already back at work, furiously making rat pies for the hungry people of New York City. You could count on the good people of New York to never remember a face.

The crowd swirled around me as I reholstered my gun, and then Nad was at my shoulder. "Good work," he said.

It didn't feel good. "Hell," I said. "I need a drink."

II

AN ENDLESS TRAIL OF SUNSETS

00000

‖‖‖‖‖‖‖‖‖‖‖
_____

Pickering's was a good place the System Pigs hadn't noticed yet, below the radar of the entire System of Federated Nations. It was semilegit, with some ancient liquor license and a paper deed, somewhere, or so rumor had it. It was located on the first floor—the only floor left—of a burned-out hulk of a building that looked, from the outside, ready to collapse at any moment. Liberal bribes to the Crushers kept it open, at least for the time being. Pick himself was the oldest man I knew: fifty if he was a day, ancient and always pissed off, a fat, slouching blob of a man with white, yellowing hair and gnarled, painful-looking hands. I'd never seen Pick stand up.

Pick had just two rules: You paid your bills, and you took fights outside. Inside, it was civilized. Pick didn't use Droids, either—the only waitress was a living human being, and she would slap your hand to prove it. The place was thick with smoke and plotting, and nobody looked around too freely. It was best to mind your own business and keep your hands on the ancient wooden tables scrounged from the wreckage of riots past. Pickering's was not a gentle place—these days you either had a job or you didn't, you were either System Police or a criminal. You had to be, and Pickering's was full of the thin, gray people like me, people not above killing someone, stealing something, starving to death over the course of an entire lifetime. People got killed in Pickering's. Even the most civilized places had their moments.

Nad and I had found some space at a table in the back near the door, where Kev Gatz was already half in the bag and in no condition to resist our invasion. I shoved my way onto the side facing the door. Over cups of Pick's bathtub gin we got shitfaced and sat talking about Monks, Nad's current obsession beating my weary boredom. Besides, I was hoarding the pitiful yen I'd earned for the Little Prince—a job I wasn't proud of and didn't want to think about—and Nad was willing to buy a few rounds, so I let him talk, even though he was telling the story of Kitlar Muan again and I wanted badly to twist Nad's nose and tell him to shut the hell up, but free booze was going a long way with me after my day.

"Who the fuck," Nad wondered, "would have their heads sliced open and their brains stuffed into a can?"

Kev Gatz sat in silence. Gatz was . . . special. We called him the Pusher. He hardly ever spoke, a thin shock of gray hair sitting on top of a head that looked like the skin had been stretched thin over the bones. He was wearing dark glasses—Gatz almost always wore his glasses. He sat so still it surprised you to notice his drink disappearing, as if he was waiting for you to look away before making any moves.

"Nad," he croaked, "shut the fuck up, okay?"

I swirled the liquor in my cup and looked around the place, feeling tired. The cream of Manhattan's thieves and murderers in one place, getting stoned and making noise. An SSF raid would clear a lot of dockets, I thought. The Pigs would pay a hard price for it, though, considering the sheer amount of hardware hidden away in holsters, secret pockets, spring-loaded sleeve units. Not that a raid was likely, the way Pick greased the Crushers to pretend Pickering's was a black hole. A few people nodded at me as I moved my eyes around, and I gave them your standard-issue hardassed nod back, well-practiced.

I took a breath, closed my eyes, and swallowed my drink in one fast motion, not breathing again until it had hit my stomach like acid, like lead pellets. I winced and slammed my cup down, fighting my body's natural urge to reject it all, and presently the sting faded into a warm glow, and I relaxed, signaling Melody for another round and pointing gleefully at Nad.

Nad hadn't taken Kev's advice. As he rambled on about the Monks and how much they freaked him out and how anyone who volunteered for that shit was crazy, the door opened behind him, and with a blast of rain and wind from the black night a Monk stepped into Pickering's. No one took much notice at first—the Monks liked to just stop into places sometimes, say their piece, and leave—and it paused right behind Nad, cocking its plastic head and listening. I had a weird gut reaction—my balls tightening up and all the hairs on my arms standing up. I thought of the three Monks keeping pace with us earlier, and sat up straighter, eyes fixed on the Tin Man.

"I appreciate your aversion to the concept," it said in the standard deep, modulated artificial voice. "I myself once shared it."

The place quieted a bit. It didn't go silent, but the whole place's attention shifted, you could tell. The Monks did enter public houses, make their usual speeches, and tolerate being ignored, but this was a little different. None of us came to Pickering's for *different*. We came to make deals and plot strategies and drink until we couldn't see straight.

Nad grimaced but didn't turn around. He shrank visibly before us, collapsing down onto the carved-up table.

"I would like to speak to you about immortality, if I may, Mr. . . . Muller, isn't it?" the Monk continued. They always knew who you were. Wireless data feeds with mother church, Optical Facial Recognition; they snapped a photo of your face and had it OFRed in seconds, like Droids. But they weren't Droids. They were cyborgs—robot body, human brain—and they all used to be regular folks, like me. "It will only take a few minutes, and I would appreciate your time."

The whole place was watching Nad out of the corner of their eyes—too cool to actually look, but interested anyway. The preaching on the corners was pretty normal, but I didn't think I knew anyone who'd witnessed an actual attempt at conversion. There were more and more Tin Men on the streets every day, telling you how great it was to be immortal, to be nuclear-powered and free from pain—and fuck if I didn't sometimes think, *Damn, what if the motherfuckers are* right? —but they always popped up as if by magic, converting overnight, like Nad's friend Kitlar Muan. Curiosity ate away at the blank-faced cool we all tried to project twenty-four hours a day.

Nad wasn't enjoying the attention. He wasn't a tough guy. His response, murmured into his cup, was barely audible. "No. No, I'm a busy man . . . "

I kept my eyes on the Monk and moved my hand into my coat pocket out of sheer, dumb instinct. There was nothing to fear, the Monks never *did* anything. But I was tense as if someone had a gun on me.

"I understand," the Monk replied immediately, pleasantly. It stood perfectly straight, and the etched smile on its face didn't twitch. "Truly, I do. Time is your curse, Mr. Muller. Lack of time. Everything requires time, and you have so little. This leads me to the fundamental question the Electric Church poses: How can you be saved when you have no time? How can you possibly combat your sins in the time allotted you?"

The place was almost quiet by then as people gave up trying to be cool and just twisted around to watch the show. As the Monk moved, the soft whirr and hum of tiny motors and hydraulics could be heard.

"Consider the technological advances of the human race in recent centuries—quantum computers, limited teleportation, genetic engineering—we are a race designed to plumb the mysteries of the multiverse. It is God's plan that we do so, that we investigate and harness the forces of nature. Why were we designed this way? We are meant to find salvation through our progress. But computers cannot output salvation. And we cannot teleport salvation into this room. We cannot splice salvation into our genes. Salvation must be *attained*, Mr. Muller. But so few of us achieve this. Do you know anyone who has been saved?" The Monk stared at Muller for a moment, then turned to regard the whole place. "Have you? You? Anyone?"

The Monk shifted slightly, his robe rustling in the stillness. "Of course not. You have not lived long enough. You must work, earn yen, live. You must rest. You must eat. You must dress yourselves and relieve yourselves and fight and love and struggle, struggle, struggle." The Monk's voice rose in perfectly calibrated waves, its bass reinforced electronically, booming through the room. "I represent the first step in the correct direction. God has planned for us. This is the Way."

Its voice suddenly dropped until it was just loud enough to be heard throughout the room. "I am *time enough at last*. I am immortal. I am impervious to time, to hunger, to lethargy, to apathy. Only through eternity can you be saved, my friends. Salvation cannot be attained in a mere century. You, Mr. Muller, may live to be ninety or one hundred. A woman in Minsk is 126 and still working for the System Police as an FLS radio operator. One hundred and twenty-six paltry years is not enough time. *Five hundred* and twenty-six is not enough time. Salvation is not easy. Salvation is complex, the most complex puzzle ever devised. A thousand years, and perhaps we can begin to decipher the first word of the question. A million years, we may begin to work on the answer. Perhaps when the universe has collapsed in on itself, and all the worlds scattered throughout have been eaten by hungry suns, perhaps then we will be on the verge, about to triumph and join the angels. I can only hope we have not been too slow to realize the truth, that we do indeed have enough time."

The Monk paused and scanned the room. No one had moved an inch. I felt like something huge and invisible had launched itself at my back.

"What I am sure of, Mr. Muller, is your puny lifespan is not enough. You can barely perceive the need *for* salvation in that time. When you do, when you're lying old and frail, and you realize there is indeed a question in need of an answer—it will be too late. *You will not have enough time.* Unless," the Monk returned its mirrored glass gaze to Muller, "unless you realize the truth and join the Electric Church. Accept Salvation through Immortality. Learn the *Mulqer Codex*, and prepare for eternity. That is your only hope."

The Monk paused again. No one moved. We didn't dare.

"Thank you for your time," the Monk finally said and turned away, exiting the bar in a flash of rain and darkness.

For a few seconds, the whole place remained still and relatively quiet. Nad just stared down at the tabletop, unhappy. Then, from somewhere in the back someone shouted "Holy shit!" and the whole place erupted into laughter, and the hum of conversation returned to its usual level: deafening, and now punctuated by plenty of pithy comments about the Monks. I couldn't relax. I drank three more gins, fast, and felt nothing. I couldn't explain why, but that Monk had set off all my alarms.

People started buying Nad drinks out of pity. Nad was almost a mascot in the bar, this criminal failure who couldn't shut up, and seeing him quiet and subdued generated more warm feelings in the place than I'd thought possible. Inspired by this, Gatz, Nad, and I huddled together and took our drinking seriously. By the time Pickering's closed, it was just the three of us sitting at a long creaking table.

"Come on, Nad," I said, standing up to see how bad off I was. After hours of Pick's gin, the world was made of soft rubber; everything was hard to accomplish but nothing hurt too badly, so what the fuck. "Come on, I'll see ya home, then, eh?"

We saw Gatz off. He was stumbling this way and that, but no one fucked with the Pusher, even though he looked like a junkie, all gray and sinew, those stupid sunglasses on at night. So I just let him stumble home to puke and sleep it off.

Nad was in a bad way. Too drunk, too freaked out, mumbling to himself and white-eyed. I thought I'd see him home, make sure he didn't get rolled—honor among thieves, at least thieves that were also your friends. Nad and I, we went back a ways. We were old enough to remember better days, before the System, before the Joint Council, the System Security Force, all the bullshit. We remembered our dads having jobs. Not good jobs, but jobs. I didn't know what Nad's friendship was worth to me when push came to shove, but fuck, it was just a walk home. It was worth that much.

It was late. The Normals were all asleep. It was just me and Nad on the streets, listing this way and that. We knew the area, and while that wouldn't save us from getting popped, it at least meant we'd see it coming, even half-assed drunk. So, when there was a noise behind us, a scrape of a heavy boot, I was more annoyed than anything else. I was tired and putting on my hardass face took effort.

"Back off, shithead," I growled over my shoulder, pushing Nad forward to keep him in motion, "or I'll fucking tear you up."

It was all a pissing contest. It never stopped. You couldn't go soft, not even for a minute.

"Mr. Muller interests me, friend. Move along," the Monk said softly. "Mr. Muller, let me show you an endless trail of sunsets. Let me save you."

III

THEY THINK THAT BECAUSE
THEY *ARE* GODS

10100

We both froze. The Monk was about half a block behind us, its scary-pale skin shining in the moonlight, its glasses mirroring night, nothing but blackness. It was fucking smiling, false teeth dull in the weak light, its eyes just humorless shadows.

Nad vibrated next to me, stiff, making a soft choking sound. My head hummed, struggling to throw off the booze, my heart pounding with a sudden adrenaline dump—pumped up and exhausted at the same time, the prefight warmup I'd been through too many times to count.

"No thanks," Nad whispered.

"Ah, Mr. Muller," the Monk said, its smile widening—the fucking cyborg was grinning at us. "I insist."

I stepped in front of Nad. I didn't feel drunk anymore. "Sorry, *friend*," I said coldly, in my best pissing-contest voice. "He said he wasn't interested."

The Monk didn't move, but I had a sudden sense that it shifted its attention from Nad to me. After a second its head twitched slightly, and it spoke to me.

"Avery Cates," it said, still grinning. "Twenty-seven years of age. Last official record logged with SSF dated eight years ago. You're quite a mystery man these days, Mr. Cates. But you've been busy, haven't you? Murder-for-hire, robbery, smuggling, theft of many varieties. Mainly murder, though. Oh, yes, you're quite famous, aren't you? Tell me," it said, taking a step forward, "do you think you're going to have enough time to ask forgiveness for all of *your* sins? Let me bring you to the end of time, Mr. Cates. Let me *save* you."

In a second everything had shifted. One moment, I was defending my old friend. The next, the Tin Man was talking to *me*. And I knew Nad was in no shape to defend anyone. I kept my eyes on the fucking machine, standing on the permanently damp street, the ancient, rotting buildings rising up like canyon walls ready to bury us. The usual dance wasn't happening: Normally you could tell the other guy was just as scared as you were. The Monk didn't give that vibe. The fucking Monk didn't give *any* vibe, and the vacuum standing in front of me was suddenly disconcerting in its blankness.

But that was okay. I hadn't become so famous—in certain circles—by accident. I smiled.

"Immortal don't mean *invulnerable,* friend," I said clearly. "Two more steps and your own plan for salvation might not work out exactly the way you thought."

One thing you learned early in New York was to never appear weak. Never look afraid. Never admit defeat. Defeat was you choosing to spare someone's life, or choosing to be magnanimous for a change, let things slide. Maybe they didn't believe the tough-guy act, but it put a little seed of doubt in their brains.

I was twenty-seven. I was *old*. All my brothers were dead. Nad and Kev Gatz were my only old friends left. Most of us died before we were twenty. I had no reason to fear the Monk, of course, and yet inexplicable fear poisoned me as I stood there. But I chalked up a lot of my longevity to never showing fear—so fuck this pile of circuitry and surgery.

It paused. On a human, I would have interpreted this as weakness, hesitation. The Monk, though, might very well have been analyzing new data, or simply taking the moment to do a few more computer analyses. This was just a Monk; there was no reason to worry. Me, I kill people. No bones about it: That's what I do. The Monks just talked you to death.

I had a sudden flash of memory: some lucky bastard sprinting from a bar raid, somehow getting past the noses of dozens of Stormers and System Pigs and breaking free into the night, passing by a trio of Monks. A gesture, so far away I hadn't been able to make it out, and the lucky bastard going down, disappearing.

I steadied myself and flexed my hands. My brain told me the Monk wasn't a threat, none of them were, but my gut told me this was a fight, and I knew how to deal with situations like this. I didn't move. I didn't have superhuman reflexes, and movement just telegraphed intention. I stood perfectly still and watched it. Nad started clucking in his throat again.

When the Monk moved, it moved faster than I thought possible, but I was ready, even as part of my mind sputtered in shock. Its hands came up, each with an automatic gleaming wetly. Its robe billowed out, catching a draft—but it was strangely silent. There was no grunt of effort, no shout of triumph, nothing. It was like watching a Vid with the sound off.

People think the best thing to do when a gun is pulled on you is dive to one side, but that doesn't work. A patient Gunner, a trained Gunner, doesn't come up shooting. He comes up, tracks your movements, and chooses the best time to pull the trigger. You don't shoot at where your target *was*, you shoot at where he's *going to be.* You only shoot blind when you're desperate. I used my head. It was the only reason I was still alive.

I threw myself forward and down, pulling Nad down with me. It's usually the last place a Gunner expects, and that buys you a second or two. With other adversaries, a second or two is often enough to change the equation. With the Monk, it just meant that Nad got shot twice in the chest as he fell on top of me.

The only chance I had of staying alive was to keep moving. Nad was a heavy piece of dead fucking weight, though, and as I tried rolling to my left he weighed me down. By the time I finally broke free of him, his sticky blood all over me, debris from the street sticking to my soaked clothes, I was sure the headshot was coming—except no, it wouldn't be a headshot. They needed the brain. I panted, scrabbling, ripping a fingernail on the concrete, *get up get up*—If I'd been in the Monk's shoes, I'd have been able to take at least three shots by the time I rolled behind cover; I winced spasmodically, imagining the impact.

Then, somehow, I was behind a trashcan, still alive, filthy but breathing. I came up with my own gun. Worrying about why I was still alive would come later. With the copper smell of blood in my nose, I swallowed puke and forced myself to be still. I peered over the trashcan and got ready to sell myself dear.

I wasn't alone anymore. The alley held me, the Monk, Nad's corpse, and someone else—and the mystery of my survival was clear: An unknown quantity had entered the equation, and the Monk was playing it safe for the moment. I couldn't see the new person clearly; he was on the other side of the Monk backlit in the wash of streetlight. I knew two things right away: The sound of shots fired didn't faze him in the least, and the Monk had forgotten all about me. This led me to conclude that the new guy was a System Pig, an SSF officer. I didn't relax at all. If it had just been a Crusher walking a beat, it wouldn't have worried me, but in my experience, the elite SSF officers never improved situations, and their presence usually increased my personal chances of getting killed. Everyone complained that the System Cops thought they were gods, but I thought, fuck, they think that because they *are* gods.

They try to teach all the young kids that the SSF exists to protect them from dangerous fuckers like me, but that isn't really true. Most of those kids are going to grow up to be dangerous fuckers like me, anyway, since there's nothing much else to do these days if you want to eat. So the SSF is really there to fuck with everyone on the bottom 99 percent of the pyramid.

Cowering behind my trashcan, fully aware that I should be dead already, I was for the first time in my life glad that the SSF existed. And that the System Pigs were such fucking badasses. Nad was dead, but maybe this guy could help keep me alive. And then I thought of the last few weeks, of all the money and effort I'd had to put into distancing the name Avery Cates from a dead SSF officer shot on the East Side in a botched assasination, and dread replaced my relief, black tendrils inching through the cracks.

They started *talking*. It gave me time to think, but how fucking weird. The Monk and the System Pig (taking a break from busting heads for shakedown money) meet in a dark alley, guns drawn, and start *chatting*. I knew they were frisking each other for backup and telecom, making sure they weren't each going to have a goddamn army on their heads if they made the wrong move, but it was still creepy.

Time to think. Why in fuck had the Monk killed Nad? The answer was fucking surreal, but it stared at me. The Monk was recruiting him. I'd heard the rumors, and I knew a little something about anatomy—when the Monks had been a fairly new phenomenon there'd been all sorts of articles about them in the Vids, the underground, off-net Vids, technical specs and theoretical designs and treatises on brain chemistry and how a human brain could be transferred from a skull to a CPU. You could shoot a man dead in an alley and have him up and running in a Monk body in a few hours, with minimal brain damage. Damage that maybe could be fixed through circuitry, who the fuck knew. Someone you used to pal around with, get high with, woke up one day feeling spiritual and signed up for their metal body, for no reason, and next thing you knew they were doing the ritual introduction, *Hiya, I used to be your pal, now I'm a Tin Man, let me chew your ear about eternity for a while.* Except now I knew the reason. And people like Nad—people like *us*—were meaningless, in the grand scheme. No one would miss us, no one would bother investigating us.

It'd killed Nad Muller to recruit him. Nad was going to wake up tomorrow a Monk. And me? I got the feeling I hadn't been chosen.

I had better things to think about, like lines of sight and escape routes. I needed contact with a System Pig like I needed a hole in my head, and here were both possibilities staring me in the face. It was a banner fucking night. I wished fervently that Kev Gatz had hung around, the fucking freak. He would have come in handy. I squeezed my gun tightly to keep my hand from trembling.

"Hello, officer," the Monk said, calm and cool. "This man appears to have been attacked."

Motherfucker, I thought, *it's just buying time.*

IV

WRONG IN A GLORIOUS WAY

01000

The cop knew the Monk was just buying time, too. System Pigs generally didn't do undercover. They strutted around and no one dared fuck with them. You could pick out a System Cop a mile away, and that was just how they liked it. They stepped out of their cars and everything stopped, hardasses standing around whistling like there was nothing in the world could get them to commit a crime. This one just stood there for a moment, looking the scene over, before responding to the Monk.

"Identify yourself," the cop said. The street was quiet and very dark, but his voice was clear and steady. Human.

I pictured the street and considered my options. If I stood up, I'd just get nailed by the cop, distracting him in the process. This was my best opportunity to just leave the fucking Monk to whatever it was going to do. I didn't know. I was paralyzed.

"I am Brother Vita," the Monk replied immediately. "Brother Jeofrey Vita, of the Alpha Brethren, the Electric Church."

"I can see you're a goddamn Monk," the cop snapped. "What happened here?"

And I knew right away the cop wasn't linked up. He was either on his way to something, or off-duty, or doing something he didn't want the Worms to find out about—whatever, he wasn't linked up.

After what I'd just seen the Monk do, I knew he was a dead man.

That was my cue. No link meant he couldn't beam my picture in, meant I could walk away from him and let Brother Vita do the deed. But fuck if I could move. The fucking Monk was *fast*. If I'd figured out the cop was unlinked, the Monk couldn't be far behind, and I didn't have any doubt that the Monk could nail the cop and shoot me in the back without breaking a sweat. If it did sweat. I crouched against the dirty pavement and tried to think of something to do that wouldn't end up with me getting shot. Nothing came to mind.

For whatever reason, the Monk didn't make a move. It played along another moment. "I don't know, officer. I found this man here, and was about to contact someone."

It sounded eerily human.

The cop grunted and pushed his long coat back from his sloppy suit—nothing I or anyone I knew could afford, but *looking* cheap nonetheless—and knelt near Nad, paying no attention to the Monk. A watch glittered dully on his wrist as he lifted Nad's jacket to inspect the damage.

"Modified Roon," the cop said thoughtfully. "Funny, I've heard that's the kind of illegal weaponry—"

The Monk pounced, whipping up one arm so fast I thought I must have imagined it, a *blur*. I was mesmerized. Blink, the Monk standing there watching an officer of the law at work.

Blink, the motherfucker has the Roon *out*, like he's saying, inspect *this*, fucker.

I nearly shit my pants. Fucking System *Pigs*, man. They were not to be fucked with. A System Pig shows up, you look at your shoes and blank out your mind, *everyone* knows that. But I'd never seen anything as fast and blank as that Monk. The cop moved immediately.

The Monk fired, and the cop rolled and threw something at the Monk—I couldn't see what—but it hit the Monk on the wrist, knocked its aim off, and then the cop was in shadows, and firing at the Monk. Firing fast. Blam blam blam blam blam—five muzzle flashes in the dark, lighting up the street, showing the Monk in jump cut, moving, dodging, rolling.

When I saw the cop had missed the Monk five times, fuck, something in me finally realized that this was my one and only chance. Whispering prayers to the cop-gods that the Pig had enough in him to give me one stinking, solitary *minute*, I turned and ran.

I'd bet my last yen I'd see Nad again with freaky mirrored glasses and plastic skin, but I had no fucking desire to join him. Avery Cates was an old man because he knew when to run, believe it.

I ran. Behind me, one last blast and then horrible silence. Within seconds, *seconds*, there were steady, heavy feet behind me. My legs didn't want to move after a night of sitting and drinking; I felt like I'd stepped into a river of muddy concrete, the whole city sucking at my heels, urging me to kneel and kiss this metal freak's ring.

"Wait, Mr. Cates," the Monk called out. "Would you take confession? When contemplating eternity, it is advisable to map out a personalized plan of salvation."

I kept waiting for the shot. I was sweating, soaked through, and I'd gone through drunk, hung over, and thirsty all in about five minutes, my body flushing toxins overtime. I'd pulled just enough ahead of it to queer its aim, or my erratic course was helping, or, fuck, maybe I knew the streets just a little bit better. These were old streets, ancient, back when everyone got around by car, before hovers, before everything else went bullshit and crapped out. Going back to when New York was a much smaller city, not the entire Eastern Seaboard, with Trenton as a neighborhood. I strained my mind for advantages, and thought of Kev Gatz, who crashed nearby; he'd always been a freak, but he was my best hope. He was twenty-three and looked likely to die within the next five years, but he'd looked like that for as long as I knew him. Just another faceless piece of shit swarming through New York, except something in his head was wrong.

Wrong in a fucking glorious way, because Kev Gatz was a psionic. If I could get to him maybe he'd be able to Push the Monk. It wasn't much, but it was the only asset I had.

I rounded a corner with a five-second lead, and I knew exactly where I was and I knew, with a jolt of something approaching joy, that there was an old Safe Room nearby. Not wasting any time, I pounded down an alley, and then immediately bolted down a second alley. Both were just wide enough for a man to run through if he was very careful. You could walk past both a thousand times and never see it.

"Do not flee your destiny, Mr. Cates," the Monk said, closer than I'd expected. "Can you outrun oblivion? Think, and submit."

Think and submit, holy fuck. I wish that Pig had taken your fucking metal face off. With a solid kick, I knocked a cheap wooden door off its hinges, revealing a rotting stairway. I pelted up, my weight making the ancient wood sag and dance in unexpected ways. I was turning the third landing, lungs burning, legs aching, when I heard the creak of weight on the stairs below me. I made a desperate leap into a spare, battered room of white plaster and rotten wood flooring. No hesitation, no mistake: I had my five—maybe four—seconds to save myself.

I hit a spot in the plaster that looked like every other bump on the wall, and kept running, leaping into the far wall. I skittered onto a dusty metal floor like a cannonball, getting scraped up pretty badly in the process, and curled up into a ball. I smacked into something unyielding, my whole body lighting up red.

Lungs burning, I froze. Sweat poured into my eyes. I didn't even allow myself to blink.

There were Safe Rooms all over this area. Everyone floating under the SSF's radar had hired Techs to come in and set one up at one time or another, cash only, one day's work, to spec. Heat shielding, signal fuzzing, holographic obfuscations, soundproofing—once you were inside one of these rooms, the System Pigs would need to start knocking out the walls, or shooting into them, to find you. They weren't comfortable, but they did the job.

A moment later, the Monk was in the room. I clenched my teeth against the desire for a breath. A single, deep breath. Anything. I wished I could suck oxygen in through my pores.

Then, heavy footsteps, moving around. And something else, distant, weak, like hope: the displacement of an SSF hover.

Another moment, the two of us still and silent, me with my vision getting blurry around the edges. Inside the Safe Room, I couldn't be seen, but I couldn't risk the noise of my breathing, not with a goddamn cyborg looking for me.

"Why hide, Mr. Cates?" the Monk said. Amazingly, it almost sounded sad. "Oblivion comes to us all. End this game with dignity and embrace your destiny. It appears our friend from the SSF was linked up after all. That is unfortunate, as it means I cannot spend a few profitable minutes shooting randomly into the walls. That would attract attention, would it not?" There was a pause. "Well, as a dutiful citizen of the System, Mr. Cates, the least I can do is pass your name on to the local SSF office and suggest you might have been in the same location as a recently murdered officer. The Electric Church takes citizenship very seriously. Good-bye, Mr. Cates."

I heard its heavy tread retreat from the room, and then down the stairs. The hover was close. I imagined bright blue light flooding the room, searching for the dark figure of the Monk. I held my breath. I held my breath until I felt like biting my tongue off. I held my breath until my vision fogged and my brain blanked, and I finally passed out.

V

MEN WITH JOBS, THE VANISHING SPECIES

00101

It was too bright, too open. I mashed one finger down on Gatz's buzzer. I could hear the soft female voice of his apartment's Shell calling out, "Visitor at the door! Mr. Gatz. Visitor at the door!" Gatz liked to set his Shell to "female" and talk back to it, cursing and calling it names.

The gray mass of people pushed past me in both directions. Millions of people every day in New York had no jobs, they just darted around looking for something to steal, someplace to sell it, and maybe some free grub here and there. I felt exposed, and my head ached. I suspected the Safe Room was the only thing that had saved my life from the assorted other bottom-feeders, most of whom would have slit my throat out of simple fear if they'd been able to see me.

I leaned on the button again. That flirty fake voice was

starting to bug me, it was so fucking cheerful. There was nothing to be cheerful *about*.

Finally, the front door buzzed. I stepped inside quickly and shut the door behind me, scanning the crowd before mounting the broken escalator and humping it upstairs. Gatz shared the room with two other people in shifts of eight hours. It was just a room with a cot in one corner, a couch that didn't look too moldy, a kitchen module, and a water closet. Grim, but it was off the street and behind a thick metal door, which provided at least minimum security against the sneak thieves, cutthroats, and other desperate creatures.

Gatz opened the door and stepped aside, waving me in. He wore just a pair of shorts, and his thin, wasted body glowed with ghostly pallor. He was wearing his sunglasses, which relaxed me, because Gatz needed to look you in the eye in order to Push you.

I didn't really understand the Push. I'd only experienced it once, really; Kev Gatz had been a new face around town back then, a skinny asshole with an attitude. Like just about everyone else, I'd become determined to teach him a hard lesson—you had to hit people first, never let them think you were soft. When I came after him he just took off his shades, and the moment he got a good look at me I felt this calm, peaceful feeling spreading over me. I was suddenly content to just stare at Kev. I didn't feel anything, want anything, think anything. I was just there.

To Kev's credit, his revenge wasn't anything terrible. He sent me away relieved of all my money and gave me a task: Write *I will not try to shake down Kev Gatz ever again* one hundred times on paper. I was on line thirty-three before it wore off, and I stopped in the middle of the word *try* and just blinked, everything rushing back to me. The motherfucker—he made me laugh, and when I met up with him again I had to admit that aside from being bug-eyed afraid of looking him in the eye even by accident, I liked that about him.

I sat down on the couch and put my feet on the cot. I fished out some precious cigs and offered him one, which he took silently, sticking it behind his ear. He slumped back down onto the bed next to my feet and squinted at the Shell's screen. "Fuck, Avery, I've got forty minutes before the Teutonic Fuck gets in."

The German. No one knew his real name. He worked free-lance security around the city, cracking heads and guarding drug mules. He was obviously augmented, illegal all the way and probably going to die young. Augments bought on the black market were almost always deadly. Currently, however, the German was a mass of rippling muscles and rage, and he'd made it known to Kev that if Kev wasn't out of the room when he got back, he'd toss Kev out the window, because the German needed his beauty rest.

"I'm in trouble, Kev," I said, lighting my cig. "I need help."

Kev nodded. "How much you paying?"

Ever practical, that was my Kev. I did some quick mental calculations. "Forty."

"Forty," Kev repeated, liking the number, "for what?"

"I gotta get out of New York for a while, and it might be tricky. I think my face is in the air with both the SSF and the Electric Church."

Gatz was scratching his eyes under the dark lenses. "The EC? The fucking plastic Monks standing around telling us how great it is to have mechanical brains? You serious?"

I gave him the short version of my evening. It was hot as fuck up in his little room, and rivulets of sweat were burrowing through my body hair. It smelled like three unwashed men had spent the evening farting continuously, and I fought the urge to just hold my breath.

"Holy shit," was Gatz's only comment. "You *are* fucked, Ave. How long you think you have?"

I shrugged. "No time at all, I'd say. I gotta go underground *right away.* And I'll need your special talents to make that happen." I exhaled smoke into the room. "So, move."

"What the fuck do you expect *me* to do? I'm not muscle, Ave."

He was, though, in a way. "Kev, I need you to be my guardian angel. Make people leave me alone without getting into gunplay or such shit." I also wanted someone I thought I could trust, and there were precious few of those, but I felt a weird affection for Kev. It was like having a pet.

He shook his head. "Fuck, man—Ave, you're a friend and all, but this is a lot of danger for forty. System Pigs? I don't know."

I decided not to tell him the SSF was probably the lesser of two evils here, from what I'd seen and heard of the Monk. I was pissed—I'd done Kev plenty of favors. He owed me, and to find out he had the same short memory as the rest of the shit out there made me angry. I waited a moment, until the gaunt little fuck started stretching, scratching himself. Then I dove forward, pushed him up against the outdated Vid screen on the wall, and had him by the neck, and I made sure he could feel my breath on his face. I used my thumb and kept his face turned away from me—it was dangerous not to control Gatz's field of vision. No one knew that better than me.

He couldn't explain it, the Push. Kev didn't even know how old he was, precisely. He'd always been plagued with headaches, bouts of hysterical blindness—he'd always assumed he had a tumor or some other terrible malfunction and wouldn't live long. Then one day, he was getting his ass kicked somewhere, and he was just staring at the guy, wishing the guy would stop hitting him . . . and the guy stopped, just stood there.

"Listen to me, you little shit," I rasped. "I am in deep shit here. Deep fucking shit. I need help. You won't lift a finger for me unless I'm fucking bleeding for you? I've saved your ass how many times? Put that shit aside. You think I won't fucking hurt you if you leave me hanging in the wind here?"

His breath whistled in and out of his nose; he didn't even try to struggle. I knew how to beat him. "Fuck, Avery, fuck, come on! Get off me! Of course I'm gonna help you—of *course* I am."

" 'Cause normally I don't mind your bullshit," I went on as if he hadn't said anything. "Normally I let your bullshit slide, Kev. You being all fucked up all the time. You acting like just because you got the Push, you can do anything you want. I let it go. Okay? But I am in some deep fucking shit here, asshole, and I will *not* tolerate being kicked in the balls, all right?"

For a second there was just Kev's whistling breath. Then: "Look me in the eye when you say that, Avery."

Kev did not possess what you might call a sophisticated brain, or any desire to plumb the mysteries of his life. Once he determined that he had this power, he accepted it as the way of the universe and just used it as best he could, to survive. If it didn't leave him a shivering, weakened shell every time he Pushed someone, he'd probably be the biggest fucking criminal in the world right now. As it was, this incredible power gave him just barely enough of an edge to keep him alive a little longer than otherwise would have been possible.

The Joint Council had declared all active psionics property of the SSF, and the System Pigs kidnapped anyone they heard about. Gatz was the only psionic I knew of who wasn't chained up in some SSF training course or research lab, learning how to keep the System spinning.

I kind of liked that about him, too. When he wasn't kicking me in the balls, at least.

I gave him one good knee in *his* balls, just enough to make him cry out in pain, and then I was off him. "Fuck you, Kev. Keep those shades on, or I swear I'll make you regret it."

Desperation came off me in waves. I hoped Kev, with his fucked-up senses, might mistake it for anger, or danger.

"Jesus, Avery," he complained, rubbing his neck. "You could have snapped my windpipe, you know? There's no need for this shit."

I took a deep breath and retrieved my burning cigarette from the floor, where it had charred a small black circle in the cheap, sagging floorboards. "Sorry, Kev. I'm on edge." I'd re-established the natural order between Kev Gatz and me, and now we were friendly again.

"Yeah." He stared at the ground for a moment. "So, what do you need?"

"Aside from those googly eyes of yours, I think your friend Marcel would come in handy right now. I need to get the fuck out of town and come back as someone else. Someone new."

He turned his head back to me and pulled a stained shirt from the floor. "Augments? Avery, I would never have thought you'd —"

"Desperate times, *mi amigo*," I said, and I meant it: I wasn't one to be a hardass for no reason. I was exhausted by the performance. "You'll arrange things with Marcel for me?"

He nodded. "Okay, Avery. I'll meet up with you tonight."

And we shook on it, because we were old friends, the Pusher and me.

I didn't make it five feet out of Gatz's building before I noticed a pair of cops on my trail, not Crushers but the elite plainclothes officers, arrogant and worrisome. The System Pigs could be invisible if they wanted, if there was a tactical reason to blend, but many times they didn't give a shit, because what *rat* was going to go after the mighty officers of the SSF? These two might as well have had signs on their chests that said POLICE, with their dark long coats and their suits, their shiny shoes and their smug faces. They looked prosperous, men with jobs, the vanishing species. Besides, I recognized one of them, a blond with the blank look of a sociopath: I'd seen him outside a raid on the East Side, a while ago, and while he'd never seen my face, he'd come pretty close to killing me.

I marked them and kept walking, steady, slow, because it was always best to know where the fucking cops were. I went over my options: I didn't have any. They would come, and I would have to take it. Every fiber of me wanted to run, and I stopped myself with effort. It would take a while, because the System Pigs were careful, and cruel.

Half an hour later I was walking, head down, and somehow they were ahead of me, a wall of cop suddenly rising up in the middle of a street that was quickly becoming deserted, the soft breeze of fleeing people ruffling my hair. I actually stopped short and blinked up at them, confused.

"Avery Cates," the tall, blond one said. "The famous Gunner. Got a minute?"

I shrugged. "Always, for the SSF, officer." It pissed them all off to be called *officer*.

The blond grinned. His eyes danced, jittery, not really moving but not really focusing either, and were a bright, electric blue that made me wonder if his parents had had a little illegal augmentation done. His partner was fat and shorter, a lazy man's scum of beard on his face. He stared at me with steady, dead eyes.

"Captain Barnaby Dawson," the blond snapped. "This is my partner Jack Hallier."

I looked at Hallier. He didn't twitch a muscle. We were on Eighth Avenue, a section of Old New York that was still populated. Every other building was emptied and ruined, a scar from the Riots, but others sported gangs of people hanging out the windows, idle, bored, poor. The street had once been used for vehicles, I remembered, but had been narrowed by enterprising squatters who'd built junk shelters up against the old buildings, some used for selling scavenged shit. When the SSF wasn't around, it was packed tight with people, but we had two blocks all to ourselves, trash swirling around our feet. Even the Crushers had beat it.

I nodded pleasantly. "Officers."

Hallier whipped his hand out and slapped me across the face. My vision swam, my head jerked around, and I felt my teeth dig into my cheek, bringing out coppery blood. When I got my head back around, Dawson's finger—immaculately manicured—was under my nose.

"Watch your fucking attitude, Mr. Cates," he said, his face still as stone except for his dancing eyes. *Great,* I thought, *a psycho. Just my luck.*

I didn't say anything.

"You know a guy named Nad Muller? Lowlife piece of shit with sticky fingers?" he asked.

I nodded. "Yeah, sure. He's fucking dead. They found him down on Prince Street, popped."

Dawson nodded, his eyebrows raised. "Yeah, sure, you were there, shithead."

I kept my bruised face blank. "No, sir," I said, and braced for another slap.

It didn't come. Dawson looked at Hallier in apparent amusement, but Hallier was still just staring at me, dead eyes, mouth slightly open, like he was trying to use his mental powers to lift me off the ground.

"Huh," Dawson continued, turning back to me. "Avery Cates, aged twenty-seven, born in Old Brooklyn, twelve years of education, suspect in fifteen unresolved homicides, two dozen lesser offenses. Arrested six times, never convicted. Known as a more-than-competent Gunner, good for kills or bodyguarding or other related jobs. Good reputation on the streets as a straight shooter, trustworthy, always does the job and never reneges, reasonable pricing. Well-known even outside New York." The fucking Pigs and the fucking Monks. They thought having a wireless linkup to huge databases plugged into their ears made them special, and they loved to play mindreader. "Wanna know your shoe size, asshole?"

I shook my head. I wasn't enjoying this.

Dawson pushed his finger into my chest. "You were there, Cates. We *know* you were there." Hallier's hand was suddenly on my arm, shoving me. "So let's take a walk and you can tell us all about how you watched an SSF officer get killed."

"Ah, *fuck*," I muttered. I knew how this was going to end, with me kneeling in an alleyway with a gun pressed against my head. Fucking System Pigs. They didn't fuck around. I tried to think, but the fat cop was pushing me hard and Dawson's dancing eyes were hard and unhappy.

"Officers!"

We all paused, and I glanced up to see Kev Gatz running toward us. My odds had just improved immensely. Dawson and Hallier stopped and watched the skinny freak approach, and I looked down at my shoes.

"What is it?" Dawson snapped. If Gatz didn't have something useful to say in a second or two, they'd probably drag him into the alley with me and put one in his head just for slowing them down.

"I have information," I heard Gatz begin, and then there was silence. Hallier's hand loosened on my arm, and I looked up at the two cops, who were standing slackly, mouths slightly open. I risked a quick glance at Gatz; his sunglasses were back on.

"They're Pushed," he said breathlessly. "What should we do with them?"

I took a moment to collect myself, cold sweat dripping down my back. The two cops were just standing there, vacant. It took a lot out of him; even getting people to do minor stuff left him exhausted, but fuck if it wasn't a useful little talent.

I looked around. "We gotta get them off the street. Come on."

He nodded. "Follow us," he said to the cops. They nodded and lurched after us, heavy and sleepy. I scanned the block for a good location and chose an abandoned building nearby, crumbling old-world mortar and dusty air. With the System Cops, I knew no one was watching us too closely, or would think twice about them apparently dragging us off the street—that was standard procedure for SSF summary executions. A wide doorway had been boarded up in more optimistic times; I kicked the rotted boards out and we herded the piggies into the dark maw of the building. Gatz had our cops sit down on the floor, and I began to pace.

"How long will they be pacified?"

Gatz was leaning against a wall. "Few more minutes, Ave," he panted. "It's hard."

I paced back and forth. "We can't kill them," I muttered. You didn't kill System Cops, at least not after being seen out in the open with them by half of Old New York. It was unhealthy. The good people of New York never remembered a face . . . until the SSF started knocking heads and taking names.

"On the other hand," Gatz said slowly, "you're already fucking famous."

He had a point. When a pair of SSF show up and tell you your life story, the chances you're going to be left alone for the rest of your short, miserable life were pretty low. Maybe slitting their throats carried a low risk after all. But I shook my head. "Man, they sent two of them just because they thought I *might* have seen something. Two of them don't check in, they'll send a fucking army after me. I need to get them out of the way without being involved."

Just beyond the crumbling old brick walls there was the usual noise of the world, and inside there was Gatz, dead skinny and wearing out way faster than was fair, and two comatose System Pigs who had to be dealt with. On top of that, I had an entire religion . . .

I paused, an idea forming. I smiled at Gatz.

"What the fuck you laughing about?" he demanded.

"Get them up, okay? Get them walking, and follow me."

VI

CALM, DEFEATED HAPPINESS

00000

||||||||||||||||||||||||||

The streets of New York were always crowded, because no one had anywhere to go. Hovers zoomed by overhead, rich-kid's toys. Nothing commercial went by hover—all the shipping was automated, on specialized underground routes, though garbage was sometimes hauled in the air. The fucking robots had all the jobs; they were self-healing, intelligent, learning machines that never tired, never showed up late or hung over.

The street was wide, banked by tall, sagging old brownstones that looked moments from collapse. We followed the Pushed cops at a short distance, Gatz stumbling as he struggled to maintain a constant hold on them through his exhaustion. Trash swirled around our ankles, and every step was a push past shoulders and glares, everyone trying to out-tough each other until they saw the cops and suddenly got polite. I scanned the streets until I found what I was looking for: two Monks moving easily through the crowd with heavy tread, all the nervous humans making a small corridor for them to pass through, afraid to even touch their smooth, pale skins.

I nudged Gatz and the four of us started to follow the Monks. The Monks turned to glance back at the cops and then resumed their steady pace.

After a few moments, Dawson started to slow down, the tall blond looking up and back at me as if he'd never seen me before. His eyes sharpened.

"I'm going to eat your fucking kidneys, asshole," he growled. "I'm gonna—"

"Kev," I whispered.

Gatz nodded wearily and Dawson suddenly snapped forward again and picked up his pace. "Sorry," Gatz muttered, "It's . . . pretty fucking hard."

I ignored him, waiting. I knew how his Push worked, the mechanics of it: He needed eye contact to establish his hold on you, but after that initial lock he maintained control just by concentrating, and the effects lingered for a few minutes even after he let it go, which was ideal for my purposes here, as we wanted to put some distance between us and these Pigs. When I thought it looked like the right moment, I nodded at Gatz, and he stared fixedly at the backs of our captured cops, Pushing them to act out the little script I'd hastily written. Dawson and Hallier suddenly animated, reaching into their coats and pulling out their guns. The crowd scrambled. Shouts of "Cop!" went up, and we were standing in a swirling mass of confused humanity.

"Police!" Hallier croaked in a voice that sounded like it wasn't really meant to be used. The Monks didn't hesitate. They moved, *fast*. I was surprised that they didn't draw their own weapons, but rather ducked and ran as Dawson and Hallier pumped shells after them in precise, hypnotized sequence, Pushed. It was perfect. The Monks wouldn't take this lying down. Once away from the public eye, they'd draw their own weapons, and my two pet cops, under Kev's watery eyes, wouldn't be any match for their digital reflexes. The cops would be eliminated, and I wouldn't be implicated. The end result: two System Cops taking shots at legally recognized reps of a sanctioned religion, and poof! Dawson and Hallier out of my hair for good.

As the cops ran after the fleeing Monks, I grabbed Gatz by the collar and pulled him after me. I didn't wait to find out what happened. We ran like hell, Kev wheezing like an old man, me snarling behind him. We melted into the city and I thought I'd be on a plane out of the continental area, under a new name, within hours.

Two hours later, Gatz and I were crashing in a borrowed apartment for a few hours until it was safe to venture out and try to contact Gatz's Splicer friend, Marcel.

"Jesus fucked, Ave, isn't that one of the Pigs we got rid of today?"

I looked wearily up at the Vid. It was an older model, with no advanced features and just a sixty-inch screen, but that also meant it didn't have any of the tracking features the newer Vids had. On the screen, crisp and clear, was the oddly unhandsome face of Barnaby Dawson, blond and blue-eyed. He was staring straight ahead like he was pissed off at the camera.

I moaned, and gestured the sound back on.

"... dead. Representatives of the Electric Church issued a statement from London condemning the actions of the SSF captain, and demanding that he be immediately suspended from duty and tried for murder. No explanation for the illegally modified firearms found on the Monks' bodies was included in the statement. The Electric Church is now listed as the sixth-largest religion on Earth, with about nine hundred million registered members. Brother Kitlar Muan, spokesman for the Church, refused all requests for an interview . . . In Minsk this afternoon another food riot was forcibly . . ."

I waved the sound off again as Dawson's face was replaced by a video of a riot, people shouting and bleeding and generally getting their asses kicked by SSF, which was how all the riots ended. I looked down at the floor.

Dawson was alive, and I was fucked. *We* were fucked, but my interest in Gatz's well-being ended well short of including him in my own worries. I liked Kev a lot, which meant I'd try my best not to kill him. It didn't mean I'd lose sleep over it if I did, accidentally or otherwise, as useful as he was. Dawson was alive, Hallier was dead. They were *both* supposed to be dead. The fucking Monks were supposed to have pulled the same sort of cyborg voodoo on them that I'd seen, and Dawson was supposed to have gone down a Burned Badge who flipped out on the Monks and got fed some bullets as a reward. Having the motherfucker still *alive*—and being tortured in a fucking DIA Blank Room, a room that survelliance could not penetrate and that didn't exist in any official building plan or document—had not been the plan. I began rocking gently back and forth.

"Fuck, fuck, fuck," I moaned.

Gatz was up, rubbing his bare arms in agitation. "Avery, we ought to get moving. *Now.* Find Marcel before your name gets on the street connected to this. Marcel hears you're fucking marked with this shit, he won't touch you." Gatz shook his head, glassy-eyed. "No one will."

He was right. It was one thing to get hassled by the System Pigs; everyone did. It was one thing to even get charged with something—everyone did, eventually. But to really piss off a cop, to maybe get your name thrown around a DIA Blank Room, to maybe have the whole fucking SSF on your ass for revenge—shit, I wouldn't want to be seen talking to me either. Even the Crushers would stop taking your bribes.

I looked up and rubbed my stubble. "Okay, let's move."

It was good to move when you'd decided the time had come, because people who hesitate tend to get popped. I grabbed my coat and started walking, and Gatz was right behind me. Down the escalator, shrugging our coats on, and then into the street, still a mess of humanity pushing against the walls around them and looking for a way out. The whole fucking world was like this. There was no place left to go.

We'd only made it about six blocks against the tide when Gatz stumbled and put a hand to his head, just fingertips on his forehead, and winced. "Oh, shit, I feel like shit."

I was debating whether I wanted to go check on him or just leave him be, whether I really needed an introduction to Marcel after all, fuck, he'd know me, *everyone* in New York knew Avery Cates. But then I heard it: hover displacement. And then everyone in the street was moving and shouting.

"Police!"

"Cops!"

"*Policia!*"

"Pigs!"

"SSF!"

A second before the searchlight hit me, I closed my eyes and knew I was fucked.

The light made everyone scatter, and within seconds Gatz and I were standing in a bright pool of light, and the rest of the fuckers were crawling along the edges of the light, staying clear of it. Figuring, fuck, if the Pigs weren't interested in them, why *make* them interested? Fucking roaches, running from light.

I adjusted my sunglasses and considered. The hover was about ten seconds from close enough to drop Stormers—but they could always shoot you down in the street, too. The fucking cops could do whatever the fuck they wanted. If they hadn't shot me yet, I reasoned that they weren't going to, so I stood there, and kept my hands in the open.

The fucking hover *landed.*

I'd never seen an SSF hover land in the street. People went diving in all directions as it settled heavily on the asphalt, just a few feet away from me. Displacement kicked up. It was like standing in the path of a hurricane for a moment, wind whipping mercilessly, my face trying to peel off my skull. The street was just barely wide enough. The fucking bastards kept the searchlight on me and Gatz, trying to blind us. I'd had my glasses made specially for that, though, and I could see fine.

Little things made you feel good, when it came to the System Pigs.

The hatch popped open and two Stormers were out, darker than shadows in their black Obfuscation Kit, the uniforms taking on the color and texture of whatever they were standing in front of as they moved, giving me an instant headache. In ObFu, the bastards could stand against a wall and blend in like goddamn chameleons, and you'd never see them until they moved for you.

These two just knelt and covered me and Gatz with their KL-101s, automatic rifles with built-in grenade launchers. I made a mental note not to move. I knew I should be terrified, but I just felt empty. And tired.

"Weapons!" one of the Stormers shouted. "We want to see weapons!"

I nodded and slowly pulled my gun from its shoulder holster, my backup from the small of my back, and a razor from my boot, leaving them on the ground in front of me. Gatz just shook his head.

"Weapons, fuckface!" the other Stormer shouted.

"I don't have any!" Gatz shouted back, bless his soul.

The Stormers looked at each other, apparently having never heard of such a thing. Gatz relied on the Push to get him by. After a moment, however, the decision was made, because a couple of hapless Crushers in their loose, generic uniforms were dispatched to give us both an old-fashioned frisk, rough and thorough. Satisfied, they signaled and a System Cop emerged from the hover and stepped forward, looking dapper in a perfectly tailored suit and a mind-blowingly expensive overcoat. He glowed with health.

I hated him, hated them all, strutting around wearing more than I fucking earned in a year, and me earning it with blood everywhere, staining me forever. Mother*fucker*.

"Avery Cates, Kev Gatz," the mother*fucker* drawled. "Elias Moje, colonel, SSF." He nodded curtly. "Come on, then." He was about my size, but broader and heavier, carrying himself like a man used to throwing his weight around and getting the desired response. His salt-and-pepper hair was cut close, and a neat beard pointed downward from his chin. He grinned, but his eyes didn't. His suit was tailored, the material expensive, but what really drew the eye was his walking stick: black and shellacked and covered in thorns, its pommel a thick, heavy knot.

Outside the bright circle of light, I could see the gray mass of people moving like water, roiling, scrabbling, looking over their shoulders at us. I smiled at Moje, enjoying the curiously numb feeling that smothered all the fear, all the anger. "Nervous?"

He blinked, and then laughed. He threw his head back, and a rich, easy laugh emerged from him, spilling out in bubbling waves. "Mr. Cates, that's *hilarious*. Now, move it. You're late for an appointment with DIA Chief Marin."

I had already started to head for the hover—when the SSF sends a fucking *hover* to pick you up, you're already in deep shit and struggling will just make you sink faster—but the name *Marin* made me stumble a little.

All I knew about Dick Marin was what everyone else knew. He was the director of the SSF Department of Internal Affairs.

It was likely that Marin was the most powerful man on the planet, aside from twenty-five old bastards from around the world who called all the shots, the Joint Council (theoretically elected, but I couldn't recall an election). The DIA had been formed as a check on the System Cops, who were otherwise almost totally autonomous. The SSF had authority over everyone—the entire System. The DIA was the only body with authority over the cops. And at the top of *that* pyramid was Director Richard Marin. The facts on Marin were scarce: He'd been a real shitheel cop, a total bust, incompetent, lacking the usual cruelty and arrogance, his career saved only when he got shot about six million times in some remote hellhole in the Pacific. After years of physical rehab, he'd emerged as the newly minted director of the SSFDIA, the King Worm, newly molted. That was it for sure-thing facts.

Walking slowly toward the hover, knowing that I would be on all the Vids in a few minutes, I closed my eyes. I thought, with calm, defeated happiness: *I'm fucked.*

VII

GRIN ON THE TOP OF MY HEAD LIKE HEAT FROM A SUN

00101

I'd never actually been in a Blank Room. It was all in gray. Everything, gray. After about ten minutes I started to wonder if I was going blind. I was starving; I hadn't eaten since yesterday, and felt thinned, wasted. There was an almost imperceptible hum in the air, but whenever I concentrated, it seemed to disappear.

They left me for a long time, just me and the cup of coffee. I didn't know what they did with Gatz, and I didn't worry over it for very long. The coffee confused me. I hadn't had real coffee in months, and the smell of it made my stomach hurt. I'd never been brought in by the System Cops and not beaten up.

When the door *snicked* open I didn't get the goon squad I'd expected. Instead, I got a single man. Short, well-dressed, wearing a pair of snazzy wrap-around sunglasses, and moving in sudden bursts. And smiling. He entered the room at a brisk walk and didn't stop until he was looming over me, holding out one hand.

"Avery Cates, glad to meet you. I'm Richard Marin, director, DIA. You can call me Dick."

His grin was persistent, and creepy. I stared up at him for a moment, jaw hanging and eyes burning dryly.

"It's customary to shake a hand that's offered you, Mr. Cates, even if it belongs to a policeman," he prompted. "And I'm in a rush; I'm attending a Joint Council subcommittee meeting in Delhi right now."

I reached forward and took his hand limply. This was the goddamned King Worm, and I was shaking hands with him and sipping coffee. I was suddenly very lightheaded. Blood roared in my ears.

"Pleased to meet you, Cates." He began pacing. "Let's see if I've got this right: Avery Cates, age twenty-seven, born in Old Brooklyn about five years prior to Unification. Some early education but not much—in a formal sense. Short sheet, listing some early B&Es and a few bigger jobs . . . then, nothing." He turned suddenly to offer me a twitchy, sudden smile. "Nothing official, of course. In reality, Mr. Cates grew up to be quite the little murderer, didn't he? A shrine to Cainnic Orel and everything."

"I don't think you've ever had the world's most famous Gunner in one of these rooms, Marin," I said weakly. As I got older, I thought about Canny Orel a lot, out of simple desire to be an old man myself. Stories had it he'd been a Gunner before Unification. Although born in Philadelphia, supposedly he'd served the Irish government in the struggle for independence that followed, working for the Saoirse, the Irish Black Ops organization, murdering several early Joint Council members. When Ireland had finally succumbed to Unification forces and been absorbed, he'd survived and formed the Dún-mharú, and had become rich and famous and retired fat. So the stories went.

Unification hadn't been easy, I remembered. There'd been nothing but war, then nothing but bombs going off and officials being murdered, and it wasn't until the SSF got created and funded that things began to settle down. I had a lot of vague, unhappy memories of Unificartion, the last years of struggle.

For a moment he just grinned at me. His teeth were perfect, white and straight. His skin was smooth and pale. It was like a mask being thrust into my face, and a shiver went through me. Then he whirled and continued pacing.

"Forget it! It's true, and let's just agree that if you *are* a contract killer, independent, you are a *very* smart one. Still, current statistics suggest that you will be dead within three years. You're actually pretty old for a Gunner as it is."

He paused, staring at the far wall as if there was something there. Just when I was gathering myself to try to say something, he whirled again, pinning me with his mirrored sunglasses. *Just like a fucking Monk*, I thought.

"Mr. Cates, why did you set up two System Security Force officers to be killed?"

He was smiling, and then, like a jump-cut, he wasn't. "You were half-successful: Jack Hallier is, in fact, dead. Shot in the head by Monks who were, officially, defending themselves from madmen. Barnaby Dawson—the *other* madman—fled the scene shortly after Hallier's demise, but we tracked him down pretty easily. I've had him in a room very much like this one, being beaten to within an inch of his life by a fellow I affectionately call Mongo, and while I personally believe that Captain Dawson is no longer *capable* of lying to me, the story he tells me, over and over again in a sort of mumble because of a few missing teeth, is so *fucking* unbelievable, I had to have you brought in just so someone else would be in on the joke."

I stared at him, and he fucking smiled again. I felt shivery and weak, as if I was hollow inside.

"You're almost a legend. I can't remember the last time someone killed *three* SSF officers in the space of a few months!" I froze, cold shock splashing through me, and he nodded crisply. "Colonel Janet Hense, of course, and the unlucky Officer Alvarez found next to your friend's corpse. The teeming masses will write songs about you. Tell me about Mr. Gatz," he said suddenly, without pause or transition. "We have very little information on him, and he seems to be a good friend of yours."

I cleared my throat.

"A psionic, yes?" he said happily, almost dancing as he paced around me. "One that slipped through the cracks."

I nodded, struck dumb by the onslaught.

"And he took limited control over Dawson and Hallier and forced them to act contrary to standing order 778 concerning legal representatives of a legally recognized religion—a religion that has a lot of members, and thus, a lot of influence. Mr. Cates, what you and Mr. Gatz did was very, very bad for us."

His manic grin made him seem almost happy about this. As I stared up, his expression switched off again, and he leaned down, putting his hands on the table in front of me.

"Dawson and Hallier are the worst of the SSF, Mr. Cates. They're ignorant and arrogant and too willing to hurt people. But I don't care about them. What I care about, Mr. Cates, is the reason you were found by these two assholes in the first place. What you saw the night Officer Alvarez was killed." The grin came back, exactly as it had been. "I tried to get to you first, but those assholes had nothing better to do."

Suddenly he straightened up and stared over at the corner for a full six beats of my straining heart. Then it was back to me again. The motherfucker was crazy.

"Let me tell you what you saw," he said cheerfully, standing up. The lights dimmed suddenly, and one of the gray walls bloomed into bright light, a Vid. It hurt my eyes at first, but I welcomed the change of scenery.

"You saw a Monk recruiting a new member by killing him. The Monk shot him and would have had the corpse retrieved within moments. The victim would have reappeared the next day as a Monk—happy, content, and complete with cover story concerning his epiphany. This is how the Electric Church operates."

The screen flickered and a chart appeared, boring cubes and gridlines.

"The Electric Church is the fastest-growing organization in the world. It is growing so quickly, Mr. Cates, that it is currently estimated that it will be the world's largest religion in five years. In eight years, it will be the world's *only* religion."

I blinked, almost got my mouth open before he whirled back to me, his skin pale in the gloom, his glasses pitch black. "I *know*. A religion that did not exist seven years ago, subsuming the world in ten. Unbelievable! Is it because the idea of salvation through eternity is so seductive? No, Mr. Cates. The Electric Church is growing so quickly because it forcibly recruits new members. They murder their new members, they perform surgery on their new members, and they control their new members postprocess via hardwired circuitry."

Suddenly he was right on top of me again, leaning down. "In other words, Cates, I believe that inside most of those Monks is a horrified, tortured human mind that is used like a puppet, with a gibbering ineffectual terror. I think that Dennis

Squalor is possibly the worst mass murderer in the history of the human race. Worse," he leaned back again, smiling. "Worse, Mr. Cates, I think that if action isn't taken soon, the Electric Church may soon be beyond the authority of the SSF. Beyond *my* authority. And that doesn't sit well with me."

I cleared my throat. "Dennis—" I managed, and Dick Marin animated again, leaping up as the Vid wall clicked, and a picture, old and grainy, shot from some distance, appeared in place of the chart.

"Dennis Squalor," Marin said briskly, pacing up and down, "Founder and chief prophet of the Electric Church. He reminds me of you, Mr. Cates. Not a lot of information on him past the age of twenty-three, which is when Unification was achieved and he disappeared, returning—on various paper trails, at least—only when the Electric Church applied for formal religion status within the System. The Electric Church enjoys protected status as a religion, and it isolates Squalor pretty effectively. Of course, I know more about him. I know everything, but it's need-to-know and you . . . don't need to know."

He spun and almost threw himself at me. "Imagine, Mr. Cates—you were there, it shouldn't be a problem— imagine, you're walking home late at night. A Monk appears and the next thing you remember is waking up, trapped inside a metal and silicon body, with your higher brain functions looped through a container circuit. You try to move, but nothing happens. You try to speak, but the words that emerge from your mouth are not your own. *Your brain has been kept intact merely to pass all known identification systems.* Think on that, Mr. Cates."

I didn't want to. Instead, I thought about getting out of the Blank Room, getting back to a world where there was color and nuance. I cleared my throat, and when that did not start the madman jumping around again, I ventured to try my luck at a sentence.

"What is it, *exactly*, you want from me, Mr. Marin? I appear to be a little bit below your level."

Marin nodded. "What do I want with you? Mr. Cates, I want to hire you."

I blinked. The motherfucker was *insane*. The whole world was being run by this insane little shit. "You want me to Gun for you?"

"Of course not, Mr. Cates. You would be voluntarily choosing to do a few things, which will in turn have some unexpected benefits for you, which might, after an exhaustive and death-defying investigation, be traced back to the SSF. Not to *me*, mind you, but to the System Security Force in general. You'll do this because it'll be lucrative, and because I can have you killed just by letting your case proceed. You're a cop-killer, Mr. Cates. I am all that stands between you and execution. Take this on, and not only will your involvement in the deaths of officers Janet Hense, Jack Hallier, and Miguel Alvarez remain secret, you'll get paid, too."

He stopped, and just grinned at me. Fuck the Blank Room, this cocksucker's *grin* was freaking me out. I knew I'd break in no time if he just sat there and grinned at me, his head cocked to one side like a fucking ventriloquist's dummy. I felt an almost-irresistible urge to grin back, and I knew if I did I'd never be able to stop.

"You'll clear me on three dead cops?"

Marin *shivered*, a subtle vibration that rippled through his whole body in a second. "Collateral damage, Mr. Cates. I could not possibly care less about three dead cops, if you pull this off."

I licked my lips, and he spun away again. "Actually, I've already hired others to do this job. There are a *lot* of Gunners out there, Mr. Cates, and I've hired quite a few in the last few months. Most with much better skill-sets than you, I think. They are all dead now—assumed to be, in some cases, as no body has yet turned up. I've been forced to shift down to the second tier, and there you are—you have a rep for being very good, physically, and smarter than most. I've reviewed your arrest file."

Behind him the screen lit up with a quick flicker of my various busts, fifteen years of my life told in progressive mug shots.

"You're smart, Mr. Cates, but something's holding you back, yes? You fulfill your contracts and play by rules—you're trusted out there. Which is rare, these days. Criminals fear each other, they respect force, but very rarely do we find a criminal who is *trusted*." He whirled to grin at me again. "You're unique, Mr. Cates: a thinking killer. I hope maybe your approach will be more effective."

"So you're hiring me because I'm a mediocre Gunner," I croaked. This sounded interesting. My day was improving. "How rich?"

Marin nodded, once, curtly, and produced a slip of paper from one pocket, which I was amazed to think he'd had waiting for this moment, ready. I took it from his cold fingers and stared down at the unusually large sum written upon it. I thought at first it must be one of those imaginary numbers I'd heard about in school.

"Deposited into a secure account under any name you wish, within two hours of proof of completion. Do we have a deal?"

I kept staring at the number. "I have one requirement."

Marin was silent, but I could feel that fucking grin on the top of my head like heat from a sun. "A requirement, Mr. Cates?"

"Gatz," I said, looking up and squinting into his smile. "I need Kev Gatz. He gets out with me, and he gets a cleared file, too."

Dick Marin laughed, a single bark of noise. "I *see*, Mr. Cates! A reasonable request. We have a deal?"

I didn't answer right away, and then frowned. "Wait a sec—who am I supposed to kill?"

Marin might have blinked behind his glasses, I couldn't tell. "Why, Mr. Cates . . . I want you to assassinate Dennis Squalor. Of course."

I blinked. "Jesus fucked, *why*?"

Marin didn't answer right away. He stared just over my head for a moment, once again listening to something only he could hear. Finally the King Worm shivered and returned his attention to me.

"Why? Mr. Cates, haven't you been listening? The Electric Church is using its status as a religion as a *cover*. Dennis Squalor is not converting fanatics, he is aggressively acquiring slaves. If I do nothing, within the decade we're all working for him—and digitally prevented from doing anything about it, or even complaining. Time is short. I have no evidence, which restricts my options, and he's got the political acumen to make trouble for me if I act without evidence—highly unusual for me, and highly inconvenient. I have got to go through back channels. Buried channels. *Nonexistent* channels. I am seeking a loophole. If Dennis Squalor goes down, the resulting confusion will give me the leverage to order a full investigation, temporarily suspend the EC's exempted status—don't worry over *how*. You just do your part. Kill the high priest.

"Let's be clear." He was suddenly calmed and relaxed, orienting on me as if really noting my presence for the first time, his manner suddenly fluid and focused. "There is nothing official about this. You will be denied. I can offer you no help. On the other hand, you are free to act. I am not concerned with collateral damage. If SSF officers take notice of you, I will do whatever I can to help you. But a man like you knows how to avoid the cops when necessary, doesn't he? And if you succeed, Mr. Cates, all will be forgiven, no matter how messy."

I shrugged, trying to smile back at him. "I'm here, though, right? Is that how you keep things secret, by sending a goddamned hover to scoop me up in the middle of the street?"

In the face of that shining sun beaming from Marin, my own grin felt weak and brittle, and quickly faded away.

"Colonel Moje is . . . overly enthusiastic, sometimes, I admit. But no one knows, or would believe, that SSFDIA Marin is behind this, Mr. Cates. SSF officers often disparage the use of uniformed officers—what do you call them? Crushers?—to acquire assets, and misuse hovers and Stormers like that just to make an impression. To over*awe* the population, you see. A show of force is very effective for that. As far as anyone outside this room is concerned, Mr. Cates, you were picked up for questioning concerning the Dawson and Hallier incident, and released."

I thought about pointing out the sheer implausibility of this story, since the Pigs hardly ever released anyone, but didn't want to tempt this madman into going for a more realistic approach. Like beating me within an inch of my life, just for effect.

Marin leaped up and the door *snicked* open again. "We have a deal, then, Mr. Cates?"

He was walking briskly to the door. "I'll need start-up costs!" I shouted.

And he was out the door, which snicked shut again. I waited a moment to see what would happen, but nothing did. I glanced down. My coffee had gone cold.

VIII

THEY MAY NOT BELIEVE
THEY'LL SURVIVE

01110

"So, what's the deal?"

I didn't look at Gatz. I sucked on a cigarette and considered my options. They were very few, and it didn't take long, so I kept going over them again and again, to keep myself busy.

Marin had transferred a few thousand yen into my account, not much but a start. I had a few thousand scattered here and there, as well, and after a few debts were collected I figured we had about ten grand to get started with. You could have a pretty swanky night in Manhattan with ten grand. Almost everything else cost about twice that. Still, it was a start, and I figured whatever we couldn't afford Gatz might be able to finesse.

"Avery, come on," he said, struggling to keep up with me, turning his head this way and that as we walked down

Broadway, ruined buildings on either side of us. "We got pinched, we got released. No one even *talked* to me. So what's going on?"

I exhaled smoke into the densely polluted night air. "We've got a job, chum. We're working for the Worms."

He stumbled and I gained a step on him. "Are you fucking kidding me?"

I shook my head, my eyes scanning the crowd that pushed past us. No one took any notice, but you never knew. "No kidding. But the catch is, we're on our own. No one's going to acknowledge us. And the shit we'll be doing is going to be kind of high profile, some of it, and might attract trouble."

"So what the fuck is it?"

All of a sudden, we were partners. Gatz had proven to be a reliable buddy so far, I had to admit, but I wasn't used to having a partner.

"Let's get a drink."

At Pickerings, where all ventures great and small in our neighborhood began, I explained everything to the twitchy little fucker, who sat with his glasses on, slumped back in the booth, his gin and ice untouched, a layer of sugar floating on top—without the sugar, the fucking stuff would blind you, no shit. In the gloom and smoke of Pickering's he looked like a reverse shadow, pale and blurry.

When I was done, he leaned forward and took a long drink from his lukewarm cup, coughed a webby, chunky cough that didn't inspire confidence, and leaned back again. "Fucking hell," he murmured. "What now?"

I waved at Melody and held up two fingers for a second round. The thing with the unlicensed liquor was, once you started drinking you might as well get trashed, because it was going to hurt like hell when it wore off no matter how much you drank. In the light of day, Pickering's looked almost clean, its scavenged tables gouged with a million carved messages, its bare concrete floor still reeking of the morning's bleach. The whole place looked like it might collapse in the next stiff wind. Pickering's was the very edge of halfway-civilized New York; two blocks south and you were in no-man's land.

"We're going to need a team. This is fucking huge."

"A team," he murmured.

I held up my hand and began ticking off fingers. "I'm the Gunner—okay, fine. You're the secret fucking weapon, Kev, off the charts. You can handle all sorts of unexpected situations, just like you handled those two System Cops for me. But that leaves a lot of jobs for us. We'll need a technical guy. We'll need a transportation guy. I can do security, too, unless there's someone brilliant just kicking around New York. "

Melody brought our drinks and set them sloppily on the table and had already half-turned away when I snaked out a hand and grabbed her arm. "Mel," I said just below the din of the crowd. "I need to talk to Pick."

She blinked down at my hand; a spongy, pale girl getting slowly fat, missing one front tooth. "Yeah?"

I nodded. "Yeah."

She nodded, and disappeared. Gatz and I sipped our drinks uncomfortably for a few moments, and then she reappeared, swimming up from the crowd with a dirty towel in one hand, the other extended, its finger curled at us.

"Come on, then. He ain't gonna live forever."

Gatz and I got up, shrugging our longcoats back into place. I checked my weapon—Pickering's wasn't a good place to be unarmed—Gatz looked like he was negotiating with gravity to stay off the floor, and we followed her through the crowd, around the back of the bar, and through a nondescript steel door she held open, smirking at us.

"Be careful," she said, smirking, as I passed her. "He's in a mood today."

The back office of Pickering's was small and crowded, dimly lit and choked with dust. Old Pickering had once been a biology professor of some sort, back in the day. In the gray years just before Unification he'd lost his position and had begun a career in crime—and been pretty good at it, at least the nonviolent sort. Good enough to open his bar and retire, kind of, becoming a central gathering point for everyone in Manhattan. Old Pick knew everything that happened in Manhattan, and everyone.

The place was filled with paper and boxes. I remembered how to read, but didn't get much practice these days, and didn't bother deciphering the lettering on everything. Pick had his reasons. In the far corner, bathed in the bluish light of an ancient cathode-ray monitor, which was connected in turn to an ancient, tiny computer, pre-Unification, was a huge wooden desk, piled high with more paper and dominated by a huge round ashtray, in which sat a day's worth of cigarette butts, a huge pile of ash, and cheap, unfiltered remnants. Pick himself was a fat, immobile man with long, dirty gray hair and a round, punched-looking face. He managed to give the impression that he hadn't stood up in years, that the office had grown around him organically. He didn't turn around as we entered. He didn't look like he *could* turn around, this fat blob of a man hunched in front of a fucking keyboard—a *keyboard!*—and staring at the ancient screen.

"That's primitive," I said lightly, like always—we had a running joke. I snaked my way through the piles of crap.

Behind me, I heard the hum of the bar, distant; the room was reinforced and bugproofed.

He grunted. "Fuck you, Cates. It's pre-Uni, so it's clean of trackers and serials and spyware, yes? Can't do much, but what it *can* do the fucking System Pigs can't see. So fuck you."

I leaned against a tall pile of boxes next to his desk and tried to look casual. "You're looking fat, Pick."

He scowled and leaned back from his work. "All right, I see I'll get no peace until you have my undivided attention. What can I do you for, Mr. Cates? And, uh," he peered thickly at Gatz, his jowly face screwed into a permenant frown of concentration, "Mr. Gatz? The infamous Mr. Gatz, the man with the googly eyes. Your name's come up."

Gatz sank against a tall pile of paper. He looked ready to quietly expire. "Oh yeah?"

Pick nodded, turning back to me. "So?"

"I'm putting together a team."

"Yeah? Pay, or share?"

"Share. I've got some startup costs, but not much."

"Score?"

"Huge, potentially. Also hugely dangerous."

"Hmmph," Pick grunted. "Typical. Listen, Cates, you ever get tired of running in the hamster wheel out there and decide to do some real work, let me know. Okay. Let's hear about it."

I shook my head. Pick was of the opinion that we would all be better served by trying to destroy the System, and I'd heard his speech many times. "Uh-uh. That would ruin the surprise."

He grinned, his teeth the strong white ones of the older people, pre-Uni people. My own were yellowed and ached a lot. Gatz had about ten teeth left in his mouth, mostly in the front. We didn't get to eat often enough to worry about our teeth. In the middle of his cauliflower face and steel-gray hair, they were shocking and looked fake. Everything real looked fake, these days. Fake looked real. "I'll find out, soon enough," he declared easily. "Okay, what you looking for?"

I gave him the general outline of our requirements, keeping it vague and terse. Pick was right: He'd know everything soon enough. The man was a lightning rod for information around these parts; it was part of his livelihood, because everyone knew he knew everything.

The fat man whistled. "That's quite a team. Getting good people to work on commission's gonna be hard."

I nodded. "I've got a good rep. Remind people of that."

Pick held up his stubby hands, his panting breath loud. "Hey, Avery, I'm not saying you don't have a good rep. One of the better reps I know of. People will believe you'll pay them—but they may not believe they'll survive."

I shrugged. "Not my problem. Who's in town?"

Pick was a living, breathing directory. When people drifted into town, or got out of jail, or came out of retirement, Pick knew moments later, somehow.

He smiled at me. "Standard fee, of course?"

I fished out my newly fattened credit dongle, slightly dulled and battered over the years, but still functioning. "Of course."

He took it and slid it through the equally aged and battered reader built into the desk. He began punching buttons on the reader. He handed the disc back to me and then collapsed back in his chair. "Let's see . . . no one sitting out in the bar is right for this, but there's always people available in the city. You want the full list, or you want me to edit it based on who I think you can actually get?"

I was pressed for time, with the King Worm breathing down my neck. "Edit it, Pick. I'm in a rush."

He nodded. "For a Techie, then, I'd suggest Ty Kieth out of Belfast. He's on the run and living under an assumed ID over on Charlton. Heard of him?"

I squinted at him. "London Museum job, couple of years ago. A few other things."

Pick nodded. "He's good, but hard to like. Does his job, but pisses people off. He needs work, I happen to know."

I nodded. "Okay."

"Transportation." He sighed, rubbing one of his many chins. "That's tougher. Things ain't what they used to be, in that area. Fucking Joint Council's spent the last five years mandating DNA locks on all vehicles. Jumping hovers just isn't all that easy anymore . . . but, there's an old team laying low up in Chelsea these days. Retired, but always liked a challenge. If you floated it as a *challenge*, you might have some luck. Ever hear of Milton Tanner?"

I shook my head.

Pick snorted. "Fucking kids. Before your time, I guess. Take my word for it, Milton and Tanner are your people."

I shrugged. "Like I said, I'm in a rush. I'm prepared to accept your opinion."

He ignored me. "Security's always the problem, isn't it? Fucking security experts are all fucking ex-SSF, all fucking assholes. Macho bullshit. They all think security's the most important aspect of any job, and they always want to run every job, huh?"

I shook my head. "I'll handle security myself. Whatever this guy Kieth can't handle on the side, that is. Security's all tech these days anyway."

Pick rolled his buggy, porcine eyes. "Like I said, security's all assholes. Shit, Cates, I thought you were world-class. You're just a shitkicker after all, huh? Handle security yourself, you cheap bastard. That don't impress me."

Impress him. "I think I'll manage, thanks. Give me three backups for each, too. I'll take a hardcopy of current contact if you have it. Put the word out, too. I don't think I need warm bodies, but just in case I'd like it to be known that we're in business, okay?"

Pick nodded, sour, mouth kinking up in one corner as he swallowed bile. "Fucking hardcopy."

I shrugged. "I got no memory." I gestured at Gatz. "He's barely got a brain."

"Everything's going to fucking hell," Pick complained, gesturing at the hardcopy as it rattled out of the ancient printer. "Twenty years ago, we fucking knew how to fuck with things. These days . . ."

I pushed off from my perch and grabbed Gatz by his collar, pushing him toward the door. "Wasn't the fucking System back then, was it? Everything was better, yeah yeah, I heard it all. We all went to school and had jobs and were fat on milk. Fuck that."

The door opened for us as we approached. Behind me, Pick coughed loudly and then growled, "Fuck you!" And then we were back in the crowd at Pick's, where every fucking lowlife in the place was already staring at us hungrily, wanting in, word already going around.

IX

IT'S *THE HIGHEST LEVELS* AND LEAVE IT AT THAT

00100

Charlton Street was mostly residential, packed with sagging old brick buildings with no amenities, rooms rented by the night. Ty Kieth was in number 3224, up on the tenth floor, waiting out some overseas heat. We were expected, so we just stepped onto the escalator. I'd come armed, of course; not with anything insulting, just basic protection. And Gatz, of course. He slumped against the escalator railing next to me, dead weight borne aloft on metal tracks. On floor ten I had to grab at his collar and lift him off the fucking thing. Dragging him behind me, I found the right door and knocked, carefully. Pushing Gatz to the other side, I moved to my left and stayed out of the way, just in case Kieth was one of those touchy types who liked to answer the door with a shotgun blast.

To my surprise, the door opened without incident, and a short, bald, unshaven man stood smiling in the doorway;

not a care in the world. His nose was abnormally long, and I wondered if he had trouble hitting things with it as he moved about. As he spoke, it wiggled hypnotically.

"Hello hello. You must be Avery Cates, Gunner Extraordinaire, come to interview me. Don't be shocked, mate; I've got my eyes and ears in the air and watching at all times. If you were coming to kill me you would have brought more iron, and if you were bringing me some Piglet tracking device I'd have sussed it out of your magnetic field, trust me. Come on in, then. Let's talk." His voice was vaguely accented and precise; he enunciated every word and spoke very fast.

He disappeared into the room, leaving the door open. I glanced at Gatz but he just shrugged. We stepped into Ty Kieth's hideaway.

It was a small room, but the entire far wall was covered by stacks of electronics. Monitors showed us six different camera angles, starting with Charlton Street and working their way up to right outside his door. Black boxes with no obvious purpose hummed, red and black wires running between them. One small corner of the room boasted a creaky cot with a bare, thin mattress. Otherwise the place was empty and humming with electric radiation, black noise that cut through me, mutating cells and raising the hairs on my arms. Fucking Techies, knew everything but they were all racing against the tumors in their heads from the black noise.

"Word is you've got a job for Ty, eh?" Kieth said cheerily, punching buttons and making gestures near his equipment as he studied a green-on-black screen, lines of code streaming by his amazing nose. "Ty's hiding, of course, you know that, eh? But he's poor. Poor old Ty, he needs money. So maybe we can work something out."

I watched him for a moment. "You always do that?"

"Eh?" he said without looking up. "Do what, then?"

"Talk about yourself like that."

He shrugged. "Guess so. Never think about it. Spend a lot of time alone."

"Huh." I considered being stuck with this guy for weeks, months. "What're you hiding from?"

"Pigs," he said simply. He turned his twitchy nose toward me. "You want to see all the Pigs on the street?"

I frowned. "Huh?"

He beckoned me to a small, ancient monitor you had to lean forward and put your face against, cupping your hands around your face to amplify the dim image. "Take a gander, Mr. Cates."

I moved up and leaned over. A grainy black-and-white image of Charlton Street came into focus. It was poor quality and I could just make out the rough details. Most of the people were a dull, muddy gray, but three—two men lounging together against a wall, and a woman sitting at a street café, smoking a cigarette—glowed with a sickly green aura.

"SSF uplinks operate on a specific frequency and radiate a signature, chum," Kieth said happily. "They fucking *glow* if you know what to look for. I think these three know I'm here, actually. They've been hanging around the past few days."

I straightened and laughed a little. "Kieth, this street probably has a dozen fugitives hiding out. Why think it's *you*?"

He grinned. "Yer right, of course, Ty's unimportant—a speck. Lord knows he didn't have to flee Fortress Europa for a fucking *reason*, lord no. Only important fucks like Avery Cates get sucked up into SSF hovers like royalty and spat out a few days later with all his fingers and toes."

I reached out, fast, and pinched him just below the Adam's apple. It was huge, and tempting, and you practice shit like that in my business. Cut off his voice, his breathing, nice and neat. His eyes bugged out and the room was suddenly filled with a low hum and nothing else. Techies: They always forgot they were flesh and bone.

"Listen to me, shithead," I said easily. "I can just wait ten minutes and you're dead. Okay? I can twitch my hand, and crush your windpipe, and you're dead *faster*. Okay? I'm going to let go, now, and when I do, take a moment to get your breath back, and then tell me why the fuck you're on the run, okay?"

He stared at me, his mouth working. I waited.

"You know I can do this, right?"

He nodded.

"Okay." I let him go. He dived backward, coughing, and found a resting point against a stack of his equipment. He massaged his throat and glared at me.

"No call for that, eh?"

I settled myself casually. I was dancing, playing my part. "I need to know what baggage you're bringing. I've got enough attention coming my way, okay? I don't need your minders piling on with *my* minders, and making this into a fucking SSF party."

Kieth smoothed himself with elaborate ceremony and seemed to have completely regained his equilibrium, which was impressive. "Listen, mate, it won't be any worries, you understand? I can lose my little escort any time I want. Why do you think they're hanging around instead of cracking heads? Because word on the street is, I'm here, but they *can't fucking find me.*"

"Dig," he said, gesturing at one of the black boxes he had piled around. "See this? I can make this whole room disappear. They walk right by, every time. And this." He gestured at a smaller box. "Jams everything they throw against me. They're not stupid, you understand, they *know* I'm probably here. They just can't figure it out. Illegal, of course, every chip and nano-chain. No civilian supposed to even know this stuff exists."

This was interesting. I was beginning to regain my faith in Pick's recommendations.

"A Safe Room, huh? There are ways around Safe Rooms, Kieth, if the SSF has the energy and the motivation. You get blueprints, you do soundwave imaging, compare the holes you get on the screen with the holes you can see."

He sneered. "Safe Rooms—I've seen the rooms you folk in this godforsaken city call *safe*. Amateurs. Two-year-old tech, my friends. The only thing keeping you alive in those rooms is the fact that the SSF has a shrinking budget these days and the JC won't vote 'em enough skag to buy the necessary equip, see? If the Pigs are *really* searching you out, they could find you in a blink. This building," he swept a hand around impatiently, "is pre-Unification. There aren't any plans left. Ty checked. It's been burned, ruined, and rebuilt out of rubble. Our friends the Pigs would spend days digging into the walls of this place investigating every single anomaly."

I nodded. "Okay. I believe you. You interested in our work?"

He glanced at Gatz and then back at me, feigning relaxation. The way he watched my hands, though, I knew I'd at least made an impression. "Now, that depends, don't it? How about you give us a few details, then, and Ty can make his decision about that. Just the basics, nothing that could gum up the works."

"Assassination. Deferred but large payment. Very difficult. The target is Dennis Squalor."

Kieth became quite still, his nose oriented on me like an antenna. "The fucking Monks," he murmured. His watery eyes unfocused, going soft and dreamy. His nose quivered. "Who's hiring, then, mate?"

I considered. Having my employer common knowledge would be problematic in so many ways it was dizzying to contemplate. I was with Marin: No one would suspect—or possibly believe—that the SSF was behind it all. I shook my head. "Need to know," I said steadily. "*Mate.*"

Kieth grinned. "I get it, I get it. Ty's not stupid, but it never hurts to ask. We'll just assume it's *the highest levels* and leave it at that." He seemed suddenly calm and cool again, happy. "The fucking Monks. Oh, I'd love a crack at them. Cyborgs. Highly advanced. I've read specs and some papers, but the actual wiring is secret, you know. No one gets a gander. Secret, secret. Too many secrets." He appraised me again. "What's my end?"

"Large," I said. I gave him a number, and enjoyed they way his nose quivered. "But I can't promise anything. All deferred to after the job."

He nodded like he wasn't concerned. "Yes, yes, but what Ty wants to know is, can he have a Monk? I want a model for examination. Lots of tasty stuff in there, lots and lots of interesting tech. A man could get famous, publishing something with those specs in it, yeah? Don't you ever wonder?"

"Wonder what?" He spoke so fast I was having trouble keeping up. My hands twitched with the urge to slow him down.

"If they're really true believers, or if they're fucking robots, mate! Give me a few hours with one, and I'll tell you. I'll tell the world."

Kieth was a True Believer, a fanatic in the Church of Tech. I decided it wouldn't hurt to have one floating around. "Mr. Kieth," I said carefully, "I can almost guarantee you a Monk of your very own."

"Plus my share of the profits, yes?"

I nodded. "Of course."

Honor among thieves. He studied me for a moment, and

then glanced at Gatz. "And what's his role in this little theatrical put-on, eh?"

"Kev Gatz, Ty Kieth," I said by way of introduction, keeping my eyes on the Techie. "Kev's with me, and he's going to be very useful."

Kieth glanced back at me and winked. "Need to know again, eh? Well enough." He held out his hand. "Good to meet you, Gatz."

Kev stared at the hand like it was covered in sores, and then slowly unspooled a cadaverous hand to take it, shaking listlessly. Kieth looked back at me as he pumped Gatz's dead arm.

"I'm in, Mr. Cates, no worries. I've got enough info for the beginnings, see, so I can start scaring up skag we'll need. Let me know if you have any specific requirements, and if you have any cashola to get the gears started. I assume you'll be covering my expenses?"

I shook my head, trying hard to conjure up some simulation of regret. "Sorry, Ty. Your end is your end. I can't help you."

He scratched his head. "Eh? Well, there's a bit of a sticky nit, isn't it? Since I'm flat broke myself, having put most of me rainy-day funds into these luxurious accommodations in order to, you see, avoid the long-if-easily-befuddled arm of the law." He nodded. "All right then, it's back to basics: Ty'll steal what he needs. What's the good word, then, Cates? When do we start?"

I gestured and began following Gatz out of the room. "I'll be in touch, Kieth."

I could almost feel him grinning behind me as he said "Naw, you won't, Mr. Cates. Step out that door you'll ne'er find me again, eh? I'll find *you*."

And the motherfucker was right—the moment I stood in the hallway with Gatz again, I turned to look at the door we'd just passed through, and it was gone. I put a hand against the wall and it felt solid enough.

"Looks to me like you just hired the right guy, Avery," Gatz said laconically.

"You were a shitload of help," I said, running my hands flat against the wall. It was fucking *gone,* and all of a sudden I was in total agreement with Gatz. Whoever the fuck Ty Kieth was—and his anonymity spoke well of a Techie—he was fucking good.

"Yeah, well." He shrugged. "I don't know shit about this shit."

I turned away from the wall, imagining Kieth laughing at me inside, watching me pressed up on a plasma field with my nose squashed against invisibility. Fucking Techs. They thought they ran everything, and it was galling, because they did.

"Come on," I said, pushing him toward the escalator. "We've got more people to dicker with."

"Come on, Ave," Gatz said with a crooked, crazy grin. "Everyone wants in on this." He shook his head. "Everyone. They'll fucking pay *you.*"

X

YOU ARE NOT A BAD MAN.
/ AM A BAD MAN.

00000

Gatz and I got out on the street and I looked for Kieth's three cops. Even though they'd been clear as day on his little monitor, I couldn't find them. It freaked me out. System Cops are not subtle; they do not deign to fucking worry whether we see them coming or not. Seeing three of them do the undercover thing made sweat pop out on my forehead, because the only thing that made it possible to deal with them was their arrogance.

I swallowed hard. Gatz trundled along behind me, and who knew what the fuck that freak was thinking?

Your whole view of the world changes when you've killed someone for money. You can solve anything through murder. Someone shoves you in the street, you can follow them all day until they're alone in a darkened stairwell—and *pop*! Problem solved. Someone shortchanges you or doesn't pay up, you could wait for them, and *pop!* Problem solved. When you killed someone for money, you realized that the world was just a fucking machine. Push here, something happens. Pull here, something happens. Push and pull in a coordinated sequence, and you could make just about *anything* happen.

Your behavior changes, and thus everyone's reaction to you. I walked with Kev Gatz through the crowds, hundreds of people just like me and him, nothing better to do, lean and hungry. But everyone got out of my way. Everyone made room. When you killed someone, you were a god, if only for a few moments. It clung to you afterward, the faint scent of godhood. All the gray people around me could smell it, and they shied away.

You didn't just walk in Manhattan, not these days. You *performed*. You did a little performance just to get across the street. I scanned the crowd, hardassed, trying to project complete disdain. The thieving, roiling mass of arms and sticky fingers was my enemy and they were all looking to get over on me. You couldn't let that happen, because if you let one of the bastards get over on you the rest swarmed.

Gatz and I made our way on foot like all the other shlubs, pushing and shoving our way through the wall of meat. The problem with being hardassed all the time was *everybody* was hardass all the time. And I had a rep that inspired people to be twice as fucking rude to me just to show they weren't afraid. Fuckers.

So it was pretty obvious what was going on when the crowds kind of miraculously began to thin, and Kev and I found our way much easier.

I glanced at Gatz. "Fuck me. We're going to start getting a reputation."

Gatz looked like he'd swallowed a stone. "Start?"

By the time the cop cleared his throat behind us, the street was deserted except for a trio of Crushers who lounged against a crumbling wall, looking unwashed and grubby in their ill-fitting uniforms, their faces careful and stiff. Otherwise, we owned the street. I could have set up a table and had high tea with the Pig and no one would have bothered us.

I turned. "Colonel Moje," I said. He was about three feet behind us as we turned. He almost shone in the dirty gray light of Manhattan. The man could wear a suit. It was dark purple, pinstriped, with stylishly flared lapels and cuffs. He carried a dark black walking stick like a scepter, waving it unnecessarily. "How fucking delightful."

He grinned, his beard trimmed expertly, the flashes of gray in it giving him a distinguished, professorial look. Then he tossed the stick in the air, caught it deftly, and swung hard, hitting me in the stomach.

I exhaled my kidneys and went down to my knees like a sack of shit. I tried to breathe, experimentally, but it felt like a small rubber cork had been shoved down my throat.

"Mr. Cates," Moje said, breathing hard. "My name is Elias Moje, please don't ever forget it, because you have been *brought to my attention.*"

Oh, fuck. I thought. *This guy takes himself pretty fucking seriously.* At my altitude all I could see were his shiny, shiny boots.

"I was inspired by certain parties to pull your file, Cates, and spent an afternoon reading it. You think you're *world-class.* You think you're a *bad man.* Let me tell you something, Mr. Cates: You are not a Bad Man. *I* am a Bad Man."

With a large rock lodged somewhere in my windpipe, I could only stare at his incredibly shiny shoes while dark red spots crowded in on my vision. I thought, *Shit, who's paying this son of a bitch to run me off this job?*

"I know that you're working for Marin, that *fuck*," Moje hissed. "I'm telling you to back off. Don't get into shit with the Electric Church, got it? I'm telling you to go away. Go hide somewhere."

A pinhole opened in my throat and I sucked hoarse, wheezing air through it. Moje nudged me roughly with his boot. "Got me, shithead?"

I put my hands palms-down on the pavement and panted, the pinhole getting wider. "Yeah, I got you."

"I'll be watching you, Cates. Behave yourself."

I watched his boots scrape their way off, and Moje receded into a smaller version of himself, and was then swallowed by the suddenly returned crowd. Gatz eventually helped me up, and I wiped spit off my chin and watched where Moje had been, burning with a shameful fury.

"He doesn't like you," Gatz offered.

"Lots of fucking help you were," I snapped. "And it has nothing to do with me, fuck. That bastard's getting paid."

It was pretty common for corporations or very rich private citizens to hire System Cops as bodyguards or what have you—officially illegal but the DIA winked at it, usually, if they even knew about it. Whoever'd paid Moje had obviously cheaped out and not gone full-price to just have me murdered. Or maybe they just thought I was your typical street rat, and easily scared. Or maybe they *had* paid Moje to kill me, and he was just trying to rip them off, take their yen without breaking a sweat. Or maybe Moje was too terrified of Dick Marin to just kill me—who knew? And if that was the case, who would terrify Moje enough to even get him to go this far against the King Worm? Thinking this, it hit me: If Moje wasn't collecting a check from the Electric Church, I'd eat my fucking shoes. If the stupid motherfucker thought his sad display of power would somehow make me less terrified of Dick Marin, the stupid motherfucker was in for a lesson.

We blended again, becoming just another pair of unhygienic assholes in the mass. Milton Tanner were living a straight life up in Old Chelsea, running what, from all reports, was a profitable store selling artistic little bric-a-brac to rich fucks. I hadn't heard much about Milton Tanner, as they were before my time, and were over forty, to boot, adding a layer of unbelievability to it all. I didn't know *anyone* over forty, except Pick. It was like Gatz and I were going to meet a leprechaun.

The streets thinned out as we headed uptown, and the empty shells of buildings gave way to merely decrepit, sagging old stone structures that should have been blasted away and replaced with the shining new metal ones, except that everything ground to a halt twenty years ago and never quite got started again. Even those shining new buildings uptown were starting to look a little run-down.

The shop was called Tanner's, and the windows on the street were big and clear and unbroken, filled with the most ludicrous bullshit I'd ever seen. Little figurines, wooden jewelry boxes, crap like that. I felt grimy and dirty, and self-conscious — we'd lost our camouflage and stood out against affluence, even the very edge of affluence. I looked at Gatz and he just shrugged raggedly. I squinted at him.

"When was the last time you ate, man?"

He shook his head. "Food just makes me sick."

Tanner's was warm and inviting, filled with all kinds of useless crap. Furniture, lamps, knick-knacks, art pieces lined the walls and tables. There was barely any place to walk. I felt huge, shouldering my way through all the dusty shit, my eyes scanning the ceiling for the obvious security measures. Just as I was wondering where in fuck Milton and Tanner *were*, I turned a corner and stopped short, finding a tiny, craggy old woman blocking my way, arms akimbo.

"I *hope*," she snapped, "that you didn't come in here thinking to be robbing us, kiddo. You're on the system, and you wouldn't get far."

I smiled. "I look that desperate, eh? To rob this fucking place?"

It was insulting. I was a Gunner. I worked for a living. I didn't have to steal.

She looked me over from foot to head. "You look like a punk."

That was insulting. I turned the smile off. "I see the fucking cameras, Mother, and I see the field trips embedded in the walls. I didn't come here to rob you. Pick suggested your name for a job."

She shifted her weight slightly and suddenly seemed quizzical, less pissed off. She even smiled a little. "A job? What the hell do I want a job for? Do you have any idea how much money we make with this place?"

I looked around. "This crap sells?"

"It sure does, kid," a voice came from behind. I turned, startled, and found the same woman standing behind me. She was even standing arms akimbo, and a brief moment of complete confusion shuddered through me. Fucking twins.

"All right," I said, nodding. "Which one's Milton and which one's Tanner?"

The second woman shook her head. "Doesn't matter."

The first said, "Come on in the office, then, sonny, and we'll talk business."

The second added, "Bring your scabby little friend, too."

The first, "I don't trust him out here alone. Sticky—"

The second, " —fingers."

"Don't worry," I said, gesturing at Gatz, who was, indeed, examining some of the shit closely, as if it might profitably disappear into his skeletal hands. "He's coming. I insist."

The two women cackled simultaneously, freaking me out. "He thinks—"

"—he's got—"

"—some pull, like it ain't us—"

"—that's got the guns on him!"

I scanned the room again, gritting my teeth against the embarrassment of having to. I didn't see anything. I looked back at the first one. "No fucking way."

She sneered at me. "Gunners."

The back office was plush, carpeted, and climate-controlled, dominated by a huge wall-mounted Vid and two oversized wooden desks, ornately carved, pushed together head-to-head. The twins each took a seat and left Gatz and me standing. I glanced around, shrugged, and shoved a pile of papers off one of the desks with a flourish, hefting myself up onto it, facing them both simultaneously. I was about as uncomfortable as possible, but I wasn't about to tell them that.

They looked at the papers on the floor sourly. The second one said, "Your boy's gonna clean that up before he leaves, yeah?"

I blinked. "Probably not. And I'd like to see you make him. I'm here with a job offer. You interested, or are you making so much skag with this bullshit you're just enjoying breaking my balls?"

The second one shrugged. "Sonny, we *like* breaking balls."

The first one nodded. "We earned it."

"Wasn't for Pick, we wouldn't even talk to you," the first one said. "He's the only fucker we know of 'round here that's *older* than *us*."

"How do you know Pick?" I asked, to be polite. Polite did wonders for the oldsters. Anyone who'd been an adult before Unification, a few *yessirs* and *noma'ams* could go a long way.

"School," they said simultaneously.

"We worked with him on some government projects, back when things were still sane," the first one continued.

"Genetics," the second one added. "It was amazing to have the chance to work with him."

I tried to picture these two as scientists. It was an amusing image, these two leathery old broads rubbing their chins wisely, wearing white coats or some shit. It made sense, though; a lot of the best crooks after Unification had been real brains, scientists and economists and shit. Unification had done some weird things to people, people you'd never expect. It had killed my father, who'd seemed tough as steel to me when I was a kid, and it had turned these two freaky twins into thieves, and good ones. It was hard, after twenty years of living life on the streets of New York, to picture these two as fancy academics, but I'd seen stranger things.

"Fucking Joint Council tried to recruit us all," the first one said with a grin full of shockingly good teeth, yellowed but strong and unbroken—sort of like the women themselves. "We were living in a commune upstate—remember?"

The second nodded, her eyes on me. "Sure, sure—Freedom Gardens. Naked fucking kids, every-fucking-where."

"We were living up there with Pick, just watching everything happen, after the schools were all shut down and our funding cut off, and the JC sent a couple of shiny new undersecretaries up there to offer us all jobs. Some project they were all working on, right after the JC formed, something top secret, very hush hush."

They both grinned. "We told 'em to stick it!"

They glanced at each other without moving their heads, just eyes sliding to the side. "Shit," the first one said with a sigh. "They fucking raided the place a month later. Pick had a bolthole and we got out, but they tore the place down."

"We've been making our way off the books ever since."

"In other words, kid, Pick and us, we go way back. And that's the only reason we're talking to you, okay?"

"So get—"

"—interesting *fast*."

I shook my head. "You're talking to me because you're *intrigued*. Look at you. Sitting here rotting away selling bullshit to people you used to rob." I grinned. "Come on. You know me. You know I don't waste time."

They looked at each other. I could almost hear the static of communication between them. They looked back at me, creepy as hell.

"We heard the name, Mr. Cates," the first one said. "You call me Milton."

I winked at the second one. "Tanner. Let's hear it."

They may not have bought the act, but they bought the job. When I was done with my high-concept gloss on the whole mess—boiling what was likely months of work and endless complexity into two sentences—they looked at each other with that crazy light of excitement and greed I recognized very well. Every crook got that look when you really got him interested.

Milton—or Tanner, who the fuck knew?—leaned back and regarded me. "You're either the most fucked-in-the-ass Gunner I've ever met, Mr. Cates, or onto something great."

"He's fucked," Gatz said lazily. "Obviously fucked."

"Either way," the other one said, "we want to be there to watch."

"What's our cut?"

I gave them a number, and for the first time since we'd walked in, they were silent, staring at each other, using that twin telepathy to hash it out with waggled eyebrows and dilated pupils, Morse code. Finally they looked back at me.

"We're in, Mr. Cates," they said simultaneously. "When do we get started?"

"Tomorrow night," I said, sliding off the desk and making for the exit. "I've got a few arrangements to figure."

From behind, I heard one of them call out, "Word is there's a System Cop's got your name tattooed on his ass. You still gonna be alive by tomorrow night?"

I didn't look back. "Probably not."

XI

JUST SOMEONE WE THOUGHT WAS DEAD

10000

Outside Tanner's, Kev and I paused a moment. I watched the gray, sullen faces of people who marched to jobs working for people just slightly less poor than themselves. Or thieving and mugging and murdering their way through life. Few of us managed what Pick had managed, a little emperor of information in his back office.

I glanced at Gatz, who looked like he'd fallen asleep standing up. "Shit. I need a drink."

He nodded. "What the hell. I don't have any appointments or job interviews today."

We started walking. I felt nervous, exposed. I'd imagined I'd stayed outside the sphere of the SSF's attention because I was smart and careful, but here we'd located several famous people on the SSF's most-wanted list in almost no time. It suddenly occurred to me that the System Pigs might know a lot more than they let on, and just let us all scamper about to see where we'd go, that maybe I wasn't as hidden as I'd thought. After all, we had engaged Pick in fifteen minutes of conversation, paid him a few thousand yen, and had the location of several desperate criminals. I had an uneasy feeling Pick got his info direct from the SSF databanks, and that maybe I was in there, too.

It never took long to find a booze establishment in Old New York, the ancient core of the city. This one looked nicely squalid—a transient, illegal bar, not like Pick's, which was mostly legal and had bribed its way to a truce with the Crushers. It was one of the hundreds of illegal, unlicensed places that sprang up for three weeks, raked in cash selling sewer liquor to anyone with yen, and then disappeared just before the System Pigs took an interest. It was an old bombed-out relic from the Riots that looked ready to fall over in a heap, its windows ragged empty spaces. Scavenged tables and chairs had been scattered amongst the debris, and an open fire crackled in a trashcan in the middle of the room. I paused to admire the hand-lettered sign leaning up against the outside wall: LIVE MUSIC EVERY NIGHT. SITTERS MUST DRINK FAST.

I turned to Gatz to say something about this, but the freak had kept shuffling forward and was already inside. I quickly followed him in. The only other customer was an Asian-looking kid, apparently asleep at a table, legs up, mouth open, sunglasses obscuring his face, empty bottle between his ankles. I walked up to the makeshift bar while Gatz took a position near the door and removed his own glasses. Good lad, guarding my back.

The proprietor was a short, round, red-faced man who beamed at me with alarming jocularity.

"Welcome! Welcome to Rolf's by the Sea." He winked. "The Sea of Humanity, that is, flowing by our hallowed windows every day. We serve anything you want, as long as it is potato vodka. But we will call it whatever you wish."

I asked the obvious question. "Where in hell do you get potatoes?"

He winked one bleary eye. "We call anything used to make our fine liquors potatoes, sir. It is a generic term."

I nodded. "Okay. Give me a bottle."

He nearly farted in excitement and scurried away, opening a well-locked, reinforced door and disappearing into the room beyond. Real restaurants had fancy delivery mechanisms and Droid waiters, but who could afford shit like that? I drifted to sleeping beauty, pulled out the empty chair, and sat down.

"You have to sit here?" he said without moving.

I blinked. "No."

I grinned as the blobular Rolf arrived with amusing pomp and ceremony. The kid straightened and leaned forward, folding his legs underneath the chair with surprising grace, and said, "I wouldn't mind a blast."

I looked at him. He couldn't be more than a teenager, maybe eighteen at the most, but he was already ruined. Broken teeth, sallow skin, red eyes—a fucking waste. You could tell some-one's status just by looking at him, because there were only two kinds of people in New York—maybe in the world—these days: Rich and Poor. If you were rich, you glowed with health, you benefited from organ replacements grown from your own DNA, noninvasive life-extension therapies, effective and current vaccinations—the whole deal. If you weren't rich, assuming you made it out of childhood to begin with, you ended up looking like this kid. Like *me*. A walking corpse. You either had more money than I could even *imagine*, or you had nothing. That was it.

You sometimes got a slummer in the gin mills, a rich fuck prowling around in a costume, pretending to be poor. That's all they ever did—pretend. When you're that rich, there's nothing else to do. Everything you did, by definition, was pretend, because you didn't *have* to do anything. If you worked a job, it was for fun, because the jobs didn't pay shit. Droids did everything better; humans were just expensive, unreliable, and, to be honest, prone to robbing you blind.

You were either rich, cop, or little people. It always pissed me off when I saw some rich fuck pretending to do a job. There were people shuffling along outside right then who would kill for a job, any job. The only jobs left were in the Vids and the SSF. You could get into the SSF as a Crusher, a beat cop, which was better than nothing, but all it did was make your daily struggle for survival legal. Everything else you had to be rich in order to get the damn job. It made my blood boil.

I shrugged and slid the cup over to him, uncorked the bottle, and poured him a blast. He took up his cup, nodded at me, and drank. I took a hit from the bottle and winced. The stuff tasted like piss. Warm piss. "How old are you?"

The kid scowled, squinting into the cup. "What is this, a *date*? I'm nineteen."

I nodded. About right. Hadn't known any world but post-Unification. Had spent his whole life running through the sewers, terrified of the light because it usually turned out to be an SSF hover. I stood up. The booze was eating me from the inside, and I wanted to just puke it all back up. "Keep the bottle," I said, feeling tired.

He was already pouring himself another. "Fuck, man, I owe you one."

I started for the door. Fuck it, he'd be dead before long anyway, just like everyone else. Behind me, I heard a fussy, chubby little commotion.

"Sir! There is the issue of the bill!"

I paused next to Gatz and glanced at him out of the corner of my eye. "Kev, pay the man."

Even though Pick had never been a *physical* kind of crook, the kind that waves a gun around and beats the tar out of people, he had everyone's respect for the simple reason that he had survived the streets of New York long enough to grow old, and he knew everything. As a result, anyone in New York who planned to separate some citizens of the System from their yen came to Pick's.

A lot of jobs had been planned at Pickering's. Most if not all of the major schemes attempted in New York in the past decade had probably been started over rotgut gin at Pick's, and I figured I could do worse for a portent. I slipped Melody a few yen and reserved the back room. Once we were seated back there, I ordered Gatz a bowl of whatever Melody had going in the kitchen and sat there while he ate. It was slow going at first, but some ancient instinct kicked in and by the end he would've eaten the bowl if that hadn't cost extra.

I hadn't even gotten around to my glass of booze when Ty Kieth appeared, lugging a huge black bag. It was amazing: I *slept* with everything I owned. No one owned anything, anymore; the best you did was work some rich fuck's property and get some crumbs in return. But Techie freaks like Kieth could always scavenge tons of skag.

"Cheers," Kieth said breathlessly, dumping the bag on the floor and tearing it open. "Give Ty a moment while he scans and cleans the place. Ty doesn't make a peep in public until he's safe."

I nodded, raising my glass and taking a sip—always a mistake; Pick's gin was meant to be bolted, winced over, and held down by sheer force of will. "Knock yourself out."

He began extracting a startling amount of equipment and laying it in a perimeter around the room, pausing each time to spin around with a handheld device in one hand. Gatz and I watched him silently. When he was done, he grinned and dropped heavily into a chair.

"Well, that's done. We can speak safely now." He winked at me. "You're a hot name, you know that? Everyone knows Avery Cates out of Old New York has something big brewing."

I choked a little on my drink. "Great."

Milton Tanner arrived without fanfare and leaned up against a wall, arms crossed, looking very unhappy. I muted the huge Vid installed in the wall behind me with a gesture.

"Okay, since you're all here I assume we're all on board, yes?"

Ty Kieth attempted a smile, nose quivering. "I think we're all desperate enough to be in this."

"You don't speak for us," Tanner growled. I saw Milton's lips move, silently. "But yeah, we're in."

I didn't give a shit *why* they were in. "Okay, let's get started. I have three items to address here. Number one is, as of this moment, you are all in my employ. This job has begun, and if you have any problems with me or taking orders, walk away right now."

I waited again. Stony silence.

"We'll make introductions later. The second item is this: This is not a democracy. The money flows through me, so if you want your share, do what I say when I say it. Your expertise is needed and I'll ask for it. But don't argue with me. Questions?"

I waited again. After a moment, to my surprise, one of the twins raised her hand.

"Okay, we're experts, Mr. Cates," she said crisply. "I know who Kieth is by reputation. Who's the zombie?"

I glanced at Gatz and grinned. "Kev Gatz is who you deal with if you piss me off."

We all stared at Gatz for a moment. He appeared to be asleep.

The sisters looked at each other for a second and then looked back at me. "Okay."

I nodded. "The final item is this: How we're going to proceed. We need information. The Electric Church is a protected state-registered religion under laws 321 and 322 promulgated by the Joint Council. There's no detail concerning their activities or facilities. We need to do some recon." I paused, finally knocking back my drink. It burned, and my eyes watered. "We're going to begin the discovery process by acquiring a unit from which to extract information."

I waited again. Everyone stared at me and Kieth became excited, glancing this way and that to gauge the reactions of the others. "Wait a sec, Mr. Cates, are you saying we're going to acquire a fucking *Monk*?"

I nodded. "That's priority one. We need to identify a unit, snatch it, and then it'll be up to you to dissect and get whatever you can from it."

Gatz suddenly animated, sitting forward with a scrape of

gritty dust beneath his boots, looking over my shoulder at the Vid. He didn't move any more than that, but a vibrating stiffness settled on him and made me watch him from the corner of my eye.

"We can't do this here in New York, though," I said, ignoring Gatz. "As Mr. Kieth has pointed out, I've attracted the attention of a System Cop named Moje."

Milton and Tanner moaned in unison. "Elias Moje," Milton said. "We know that cocksucker."

"So the idea is, we leave here tonight with an action plan for acquiring a Monk," I concluded.

"Ave," Gatz croaked. I glanced at him. He was still staring over my shoulder. "We got a situation."

I twisted around to view the silent screen of the Vid. I almost jumped out of my skin, because a three-foot-high image of Barnaby Dawson's face filled it. I gestured the volume back on.

"*. . . custody and is at large. SSF spokesmen could not explain how Captain Dawson escaped from custody, but did issue a warning to the public that the former SSF officer is armed and dangerous. They note that Captain Dawson had been in Internal Affairs' custody being investigated for several infractions of the SSF Binding Charter, including murder, trafficking in illegal and/or stolen goods, torture of suspects, misuse of authority, cat —*"

I gestured the sound off again.

"Another SSF friend of yours?" one of the sisters asked with a raised eyebrow.

Her sister raised the opposite eyebrow. "I'm thinking we should get hazard pay."

I stared into Gatz's blank tinted lenses for a long moment. Then I shook myself. "Just someone we thought was dead. He doesn't factor into this." I took a deep breath. "Action plans for acquiring a unit. Let's hear 'em."

Dawson's face, with his crazy, dancing blue eyes, stayed in my head. I knew I'd be seeing it again soon. If there was one rule every one of us scrabbling for survival at the bottom of the barrel lived by, it was *Never* fail *to kill a System Cop.*

XII

FORCED INTO THIS LIFE BY THE EVIL WORLD

10010

"Kieth really came through, huh?"

I glanced at Milton—I assumed it was Milton—but didn't respond immediately. In my ear, the commlink hummed with dead air, the sound of the city's wind rushing by. I looked back at Gatz.

"Everyone came through," I said curtly.

Kieth had produced an astonishing amount of high-quality tech in a few hours, including the wireless commlinks we all sported, a tiny earplug and ambient microphone that picked up the slightest whisper. Milton and Tanner had somehow found the perfect transport for our quarry. I had armed us, finding just about everything on my wish list in hours—word was out that I was a dead man, on the SSF's shitlist and in over my head, but word also said I was a *rich* dead man, so transactions were easy, even with my credit. Kev Gatz, although his role in our first foray into world-class criminal activity was a passive one, took it without complaint. He was now standing out on the ruined street, looking like he remained upright through simple habit.

"Where the hell are we, anyway?"

I ground my teeth. Milton never shut up. Separating the twins had been a mistake: She chattered aimlessly, and I thought she didn't know what to do when her sister wasn't standing right next to her. "Newark," I said stiffly. "What's left of it. Riots nearly burned it to the ground. No one really lives here anymore, except a couple of villages built out of borrowed stones."

She nodded. I hefted the sniper rifle I'd acquired and examined its action for the hundredth time.

"You know how to use that, sonny?"

"Yes."

"I know it's old, it's from the Iraqi Wars. Fucking ancient. But the shells are armor-piercing, and it'll fire. You know what the Iraqi Wars were?"

I closed my eyes for a dangerous moment, gathering strength. I was Gatz's lifeline; if this went wrong and it looked like the Monk was going to start tearing new asses, I was going to blow its head off. "Yes."

"I wasn't sure. Can you read?"

"Of course I can read."

"Just checking. You're just a kid, and the lack of education is shocking these days." She paused for a blessed moment. "You ever wonder about them? The Monks?"

I gritted my teeth again. I imagined death, imagined my breathing getting harder, more labored, my mind dimming, everything going dark . . . I pushed the thoughts away, my heart pounding. Swallowing thickly, I oriented on Gatz, who still stood in place, like a statue. I knew the Monk would come if we managed to not set off any alarms. It had harangued Gatz earlier in the day, just like the Monk had harangued Nad Muller. It was coming.

Milton's voice swam back up from the muddle. "You ever think about your sins?"

I forced a laugh. "Sins?"

For a moment, a blessed moment, she was quiet. Then she chuckled. "I guess you're one of the good guys, huh, Cates? Forced into this life by the Evil World. Every person you cut down, they deserved it, huh? I'll tell you something; no one deserves it."

"Shut up. Something's coming."

Gatz leaped into action by raising his head and removing his glasses. It was instinctive with him, unveiling his only weapon, even if it wouldn't do him much good. I fit the rifle's stock into my shoulder, rested the barrel on the low wall of crumbling brick, and squinted along the sight. After a moment, it appeared.

Tall, its black robes melting into the night, its waxy white face shining like the moon, its eyes behind dark glasses a band of void.

"Mr. Gatz," its voice came, silky and perfectly modulated. "Let me show you an endless trail of sunsets. Let me save you."

I waited for Kieth. I expected him to jump at it, hit the spot immediately as we'd discussed. But there was nothing. I'd give Kieth as long as I could, until the Monk made its move. Kieth knew his window. I'd give it to him.

Gatz didn't say anything, or move. He stared at the cyborg with his slitted, yellowed eyes.

"Ah, you are ready," the Monk said. "That is good. Too many flee from salvation. You will soon be free from doubt, Mr. Gatz. You will soon be assured of grace."

"Come on, Kieth," I murmured, sighting the Monk's grinning latex face. "Don't fuck this up." He had about five seconds before the Monk blew Gatz to hell.

The Monk hesitated. It was a strange sight. It looked like it was about to say something, and then . . . froze. I'd never seen a Monk go still like that.

"Cates," Milton whispered next to me. "Cates, it's gonna blow his chest open. *Do it*, for God's sake!"

The next two seconds were a blur. The Monk moved as if encased in sudden jelly. Kieth appeared, moon-faced and bald, holding up the handheld trigger. A split-second of complete silence, and my earpiece went dead and the Monk crumpled to the ground.

"EMP discharged!" Kieth shouted. "Seven minutes to brain death! Let's *move!*"

The electromagnetic pulse disrupted electrical systems, causing most to just shut down completely, causing all of them to malfunction to some degree, but did no physical damage. Kieth had insisted an EMP would knock the Monk on its ass, and there it was, prone and unmoving, gun in hand. As Milton and I leaped from our hiding place, the roar of the transport hover filled up the empty space—a slow garbage-detail hover, normally completely automated. Kieth had wired it for manual operation after Milton and Tanner had acquired it, and Tanner piloted the gerrymandered ride with a light touch I had to admire, setting the behemoth onto the pavement, just feet away from us. The huge, slimy hold that normally contained whatever garbage the shiftless citizens of Newark generated opened like a mechanical flower. As Milton and I ran by I tossed the sniper rifle in.

As I moved past him, Gatz said "I felt something, Ave. I felt like . . ." He shook his head. "Forget it. Probably my imagination."

I nodded. "Get it in!" I shouted. "Move!"

I took its arms, Kieth and Milton each took a leg, and we lifted it about an inch off the ground and grunted.

"Holy shit!" Milton gasped. "Doesn't the Electric Church know about *alloys*?"

As fast as we could, we dragged the Monk into the garbage hover, the last few feet an effort of pure willpower. Gatz clambered up behind us.

"Thanks, mate," Kieth wheezed to Kev. "Without you it would've been impossible."

"Let it drift," I advised. "Five and a half minutes left. Tanner! Let's displace, and be careful not to activate the compressor!"

Kieth eyed the huge hydraulics, which normally crushed the trash into tiny cubes, and his nose quivered in terror. He shook himself and tore open his backpack, pulling fistfuls of tools from it. "Give me the time every half-minute," he ordered. "First, we have to disconnect the communications and tracking bugs, or the moment our friend here comes back on line, we're dead men."

"Five-fifteen," I said, glancing at my watch. The hover lurched, and my stomach dropped into my shoes as it rose into the air. "Tanner!" I shouted again, feeling undernourished and exhausted. "Stay to the usual routes as much as you can."

"Yes, Dad," she shouted back. "Now shut the fuck up and let me drive."

The hover, lacking any of the amenities of a manned transport, made so much noise I felt it vibrating through my body. I watched Kieth work.

First, he produced a small laser-powered cutting tool. "The abdomen's where the main tech will be; it's the largest part of the body," he muttered, sweat dripping of his nose. He tore the black fabric of the Monk's robes, revealing a smooth, mannequin's body, crisscrossed with compartments and openings. With a blue flash, Kieth fired up the cutter and set it against the latex skin, right below the shoulder.

"Five minutes," I shouted.

Kieth didn't blink, and cut with maddening care, the bright blue beam of razor-sharp light inching its way around.

"Can't rush these things, Mr. Cates," he muttered. When he completed the oblong incision around its chest, he produced a large suction cup with a handle, which he hammered down onto the Monk, lifting the outer shell up and tossing it aside as well.

We all stared. The Monk's insides were inscrutable; five black boxes of varying size, connected by what appeared to be pipes of plastic.

"That's the fusion power source," Kieth said, tapping the largest of the boxes with a long metal tool. "Can get you ten for a million yen in just about any city in the System. The pipes are data buses and power lines, bundled. Give Ty a moment here to suss out a few things."

"Four and a half," I said, fighting an urge to jump up and pace.

Kieth's mutterings became inaudible, his lips moving as he ran his fingers over the piping, each section popping open under his learned touch, multicolored wires bulging out in a confused mess.

"Fucking thing's a walking arsenal," he said suddenly. "Cates, you've been lucky. These bastards have more firepower than you'd imagine, hidden in the arms and legs." More lip-moving, and then, with a grunt, he leaned forward with his odd, long tool and touched a small black dot on the side of the cavity. There was a flash and a scent of ozone.

"Got one. Kieth knows what to look for now." More flashes as he jabbed the tool here and there. "Milton, how about handing Ty that small gray box with the red button?"

Milton twisted her wiry frame around and rummaged around the bag and tossed the box to Kieth, who caught it smartly in midair. Kieth waved it around inside the Monk's cavity and nodded. "He's quiet. Can't talk to Mother Church, at least. Ty doesn't think he can be tracked, either."

"Three and thirty. What the fuck does the word *think* mean in that context, Kieth?"

"It means it's always possible they can track him in any number of ways. Radiation signature. Brainwave scan. Inter-valed Call-Home Beacon. It would take Ty a few hours to rule out every possibility, okay? And we have three minutes. And I've still got to resuscitate him. We don't have time. Proceeding to resuscitation."

More tools, Kieth's hands moving in a blur. We didn't know for sure how the Electric Church kept the Monks alive, their brains at least. I sighed and rubbed my eyes. They felt like someone had poured sand into them.

"Bind it up, Milton."

As Kieth worked, Milton tied its hands and ankles with heavy wire.

"Here we go, gents," Kieth shouted. "Be ready!"

"Milton!" I shouted.

"Okay, okay, damn!" She scrambled back and produced

a heavy pistol, known on the streets as a Tank Stopper. Also ancient, but it would turn the Monk into spaghetti code with one shot.

With a deep breath, Kieth made an adjustment. Nothing happened. We stared at each other, like eyeball Ping-Pong: I looked at Kieth, he looked at me, I looked at Milton, we all looked at the Monk. Without warning, it spoke, calmly, its voice automatically amplified, like magic.

"I detect that I am bound, and that my system integrity has been compromised," it said. "Explain this."

We all sagged backward, letting out our breath. If it had been able to attack, it would have, I was sure.

"You've been kidnapped," I shouted back, panting with reaction, the tension running through me. "Now shut up. You'll find out what it's all about soon enough."

A few seconds of noise ticked by. I was sure the creepy thing was studying me. "Very well," it said finally, its voice clear above the din. "I will wait. I have time."

XIII

HELLO, RATS. TIME TO RUN.

01001

"I assure you, this is not necessary. I would not harm any of you. Life in all its forms is sacred to the Electric Church. Mr. Gatz, I appeal to you."

I was busy helping Kieth unpack his gear and trying to breathe. The warehouse was a shell, a huge spiderweb of beams and tattered insulation, set on fire at least once in the distant past. There was plenty of evidence that it had been used many times by people like us, scuttling along under the SSF's radar.

"What's your name, Monk?" I called out, fighting the urge to cough up a lung. The dust we were stirring up was thick and sulfurous, decay itself. While Kieth and I slapped units together and dragged cable, Milton was double- and triple-tying the Monk to an ancient rusted barber's chair we'd found in the debris, its padding eaten away. Tanner was going over the garbage hover, stripping off unnecessary weight and rerouting the wiring more efficiently. Gatz sat cross-legged in front of the Monk, staring at it intently, the weird bastard. Altogether we were stirring up a decade's worth of particles.

The Monk turned its white head toward me. "I am Brother Kenneth West, Gamma Brethren, the Electric Church."

"Well, West," I wheezed. "I know you're talking to my associate there because he's the only one of us you managed to run through the EC's databanks before we snuffed your connection, but don't waste your time. He can't help you, even if he wanted to. Which I doubt he does."

The Monk stared at me for a few moments. "You are in charge here? Then I shall speak to you. Why have I been abducted? Why have I been tampered with? This is in direct violation of a number of System laws, most notably Joint Council edicts 321 and 322. Tell me," it went on, its voice maddeningly calm and fluid, "do you fear eternity so much, that you seek to prevent me from attaining it?"

Its serenity bugged me. It was programmed, I knew, but it still bothered me. As Kieth and I pulled the last of his black boxes from its sheath, I left the bolting and connecting to the short, bald Techie and walked over to stand in front of the Monk. It looked back at me with its blank, dark-lensed stare, cocking its head in curious birdlike movement that struck me instantly as somehow familiar.

"Eternity is actually just fifth or sixth on my list of heebie-jeebies, West. Right below bugs crawling into my ears while I'm asleep and above getting gutshot by a Monk and having my brain sucked out of my skull." I put on a bright and cheerful expression. "That leaves lots to be more afraid of. Milton, take those fucking glasses off."

"Yessuh," Milton muttered, ducking her head in a mock bow. "As you command, suh." She reached up and tore the glasses roughly from the Monk's face. A split-second of complete stillness enveloped us.

"Ah, fuck," Milton grunted.

The Monk had no eyes. In the sockets were small, delicate-looking lenses, cameras, which moved this way and that on tiny motors, probably nano-based. They protruded from empty, dark sockets, moving with subtle jerks, almost subliminally. I didn't want to look at them.

"I assure you," the Monk said evenly, "I see perfectly well. I do not know why you despise my religion. It is a better existence. An eternal existence, one that leads to salvation. I would be very willing to discuss these things with all of you. You may even leave me bound, if it comforts you. Those who have no hope are often afraid of what they do not understand."

I rubbed my own eyes. "Kieth, you'll be okay with it alone? We need to acquire some equipment, and it's slim pickings in Newark-fucking-New-Jersey, population fuck-if-I-know."

"Ty's secure in his damnation, Cates. Ty works better on his own, anyway."

"Milton, Gatz, come on. We've got a laundry list before we try to skip the country."

Milton gave one final tug to the Monk's bonds and then popped up. "Yessuh. I'm a-comin', suh."

Gatz swiveled his skeletal head around to face me. "Ave, I'd like to stay here, if it's okay."

I eyed him. "Yeah?"

"I'm working on something."

"All right," I decided. I never knew what was going on behind Gatz's sleepy face, but I knew enough to respect the rare moments he actually expressed an opinion. "Let's go, sister."

"Cates," Milton said, "keep calling us *gals* and *sister* and you're going to end up a eunuch before this is all over." She said it cheerfully, like it wasn't meant to offend. I just shook my head, thinking I probably wouldn't even notice.

Silently, we exited the ruined warehouse, picking our way over the rubble that had once been Newark. A lot of cities had been hit pretty hard during the Riots, before the SSF organized effectively. Newark had actually organized as an independent city-state for a few months, refusing to acknowledge the Joint Council or the National Governments. The SSF hadn't left much standing once they'd gotten around to putting down the rebellion, so Newark didn't have much by way of infrastructure anymore. Wireless phones were illegal and hard to find, anyway. Easier to get closed-circle commlinks like the ones Kieth had supplied, but those only worked with links tuned to the same frequency. I was out of ready cash, and had no contacts in Newark—if there were professionals to even contact, in this wasteland—so we'd just have to scavenge for the remainder of our requirements. Which wasn't too bad. The wasteland was also a jungle of ancient, rusting tech, a lot of which could be cannibalized and used.

"What if we unplug that poor bastard back there and find out he's a true believer? Waiting out Eternity, hoping to shake God's hand?" Milton suddenly wondered.

"For God's sake," I complained. "I . . ." I paused, cocking my head.

"I what?"

I held up a hand and drew my gun. "Shut up. Listen, for a change."

We stood for a moment amid broken stone and twisted metal, lit by the moon and nothing else, the faint outlines of a street stretching out before and behind us. I could hear Milton's breathing, loud and ragged, the sort of breathing that made my job easier, usually. I closed my eyes and just listened. When I popped them open again, my heart was pounding. I shoved Milton's shoulder roughly.

"Run."

I took off without waiting for her, diving into the only cover we had: the buildings, empty, smashed open, easy to jump from one to the other. Milton was right behind me, but making more noise than I liked.

"What is it? Cates! What is it?"

"Hover displacement!" I shouted over my shoulder. "Distant, but coming."

She didn't say anything. She knew what that meant.

I raced through our slim list of options—where could we run? Back to the others so we could all get smashed? The System Pigs weren't out here by accident; there was nothing to patrol out in fucking Newark. Out here, without crowds and Vids and that peculiar gossip of the crowded cities, whatever thin protection they afforded us was gone. Out here, the cops wouldn't even feel the need to march us out of sight before shooting us.

We ran. I had plenty of experience running, and I moved as best I could, leaping through empty, crumbling windows and forgotten, sagging doorways. I crashed into walls and tripped over rubble, and before long the roar of the hover got close, and the stinging white light of the search lamps began to track us.

The hover's PA system crackled to life. "Run, you fucking rats, but we're on you now!"

I tripped at the sound of the voice and went sprawling, my teeth clicking shut, hard, on my tongue, my gun skittering away. Elias Moje. The smooth, well-fed voice was unmistakable. Milton leaped over me and ran three long steps before skidding to a halt and hesitating, looking back at me.

"Go!" I shouted, staggering to my knees. My head was ringing. "Don't be an ass! GO!"

"Fuck," she hissed, and spun back to me. She plucked my gun up, grabbed me by the coat and pulled me to my feet with surprising strength. I spat blood as she handed my gun back, and then she was on her way again, running blind. I sprinted to catch up, my mouth full of the coppery taste of my own blood.

The SSF had a million ways to nail you, of course. They weren't burdened by ancient concepts of warrants or rights or due process. They could arrest you for no reason and hold you indefinitely without a charge. They were licensed to kill and had nothing more than paperwork to deter them. They played nice with the lords and ladies, the rich and powerful, sure. People who could push on Dick Marin and get Internal Affairs to investigate something. But for me? For all of us scuttling through the packed cities picking up a wage here and there, robbing for food and terrified? They did whatever they liked.

Milton and I darted through empty buildings, taking random turns and trying to stay under cover of crumbling roofs as much as possible. After a few minutes, I stopped and held my hand up for Milton who, an old pro, stopped on a dime, panting. I tried to control my own breathing, and listened.

Nothing. Silence.

"All right," I said. "Let's hunker down in here for a few minutes, and then we'll make our way back. Pick up what we can along the way."

She nodded, raising an eyebrow in a way I already recognized as a Milton Tanner trademark. "That's the most amazing plan I've ever heard, chief."

"Just keep your eyes open," I muttered, spitting blood and finding a wall and settling down against it, catching my breath.

I contemplated a short, unhappy life spent being chased down by Colonel Elias Moje, and decided I'd have to do something about the bastard.

Milton started to move out into the open, but I put a hand on her shoulder and held her back.

"Just wait a moment. Make sure the coast is clear."

She settled down. Useless, of course; if the SSF wanted to stay hidden, there was no way my eyes and ears were going to pick them out. But old habits died hard, and even futile exercises sometimes yielded fruit. So I waited, counting in my head as I let my eyes roam the street outside our warehouse and let my ears soak in the windy silence of the ruined city.

We'd gotten pretty lucky on the walk home, finding a few useful items and a lot of garbage we didn't know what to make of, brought back to Kieth for inspection. There'd been no sign of Moje, but I didn't think he'd just give up, go home, and have a cocktail. He was in for the haul, and he had a perfect opportunity here in Newark to kill me without details getting back to Marin. I scanned the black sky and sighed.

"Okay."

We stepped into the warehouse carefully, nervous, but everything looked okay. Tanner, Kieth, and Gatz were gathered around the Monk, who remained tied to the barber chair. I tossed my skag onto the floor with a crash, and they all jumped and whirled. Tanner had a gun trained on me, instinctively, and sagged in relief.

"Fuckhead!" she snapped. "I could have shot your fucking head off."

"You haven't been converted, have you?" I asked, striding forward. "Things looked pretty reverent in here."

"Avery," Kieth said slowly, glancing back at the Monk. "Mr. Gatz has something to show you."

I raised an eyebrow and looked at Gatz, who stared back at me from behind his glasses with what I could only assume was . . . excitement. Having never seen it in Gatz before, I had to assume what the faint coloring in his face meant. "Let's have it, Kev."

Gatz licked his lips, but as he drew in breath to tell us, the dim warehouse flooded with the familiar antiseptic white light.

"Hello, rats," Moje's voice boomed from the night. "Mr. Cates, I gave you a *warning*. I am *very* disappointed to find you here. Time to run."

XIV

SO I CAN KILL YOU *AGAIN!*

00100

"Son of a bitch," I muttered. I ran my eyes over the place, made my decision immediately. "Kieth, Milton, Tanner, take the unit and get out. I don't care where right now, just *get out.* Kev, you're with me. The Pigs want me, so they'll follow us. Kieth, wait a minute until the hover goes after us, then get the fuck out of here."

I looked around again. "We meet in London as planned. I'll find you. And if you fucking screw me, I will find you faster. Move!"

"We're gone!" Milton shouted, leaping into the garbage hover. "Gonna stay low, a few feet off the ground, and follow the streets. SSF won't pick us up on their screens that way."

"You'll *what*?" Kieth said, aghast. "Fucking crazy bitches, you can't steer this thing through *streets.*"

"Watch us, little man. Get your science project on board and stop bitching."

Gatz and I ran out the back way. The search lamps hit us immediately, and we pushed into the maze of ruined buildings moments before a burst of gunfire chewed up the rubble behind us. The taste of grit coated my throat as we scrambled through what was left of the ruined city, and we barreled through dark rubble-strewn rooms without regard or thought for the half-million things a man could trip over and impale himself on.

The roar of hover displacement was right behind us. I just ran as best I could, ducking and diving through the endless blasted buildings until we found ourselves back on the remnants of Newark's streets, facing a blank wall, undamaged. We skidded to a halt and stared around helplessly, and I imagined I could feel the hover cresting the building behind us, searching the ground. My eyes fell on a manhole cover set in the ground, obscured by debris. I shoved Gatz.

"Go! The bastard's after me. Go and I'll meet you in London!"

Gatz nodded as the white light, pure and painful, swallowed us. I backed away quickly, trying to stay in the shadows created by the buildings. Gatz glanced back at me as I stepped carefully backward, and I stopped moving, a familiar feeling of listless cooperation stealing over me for a second. He winked and dropped the glasses back in place. I stumbled back into motion.

"I'll see you there, Ave!" Gatz shouted over the roar of the hover.

I didn't stop to think. I turned and dived for the manhole cover. In New York we often used the old sewers to get around. Hell, staying alive in the System when you didn't have money was a full-time job, and back when I was fifteen and running with the Snuff Thieves pulling the old dust-in-the-eyes-credit-disc-in-the-hand routine I'd learned that there were hidden roads under the streets. We kids used to *live* in the damn sewers. But the SSF had caught on and started wiring them up, motion detectors, motion-activated cameras, random patrols. It was illegal to travel the sewers—just one of the endless stream of laws by the Joint Council. There were at least ten new ones a week, along with countless amendments. My coat, filled with various tools for various occasions (you didn't live to be a spry twenty-seven by being unprepared for bad news), produced a simple hooked wrench that fitted into the small opening in the lip of the cover perfectly.

"Hey, rat!" Moje's voice boomed over the noise as the hover cleared the building, its spotlight finding me and lighting up my world like noon in Times Square. "If you make me go down into that shit, I will have doctors resuscitate you after I kill you so I can kill you *again!*"

I flung the cover up and away, losing my wrench in the process. I shoved my feet in and hugged myself, sliding down into the darkness as bullets once again cracked the pavement. I could tell immediately that these sewers were deeper than those in New York, and I just closed my eyes and waited for impact.

When it came, it hurt like hell, but it didn't kill me. I hit water, and after it smacked me in the back like a block of cement, I sank and choked immediately. Avery Cates, world-famous Gunner, drowning in four fucking feet of ancient shit.

The humiliating thought of my shriveling reputation spasmed me into determined thrashing, and I started to kick up to the surface, coming to my senses and changing direction after a few kicks. If I were Moje, I'd order my Stormers to fire down into the water for a moment, try to hit me before I even surfaced. I swallowed ancient shit and kicked for all I was worth in a random direction. All the other bullshit aside, I was running for my life now. Who gave a fuck if the Monks swallowed the world, or if the Joint Council finally made all of us illegal, or if the SSF tore my arms and legs off for spite after I was gone—it was a matter of whether I would live to see the next hour or not.

My stomach turned from what I'd swallowed, my lungs burned, and I couldn't seem to order my eyes to open, to see the actual filth I was swimming in. I just swam until my hands and knees scraped stone, and stood up in shallower water, only up to my waist. The walls gleamed with slimy, reflected light smeared over the old bricks, stretching off into blackness. There was no chance of secrecy, of being careful; I had to breathe. I sucked in air loudly and flailed around in the water for a few seconds, orienting myself. The shaft of bright white light coming down through the manhole was about fifteen feet behind me. The fact that I was still alive indicated that the Stormers hadn't come in after me yet. The sound of the hover indicated that they were coming, probably fast.

I pulled my backup weapon, aimed at the pool of hard light directly below the manhole. The Stormers would be close to invisible in their ObFu Kit. I kept my hands still and waited . . . waited . . . waited . . .

Two splashes, one on top of the other. I put four shells into each spot, turned, and ran for all I was worth through the water. It smelled like something had died down here, the air burning my throat. Before I'd gone more than ten or fifteen more feet, I heard a third splash, then a fourth and a fifth.

Everything was in slow motion, every ripple on the oily water, every jagged edge of the walls standing out in harsh relief as my mind raced and my heart seized up—I had just killed an SSF officer. This would make the fourth I'd either killed or caused to be killed in recent months, but the first had been an accident, a mistake, and I'd spent a lot of time and sweat erasing any connections between it and me, lying awake at nights listening for the sound of a hover, the whipping sound of Stormers sailing down on wires to raid my building, grab me up, and execute me on the fucking roof. The second hadn't been my fault, though the Pigs, in their infinite Drum Trial wisdom, wouldn't care. And the third I'd done remote control—I was blocks away when it'd happened, and if that crazy bastard Dawson had done his duty and died, too, no one would have known of my involvement.

But this, this was different. I'd reached out, personally, and taken this one. There would be a record of who they'd been chasing. Moje would be more than happy to spread the tale. I didn't think even the unofficial patronage of Dick Marin could save me if it became general knowledge.

My arm ached from holding the gun steadily in the air—I had just killed a motherfucking System Pig. As the implications hit me I found myself running on autopilot, my mind paralyzed with an odd mixture of dread and relief. I had killed a cop; any thin barrier between me and the vengeance of two million Pigs all over the world was gone, burned up in a muzzle flash. The System Pigs could be bought, they could be fooled occasionally, and they sometimes tolerated things out of laziness or for profit. But people who killed SSF—the few who had been stupid enough these past twenty years—they were hunted.

And made examples of.

"Better run, rat," Moje shouted, receding behind me. "You're a cop-killer, now. Two of my team! We're gonna have to punish you for that."

Two down, I thought, recovering as I pounded along. Forget the dead cops—it couldn't be helped. Besides, when they
started sending the Stormers into the fucking sewers after you,
you were pretty much on the SSF shitlist anyway, so how could
a couple of dead cops make things worse?

Thinking such cheerful thoughts, I added the attrition of
Moje's team to my slim list of advantages. It didn't do me much
good; I didn't have any other plan. I had no idea where the
sewers led, where I'd be when I emerged, or if I'd be able to stay
ahead of my pursuers.

You're screwed now, Avery, I panted to myself as I ran. *Shoulda
known twenty-seven was too old. You've pushed your luck.*

I imagined a bullet in the back of my head. I imagined falling down and drowning, the inky blackness creeping closer. I
imagine being paralyzed, everything slipping away, and I wondered if I hadn't made a huge mistake rejecting the Monks. A
thousand times, I'd walked by them preaching on the streets.
A thousand times I'd ignored them. Even knowing how they
acquired most of their members, the crazy thought that maybe
it was better to live as a Monk than to die. Always the craziest
thought: Fuck, man, what if they're *right*?

The sewers were tight, barely man-sized tunnels, and I had
to crouch to be able to move through them. The water slowed
me down and pushed against me, sucking hungrily and soaking my clothes. The bottom was slick slime and I lost my footing frequently, especially when I found intersections of tunnels
and made sudden decisions to take one. And all the while,
Moje shouted after me, over the splash of their pursuit.

"You didn't think you were just going to walk away from
me, did you? Here we come, rat!"

I stumbled, finding myself in an open area, spilling out into
a round area where a lot of tunnels seemed to connect. The

air sweetened, and looking up I could see another manhole. Behind me, I could hear shouts and lots of confused movement, and figured I'd lost them for a minute—at most. There were only so many possible paths, and I knew Moje would catch up soon enough. This was a junction, which meant that picking a tunnel randomly might lead me back the way I came, right at Moje and his Stormers.

I looked up at the manhole. There was a narrow, crumbling lip of stone halfway up, and I thought if I could get a foothold on it I might reach the manhole and push my way out. It wouldn't be easy. I felt tired just staring up at it.

Shutting my eyes, I got ready. I could hear Moje and his men sorting themselves out, coming closer. I stashed my backup in one pocket and thought if I couldn't do it, I wasn't going down without a fight. And I thought, *If a Monk were to somehow pop up out of nowhere and offer me salvation, save me from having to pay for twenty-six dead people and a slew of other crimes, I'd do it in a heartbeat.* Taking a deep breath, I began calculating angles, probable entries, and how I would approach me if I were wearing ObFu Kit that made me blend into the walls.

I picked my spot—a section of wall where the mortar between bricks had chipped away, leaving shadowy gaps—and launched myself at it. I managed to cram two fingers into one of the gaps and get one foot hooked on the tiny ledge. Heart pounding, I pulled and pushed and pushed myself up until I was almost standing, pressed up against the slick wall.

I twisted and stretched out one trembling arm for the manhole cover. Almost . . . almost . . . with sweat running into my eyes, I gathered myself for one final effort when there was a scrape from above. I froze, swiveling just my eyeballs up to look. The manhole shifted, then tore away, revealing the dark blue night sky. A pale and ridiculously genial face, hidden behind fashionable sunglasses, appeared over the rim. I stared in complete speechless shock.

"Come on," Dick Marin said. "I'll pull you up. I don't have all day; I'm about to deliver a speech to A-Level SSF chiefs in Sydney."

XV

CONSIDER THIS YOUR HEALTH PROGRAM

00101

I stared up at Marin, my whole body quivering with effort. His pale face disappeared, and a sturdy-looking rope slithered down toward me.

"Come on. I'll pull you up."

The splashing and shouting of Moje and his Stormers straightened itself out—they were on my trail again and getting closer. Probably using heat-tracking goggles: I only had a few seconds. I stared at Marin's rope in disbelief. *What the fuck is the King Worm doing in Newark? How does he think he's going to pull me up?*

"Cates! Come on! I don't have time for your existential bullshit."

I shivered, shaking off inaction. I reached up with my free hand and took hold of the rope. It felt oddly slippery and surprisingly strong. I looked back the way I'd come, Moje and his men so loud I couldn't believe they hadn't arrived yet, the acoustics of the sewers making them sound much closer than they were. I wrapped the rope around my forearm a few times and gripped it, giving it a strong pull to judge it, and looked back up at the director of SSF Internal Affairs.

"Whatever you've got up your—"

Marin pulled with a grunt, lifting me off my feet. To my amazement, I rose steadily upward. Within seconds I flopped on the damp, ruined streets of Newark again. I looked up at Marin. He stood grinning in an ObFu Kit; my eyes ached looking at him. The ObFu shimmered in the night, his head seeming to float disembodied in the air.

He had a length of cable wrapped around his waist. My eyes moved beyond him, where a shining, unmarked SSF hover sat on the street, running lights still on. The cable led to a winch on the rear of the hover. The motherfucker had simply used the winch to pull himself—and by extension, me—away from the manhole.

I released my grip on the cable as he untied himself with a quick motion, and the cable snapped back as the winch collected the slack. "Come on, Mr. Cates. Your friends won't get out of the sewers for a few moments, and I'd rather not be seen here. I'll give you a lift."

Without waiting for a response, Marin turned smartly and marched back to the hover. I lay panting in the mud and rocks, wet up to my shoulders, bowels loose and legs shaky. Without exaggeration, I figured if I hadn't been able to push up the manhole and pull myself up, I'd been about fifteen seconds away from death. I might have gotten one of the Stormers, maybe even two in an incredible burst of luck. But I'd never have gotten two Stormers *and* Moje.

"What about Moje?" I gasped, pushing myself up to my knees.

"I do not personally worry too much about Colonel Moje. Get in. It's better for me politically if I'm not seen here, and it'll enhance your reputation."

I struggled to my feet and walked shakily to the hover, betting on Moje's not having an easy way up out of the sewers. It was a small vehicle, big enough for two or three people and some gear. I climbed into the cockpit next to Marin and the doors sealed behind me. The inside was spotless, painfully clean.I sat dripping and reeking and felt angry at myself for soiling something so perfect, so beautiful.

Marin put the hover into motion and we rose into the air like a bubble. I barely felt anything. The SSF always had the best tech. Kieth might sneer at it for being two years out of date, but the endless supply of spotless, perfectly working tech the SSF had was awesome, beautiful in its perfection after the rusty, cobbled-together shit I had to make do with. Looking at the hover was like squinting into the sun of power and wealth.

"Where to, Cates? Anywhere in the general area. This unit won't take us cross-country or over large bodies of water, but within reason I can take you anywhere."

I looked at him. Marin cocked his head as if listening to someone in the rear seat, and then smiled, one of his sudden grins. One second he was squinting into space, the next he was beaming.

"Cates, you're an employee of mine, more or less. I told you I'd be keeping tabs and helping out where I could. That arrogant fuck Moje is lazy, and he uses SSF channels to organize his team for his superlegal adventures. I happened to be within a hop skip and a jump of here, so I thought I'd glance in on things. And down there your heat signature was like a bright light moving underground, so I just tracked you until you were underfoot. No mystery. Besides, several of the other assets I've put in play on this project have already been terminated. Sloppy work, mostly." He looked at me out of the corner of his eye for a second, and I got the message: Getting trapped in the goddamn sewers of Newark, of all places, was pretty sloppy, too. "So I thought I'd preserve you to fight another day."

I gritted my teeth. "I was seconds away from extricating myself without assistance."

Marin grinned. "You're welcome." Without warning his face became grave again. "Two Stormers, huh? Not bad."

"Lucky shots," I said tiredly. "ObFu doesn't help if you're splashing around."

Inside the hover it was easier to make out the outlines of Marin's body, though a casual glance made it look like his head and hands were floating.

"Where to, then?"

I thought about it. I was on my own until I could get the team back together in London—assuming they made it that far—and I had no prospects or contacts in Newark. "Back to New York, I guess," I said slowly. "Moje is here and will probably spend at least a few hours making sure I'm not around. Plus all my best contacts are in New York."

A few more seconds than I thought natural went by before he nodded in stages, curtly and jerkily. "New York it is," he stuttered, as if everything were coming to him in waves. I wondered if Marin were having a stroke, and eyed the controls of the hover nervously.

I swallowed. "Thank you."

After a moment, he snorted. "Like I said, you're an employee. Consider this your Health Program."

I stared dumbly out the side window, watching what was left of Newark drift by. Health Program. You couldn't even get near a hospital without one. If you were rich enough or lucky enough or *something* enough to get enrolled in one, they surgically implanted a chip under your scalp. Every hospital and doctor scanned for chips on a constant basis, and if you didn't scan with one, you didn't get near. Some of the best-defended places in New York were hospitals, with private armies keeping people like me away. Gutshot by some asshole junkie, sliced by our psychotic, alcoholic wife, or just slipped and fell, shattering a shoulder, it didn't matter. No chip, no service.

There was, of course, a thriving black market for the chips. The real pros kept the true owner of the chip prisoner, hidden, alive or—better—dead, in order to prolong the life of the chip, which was naturally red-flagged when its registered owner turned up dead, or was found by the SSF with a cracked skull and a surgical scar. Even so, you could make a lot of money with nonguaranteed chips whose legit owners were still alive and on the loose. Desperate times, and all that.

"I have some news for you, Cates," Marin said suddenly.

"News?"

"Your friend, Barnaby Dawson. He's been converted."

I blinked dully. "Converted?" I blinked again. I sat upright in the seat. "He's a fucking *Monk*?"

Marin nodded once, mechanically, cocking his head, listening to unseen people again. "A few hours ago. We were tracking him, of course, but something went wrong. He's the first SSF officer to ever convert to the Electric Church—although technically he was no longer SSF. It's a PR nightmare, let me tell you. When he emerges tomorrow as Brother Dawson, the Vids are going to have a field day with it."

I sat back in the seat again. "Holy shit." I felt heavy and tired, numb. I kept thinking that we'd barely even *begun* the job and I was exhausted. I'd come within an inch of being killed.

I didn't look at Marin. "You know the Electric Church is paying Moje to harass me. To eliminate me."

He nodded. "Of course. But my difficulty is that, officially, I have no probable cause to act against the Church. So, officially, Colonel Moje is doing nothing wrong—you being a known criminal. I am currently powerless to officially halt Moje's activities. I could back-channel him—there are a hundred IA investigations I could launch, suspending him immediately and making that piece of shit disappear into a Blank Room forever. But that would tip my hand, and I'm not ready to do that yet."

I kept staring ahead. "I don't understand a single fucking thing about that."

Marin nodded again. "We all have our limitations, Mr. Cates."

The rest of the flight was a blur. I dozed in my seat, itching in my drying clothes. Marin said nothing more, although he hummed to himself quite a bit, and occasionally I imagined his hums were murmured words, as if he were responding to people who were not there.

Suddenly he stiffened and went silent. For a few seconds he remained that way, and I wondered if I was going to have to deadhead the hover onto the ground by myself while Marin twitched and raved in the back. Then he convulsed, a gentle, wavelike spasm through his whole body, and turned his head to me in a single sharp movement.

"I have some more bad news, Mr. Cates," he said, turning the hover in a smooth arc. "New York is on fire."

My sudden ennui shattered. I sat up straight in my seat. "What?"

"Food riot started in Battery Park yesterday. An insufficient SSF force was sent in to subdue it, and the arrogant fucks did what they always do, tried to overawe the rioters with force. Two SSF officers were killed in the ensuing melee. Over five hundred citizens were killed as well, but apparently two dead System Cops were enough to inspire everyone, and the unrest has spread throughout most of the island. The SSF is holding the crossings by force right now."

I rubbed my eyes. "Goddamn it," I muttered. "That complicates things."

Riots never lasted. A bunch of starving, ignorant people throwing rocks couldn't last long against the System Pigs, especially when the Stormers landed and brought in the hovers. But they could do a lot of damage in the meantime. I'd lived through three riots so far. One had lasted three days, and the stupid fucks had even elected a mayor to speak for them. He was dead now. It hadn't been pretty.

"I'm afraid this means I can't take you directly into New York," Marin continued. We were nearing Manhattan. I could see black smoke billowing into the air. "I can get you in close, up north-island, but that's it. You'll have to make your own way south, if south is where you need to go."

There wasn't anything north of Seventieth Street anymore in Manhattan. The Riots—*The* Riots—had razed huge tracts of the city to the ground, just like in Newark. I turned to study Dick Marin, the King Worm, sitting just a foot or two away from me, calm and silent—but smiling, for no reason I could detect.

We started our descent. "A word of advice, Mr. Cates: Be on your toes. Colonel Moje has almost certainly made your name known to every SSF officer in the area. You're wanted in several outstanding investigations, so there is no legal problem with arresting, molesting, or murdering you. But when a brother System Cop puts up someone's name onto the wire, everyone's enthusiasm level rises accordingly, do you understand?"

I nodded glumly.

The hover set down on the river's edge, grass waving in the displacement field, the worn-down remnant of a foundation not too far away, the sky filled with black smoke and light flakes of ash drifting everywhere. I took a moment to take stock. My team was scattered, I'd just had my ass saved by the biggest System Pig in the world, I had every other SSF officer in the area carrying my picture in his wallet, and the last cop I'd tried to kill was by now probably sporting a fission heart and a digital uplink to the Electric Church. I was in fine form. I was taking home the door prizes. I was beginning to think twenty-seven was where the Avery Cates train pulled into the station for good.

"Mr. Cates? Get out now, please. I have a meeting with several Joint Council undersecretaries in a moment, and I'm sure this New York situation will be number one on the agenda."

I pushed open the door and stepped out of the hover. I shut the door behind me, but Marin clicked it back open.

"Do you have a plan, Mr. Cates, or should I arrange flowers for your funeral?"

A plan? I grinned at the King Worm. "I guess it's back into the sewers for me, Dick."

XVI

THE HAND OF GOD HIMSELF

OOOOO

"Do you not tire of this empty struggle? Do you not long in your secret heart for peace? Does the cycle of suffering not cow you into desperation?"

The Monk was pretty entertaining. It stood on a wooden box, preaching. It had been there three or four hours ago when I'd first emerged from the sewers into Longacre Square, the old unused roads splitting off in all directions. It didn't move, it just kept preaching. The crowds, angry and as well-armed as they could manage, surged over everything they could, smashing and stealing and burning, but they gave the Monk a wide berth. I leaned back against the old statue of George Cohan (whoever the fuck he'd been) and smoked a found cigarette, my back aching from standing for so long. It was a beautiful day, sunny and clear. A perfect day to burn your city down to the ground.

The SSF was establishing "order" block by block. They had air superiority and squads of Stormers on the ground, so it was only a matter of time. The riot had been going on for about twelve hours, would probably be suppressed in another twelve, and I felt sorry for anyone trapped in the poorer sections of the city once "order" was re-established. SSF punitive sweeps were pretty thorough.

Across the street, the mob was smashing their way into one of the upper-class stores where the wealthy shopped. An SSF hover swooped into position with startling speed and a team of Stormers dropped from it on thin cables. I faded back, edging into shadow. It always upset the System Pigs when some of their own got killed. The accepted wisdom being that you could never let the poor fucks think they could actually *kill* a System Cop. People had to believe that the hand of God Himself would reach down and squash them if so much as a drop of SSF blood spilled. The hand of God here taking the form of a hover, some Stormers, and a group of hapless Crushers who double-timed into the square to form a ring around the firefight, facing outward to guard the Stormers' backs.

The Monk had also disappeared, but I ignored that. I wasn't interested in the Monk. I was tracking Kev Gatz's old roommate, the Teutonic Fuck. Through him I expected to find his source for genetic augments, Marcel, who Gatz recommended for just about any illegal service.

Kev had given me enough background on the German to start with, and even in the midst of a riot some of my contacts still worked. Pickering's was on a war footing, but was still selling terrible booze and information. Pick himself had come out from his little office, grunting along on comically skinny legs below his balloon body, to have a belt with me and grouse about the stupid fucks burning down the city.

The Teutonic Fuck made his living and paid for his illegal gene-spliced augments by providing bodyguard services to other, slightly-higher-on-the-food-chain hoods. Like most augment-junkies, he was all flash and no sizzle. The augments that made him a huge, rippling mound of muscle left his bones weakened and his metabolism fatally compromised, meaning he was fragile as a bird and, while strong, easily winded. During moments of crisis like this, however, there was no need for his services because all the smart hoods were holed up in secure hiding places, waiting for the storm of SSF to pass them by. In such situations, the German made up his lost earnings by pulling mule duty for a few drug cookers. Since drug use of all kinds increased during times of severe social unrest, he was working overtime, following fixed routes on predictable schedules.

As I watched, he emerged into the square with two companions, ignoring the slaughter happening a few hundred feet away. The German was easy to spy. He was between six and seven feet tall, unbelievably muscled. His arms stuck out from his sides slightly because he could not lower them any farther. He had no neck at all, just a tree trunk of tendons ending in a red, lumpy face. His hands were shovels. He carried a nasty-looking pump-action shotgun, old but serviceable, and his legs looked like they'd been carved out of stone. Like a lot of other crazy augment-junkies, he wore a skin-tight latex uniform to show it all off. He glanced at the group of exhausted-looking Crushers, and a few nodded back. At least the German's bills were paid up.

Everything twitched as he walked. There was nothing natural about gene-spliced muscles. One look at this moron and I knew he had about two years, maybe less, before some catastrophic genetic breakdown turned him into a pool of reddish pus. But he looked dangerous, and a lot of times that was all that you needed to get by. Everything was a fucking act. His two companions were oily, dirty women, obviously terrified. I'd be terrified, too, if I had enough drug condoms sewn into me to kill a fucking herd of elephants.

With a glance at the battle raging to my left, I stepped out directly in front of the trio. They stopped about ten feet away, the German leveling the gun at me. That didn't bother me. I've had plenty of guns pointed at me, and recent adventures had forced me to reconsider who really was a threat to my life. If you weren't a cyborg killing machine or an elite System Security Force officer, you just didn't get my blood pressure up.

"It not worth it, friend," the German said. His accent was so thick he seemed to be picking the words from a muddy stream. I flicked my cigarette at his feet and exhaled smoke. The cigarettes used to be better. It was like booze. Sure, you could find them, and if you had the yen you could even buy good ones—but the best were pre-Unification. Maybe that was romantic bullshit, but everyone swore they tasted better despite the age and even the shit cigs were ungodly expensive. For most of us, shit was all we ever saw.

"Listen, you Teutonic *fuck*, you know me. Kev Gatz was your roommate. We've met."

He squinted at me, his shoulders and arms twitching. It was unappetizing.

"Ya," he said at last, his flat, red face breaking into an ugly smile. "I see you before. Sure." The smiled snapped off. "Get the fuck out of way."

I held up both hands. "I just need to find Marcel."

The smile came back. "Marcel? Ya, I know Marcel. He hiding. I tell you where he is. Five hundred yen."

A wave of tired rage rippled through me. I was tired of obstacles. The grinning red potato of a face pushed the wrong button, so I took him down. It was ridiculously easy. Big men—especially big men who have paid dearly and suffered much discomfort for their hugeness—usually overestimate the amount of force required to break them.

It didn't take any special kung fu. I nodded and glanced down at the street, waited a beat, and then launched myself forward directly at the shotgun. Before the German could react, I slammed into the barrel of the gun, ramming it up into his nose. He went down, his nose shattering into a bloody pulp. I held on to the shotgun as it slipped from his fingers. Since the last thing I needed was some drug lord coming after me in addition to all my other admirers, I whipped the barrel down and held it on the two mules.

"Stay," I advised. "Our business will be done soon."

As the German writhed on the ground, an explosion went off near the store, blowing a warm wind past us. The mules glanced over but I kept my eyes on them. I kicked the German lightly and he moaned.

"You've got bones like a fucking bird, friend," I said. "Just give me the skinny on Marcel and you can finish your deliveries. Fuck with me some more and I'll break every single hollow bone you have. You understand?"

The German moaned. "Ya, ya."

"Good." There was a second explosion, a second blast of warm wind. I winked at the two mules. "No worries, then."

Everything was on fire. Outside the beat-up old hotel, every fifth building was burning, and most had already burned once or twice in previous uprisings.

"Why do they always burn shit down? Every single time things get out of hand, all they want to do is burn shit down.

Took us hundreds of thousands of years to get to this point, and they want to fucking piss it all away in an evening."

I shrugged. "None of it's theirs. Burning it's just entertainment."

Marcel was a plump man of indeterminate nationality; so used to being tracked down and accosted he didn't bat an eye when I emerged from the sewer drain down the block and walked into the old hotel he was living in. He'd made the ornate lobby his headquarters, and it was like a goddamn oriental court: People just lounged lazily around him looking bored, all of them young, good-looking, and heavily armed. Polite, too, with a few Crushers on the payroll standing uncomfortably here and there. Except for the Crushers, they'd all had a lot of cosmetic augmentation done, men and women, and drifted about in silky threads, not looking dangerous at all. Which made me think they just might be.

His people did nothing to stop me introducing myself, and for five minutes Marcel was happy to shoot the shit with me about the weather, the summary SSF executions he'd witnessed outside his windows, about the fact that no one knew how to riot properly anymore.

I'd heard of Marcel through Gatz and scraps of talk here and there, but there were a thousand operators in New York. They all thought they were the fucking Godfather and usually ended up dead before too long. Marcel had shown up in gossip about a year or so ago. He was heavy, had lazy eyes that remained half-shut, and since I'd arrived he hadn't moved so much as an inch from the plush chair he was ensconced in.

"Well, Mr. Cates—who is such a good friend of Kev Gatz that Kev never mentioned him—I appreciate the social call under such extreme circumstances, but what can I do for you?"

I nodded. "I've come to beg a favor."

The porcine little eyes widened just a bit and then settled elastically back to half-mast. "A favor, Mr. Cates? Alima, honey, go do a credit check on Mr. Cates while he tells me his tale of woe."

A Middle Eastern–looking woman sitting on the floor hoisted herself up with animal grace and disappeared into the interior of the hotel.

"I'm not suggesting there's no payoff for you," I said quickly, trying to maintain my smile, my calm, and my hardass look all at once. It was exhausting. "But there's no *immediate* payoff. Long-term, I'm willing to offer you a fair price. Double a fair price."

Marcel studied me. "Mr. Cates, your name is out there, so I believe you've got a big job on the hook. Okay. Let's stipulate you got a big payday coming. What do you need from me?"

I shrugged. "I need to get to London."

Marcel laughed. After Dick Marin's sudden barks, this sounded decadent and bottomless. His whole body jiggled with amusement. "Oh, Mr. Cates," he said finally. "That's rich. Transport's normally expensive. In these unsettled times, it's fucking impossible. I don't care what you've got on the hook. You can't afford it."

I swallowed. "You've heard of me?"

Marcel shrugged, still giggling, wiping his eyes. "By reputation, Mr. Cates. A fair Gunner. Reliable. No Canny Orel, maybe, but competent."

Canny Orel again—he was becoming my patron saint. Rumored to have killed over a hundred contracts in his time and retired rich. His name had been out of circulation for a while. When they'd been active, Orel's organization had killed everyone—criminals, cops, politicians—with legendary impunity. You never knew with old stories like that, that tended to grow with the telling. But even if you subtracted three-fourths of what you heard as bullshit, they'd still been a bunch of hardasses I wouldn't want to mess with. Anyone who had any kind of legit link to the Dúnmharú was instantly promoted to Chief Asskicker in the room. "You know my rep. You know I don't fuck around."

Marcel shrugged again, all the good humor draining from him. "A desperate man can forget his rep pretty fast."

The Middle Eastern woman re-entered the room, crossed to Marcel, and leaned in to whisper to him. Marcel's piggy eyes widened again. He looked at me for some time before speaking.

"Mr. Cates, your credit is good. I think I can get you on a flight tonight. We will have to arrange a price."

I blinked. "What the hell did she find out?"

Marcel smiled. "Only that your credit is good, Mr. Cates. Our price?"

Thank God, I thought, for loose lips. Marcel must have heard my payday was huge. And very real. I flipped open a small notebook and tossed it to him. "Write down a number. I'll pay you when my work is done."

He paused for a moment, still studying me, and then began to laugh as he laboriously wrote numerals onto paper, with a schoolboy's care. When he tossed the book back to me, he was laughing full-strength again. "Mr. Cates, are you ready to impersonate someone very rich, someone very powerful, someone authorized to fly to London during a riot?"

I glanced at the number he'd written, struggled to hide my horror, and shrugged. "Sure. Why not?"

Marcel kept laughing, and soon his entourage joined him. "Ah, Mr. Cates, what will you do about your clothes?" Marcel finally exploded. "The nobility is not accustomed to traveling through the sewers!"

I looked down at myself. I was caked in filth from head to foot.

I grinned back up at Marcel. "Well, fuck. It's a *riot*. I'll steal some goddamn clothes."

XVII

ALL HUMAN BEINGS, SAVED OR UNSAVED

01001

It was about the time they served the coffee that I really started to freak out.

Marcel had come through in spades. He didn't just get me passage, he got me *first-class* passage—handed over with a fake ID and a stern command to find myself some appropriate clothes and clean up a little. That part was simple enough. Night had fallen and the SSF was closing in methodically, not rushing things, probably because they were enjoying themselves too much. I followed a small band of merrymakers through the streets uptown and waited for them to sack an appropriate house. The owner was one of the foolish rich shits who'd decided to stay and defend his property; he popped up, silver-maned and wearing a silk smoking jacket, with a brand-new automatic Roon in each hand like he was Buffalo Bill or something. He nailed about four of the merrymakers before they stormed his windows, and the last I saw of him he was running down the street with his hair on fire.

His house quickly followed, and the merrymakers scurried out like rats in twos and threes, bearing away anything that could be sold quickly. I waited until they were all gone, judged the fire, and then went in for a quick shower and a change of clothes. Rich people fireproofed their homes, which stopped fires altogether for a few years, and even when the antiflame compounds aged and started to break down it slowed a fire down considerably—it took hours for them to burn down, and I knew you could pack a bag and take a nap before a fire became a real concern. It was burning slowly but steadily when I emerged, shaved and rubbed pink by expensive towels, wearing one of the poor sap's suits.

I couldn't bring myself to wear his underwear, and the merrymakers hadn't left anything else of value.

It would have been nice to steal a hover and arrive at the airport in style, but the SSF had grounded New York and would have knocked me out of the air immediately, so I had to hoof it. The System Cops had the Madison Square AirPad under their control, so air traffic was still moving in and out for VIPs and necessary commerce. It was a long walk, but I was passed through the gates by two bored Crushers—luckily, strangers to me—who were as polite to me as any had ever been, if still grouchy. They called me "mister" and told me to have a nice day after running yellow eyes over my ID. It was the clothes—no one saw much more than a clean guy in an expensive suit. If they looked closer they might notice the bad teeth, the scars, the accent—but they didn't look close. You could hand them a hand-written ID with the name spelled wrong and they'd pass you through if you looked rich. Looking rich was a skill any criminal worth his salt learned early.

Then it was straight onto the heavy-duty long-range hover, a comfortable seat behind an attractive, porcelain-skinned red-haired woman I recognized from the Vids, and a glass of beer pressed into my hand, all within the first five minutes. The seat was soft and supple. The air inside the hover was clean and crisp. The fabric of the poor sap's clothes was dry and sumptuous against my skin.

I began to freak out.

The woman, a few years older than me but gorgeous, twisted around to smile at me. I'd seen her reporting the news a few times, her face ten feet high, her smile permanent and frighteningly unchangeable. "Time to get out, huh? These people." She shook her head in dismay. "They're so ignorant. Burning down their own city. I think the System Police should just ship them all somewhere."

I swallowed anger. The fact that this rich bitch thought New York was *my* city made me want to grab her by the nose and smash her head into the armrest. Instead I smiled. "It's the SSF's fault. They're too slack."

She nodded, but didn't seem to like my smile. It might have been my teeth, which hadn't had the benefit of a dentist. Ever. "Yes. I quite agree," she said, facing forward again without another word. I imagined I could smell the soap on her skin. Or maybe that was *my* skin; I was so clean I itched.

The meal service started, brought soundlessly by human-looking Droids who smiled but couldn't speak, and my will to retire rich tripled. Rich was the only way to live in the System. When you were rich, the System Pigs called you sir and wished you a good day. When you were rich, they served you breakfast on the hover—real eggs, real bacon, and sweet lord, when the coffee came, hot and strong in a cup so white I had to squint at it, I lost all reason. I promised myself I would do anything it took to be rich. And then it occurred to me that I was *already* doing whatever it took.

The flight to London was only two hours. After breakfast they dimmed the lights and put on the Vids, each of us getting a small but serviceable private Vid screen. Only the Legal Vid feeds, of course. In New York alone there were fifteen illegal underground Vid feeds I knew of providing news and such on a constant basis, beaming from Safe Rooms around the city. The difference between the legal and illegal feeds was startling. The legal feeds were certainly censored, but the illegal ones had their own agendas, so who knew what to believe. I was half-asleep, feeling exhausted and beaten, when the news came on and I sat up straight, startled. The anchor was the woman sitting in front of me; the caption read Marilyn Harper. She was reporting on the riots, standing blithely in the midst of the merrymakers as they looted a row of stores. She looked smart in a short suit, her hair up, her skin too white, too pale, too clean to be standing in New York in the middle of something like that.

She signed off and I was about to try to get some sleep, when the next news segment came on and I almost puked up my breakfast. It was the Marilyn Harper again. The caption underneath was: "BROTHER BARNABY DAWSON: Former SSF cop, now Monk, suspect in two assaults."

I gestured the volume up so violently it shrieked up to full blast, causing all the other passengers to twist around in annoyance. I gestured it to a low hum and sat forward.

"—son, former captain in the System Security Force recently

detained by Internal Affairs on charges of official misconduct, is now suspected in two assaults on System citizens in New York City."

I stared at the file photograph. His crazy blue eyes seemed to dance even on the flat screen.

"The System Security Force has declined to comment on Captain Dawson. The Electric Church, in a statement issued from its London office, said only that, quote, 'No brother of the Church would ever be violent or seek to harm any other human being. The Electric Church regards all human beings, saved or unsaved, as its family, and seeks only to bring the entire human race into God's embrace.' Dawson, who served fifteen years in the SSF primarily in the New York area, reportedly identified himself several times while viciously beating—"

I gestured the sound off again. Dawson's face continued to stare at me from the screen for a few seconds as Harper wrapped up her report, and then it disappeared. I gestured the Vid off.

She twisted around again. In person, she looked older— more lines around the face—but they had that "smoothing" technology now and could make anyone look any age they wanted. "Scary, huh? First time ever a Monk is *officially* suspected of violent behavior. Guess it had to happen sometime. They start off as humans—and usually not the best kind of humans either." She studied me. "Don't I know you? You look familiar."

Fucking Vid reporter. I could have been seated behind some aristocrat, sneering at the riffraff they let onto flights these days, but I get someone who's had her nose in SSF databases all her life.

I shook my head. "No."

She studied me for a few more seconds, then made a big show of losing interest. "Must be tired. I've been knee-deep in shitkickers burning their own houses down the last twenty-four hours. Sorry to bother you."

I stared at the back of her seat. This was shit I didn't need. I knew she was going to remember my face and do some checking around. She wouldn't be a Vid reporter otherwise. I thought about Dawson, too. She was right; no Monk had ever been involved in or accused of a crime, and certainly not a violent one—not counting, I thought sourly, the millions of apparent murders they'd committed in their routine recruitment activities. Marin had told me that the Monks were controlled by a behavioral chip of some sort, that the human brain inside was probably screaming as it provided the basic operating system and motor control subroutines—not to mention the brainwave ID that kept the Monks citizens of the System. I considered the possibility that this control chip had malfunctioned somehow in Dawson's case. That he was maybe the same crazy fucker I'd tried to kill, only now in a metal body, armed to the teeth, with access to the Electric Church's database and network. Under *that* rock was the squirming, wriggling possibility that Dawson had been set loose on me on purpose, to kill me with plausible deniability for the EC.

It was certainly turning into a banner day for Avery Cates. I called for the attendant Droid and demanded a bourbon. It was brought to me immediately, a double in a crystal tumbler, frozen granite cubes instead of ice. I hadn't had decent liquor in a decade. It was smooth and perfect, and made me a little giddy. I thought to myself, *If I live to pull this off, I'll probably go*

*mad in a few years from all the meals, the booze, the fucking Droids
tending to my every need—everything.*

The landing was a little rough, the hover doing a straight verti-
cal deadhead drop in the rain, winds tearing at it. The Droids
moved up and down the aisle reassuring us that everything
was fine, that this was normal. It didn't bother me. I'd been
through worse.

From behind her, I leaned to the right and watched what
I could of Marilyn Harper. Some random jiggle of her cleav-
age reminded me that I hadn't been with a woman in a while,
but I suppressed the thought. Too many mediocre crooks just
like me had been gunned with their pants down. It was just
too risky. I was convinced that she was going to mess with
me. I knew she thought she recognized me from some SSF
file she'd seen—lord knew I was in plenty—and she was
probably thinking of ways to confirm without tipping her
hand.

Without warning, she glanced over and noticed me leaning out into the aisle, and did a double take. Then she twisted
around and smiled at me.

"There's a few things in that Dawson report I wasn't allowed
to say, you know," she said brightly. "Since you seemed interested. The goddamn SSF got a JC order to suppress, and I
couldn't put all the details on the air. The two people he beat
up? One might actually still die; he's in SSF custody and they
certainly don't give a shit about him. Both were just two-bit
hoods, known around a bar called Pickering's where all the
little shitheel crooks hang out."

I kept my face impassive. "That's interesting."

She kept her bright green eyes on mine. "Both reported the same thing: Dawson was trying to beat information out of them. He was looking for someone, someone they were known to associate with."

I wanted very badly to slap her. I licked my lips. "Really? Who?"

She smiled. "Some piece-of-shit Gunner named Avery Cates. Brother Dawson told both of them he was going to find this Cates and tear him limb from limb."

With a hollow thud, we landed in London.

XVIII

OR SOMEONE LIKE
SOMEONE I'D KNOWN

10011

▬▬▬▬▬▬

"Mr. Cates!" Milton—or maybe Tanner—shouted from outside the fence. "I do not much care for your friend."

Next to her, Gatz leaned against a trashcan and waved at me subtly, a slight lift of his hand. They stood with a small group of upright citizens waiting for passengers, the two of them looking grubby and unmutual, probably the reason that a fat System Pig had taken up position a few feet away, ostensibly watching a handheld Vid. Stationed right by the gate in front of the crowd were two smiling Monks, welcoming everyone to London and asking politely if they wouldn't want to discuss their salvation for five minutes, since next time the landing might not be so smooth.

I walked right past my lamentable partners. Tanner—some unidentifiable sense told me it was Tanner—grinned, and they followed me. I went into the nearest restroom, swept through

169

quickly, banging stall doors in to make sure it was empty, and waited. A moment later they swaggered in. Tanner was all grins. Gatz was his usual ebullient self, and stationed himself right inside the door in case someone tried to walk in, like a good soldier.

"How'd you know to meet me here?" I demanded.

"Gatz's buddy Marcel sent a message. Damn, you clean up nice, Mr. Cates."

I stared at her. "So you idiots thought you'd just show up here and meet me? Shit, I thought you girls were professionals. So in case Elias fucking Moje of the SSF got a decent look at either of you he could just connect the fucking *dots* and just arrest us all at the gate, walk us into a Blank Room, and shoot us each in the head? Is that it?"

She stared at me, a smart-assed eyebrow raised. "Yeah, that's exactly what we thought. Look, Cates, I recently spent two fucking hours being bossed around by Wonderboy here," she jerked an angry thumb at Gatz, "and I haven't slept since. I fucking *dream* about Wonderboy now. And as much as I hate having that in my head now for the rest of my life, we got our asses over here—in a lot less style and comfort than you did, apparently—found each other, dug up your travel itinerary, and established a headquarters in Covent Garden that rivals the world record for crappiness. Ty waved his nose in the air and we're wired up, communications, power, video systems, a whole lab of shit I've never seen before, or heard of. He also scavenged some security for us—just your basic movement-triggered turret systems and a couple of steel snap-doors in case we get invaded and need to slow someone down, simple stuff, that shit's just lying around—and Sis and I got us some transport. We did our *job*, okay? So climb off the bullshit wagon and let's get back to work. The sooner I get my paycheck and get Wonderboy out of my life forever, the better, okay?"

Someone tried to walk into the bathroom, but Gatz turned, raised his glasses, and glanced at them. They went away.

I sat down on the sink. "Okay. Here's the news: New York almost burned to the ground, Barnaby Dawson's a Monk but I don't think it took, because he's beating the tar out of people and telling them he's looking for me. And a Vid reporter recognized me on the fucking hover and might be a problem."

"The redhead," Gatz drawled. "I recognized her."

"Oh, yeah." I grinned at Gatz. "The Teutonic Fuck says hello."

Gatz did his best to grin back, which wasn't anything pleasant to see. "He still able to walk?"

"Yeah, but he won't ever breathe out that nose right again."

"Good. Teach the bastard to threaten to throw *me* out the window."

"Blow each other later, okay?" Tanner said, putting her hands on the top of her head and wincing as if in sudden pain. I wondered suddenly if Milton was doing the same somewhere else, silently and maybe unconsciously mirroring her twin. "Your System Pig is a *Monk*? But it didn't *take*? And now *yet another* person is trying to kill you? And we're going to see your face on the Vids?" She threw her hands into the air. "I'm following a *child*. Lord, take me now. I'm ready."

"Shut the hell up."

A few moments of silence followed, during which someone else tried to get into the bathroom, only to run into Gatz. I ran a hand over my face and nodded. "All right. You did good. The gang's all here, huh? A base of operations and everything. That's great. Brother West?"

"Still with us. Sis and I are goddamned bright chicks—we snagged an AbZero freighter unit, supposedly shipping nanotech. Too cold to open up, too cold to scan effectively, the Pigs couldn't open it. Kieth faked up the freight papers for us. Brother West traveled in comfort, and we picked him up at the hover pad easy as pie. Snagged us a brand-new hover, too. We spent a few hours going over it with a sledgehammer and a blowtorch, though, so now it looks like the original hover left over from biblical times." She grinned. "Your ride awaits, sir! Take care not to smudge your fine duds on anything as you alight the carriage."

The hover *did* look like complete crap, but ran smooth and steady. Tanner pulled up outside what appeared to be a completely respectable office building in a well-kept if largely abandoned business block, the sort of empty area with brand-new buildings that spoke of a recent cleanup of riot damage—which was more than you could say of New York, which had let most of its ruined areas rot.

"Haymerle Road!" she shouted. "End of the line."

I leaned forward. "This is where we're set up? Looks a bit too active for my liking."

She nodded. "Sure, that's what we all said. But Kieth insisted. Said that these office buildings get sealed up when no tenants are around, left in hibernation. No one comes around and checks on 'em because their security is handled by Droids connected to a private network, or some shit. Anyway, he got us in—no big deal, three-year-old tech at best—and then Ty waved his nose at the network and took over. It's an old Droid factory. When the owners check its status, it looks like a typical day, complete with faked security footage." She grinned.

"Meanwhile we got the Droids doing chores for us. I tell you, Cates, that Kieth is a genius."

We got out and I looked around. If you put a few hundred people in the streets it would have looked like some of the more prosperous sections of New York. I felt naked without people pushing and shoving at me, their dirty hands on me. Our flight over had revealed London to be half-empty, a dying city bereft of citizens. I wondered if the presence of the main hive of the Electric Church had anything to do with that.

"Where's the Abbey from here?"

She waved her hand northward. "See the spike?"

I saw, in the distance, a tall towerlike structure with a square top, a round, charred disc set in the middle. The whole thing was blackened from fire, sticking up over the very tops of the buildings on the horizon like a baleful reminder of the Riots.

"I'll get this off the street," Tanner said from within the hover. "Go on in with Wonderboy there. I'm sure Kieth can't wait to fill you in."

I followed Gatz to the door, which whisked open as we reached it. A faceless white and black Droid—humanoid torso on top of a wheeled chassis—cocked its head and waved us in.

"Come in, come in!" its synthetic voice chimed. "Welcome to the House of Kieth. Mr. Kieth is currently in the Assembly Room."

I glanced at Gatz. He shrugged as he followed the Droid in. "Kieth's got a weird sense of humor," he growled.

Inside, the building was dusty and abandoned, wires hanging out of the walls and holes gouged into the concrete where machinery used to be. A lot of factories and offices stood empty everywhere; landlords usually set up Droid armies like this to keep squatters and crooks out. The evidence of Kieth's work was everywhere: I could see the guns mounted quick-and-dirty on the walls, the steel plates ready to slam down and cut off any route into the building at the touch of a remote. I'd seen field setups in my day, and this one struck me as impressively complete and solid-looking, considering our resources and the time frame. The Droid led us along narrow corridors lit by cheap make-you-squint ambient lighting until we emerged into a huge cavern empty except for the small camp of equipment and too-bright floodlights set up at the far end like stark metal trees.

"Mr. Kieth! Authorized visitors! Mr. Kieth! Authorized visitors!"

Ty Kieth's bald head appeared over the rim of a large back cube, connected to smaller black cubes by endless cables. "Cates! Ty is glad to see you're alive!"

"Glad to find I was on the entrance list for the House of Kieth," I drawled. "Get a Vid in here, okay? We need to know what's going on." As we approached, I realized that one of the pieces of equipment was the Monk, standing perfectly still in the focus of the lights. Its face had been removed, and its torso remained exposed. "Is it . . . functional?"

Kieth glanced at it. "Sure is. We've been doing a lot of work with Brother West, Cates. I think you're going to be amazed." He glanced around. "Nice digs, eh? Between Ty and the Twins, we've rewired this whole thing and the suits that own this place don't know a damn thing! Fully shielded: We could set the place on fire and the SSF satellites wouldn't know it for days. There are five Droids, by the way. Ty calls them Bob. Bob One, Bob Two, like that. This is where they used to assemble Droids. You can see where the lines used to be."

I walked up to Brother West and stood in front of him. "What's up with him?"

Kieth sprang into animation, jumping up, wiping his hands on a rag, and running over to one of the black boxes. "He's fine, Mr. Cates, just fine. Ty's had a lot of time to dig around in there. Found the behavioral modification chip, learned how to selectively disable it. Want to see?"

I nodded. "Very much."

Although the back of its skull still looked normal enough, from the front the Monk looked totally inhuman, a mass of wires and boards for a face with two delicate cameras where the eyes should be. It stood ramrod straight. I wondered who West had been. The Electric Church seemed to draw most of its converts from the lower classes, criminals and the working destitute. West might have been someone I'd known, or someone like someone I'd known. I wondered if he'd gotten what he wanted. Or deserved.

Kieth fiddled with his equipment and began punching into a small keyboard. "All right," he said, "meet Mr. West."

The Monk spasmed, twitched, and fell to its knees with a shriek. Its hands came up and began pounding on its skull violently.

"Let me out," it said, its voice perfectly modulated and sounding strangely reasonable. As it continued to speak, the reasonable tone gave way to increasing volume and a ragged quality that made my skin crawl. "Let me out! Let me out! *Let me out! Let me out! Let me out! Let me out!*"

I reached for my gun. It wasn't there. I'd had to chuck it to get on the hover.

"It's okay!" Kieth shouted over the Monk's din. "It can't activate its weapons." He paused to stare at the Monk with me. "This is Mr. West, Cates. This is what's going on inside his brain right now. After some analysis, Ty doesn't believe his mental operations are damaged, he simply believes being

a Monk is too much to process. In short, the mod chip elimi-
nates free will, Mr. Cates, but once it is removed there's a viable
person in there. It's just a viable person who's been driven mad
by the process, and who knows how many months or years of
being enslaved."

*"Let me out! Let me out! Let me out! Let me out! Let me out!
Letmeoutletmeout—"*

I flinched away from it. "Goddamn it, Kieth, can't you shut it
up? I get the point."

He nodded, but didn't move. "Mr. Gatz?"

I glanced sharply at Kev, who unfolded himself and stepped
forward, stiff and ponderous. "Kev? What the fuck?"

Kieth held up a hand. "Watch."

Kev stepped in front of me and removed his glasses. For a
moment, nothing happened. Then, slowly, the Monk calmed,
until it was completely silent, its arms raised, its body stiff and
kneeling. After a few more seconds, it climbed to its feet again
and resumed attention.

"Kev can Push a Monk?"

Kieth nodded slowly. "It appears that the only requirement
for Mr. Gatz's ability is a human brain. And proximity."

I blinked. "But it doesn't have eyes."

"Ty's belief is that Mr. Gatz uses the eye-to-eye contact as a
focus. It isn't physically required."

Gatz spoke slowly. "I noticed it first in Newark. When the
Monk showed up, I was so fucking terrified I started Pushing without even realizing it. And I could swear for a second
I almost had that Monk by the short hairs, that it hesitated
because I was Pushing it." He glanced back at me with naked
eyes and I flinched. "Wanna talk to Mr. West?"

I nodded, my brain disconnected from the rest of me by the
stress of processing all of this new information—as if there

wasn't sufficient wattage left to manage anything else. After a moment I realized that my hands were rubbing themselves nervously together. I had to concentrate to stop it.

Gatz nodded, looked at the Monk. "Say something, West."

The Monk twitched again, and then turned its head to look in my direction. I had the eerie feeling of being stared at by something eyeless. It wiggled a little, as if losing its balance, and then nodded its head.

"For God's sake," it said, its voice terribly perfect, smooth and on-pitch, still processed by whatever hardware was built into its artificial skull. "Kill me. Kill me now. I beg of you."

XIX

WHY AM I STILL ALIVE?

00000

I stepped into the gutted kitchen area, where Milton and Tanner had scrounged a few crates together into a makeshift table and stored our meager food supplies. Food was hard to come by. Mostly, we had nutrient tablets, the kind they handed out now and then in New York when local aristocrats were moved to keep the peasant population alive for a few more weeks, for whatever obscure reasons really rich people had. The tablets kept you going, but left hunger gnawing at you. It was like starving to death forever.

Milton sat on some boxes, taking a pull from a gleaming flask. She glanced up at me from her spot at the crates and grinned. "Cheerful fucker, isn't he?"

I gestured at the bottle she was drinking from. "Give me a blast."

She handed it over. "Gearing up for the interrogation, eh? That's what we figured you'd do."

I nodded, sitting down on a box and taking a long swallow of liquor. It tasted like gasoline. I held it in by sheer will and after a moment the burning was replaced by warmth and I risked a second swallow before handing it back. "Kieth can't guarantee West's brain will last very long once it's unfettered from the mod chip. Gatz seems to be able to force lucidity onto it, but who knows how long he'll be able to manage. We need information." I coughed. "Someone will need to sit in and take notes. Kev's illiterate, I think, and Ty will be busy, so that leaves you or your sister."

She winked. "Way ahead of you, chief. Why do you think I'm in here getting drunk? It's like talking to a ghost."

I stared at the rough wood of the crates. "You believe in shit like that?"

She slid the bottle in front of me, and I took another drink. It was starting to taste better. "Like ghosts? Like a soul?" Milton's voice disappeared under the edge of the crate as she stretched out on the floor. "Sure I do, Mr. Cates. How can you not? All those prophecies are coming true."

I swallowed wrong and had to cough to clear my windpipe. "Prophecies?"

"Fucking pagan." She sighed. "Revelations. Catholic dogma. Most religions have something similar. Isn't it obvious? We're in the End Times."

I stared at the bottle. Milton's hand appeared over the edge of the crate and waved around lazily until I handed it back.

"Think about it, Cates. The dead are walking the Earth inside those air-cooled Monk bodies. You can't get a doctor to look at you or buy something high-end unless you have one of those chips under your scalp. I'm telling you, it's near over."

I stood up. "Well then, we have nothing more to worry about."

"Hey, Cates?"

"Yeah?"

"Make me a promise. I know we aren't friends or anything, but promise me something human to human. Promise me you'll blow my brains out before letting them Monk me. And my sister. Okay?"

I nodded immediately. "Honey, I thought that was understood, for all of us. Fuck, that's a standing order." I swallowed. "Be in the Assembly Room in five, okay? Take notes."

"Keep calling me *honey*," she called out after me, "and we may not have to wait for the Monks to arrange it."

I tried to find my way back, but got lost in the twisty tunnel-like hallways of the place. It gave me an opportunity to search out more of the boobytraps they'd set up in case we had to fight off a small army of SSF or Monks or whatever huge, global organization was going to decide to kill me tomorrow. They'd been busy little bastards, and the work was first-rate. Aside from the guns and the drop-plates, there were electrocution wires stretched across the floors at key intersections, ready to snap taut and murder a half-dozen men simultaneously. There were small charges embedded in the seams of the floor, ready to blow and tumble another dozen into a newly born pit. Anyone trying to force their way into the place was going to pay dearly for it.

Eventually one of the Droids found me. Sputtering programmed politeness, it led me to where everyone except Milton and me had gathered. The four of them huddled around the Monk, which stood exactly where I'd left it when I'd fled: ramrod straight, staring directly ahead under the dual influence of its mod chip and Kieth's custom instruction set.

"Well, well, the Boy Gunner," Tanner said as I approached.

"Traveling in style while the hired help suck fumes all the way across the ocean, I see," she added sourly.

"I'll kick in an extra yen to your share for pain and suffering," I announced, pulling off my coat. "Now shut the hell up and let's get started. You said you didn't think we had much time?"

Kieth nodded and danced around checking his equipment. "The brain appears to be in good physical shape, but something is decaying in there. The personality? Soul? Subconscious? Ty doesn't know. Maybe he's just too crazy, after all this time. Every time Ty unhooks Brother West from the mod chip, Brother West goes more apeshit than the last time. Mr. Gatz has been able to control West to an extent—maybe a substitute for the mod chip—but that also appears to be decaying. Ty thinks you have about five minutes before Brother West goes fatal error on us."

I stared at the Monk. It looked like a prisoner awaiting execution, head held high. I'd noticed that Kieth's third-person royal status got worse when he was under pressure. "When that happens, you can kick the mod chip back in with your new instruction set, yes?"

"Yes. I think. We won't know until we do it."

I looked around, taking stock. We were in a mothballed factory, in an abandoned neighborhood, thousands of miles from what I thought of as home, and more than likely near death. I felt a strange sense of calm, of fatalism. If the Monk jumped up and slaughtered us all, it wouldn't surprise me, and I wouldn't, I thought, mind all that much.

Milton arrived and saluted me. "Go ahead, then, Mr. Kieth," I said.

Kieth leaped up, mopping his head with the same filthy rag. "All right, then. Ty will be recording the whole episode, of course. Just in case. I will disconnect the behavioral modification chip, Mr. Gatz will assert his, uh, influence, and then you can question it."

I nodded and addressed them all. "What we need most from Brother West is information about the security at Church headquarters. Anything else is gravy. Okay? So everyone else shut the fuck up until I'm finished."

"Yeah," Tanner drawled. "Or Mr. Cates will shoot you."

I was starting to like the sisters. It also reminded me that I needed a weapon, fast. I felt defenseless and confused without something to defend myself with. "Kieth? Gatz?"

They both nodded. Kieth gestured a command carefully at his equipment, Gatz removed his glasses, the Monk spasmed again, and we all stood in silence. After a moment, the Monk shivered and turned its head, the sound of the tiny motors clear and sharp.

"Why am I still alive?" it said, turning its head back and forth. "I know Mr. Gatz. I know quite a lot about Mr. Gatz. I know the names Cates, Kieth, Milton Tanner. I do not know you."

Kieth dashed around his black boxes adjusting things with waves of his arms and subtle flicks of his wrist. "Amazing, Mr. Cates. Brilliant, really. They're using the brain's lower functions as-is—saves them the trouble of trying to program all that stuff in. They're using the brain's *memory* as primary storage, though it looks like a stream dump is sent to the EC on a real-time basis. They're saving themselves tons of money and time and effort by just using the human brain. If they tried to replicate this electronically they'd still be designing the fucking nano. The upper functions of the brain are filtered to the mod chip, which is just a null point."

"That's interesting, Mr. Kieth," I said. "Can I ask it questions?"

The Monk twitched its head like a bird, and oriented on Kieth. "Questions?"

"Will you answer questions?"

Gatz nodded. "He'll answer."

I cleared my throat and stepped forward. "I've done some preliminary research and a few walk-bys. It looks to me like the EC headquarters has a single entrance, controlled by wireless handshake, correct?"

"Probably the Amblen Protocol," Kieth said with a nod.

The Monk twitched and shivered again. "Amblen Protocol . . . modified. Custom. Dr. Amblen himself provided the algorithmic adjustments."

I shrugged. "Doesn't matter. Mr. Kieth, that means there's a transmitter chip that beams the authentication code when the Monk approaches the HQ entrance. It's probably write-twice media, programmed to flush itself if tampered with."

Ty looked outraged. "Did you just *explain* the concept to Ty? Ty's *designed* these systems, Mr. Cates."

"There is," the Monk said slowly, jerking its head twice, "a random frequency shift as well."

"Ah," I muttered, ignoring Kieth. "One entrance—what are the deterrents to herd you through?"

"The authentication handshake is wide-field. You must supply the correct response no matter where you attempt to enter."

"The response to a failed authentication?"

"If no . . . response is . . . transmitted, a suppression field is deployed. That is all that is necessary. There are of course brothers on guard duty."

"There you have it. Thank you, West." I turned to Kieth

and smiled. "We can get in. Ty, find the transmitter chip, but don't fuck with it. It will be hidden, possibly camouflaged as a different type of chip altogether. Then we can start plotting."

Kieth twitched his nose. "I can get into it. Ty can get into anything."

I nodded. "Ty's a genius, yes, yes. But if Ty fucks up even a little, the chip will burn itself and will be so much char, okay? We'll have one shot at getting the algorithm out of it. Fuck it up with your itchy trigger fingers and I'll have to shoot you. Brother West," I said, "are there any other security features we need to know about?"

The Monk oriented on me jerkily, twitching. "The power and network feeds for the handshake system are located within the HQ building. They do not connect outside the building. There is no way to cut power or intercept the feeds. If you approach without authorization, the suppression field is invoked, and you are held until the guards can respond and eliminate. Response time averages six seconds."

"Are you observed while entering?"

"Digital analysis software examines every frame of security cams, which cover every foot of the perimeter, yes."

I swore. For a few seconds we were bathed in complete silence. I looked at Kieth, who just stared back. Then I glanced back at the Monk.

"Will you help us?"

It twitched violently. "Help you?"

"Will you help us to get in?"

Another few moments of silence, marred only by the trembling hum of the Monk's motors. It was vibrating slightly.

"Will you kill me?"

I blinked, and swallowed hard. "Kill you?"

"Yes." It took a step forward awkwardly, and then stopped. "If I help you to enter the Abbey, will you kill me?" With apparent effort, it spread its hands.

Glancing around the room, I found no one willing to look me in the eye, no one willing to offer even an unspoken opinion. Finally I made fists with both hands and looked back at the Monk.

"Done."

The Monk didn't move at first. Then it nodded its head, once, the motors humming. "Done."

XX

IT HURT MY EYES A LITTLE
JUST TO LOOK AT HER

00001

"Well, this is depressing."

I ignored Gatz. He was the only one I thought I could count on to at least not slit my throat. Kieth intended me no harm, I thought, but he wouldn't lose sleep if I got hurt, either; I wasn't even sure he regarded other people as people, and not as especially well-designed Droids. Milton and Tanner were in it purely for the money, and people in it for the money could never be trusted.

That left Kev Gatz.

We stood on the Dole Line near Downing Street with every other citizen of the System. A few blocks back were the twisted remnants of a heavy-duty black metal gate, half of it torn from its moorings and the other half melted. I twisted my head and could see a jagged wall of masonry still standing on Downing Street itself, just inside those gates, where a small sign was amazingly clean and uncharred, reading DOWNING STREET, SW1, CITY OF WESTMINSTER. I considered asking when the fuck London had been the City of Westminster, and then considered my companions and decided against it. The Abbey was called Westminster, too, and the Abbey had looked like the oldest fucking thing in the world, so maybe it had been a long time ago, fifty years or forever.

I imagined some of the people on the line—snaking for miles up and down the street several times before disappearing—were actually waiting for their issue of Nutrition Tabs and Necessities Coupons, sponsored by several of the richer families in London, but the Dole Line was really just a meeting place. Most of us were there looking to make deals, usually illegal. You had the cream of London's underground standing around in broad daylight, so despised by their betters that no one paid any attention.

I was looking for guns.

Just a mile away our target sat behind a high wall and the security system: Westminster Abbey, Worldwide Headquarters of the Electric Church. The Abbey itself was largely gone, carried away by Unification and riots and the simple erosion of a population so desperate that ancient bricks became valuable. All that was left was one wall and most of one tower, upright by the grace of God or whatever, the new wall around it a cinder-block monstrosity.

I followed Gatz at a leisurely pace. He was working the line, making inquiries after a gun dealer Kieth recommended. I didn't have any contacts in London, so I took the advice offered and hoped for the best. It was a gray, rainy sort of day, a steady drizzle of subtle dispirited precipitation that soaked your clothes before you realized it.

I had Brother West in my head, the poor fuck. I'd had people plead with me *not* to kill them. I'd never had someone beg me to pull his plug. I was happy to take Dick Marin's money, I was happy to kill whomever he wanted me to in return for what he'd offered me, what did I care? But listening to West, I'd realized it really was true. Inside every Monk there was a human being silently screaming in digital, with no mouth.

I followed Gatz, my hands in my pockets, my best hard-assed mask on, staring at the Monks. A gang of them worked the Dole Line. They smiled their way up and down, politely asking if anyone wanted to hear their personal testimony. They got a few takers, thin, pale men and women with deep, blank eyes who probably thought that if they joined the EC they wouldn't have to stand in line for a whole day just to get some super-rich asshole's version of charity. The Monks were all immaculate. Clean, polished, calm, polite, well-spoken, but every time I looked at them I saw a scream. I made fists inside my pockets and wanted to rip each latex face off.

"Ave," Gatz said, gesturing me closer. "This guy knows our man."

I stepped forward. Gatz was standing with a short, gaunt, completely toothless man who sported a thin line of drool out of the corner of his mouth. He grinned at me and I wanted to punch him just to make him stop.

"You know Jerry Materiel?" I asked.

Drooly nodded slowly. "Shure, shure," he lisped. "He's on line right now, doin' bizness. I could point 'im out to you for, say, five yen."

I stared at him, keeping my hardassed mask on. I felt Gatz glance at me through his glasses.

"You want I should give him a nudge?" he asked.

I bunched my jaw muscles. "No," I said firmly. There were rules, or ought to be. Or had been, once. If you just fucked everyone you met, fucked and fucked and fucked people, where did it end? The man had made an honest offer. I fished a credit dongle from my pocket. "Five it is, friend, on delivery."

Drooly nodded happily, spittle flying, and broke away from the line. We followed him for about two minutes, an endless, featureless line of desperate people passing us, most engaged in furtive discussions, some making exchanges. The city around us looked desolate and abandoned, and incredibly ancient. On the horizon was a tall, broken tower that soared upward and ended in jagged, black-char teeth. The whole place felt like the riots had ended twenty years ago, and everyone had just left it as it was—every stone on the street, every destroyed building, every evacuated family—all just collecting dust all these years. It was a ghost city. Drooly stopped in front of a group of men who looked a little too well-fed for the Dole Line and pointed.

"Here's Jer," Drooly sputtered. "Wit' the broken nose."

I ignored Drooly's outstretched palm and stepped up to the group. One of them did have a prodigiously broken nose, sitting at a noticeable angle to his face. I nodded at him. "You Jerry Materiel?"

He looked me and Gatz up and down. "Mabe, who'el you, den?"

His accent was so thick I could barely understand him. Sifting through the mangled syllables, I squinted until I thought I looked inscrutable and deadly. It had worked before. "Avery Cates, out of New York."

He studied me for a moment, and then grunted. I knew enough about people like Jerry to determine this meant he'd heard my name. "Bawl ov chawlk, lads, eh?" The men who had been standing with him drifted a few feet away, smoking cigarettes and talking. The cigarettes marked them as fairly prosperous crooks; it had been weeks since I'd had a steady supply of smokes.

"Cates outter New Yawk, awright," Jerry Materiel grunted, looking me up and down again. "I heard you Captain Kirked the Kendish hit. That you?"

Kendish . . . I thought a moment, and then brightened. Mitchell Kendish had been a Joint Council undersecretary. He'd launched an investigation into a group stealing SSF laundry hovers and tearing them apart, selling the parts right back to the SSF to repair the remaining hovers. It had been genius, but Kendish had spoiled everything. The undersecretaries, who were the people who did most of the day-to-day real work of running the System, can usually be bribed—they were the worst in the whole damn filthy System, worse even than the System Cops because they didn't have a Department of Internal Affairs to keep track of them and meddle once in a while.

What made the whole insane machine run was bribes, really. No matter how corrupt and broken the machine was, everyone could rely on the magical power of yen and that stabilized things. But Kendish hadn't wanted anything to do with a bribe. So I'd been hired to put him away. I didn't mind; you didn't get to be an undersecretary by being a saint, and the price was right. That had been my most high-profile job—and one of the few that had gone off without a hitch, professional and dry, no mess. I thought longingly of the money I'd been paid for that. Long gone, into Pickering's, into a lot of bullshit. "Yeah, I poked Kendish."

Jerry nodded. "Awright, I know you. What kin Jerry do for Mr. Avery Cates outta New Yawk, then?" He squinted at me. I was still in my stolen duds, and they hadn't gotten too beat up yet, because I'd gone a remarkable seventy-two hours without being shot at, beaten, or chased. "Assuming 'e's gawt the bees and honey for the job."

In response, I made a show of paying Drooly, who'd been standing there grinning in five-yen ecstasy, for his time. "I've got yen," I said. "You have an office?"

Jerry Materiel spread his arms and smiled, his teeth brown and cracked. "The whole field a wheat's my office, Mr. Cates! Tell us what y'be needin'."

I had laboriously written a list onto a scrap of paper. "Any two or three of these would be fine."

He ran his eye over the list, raised an eyebrow, and licked his thumb. "Y'know what yer doin', fer sure. I'll ne' s'resurance. Say twenty would relax me on the subbeck, eh?" He produced a small hand-held credit scanner. Glancing around, I paused: A flash of red hair down the street, ducking behind something, made me stiffen. I ran my dongle through the scanner and it lit up green. I glanced back at Jerry Materiel and he grinned.

"No need to wor' abut the whoppers, Cates. They don't bust the Dole. Too borin' for 'em. If'n yer gon' wor' abut sometin', wor' abut the feggin' Tin Men."

I nodded. "I worry about the Monks," I said. "Be sure of that. I also need building plans. Old ones, pre-Unification."

Jerry winked. "My speci-ali-tee, Cates. I'll have a butcher's and see what can be done. You gawt an addy?"

I slipped him another piece of paper. "Where and when, Mr. Materiel?"

He stared at the second slip for a moment, chewing his lip, and then glanced back at the list. "Here, Mr. Cates, in twenty."

"Done." I leaned forward slightly. "Tell me, is there a red-haired woman about a block away, sort of hiding behind that ruined wall, but watching me?"

Jerry Materiel didn't move his eyes from my face, but that terrible, brown-black grin appeared again. "Lumme! She sure has been eyeballin' you, Cates, since you got 'ere. She ain't SSF, or you'da been shown the heels, right?"

"Thanks. In twenty then."

Materiel sketched a salute and melted into the Dole Line. Gatz stood close to me as we pretended to join the line. "That your Vid anchor?"

I nodded slightly. "That's her. Let's see if we can get her off the street."

We wandered. We didn't know London. In some ways, all the cities were the same: half-ruined, never rebuilt after the Riots, and continually razed a little more every time there was a food riot or something. New York, especially Old New York, the original city, before urban spread had absorbed most of the other cities on the seaboard and formed the huge, endless city it was today, was a snarling mass of people, people, people—people crushed into the streets, into the few livable apartments, into the rare legal taverns and the hundreds of temporary gin mills. The gray mass of men and women roiling through the streets was a permanent fixture. Sure, you wandered above Twenty-third Street in Manhattan and things thinned out as things got richer, but I didn't think there was an inhabitable area in New York that wasn't packed with people. London was different. It had the same razed look, the same crumbling buildings, and the same remnants of the Riots, but there weren't any *people*. The streets were comparatively empty, winding off who knew where. In Manhattan, you could let yourself be carried along by the tide of people and know exactly where you'd end up. In London, I got the feeling that it was all narrow, winding streets, and the space made my skin itch. I felt exposed. And in New York, things had been crufted back together. Rubble cleared, windows boarded up, spared furniture rescued and reused. London looked like entire neighborhoods had just shrugged their shoulders, packed up, and left.

Gatz and I wandered, keeping the dirty river on our left and letting her keep us in sight, until we were on a wide but deserted street. At one time it had edged the river, but recently the river—a dirty, brown-flavored sludge flowing stolidly past us—had topped the embankment and lapped halfway across the broken pavement. When the time was right we ducked into the shadows offered by a wall of rubble dumped there decades ago and waited. Across the river from us was a hemisphere of rusted metal, a huge spoked contraption half-buried in river sludge, leaning at an extreme angle but somehow peaceful in its stillness. It was bent slightly, and I tried, briefly, to imagine it upright and suspended in the air again, but it was hard to imagine anything whole and functioning again.

She appeared a few minutes later, clean and coiffed and wearing more on her back than I'd ever possessed in my whole fucking life. It hurt my eyes a little just to look at her, someone who ate real food, who bought new clothes whenever she wanted, some girl playing at a profession because she was *bored*. The only legitimate jobs to be had, aside from maybe being a Crusher, didn't pay enough to survive on—everyone who'd lived the streets, like me, knew that. The only people who could *afford* to have jobs were rich. I watched her pass our hiding spot, bold as brass because she was convinced nothing could happen to her, that the whole SSF would spring into action if she was so much as stared at rudely. It made my heart sing to follow her silently for a few seconds, and then reach out and wrap my arm around her neck, cupping the hand over her mouth to cut off the squeak of protest she managed.

"If I flex my bicep your neck will snap," I whispered into her ear. "You believe me?"

After a moment, she nodded.

"Good. You've been following me, Ms. Harper. Bad idea." Kev stepped in front of us. "I can't have Vid reporters doing stories on me, now can I? Let me introduce my colleague Kev Gatz. He's going to have a look at you."

She tensed in my arms, not sure of what was coming, and probably believing the bullshit the Vids pumped out about the jobless mass they ruled over: that we were without conscience, without honor, without souls. Some of us were, but I liked to think there was still honor, still some humanity. I breathed in the smell of her hair—clean and perfumed—and swallowed involuntarily, shifting my weight to keep a sliver of air between us.

Gatz lifted his shades and I averted my eyes. "Ms. Harper, look at me." He sighed.

I frowned. "Kieth said you didn't need to look people in the eye." Harper rolled her eyes toward me and then back toward Kev, trying to see us both simultaneously.

He shrugged. "I dunno. I can't do it without eye contact. It's like a block or something."

And then, just before—just a split second before—the barrel of the gun touched my ear, I heard the faintest rustle of a coat, the faintest hint of someone behind me. I barely moved my head, and the gun was in my ear. I thought, *Fucking hell, who the fuck moves that lightly?*

"Mr. Cates, a pleasure," a deep, roughly accented voice said quietly. "Please ask your friend to put his glasses back on, as I have no intention of looking at him."

I nodded, not moving. "Go ahead, Kev."

After a moment, the gun was removed. "Very well, Mr. Cates, you can move if you wish."

The voice was calm and sounded amused, as if there was no worry over me making any sort of move against him. I released the reporter, who stood there in a Gatz-induced daze, and slowly turned. A few feet away stood an old man—at least fifty years old if he was a day, with a shock of white hair over a permanently pink face—dressed all in black, quality clothes, not flashy. The gun he held casually on Gatz and myself gleamed in the damp storm-light: a silver-plated, custom Roon model.

He looked me up and down, a hint of a smile on his clean-shaven, lined face. "You move well, Mr. Cates," he said cheerfully, "but you have a bad habit of assuming that if you can't see something—say, anything *behind* you—it can't hurt you."

I studied his face—he was the oldest man to ever hold a gun on me, that was for sure. I didn't recognize it. "I don't know you, do I?"

His smiled widened subtly. "Of course you do, Mr. Cates. I've been Gunning since before you were born. I'm sure you've heard of me. I admit I've been lying low for the last few years, but I'd like to think the good work I did for the cause in Ireland is still spoken of."

I shook my head. "You're telling me you're Canny Orel?"

The old man just raised a snowy eyebrow.

Gatz grunted with sudden, unexpected animation. "Can't be. Canny Orel'd have to be like fifty years old. He's dead."

I hesitated, because in a way it made sense. Canny Orel was a man who had killed upward of three hundred people, never been tapped by the System Pigs once, who'd founded the Dúnmharú, and who had retired rich and healthy. I knew I wasn't in that class, but I'd lived to a ripe old age myself, on the streets of New York, and it took skill to sneak up on me in broad fucking daylight.

And . . . I wanted to believe it. Here was someone who'd *survived,* who'd spent his life just like me, crawling from one emergency to another, who'd killed people—but better than me, because Canny Orel had always killed people for a reason, for a cause. Not just for money. Whatever he'd done before Unification, Orel had killed for Saoirse in the cause of Irish independence. When that had ultimately failed in the face of the newly constituted SSF, he'd formed the Dúnmharú, an organization of Gunners that, while profit-motivated, had only taken jobs assassinating System officials or SSF officers. As far as I knew, Orel was the only person who'd killed SSF officers and lived to tell the tale . . . until me. So far. Canny Orel had been the best, and he'd done it for a *reason.* I wanted him to be standing here in front of me.

"Gentlemen," he said, his smile disappearing. "You can call me Mr. Orel. Now, enough of the fanboy bullshit, eh? There's business to attend to."

Sudden panic rippled through me. This was no fucking coincidence, I thought—the man had been hired, sent after me. I shut my eyes. I didn't know if it was Moje or the Electric Church or who, but someone had gone out and spent top dollar for the best there was to cut me down. At least I knew when they spoke of me back in Pickering's, I'd be the guy cut down by the legend. I'd be legend. Whoever had found him and hired him, I'd at least have that.

And I thought longingly of the Monks and their nuclear batteries. I thought of Brother West, going mad, but alive, always alive, forever. I was suddenly and inexplicably sure that I was about to die.

I eyed his gun, trying to figure a way past it, an angle. I didn't see one. Heart pounding, I nodded. "Okay." I wasn't going to beg him. I wasn't going to embarrass myself. I wanted Canny Orel to go away thinking I was the hardest ass he'd ever encountered.

"Good show, Mr. Cates." He racked a shell into the chamber. "Now tell me: Where in *fuck* is that little slimy bastard Ty Kieth?"

XXI

THE MOST LIKELY OUTCOME
OF THIS LITTLE ADVENTURE

01100

"I've heard of you, you know."

We walked through London, Gatz in the lead with his sunglasses on despite the rain. South to the crumbling bridge with cracks wide enough to require a few heart-rattling jumps, past the sprawling monument to broken glass and twisted steel railings of what had been Waterloo Station—whatever the fuck that was—and finally into the maze of twisty little streets, all the same. I'd thought I'd cleaned up pretty well, but both Gatz and I were unkempt, unshaven, and unsavory-looking compared to our new friends. Marilyn Harper walked with us, Pushed to follow Gatz and keep her mouth shut. Then me, starting to feel a little under the weather, still unarmed, and with some asshole named Jerry Materiel holding twenty of my yen, gone.

And then, shining like a new penny, Canny Orel, the most famous Gunner in history. Or at least of the last twenty years, which was pretty much the same thing.

He *looked* famous. He looked rich, fat, and sleek, although he still moved with astonishing speed. His skin was dry and papery, with a pink cast. His hair was white, but expensively cut. His hands were so quick he didn't bother to hold the gun on me as we walked, and I still didn't dare fuck with him. There was a lush, sick scent of success hanging around Canny Orel.

"You have?" I said.

"Indeed, mate. Heard a few tidbits. Always sounded to me like you were more lucky than talented. Looks like you stepped in it this time, eh?"

His voice was deep and melodious. It sounded like he was subtly singing everything.

"So, just out of professional courtesy, why are you after my Techie?" I asked.

"Out of professional *courtesy*, mind your own fucking business," he said flatly, as if he said it five times a day.

As usual, the city felt deserted. Gatz was smart enough to meander a little, buy some time. I didn't know what I was going to do, since I was convinced I couldn't deal with Orel—not without a gun, certainly, and even if I'd been packing something more than my sharp wit I wasn't sure I'd be able to tackle him.

"Your fucking Techie, Mr. Cates, robbed me blind. I've been seeking him out for months," Orel finally growled. "That little piglet can *disappear*. Say, I could give you a taste of the recovered yen, maybe, for leading me to him. A finder's fee, we could call it."

Honor among thieves, I thought. Orel felt bad about making me give up my own man for execution, and he was trying to smooth my feathers. It made me think maybe I had some small currency with the old man.

"He gave me the impression he was hiding from the SSF." I kept walking.

Orel snorted derisively. "We're *all* hiding from the System Pigs, Cates. Mr. Kieth is hiding from me *especially.*"

I cleared my throat and tried to keep my voice steady, deciding to take a calculated risk. "I don't think he's got any money, Orel."

There were a few steps in silence, rain pattering softly against my face. Then: "Well, he's your man, Cates. Perhaps *you* have some money—"

A thrill went through me as a plan began to coalesce.

"—or maybe I'll just gut the thieving bastard and sleep better at night. Who's the twist?"

I looked at Marilyn Harper's back, my thrill of hope fading a bit. "Vid reporter. Recognized me from someplace."

"Fucking dilettante," he spat. "They own fucking everything, but they're *bored.* Don't hire someone who needs a fucking job, just play at it until you move on to something else." I felt him staring at my back for a few steps. "Awful quiet and cooperative, thanks to your friend there," he said quietly. "But she'll have to go."

I frowned. "We can handle her." I had no affection for rich girls playing reporter while my friends swam through shit every day trying to feed themselves either, but there was something savage about just shooting someone who got in your way. Something primitive.

"Really? How?"

I kept my eyes on the back of Gatz's head. "We made her see things our way. Didn't we, Marilyn?"

After a moment, she nodded stiffly. "Yes."

"She's going to film my exploits," I said brightly. "I'm going to be famous."

Orel grunted behind me. "It doesn't look like your man can keep her under his thumb for long, the way he's sweating. Let's cut the crap and get to your base, so I can resume negotiations with dear old Ty as soon as possible."

Gatz started to glance back, and my heart skipped a beat, but Orel gave me a shove.

"Eyes forward, Mr. Gatz. I'd hate to have to kill you, but I wouldn't lose sleep over it either."

Orel knew more about us than I liked. At the factory, I tried my last play to save Ty as much grief as possible. The place looked sewed up and deserted as we approached. Feeling the familiar buzz of adrenaline and terror, my back to the man I was pretty sure would be my executioner, I pounded on the front door and shouted. "Kieth! Hey, Kieth, let me in!"

Orel was in motion before I could knock a second time, slamming my head into the door hard enough to knock me on my ass for a few seconds and slipping silently into the building. I spent a few moments profitably staring up into the light rain, until Gatz's sallow face filled my vision.

"Well, you sure handled that like a superhero, Avery," Gatz said in a strained monotone, most of his attention bent on keeping Harper under control. A light film of sweat covered his waxy skin.

"Fuck you," I moaned, sitting up and rubbing my head. "It's Canny Orel. The man was murdering people when I was nursing. He was an assassin for Saoirse, just before Unification.

Trained by the Irish government before it Unified. So cut me a break."

"If that's Canny Orel," Gatz said, helping me to my feet, "I'll eat your shoes." The front door of the factory suddenly popped open, and Kieth was pushed roughly out. Orel grinned right behind him.

"Come on in, Cates. I am not without honor. Let's discuss terms."

I glared at Kieth, who stared at me with wide, terrified eyes. "Fleeing the SSF, my fucking ass. I should let him kill you for not warning me about this."

Kieth didn't say anything. Behind him, Orel held a shining, silver-plated gun in each hand. "Don't worry, Mr. Cates," he said. "Kill him I shall. But as I said, we can discuss compensation. Step inside, please."

I felt feverish. Gatz and I sat with Marilyn Harper on the floor. Milton and Tanner—who had allowed Canny Orel to walk in unopposed—sat near Kieth's equipment, which hummed and beeped randomly, unsupervised. The Droids, after swarming around in a tizzy of excitement giving Kieth endless reports of intruders in the building, had finally been silenced by the Techie. Orel studied the Monk with obvious perplexity, holding Kieth by the scruff of his neck.

Gatz leaned toward me slightly, his face waxy and yellow. "I can't hold on to her much longer, Ave."

I didn't say anything.

"You've got something big cooking here, don't you?" Orel said cheerfully.

I kept my face blank. "I do. I need Mr. Kieth to do it, too. Maybe we can strike a deal."

Orel looked at me without moving his head, his eyes just sliding in their sockets. I imagined I could *hear* his eyes moving—sudden metallic scrapings.

"Mr. Cates, I can't imagine what deal we could strike. I hired this cocksucker seven months ago on a project of my own. I paid him a significant amount of money. This same cocksucker then bought himself every little toy he'd ever wanted off the black market—most of which I see here—and ran out on me. Me! I can still hardly believe it."

"Let me make you an offer, Mr. Orel," I said carefully. "If you don't care for it, well, you put one in Ty's ear and I start looking for another Techie. But I think I can get back your lost investment, which must have been considerable to inspire such passion."

Orel turned away from the Monk to face me, pushing Kieth around like a rag doll. The Gunner smiled, his eyes moving easily from person to person without appearing in any way worried. He opened his mouth to reply, but Kieth suddenly spoke up.

"He's not Canny Orel," he said.

The hand on Kieth shot to the Techie's throat and pinched, cutting off Kieth's voice and breath. I stared at the old man and the old man stared back at me, a slight smile twitching on his face.

"Care to test me?" he said conversationally, sounding bored.

"Care to test all of us?" I said, trying to emulate the smooth, steady disdain of his voice. I failed miserably. Whoever this guy was, he certainly scared the shit out of me, Canny Orel or not. "Let's hear what he has to say." I gestured at Kieth.

The old man scanned the room, did some math in his head, and then shrugged, releasing Kieth, who immediately began to gasp and cough.

"Kieth?" I prompted.

He looked up at me with damp, red eyes, rubbing his throat. "Come on, Cates," he choked out. "There are like fifteen Canny Orels Ty's seen personally. It's good marketing, using that name." He took a deep, shuddering breath, rubbing his head. "He's possibly Dúnmharú, but he is not *the* Canny Orel."

For a moment I was unable to decide if this was an improvement on my situation. If he wasn't the greatest Gunner who ever lived, that was good for me. But being faced with, say, the *third-best* gunner that ever lived . . . well, it didn't make me want to do cartwheels.

"It doesn't matter, does it, Mr. Cates? The fact remains that we have business together. The fact remains that you could not, were you to try, get the drop on me. The fact remains that I can and will kill all of you without breaking a sweat if forced to. However, Mr. Cates, as I said, I've heard of you. I've heard you play by old rules. I'll listen."

Amazingly, he sat down on the floor in one smooth motion, yanking Kieth down next to him. I looked around at my team—all of them useless, it seemed. I wasn't going to be deterred now. I didn't think I could outgun Cainnic Orel, or even an Orel-trained former member of the Dúnmharú. He was right—it didn't really matter who he really was. I was going to have to make him a partner.

I looked at him as steadily as I could. "I've been hired to assassinate Dennis Squalor. The payout is huge. We've got a plan to get close to Squalor. I can offer you your money back in a few weeks."

"Double," he said immediately.

"Excuse me?"

"Double my investment."

What the fuck. It was more money than I could ever spend anyway, and the idea of this whole thing falling apart made me sick, my stomach contracting to a spiky ball inside me. I nodded. "Done."

"Okay," he said, casually producing one of his shining guns and clearing the chamber, a gleaming bullet springing into the air and hitting the floor with a metallic clink. "Okay, Triple." He glanced up and grinned at me again.

I blinked. "Excuse me?"

"If you can double, you can triple. If you can triple, you can quadruple. Let's say quadruple."

Swallowing burning anger, I forced myself to nod against every instinct I had and every lesson I'd learned—I was getting assfucked on this deal, and instead of beating the bastard silly, I was just looking for something to lean against. "Done," I growled through clenched teeth.

He winked. "Well, Jesus, if you can quadruple, maybe we should leave the issue open and negotiate later." His broad smile threatened to turn into laughter. "No? Okay, Cates. Quadruple it is. Give me the details."

I studied him. He grinned easily, hair perfect, the clothes on his back worth more than *me*. I shook my head and forced myself to smile back.

"No."

He raised a thin white eyebrow. "No?"

I couldn't afford to show any nervousness. The only card I held was the fact that the money moved through me. If Marin found out Cainnic Orel—or one of his infamous protégés—was on the scene, I would be out. If the old man found out Marin was the bank on this job, I would be out. No matter what else happened, I couldn't give this guy any details. Even if it meant Kieth got capped.

"That's the deal. Four times your initial investment and Kieth gets a pass. You don't get anything else." I swallowed. "This is *my* job. You don't want to back off, go take the motherfucking Techie out back and get the fuck out of my life."

The old man stared at me, his smile frozen. After a moment he chambered another round, a nice little piece of theater to show just how little the fucker feared me. He let out a barking laugh, showing his strong, gleaming teeth.

"All right, Mr. Cates. All right. In your position I would insist on the same."

I tried to hide the relief that hit me like a dose of cold water. "All right. What do we call you, then, if you're not the one and only Cainnic Orel?"

He shrugged. "I think that name is as good as any, don't you? Despite what this little turd says, as far as *you* know, I am the 'one and only' Cainnic Orel. Mr. Orel will do nicely." This with a tight-lipped, smug grin that made me close my hands into fists. "I have one further condition, however: I am now part of your team."

I blinked. "Excuse me?" To our right, a strident alarm blared, the sound bouncing off the walls. Kieth yelped and leaped up. Orel let him go.

Orel climbed to his feet, grinning. "You won't give me any info, I have to hang around to protect my investment," he shouted, somehow still sounding calm. "Put it this way, Cates. Say tomorrow night you get capped behind the ear, which is the most likely outcome of this little adventure. Would naturally put the chances that I'll ever get my money in a dim light, no? As a result, I'd want to have the little cocksucker on his knees nice and quick. You see? If I'm not here, the little cocksucker might slip away again."

"Cates!" Kieth yelled from his fortress of servers. He must have hit a switch, because the blaring alarms went to half-volume. "We have a problem!"

I glanced at Kieth, then back at Orel. "Okay. Give me twenty yen."

He blinked. "What?"

"You fucked me out of twenty yen back there at the Dole. It's part of your buy-in on this deal. Now, please."

He laughed, reaching for his credit dongle. "You're either totally incompetent or a genius, Cates."

"Oh, he's incompetent, all right," Tanner said brightly. "Pretty soon he'll tell you about the growing army of System Pigs who seem to always know where he is."

"Cates!" Kieth yelled again.

I turned away from Orel as our transaction went through and walked briskly toward Kieth. *"What,* for God's sake?"

The bald man was wide-eyed, his nose twitching fiercely. A fat drop of sweat was hanging impossibly from its tip, and it looked like fresh terror-sweat springing up on top of the dried residue of his previous cycle of terror and relief. "We have a visitor. Or visitors. Not sure yet."

"I see." I looked down at the floor for a moment, fists clenched. *It never fucking lets up,* I thought. This had been my whole life, one crisis after another. Where was I going to sleep, another gun pointed in my face, was someone going to try to slit my throat—it never ended. I spun to face the rest of them.

Words died in my mouth as a distant boom thundered through the building.

"Looks like they're here!" Milton shouted. "I do hope they're friendly!"

Orel breezed past me, guns in hand. "Looks like I'm earning my keep on this team of yours already," he said with a wink, whirling around in midstride and walking backward. "With your permission, of course, boss."

I stared at Orel. "Ty, who the fuck's at the door?"

Kieth didn't even look up from his video screens. "Monks."

XXII

I'M GLAD THEY IGNORED MY *SCREAMS* OF *PAIN*

01100

"Strange, strange, strange."

I watched Orel disappear into the narrow corridor that led to the main entrance of the factory. "What's strange? And for God's sake, turn that goddamn alarm off."

Kieth absent-mindedly made a complex gesture and the alarm cut off.

"There's only one Monk."

Milton appeared at my elbow. "What do we do, chief?"

I held up a hand and squinted at Kieth. "Just one? You're sure?"

"Ty could spot a Monk the size of a mosquito out there, Mr. Cates. There's just one. It's moving . . . erratically."

Milton spread her arms. "Cates? What's the word?"

I looked around. "Hold tight," I ordered. I spun around and found the sisters grinning at me. "Give me a gun."

They both blinked, almost in unison. Their smiles faded a little.

"What?" said Tanner.

"Whatever piece-of-shit rod you overpaid for back in New York, hand it over."

They glanced at each other, silent secret twin telepathy sizzling the air between them, and then Tanner reached around herself and extracted a piece from some hidden holster and extended it to me. I reached out in horrified fascination and accepted it.

I stared at the monstrosity "A revolver," I said. "A goddamned *revolver*? Where did you even *find* this relic? Fuck, forget it." The gun was impossibly heavy in my hand—I was used to the feather light alloys of the Roon—and I suspected the recoil might knock me on my ass. Assuming it didn't just explode when I pulled the trigger. I turned to Milton. "Hold tight. Don't move. We're not being chased out of here by one Monk and a possible distress signal. Kieth!" The bald head whipped around toward me, his eyes wide. "Keep tabs on outside. Get on the PA and *warn* us if any more friends show up."

Kieth nodded. "If any transmissions occur, Ty'll see. Won't be able to decode 'em, but at least we'll know the invites are out."

I ran after Orel, trotting, the heavy, ancient gun held down by my hip, pointed to the floor. As I approached the main entrance, Orel's arm shot out from the side wall and pulled me close. My arm came up automatically and put the barrel of the gun in his ribs.

"Cates," he whispered, "you run like you're angry at the ground. How old are you again? It's amazing you're still alive."

I tried to control my panting. "A Monk. Just one."

He loosened his grip. "Just one. It can't be a rescue job on your prisoner back there, then. They'd send a dozen, two dozen." He frowned. "Maybe it's just snuffling around, caught our scent. Thinks it'll try a group conversion." He put one of his guns back in its holster. I admired the way the cut of his coat hid both holsters perfectly. "If it's just a Monk, all it can do is bore us to death."

I shook my head. "Don't you fucking believe it, Orel. I've seen those things in action. They're goddamned killing machines."

His frown deepened. "What the fuck are you talking about? You know who joins the fucking Electric Church? Beggars, dope fiends, small-fry pickpockets. Desperate people starving on their feet—that's who. You telling me some shitkicker with a tin body becomes a killing machine?"

"You don't get it, Orel. That's what Monks *are*. Doesn't matter who they *were*." I fished my wireless headset from my pocket and fitted it into one ear. "Ty? You with me?"

"Here, Cates," his voice crackled. "It's still out there, circling around. Looks like it's probing our setup." He cleared his throat, the sound painfully loud in my ear. "I bolted this place down *electronically*, Cates. Physically there are a dozen spots it could wriggle through."

I relayed this to Orel, who shrugged, pulling his second gun out again. "Mr. Cates, the main rule of engagement in a deserted neighborhood like this is simple: Control the fucking situation. You don't want the Tin Man out there coming in? Then stop hiding in here." He pushed me away. "Open the fucking door.Let's kick some ass."

A booming, amplified voice tunneled through the wall, modulated, sweetened, and shatteringly loud.

Avery Cates! Let me bring you to the end of time, Mr. Cates. Let me save you." This was followed by a strange, scratchy noise that I slowly realized was laughter. *"And by save you, Mr. Cates, I mean I'm going to eat your fucking kidneys, asshole!"*

Orel looked at me, but I kept my eyes on the door. "You, uh, *know* this Monk?"

I closed my eyes for a moment. "Oh, *fuck me.*" I looked at him. "Yeah. I think I do. You heard about a System Pig joined the Church a few days ago?"

Orel nodded once, his elegantly lined face vaguely mocking, just the hint of a smile. "Went on a rampage. A fucking malfunction or something."

"Cates! Come out and let me show you an ENDLESS TRAIL OF SUNSETS!"

"Cainnic Orel, or whoever the fuck you are," I said slowly, "I'd like you to meet Barnaby Dawson, former captain in the SS-fucking-F."

Orel raised an eyebrow. In my ear, I heard Ty groan. Orel's eyes slid down to my hand. "Mr. Cates, that is a *charming* weapon. Are you sure you're a professional? If we had a guild I might deny you entrance. Very well. Let's go out there and control this situation, and tear your old friend Dawson into small pieces so we do not repeat this episode, what say you?"

I nodded. "I don't see a choice here. Let's go."

"I'll go out first and draw fire," Orel said immediately.

I felt a brief surge of resistance to this idea, which I ruthlessly ignored. I was not going to get into a pissing contest with the old man and get myself killed for the trouble. If the world's most famous Gunner wanted to take point, I was going to let him.

With a disconcerting wink, Orel shoved the door open and dove outside, hitting the ground, gunshots drilling divots into the pavement just behind him as he rolled away. I pushed myself after him, racing in the opposite direction. The door *snicked* shut behind me. I dashed around the corner and flattened myself against the wall, thinking, *Well, if the goddamn gun doesn't explode in my hand when I pull the trigger, I guess I'm ahead of the game.*

"Mr. Cates, you've doubled!" Dawson called out. His voice was identical to that of every Monk I'd ever had the misfortune of hearing. "Didn't realize you had the scratch for an illegal clone. But you forget, I got religion, and religion tells me that the partial face shot of the first man out the door goes under the alias *Cainnic Orel,* male, born Philadelphia, aged fifty-seven. That you, Canny? I doubt it, as I'm pretty sure Cainnic got shot to pieces about six years ago in the Mogadishu operation, but we never did find a body, did we? We always assumed this was because we *hadn't left much of a body to be* found, but perhaps you've merely risen from the dead. You're still on several Most Wanted lists—"

I chanced a glance around the corner and was rewarded with an explosion of chipped stone, three shells hitting within centimeters of my face, I whipped backward, cheek stinging. I sat for a moment and contemplated something that could react that fast, that accurately, for whom shadows and rain and my own expertise meant nothing.

"Things are different, now, Cates! I'm air-conditioned and armor-plated. I'm networked and backed-up. Do you know what you *did* to me? You *killed* me. I can *remember* it—dying. Do you know what it's like to be a System Cop who loses his badge? I didn't have more than a few days to live. They were fucking *lining up* to kill me, to torture me. I had nothing. And then this grinning little robot wants to talk to *me* about salvation? I thought it would be fun to twist off his little head and see what was inside, and you know what that little piece of shit did, Mr. Cates? It fucking shot me in the *balls.*"

I needed to know exactly where the bastard was. I was contemplating another glance around the corner when Kieth's voice crackled in my ear.

"To your right, Mr. Cates, against the building across the street, in the shadows," he said, and clicked off.

I closed my eyes and fixed the location in my mind.

"You know what?" Dawson went on. "I'm—" His voice cut off and there were four quick shots, followed by what I thought was Orel cursing somewhere nearby. "I'm glad you got me booted from the force. Glad! Glad that fucking machine shot me in the goddamn balls and let me bleed out on the street. Glad they ignored my *screams* of *pain* and dragged me into a hover, and I'm glad they *sawed my head off my neck while I was still alive!*"

I felt a tingle down my spine, and then Kieth's voice was in my ear again.

"Cates! Moving—fast! It's—"

I lunged down and to the side. Behind me, the wall exploded into chips and dust. I crawled as fast as I could, pushing myself up onto my feet at the expense of several layers of skin on my palms, and ran. Hard. At the next corner, I feinted, whipping myself in the other direction at the last moment, right out into the open, turning and firing three shots as quickly as I could with the old gun, guessing on target position. I didn't wait to see what happened, I launched myself forward, running for the slim protection of the angle, putting the building between us.

"Missed me!" Dawson shouted. "But don't be hard on yourself. You don't have quantum targeting chips and night vision, you don't have weather analysis calculating air pressure and wind speed. You don't have *anything.*"

I kept running, searching for cover. Behind me five more shots cracked, then a whoop that was distinctly human.

"Orel winged it," Kieth whispered in my ear. Why he was whispering was beyond me. "But those Monks are *fast*. Superficial damage. It's still on the move, and on your ass."

I was tempted to curse him out, but that would be a stupid waste of breath, which was in short supply. I imagined the scene in my head, the positions of each of the players. I veered toward the wall of the building and reversed direction, running back toward Dawson. It was an old trick; Dawson was suddenly pinned between us. The second the dim form of the Monk resolved out of the rainy afternoon gloom, I aimed down and fired my last three bullets. Orel added a volley of his own, five more shots, fully automatic, into the same spot. I threw myself off to the side, into shadows, and lay for a moment, listening. Nothing. After a moment, Kieth's voice was in my ear.

"It's gone."

"Fuck!" I hissed. I sat up, panting. Orel appeared out of his own set of shadows nearby. He didn't even look mildly out of breath, and it bothered me. He held out his guns and dropped their empty clips.

"I can't believe what I just saw, Mr. Cates," Orel said slowly, approaching me as he reloaded. "I hesitate to admit this, but I think if you hadn't been here to distract that Tin Man, I might be dead right now. I've never seen anything move that fast."

I stared up at him. I was sick to death of being chased. If one more ghost from New York showed up, I was going to have to commit some serious violence. I accepted a hand up from Orel after he holstered his weapons. He held my hand for a moment when I was up, looking me over, and then released me to touch my cheek.

"You got lucky," he said, holding up his fingers, gleaming blackly with blood. I touched my cheek and found a deep slice. It began to throb immediately. Then Kieth was in my ear again.

"Mr. Cates, you'd better get in here. Tanner got the Vid on the hover working. There's something you should see."

XXIII

YOU'LL NEVER BE PRETTY AGAIN

OOOOO

Orel didn't say anything more as we walked in, and I stayed quiet. My cheek stung and probably needed a stitch or two. I wondered if anyone had thought to bring some basic first-aid. About ten feet inside the door, Orel stopped and turned to face me.

"That was just a probe," he said.

I nodded. "He knows I'm here, he knows the basic security of the building, he knows who he has to deal with and how good we are." I sighed. "He'll be back."

Orel nodded, inscrutable. "But not here. He's established that getting in unnoticed isn't possible, and I think you and I together were a bit more trouble than he was prepared for." He paused. "You know something, Cates? That was the first time in thirty years I thought I might get killed."

I blinked. "Thirty years? I barely make it through an evening without thinking I'm going to get capped."

He kept his gray eyes on me. "You're one of those true believers, aren't you, Cates?"

"True believer?"

He shrugged. "Revolution. Changing the world. Ending the System."

I looked down at the floor, embarrassed and resentful. "Don't you sometimes just want to give up on all this bullshit? Christ, if you were in the Dúnmharú, you must."

I met his eyes again. "Oh, yes, Mr. Cates." He pointed a finger at his head like a gun. "If I could put a bullet in the System's brain, I would. But I'm a realist. Until the right time comes, a man's got to eat."

We walked back to the Assembly Room in silence. The place looked empty except for Brother West's lonely vigil, until I noticed Gatz sitting with his head down between his knees, a bound and gagged Marilyn Harper on the floor next to him tracking me with wide, white eyes.

"You okay, Kev?"

He didn't turn or lift his head; just waved dismissively at me. He'd had Harper Pushed for a long time. Kieth's bald head popped out of the hover's hatch and he waved at us.

As we entered the cramped cockpit, squeezing in with four other people, Milton glanced at us, winked, and held a finger against her lips. I oriented on the Vid, staring at my own face.

". . . no comment. Repeating this breaking news item, our colleague Marilyn Harper, a respected and popular Vid anchor, has been reported missing. System Security Force spokeswoman Denise Proctor has announced just ten minutes ago that a suspect in Harper's disappearance has been named: Avery Cates, a native of New York City, shown here. Cates is also a prime suspect in fifteen unsolved murders going back—"

I waved the sound off. "Fuck," I breathed.

"I wonder," Tanner said with a twinkle in her eyes that was eerily matched by her silent twin, "if you aren't sending these press releases to the Vids and the SSF yourself. I wonder if you aren't a secret media whore."

I'd been letting the sisters slide because they were tough, and because I wanted to keep things jolly, but this was getting old. You couldn't relax for a moment, could never be human. You had to be a blank wall. I counted to three, quickly, in my head and lunged for her. She yelped and tried to scramble back, but the cockpit was overpopulated and there was no place to go. I had her by the nose. She twitched and a knife flashed out and stopped just short of my neck, everyone else yelling and pulling at me.

"Just keep pushing," I advised her in a calm voice cutting through the sudden cacophony, looking at her sideways, my eyes just brushing her face. I ignored the knife. If she was going to slit my throat for touching her, I'd already be bleeding out. "Just keep pushing."

I let her go, and she relaxed, tenderly rubbing her nose. I turned to find Orel leaning against the hatch, looking at me blankly. "That how you handle things, Mr. Cates? Don't try it with me."

I shook my head. "Certainly not, Mr. Orel. You, I take out on the town, buy you drinks, and then shoot you in your sleep."

All I got was a raised eyebrow, manicured to a razor edge.

"Look," Milton broke in, pushing her way forward and standing with arms fiercely akimbo. "She's got a point. You're getting awfully high-profile, Cates."

Her sister, still rubbing her nose and holding her knife, nodded. "Your face is on the Vids. That's a problem."

"Goddammit, I know it is." I looked around at each of them. "This is my job. You want to walk away, go ahead—but there are no goddamn severance packages. You're either here for the payout to defend your share or you're not, it's that simple. If this is too hot for you, bail. But don't look back. And don't ever contact me again. If you walk away, keep walking." I looked at Orel. "That goes for you too, Canny. You want your money, you stick."

His eyes were alive with energy. "And if I choose to just revenge myself on Mr. Kieth here? There are other things than money in the world, Mr. Cates."

I shrugged. "I'm rapidly shedding anything I might have left to lose."

He nodded and pushed off from the hatch, putting a manicured, heavy hand on my shoulder. He gently pulled me into his orbit. His calloused hand was heavily veined and rough, overdeveloped.

"Walk with me a moment, Cates." We stepped out of the hover and I walked with him a few feet away. When he paused, I just waited, hands in my pockets. He glanced over my shoulder and then leaned in so that we were each looking over the other's shoulder—an old habit of street hustlers, to minimize volume and watch each other's backs. Orel and I fell into it easily. It occurred to me that it might be dangerous to give Orel such a clear opening, but I didn't think it was his style to sucker-punch someone he obviously considered his inferior.

"You'll have to kill the woman, of course," he said easily.

I didn't look at him, just bunched my jaw muscles. "No."

"Bad enough," he said in a clipped, precise manner, as if he'd had the speech memorized since childhood, "your face is on the Vids—but we can deal with that. The Vids have faces on them all the time, an endless parade of Bad People Who Must Be Stopped, all right? No one really cares about yet another heartless killer—not the people on the streets, at least. But she is a danger to us. *Her*, people will recognize. You and her seen together, almost certainly. What if she contrives to escape? To signal? Finally, what if she simply causes trouble? Throws a wrench, so to speak, in the works?" He pulled back enough to glance at me, and our eyes met. "No, Mr. Cates. She needs to be dealt with. Take her out back, *now*, and do it. She is too dangerous."

I swallowed thickly. The suggestion itself didn't bother me. I'd killed almost thirty people on contract, and at least that many in the course of things. I was a killer. I wasn't an *animal*. I was prepared to argue my case to God or the Cosmos or whatever—I played by rules. I lived by them.

I leaned forward slightly, until my lips were very near his ear. "I do not," I whispered, "simply kill obstacles, Mr. Orel, or whoever the fuck you are. It is not her fault that she is here. She should not be punished for it."

"That is a mistake, Mr. Cates."

I straightened up. "Mine to make. You know your options."

He straightened up and studied me, and I stared back at him. I didn't know if he was used to being ignored, but I wasn't a starfucker. Reputations had to be maintained, and one bad night could end it. If I had to, I knew I could be Cainnic Orel's bad night. After a few moments, he smiled.

"Yes, Mr. Cates. I know my options."

I watched him disappear into the guts of the factory, followed by one of the nervous Droids, which had been programmed to stay close to us in case we got lost. I walked over to sit next to Gatz, letting out an explosive sigh.

"Bad day, huh?" he asked without raising his head.

"I didn't tip anyone with Harper," I said without preamble. "Fuck, you were there, Kev. We didn't do anything stupid. How'd they get my name? A million fucking London crooks not half a mile away, and they fish *me* out of the hat? It was our fucking friend Moje. Colonel Moje. He probably doesn't even know I really did grab her. He knows I'm in London, somehow, and he's just pinning this on me to flush me out."

"How do you know that?"

I grimaced. I'd gone from exhausted and hollow to impatient with sudden restless energy. I wanted to attack something and was frightened of the urge. "Because I know what everyone else who wants to kill me is up to."

For a few moments, I just sat there. Gatz was the one person I was pretty sure didn't want to hurt me. He maybe didn't care much if I lived, but he wasn't actively pursuing my death, either, and as sad as that was, it was the best I could do. We sat there side by side, both dirty, disheveled, and tired. We came from the same place. I felt comfortable next to him.

My eyes slid to the right, and Marilyn Harper was staring at me, eyes watery, drool pooling under her mouth from the ruthless gag. I looked away. I was amazed at how complicated everything had become. It had only been a few days. And amazingly, it would probably all be over, one way or another, in a few more.

Footsteps behind me, and I turned to find Milton and Tanner, looking clean but just as leathery.

"Come on, then," Milton snapped.

"The surgery's open. No hard feelings, brother." Tanner grinned.

"Can't have you goin' septic on us, can we?"

I blinked. "What?"

They looked at each other simultaneously, and my head ached from watching them. "Your cheek, asshole," Milton said. "Let's get you fixed up."

I sat on the crate we used as a table in the corroded kitchen while Milton and Tanner fussed over me. One of the Droids sat silently between them, bearing our meager medical supplies. When Tanner lifted a thick needle attached to coarse black thread, my hand whipped up and grabbed her wrist.

"You are not pulling that fucking *cable* through my tortured flesh, right?"

She raised an eyebrow. "Don't be a baby, sonny. You see any plastic skin grafts here? You see any laser scalpels? A Med Droid? We have," she held the needle and thread in front of my nose, "good old-fashioned needle and thread."

Milton chuckled. "You'll never be pretty again, Cates," she said. "But you'll heal. We were running on the streets when you were just bad news on the horizon. I've stitched up more people and set more bones than you could count."

I looked at her closely, the faint lines around her eyes and mouth, the lean, taut look of her. "Tell me, how'd you manage to retire?"

She laughed. "You mean, retire *alive*?"

I shrugged.

"It's like anything else in this fucking world. We got lucky."

I grimaced as her sister leaned in and began shoving the needle through the flaps of my wound. It hurt so intensely that moments after she started I was numb. I ground my teeth as the sisters stared at me, Tanner's nose still red and angry.

"What?" I grunted.

Milton folded her arms across her chest as Tanner sewed me back together. I realized with a start that as her sister leaned in and out, working on me, she moved just a bit forward and back, in rhythm. "We're here, Cates. We're at each other's throats and getting bullets thrown our way. And I have yet to hear a plan from you for getting *into* this fucking place."

I looked at her and then down at my hands, dirty and covered in scabs, some of which had been torn off and leaked blood wearily. "I've got an idea."

Tanner snorted. "Glory be."

"The bad news is, it isn't something Kieth can wiggle his nose at and make happen with geek power and a few batteries."

Tanner snorted again. "So there's —"

" — good news?" Milton finished.

I paused for a second or two. "Not really."

Tanner paused, the needle buried in my flesh and burning. "Do tell, mistuh boss."

I sighed. "Well, to start with, we're going to need some stuff."

XXIV

MAKING EVERYONE SEEM FADED AND WATERY

01110

I wasn't used to wearing dark glasses; anything that reduced a Gunner's vision was a bad idea. But with my face now linked to Harper's it was a necessary precaution. Everything felt wrong: I was wearing someone else's clothes, someone else's sunglasses, in someone else's city. All day, I watched every Vid we passed, looking for my face, and saw eyes on me everywhere.

"Calm down," Canny Orel said quietly, as we climbed over a huge shattered column that had toppled over and crashed into a building, making a show of studying the list I had laboriously written out for us as if climbing over rubble required just a tiny amount of his amazing brain. "You're like a fucking Paranoia Broadcaster. I'm getting itchy just standing next to you." He squinted at the list. "Who the fuck came up with this? What the hell are we going to do with two digital video cameras?" He glanced at Gatz on the other side of me. "We prerecording our confessions to avoid the standard SSF beating?"

Gatz didn't say anything. After a moment Orel leaned in close to me.

"I have a strong urge to pinch your friend, just to make sure he still has a pulse."

"Be careful," I replied easily. "He's getting better every day. One of these days he'll pop a vessel in your brain from across the room."

Orel chuckled. "Your bunch is entertaining, Cates, I'll give you that." He sighed, scratching behind his ear. "This is a lunatic's laundry list. You're not going to give me a hint?"

I shook my head. "Need-to-know basis, Mr. Orel."

He squinted down at the list again. "You're not going to tell me what we need," he paused, licking a finger, "tetrodotoxin for? Not to mention what the fuck it is and where we're going to get it."

We ended up on a long wooden bench on the improbably named Pudding Lane that appeared to have been launched from a burned-out church during one set of riots or another. The bench was surprisingly unscathed, just sitting on the side of the street, remaining undisturbed by one of those twists of human nature that gave me little bursts of hope from time to time. The sun shone down weakly, making everyone seem faded and watery.

"It's a neurotoxin," Gatz said, his voice scratched and acid-pocked.

Orel raised an eyebrow and looked from Gatz to me. "Why, Cates, I swear I can't see your lips move *or* your hand up his ass. All right. We're shopping for a neurotoxin, digital video equipment, and, still, a gun for Mr. Cates. Meanwhile, the other members of Team Cates are out on their own mysterious shopping excursions, leaving that cocksucking Kieth in sole possession of the Monk. I'm beginning to think I should have asked for some collateral."

"Too late," I grunted. "Anyway, here's our man."

Jerry Materiel had been watching us from a second-floor window across the street for some time. I'd let him have his recon; hell, I'd be nervous, too. Man disappears in the middle of a transaction, turns out to be the most famous crook in the System at the moment, then contacts you out of the blue to make another large transaction, *then* shows up with a strange face. I'd sit tight a while, too, see if anything shook free. I noted Materiel's boys from the Dole Line stationed here and there on the street, trying to look casual and uninterested. Crowds of people wandered by, aimless and cranky, and if I hadn't seen Materiel's boys before they might've blended in.

That was okay, too. I liked a man who took precautions, and anyone who could afford retainers was obviously doing well.

Jerry didn't emerge from the building he'd been watching from; I smiled in approval as he walked out of the one next door, smiling, looking for all the world like a man without enemies walking free and easy in the weak sun, ready to do business.

"Mr. Cates," he said, proffering a nondescript paper bag. "You absented yersef before I coul' deliver the deliverables, including a set o' blues I think you'll find intrestin'."

I took the bag cautiously and found, to my surprise, my lost gun order gleaming in its depths, along with a tattered set of schematics—paper, pre-Unification, looking ancient and delicate. Kieth could digitize them in no time. While I made a show of inspecting its contents, Jerry inspected Canny, trying to decide if we were still safe to deal with. Canny beamed back at him, pleased to be a disconcerting mystery.

"Excellent," I said, closing the bag and tucking it away. "Much appreciated, Mr. Materiel. We've got some more business for you, if you're up for it."

He studied Orel for another second or two, and then turned back to me, instantly breaking into a wide smile. "M'bizness, Mr. Cates? Certainly. What can ol' Jerry git f'you now?"

I glanced at Orel, and with a smirk he handed the slip of paper over to Jerry. On my other side, Gatz appeared to be sound asleep. Or dead.

Materiel's smile faded as he read through the list. "This is an intrestin' recipe, Mr. Cates. Damn dif'cult, too. This fir' part, fer example . . ."

I let my mind wander as he launched into the usual fence bullshit: how hard everything was going to be to procure, how hot a commodity I was, and how he wasn't even sure it was wise to work with me, all leading up to the inevitable conclusion that this was going to cost me extra. I'd bought guns and other things off the black market a thousand times, and half the time it was a simple transaction, and the other half it was like being married to the fucking fence.

Something strange was going on in the street.

This stretch of city had been hit pretty bad in the Riots, but in a selective way. A lot of buildings were scorched and crumbling, left to rot these last fifteen or twenty years, but some of them were untouched, pristine. Rubble was piled, as far as I could see, exactly where it had settled twenty years before. Some of the empty lots had sprouted into wild jungles, ignored for decades. Men and women of a familiar type—sallow, skinny, penniless, and pissed off—stood in small groups or moved along in slow, unhappy circles, scowling around. Occasionally a prosperous peasant would scurry by, slightly plumper and a little less desperate, but for the most part it was just people like me.

And, of course, the Monks.

They worked the street in gangs—I wasn't sure if I was imagining it or not, but I thought there were more of them in one place than I'd ever seen before. I thought of Dick Marin telling me that the whole world would be Monked in a few years. On each corner one of the metal bastards was standing on a box, arms raised, preaching the *Mulqer Codex*. They spoke without pause or hesitation, all of it programmed in, automatic. Teams of the things moved up and down the street, smiling their fake smiles, leaving most of the people alone but pausing here and there to accost anyone who looked particularly hopeless and miserable, gently urging them to hand over their humanity for a chance at salvation. A lot of the hardcases on the street shut up and watched carefully when the Monks approached, but glowered menacingly after them when they passed. When the Monks passed near us, I looked down at the pavement. I was worried they would scan my face and come after me. The Electric Church had to know I was in London, but there was no margin in letting them know *exactly* where I was.

As I watched, the street began to dry up. People faded into the shadows, into the buildings, walking away. I'd seen the phenomenon often enough in New York, and when I glanced at Canny I found him looking at me. He nodded, subtly, and I grimaced. It usually meant one thing: System Police were coming. I turned to Jerry Materiel.

"Cut the crap," I said, standing up. "Can you fill the order or not?"

He scratched behind his ear, squinting at the list, his face made up entirely of folds of skin and stubble.

"Well, yea, I s'pose I ken—"

Canny was on his feet, too, urging Gatz up. I held up a hand to stop Jerry in midsentence.

"How much, then?"

He looked at me from under his eyebrows. "Won't be cheap, Mr. Cates. I ken ashur ya of that."

The street was clearing out, criminals disappearing like water down a drain. My whole body tensed, heart pounding, as I waited for the hammer to drop. But I kept my face calm—the act could never fail, even for a second, or the sharks would smell blood—and half an eye on Materiel's boys, who were starting to catch the scent of doom, but were still following orders and keeping their distance.

"Name a price."

It was agonizing, watching Materiel do calculations on the fly, precious seconds getting away from us. Out of the corner of my eye, I could see even the Monks packing it up and starting to drift off to greener pastures as word spread. The Electric Church might be the world's only religion in a few years, but at present the System Pigs were still at the top of the food chain.

Materiel smiled cunningly and quoted a number that made my hair stand up on my arms. I opened my mouth to protest the obvious gouging, but Orel put a leathery, curiously heavy hand on my arm.

"Done," he said to Materiel, holding out his credit dongle in the other hand. "I'm good for it."

Materiel ran Orel's credit and smiled, nodding. "Very well, then, gentlemen. Where shall I make delivery?"

I was already moving, Gatz and Orel on my heels. "We'll find you."

When we were a few feet away, Orel fell into step next to me. "Looks like a standard SSF hunt-and-gather."

I nodded, trying to have my eyes everywhere. "I'm getting tired of running from the fucking Pigs."

"Then you should be in another line of work, Mr. Cates." He gestured behind us. "They'll be coming from over there, I'm thinking, with a hover in the air over here to herd us."

"Right. Split up," I said, turning sharply away from them and heading for a ruined wall. It looked like a good prospect for a clear way out of the neighborhood. It was best to stay low; the SSF used air superiority ruthlessly. I had gone about four more steps when I heard Orel shout behind me.

"Run, you idiot!"

I turned in time to see Orel give Gatz a shove to get him moving as a huge hover, the biggest I'd ever seen, leaped into the air above the ruined church, the roar of its displacement exploding around us, a storm of noise. The few slow people who were still hanging around the street scattered like roaches in the light. I looked down, and a dozen or so System Pigs emerged from the church, guns drawn, moving fast toward us, a cloud of clumsy and unhappy Crushers around them.

Gatz ran with surprising speed and agility, but Canny stood his ground. Sweeping his coat back to reveal his twin Roons, shining in the dirty light, he drew each and released the custom, old-school safeties with an audible *snick* of metal on metal.

"Mr. Cates," he yelled without looking at me. "You owe me twenty yen, yes?"

I kept backing away, entranced in spite of myself. "What the fuck are you *doing*?" I shouted, horror swamping my better judgment for a moment and rooting me to the spot. "Move your ass!"

He shook his head. "Cainnic Orel does not run."

I whirled and thought to myself, *Well, Christ, you're not Cainnic Orel, and fuck that — Avery Cates does.*

XXV

HAS DEFINITELY BEEN YOUR LUCKY FUCKING DAY

00101

Immediately, there was a volley of shots behind me, like fire-crackers. I ducked into the ruined lot behind the crumbling wall and pushed myself to run faster, chalky dust billowing up around me. But the fucking Pigs—despite a Cainnic Orel pretender slinging bullets at them, despite Kev Gatz scurrying away—within a few seconds I knew there were at least three hot on my trail. I tore my dark glasses off and yanked one of the guns from my sack, wondering if there was enough luck left in the universe for it to be loaded.

I didn't know anything about London—if there were Safe Rooms buried in these sagging, ancient buildings, where the sewers might lead me, if there were any friendlies nearby who might take me in. I didn't even know where to hide, and I cursed everything under my breath as I ran. I'd somehow slipped behind the curtain, and was running through a ruined section, all rubble and uncleared streets, staggered walls looking ready to collapse on top of me. To lighten the load and gain a fraction of speed, I tossed the bag with the rest of the guns and popped the clip from the old Roon 85 I'd selected—three lonely armor-piercing bullets shining inside it. Armor-piercers were rare; the cops themselves had stopped using them years ago due to their expense, and they were highly prized in the underground—Jerry must not have realized he had an extra hundred yen in profit sitting in this gun. With one in the chamber that made four shots. Three cops, four shots. It was the biggest break I'd gotten in a while, and it made me nervous.

The hover displacement in the air got louder; I knew they were trying to find me on the ground in order to guide the streetside cops. I ducked into the nearest doorway, instantly enveloped in stale, dusty dark—and blinded after the relative brightness of the day. I fumbled forward a few steps and then tripped, landing hard on a loose pile of sharp, uneven things. Instinct took over and I went still and silent, biting down on my tongue hard enough to draw blood, cutting off any noise. My breath whistling through my nose sounded thunderous. The only thing I could do was wait for my eyes to adjust and try to be ready.

It took the cops longer than I expected. After thirty seconds or so, I carefully rolled over onto my back and squinted at the faint outline of the doorway. I raised my gun just in time; a figure appeared, framed in the doorway. I pulled the trigger reflexively, the shot loud enough to bring the whole sagging structure down on me. The shadow crumpled.

I stared for a moment. Killing System Pigs was starting to be a habit with me, and yet I was still alive. I'd seen what the Pigs did to cop-killers, back in New York. They usually put the body on display once they were done with it, sometimes with an educational sign pinned to it. A few months ago I'd been sick with worry over one mistakenly killed SSF officer. Now I stared blankly and thought it likely I'd manage to kill a few more before fate finally caught up with me. No matter what I did, I was already marked for the rest of my life. The only good news was that my life was probably going to be pretty short.

I heard a scrape of boot on dust behind me, and like a wire snapping my body rushed back to me. I scrambled backward on my hands, cutting them on the broken rock, still staring at the dimly lit doorway where the cop had been.

"Cates!" an unfamiliar feminine voice shouted from somewhere within the building. "Colonel Moje sends his regards, and has a message for you: *You didn't run far enough, rat.*"

I spun around onto my hands and knees and rolled until I hit a wall, then went limp. Fuck it. Moje had pronounced his death sentence on me already. Everybody in the fucking world wanted Avery Cates dead, and after twenty-seven years maybe it was time. I could remember my father, coming home from work—a real job—and being greeted by the men in our building, shaking hands, smiling. I could remember the world before, and knew this one wasn't worth fighting for.

All this in an instant, in a heartbeat. Then it was just me on the floor, staying low, rapidly losing my sight advantage, and two trained cops trying to kill me. And then I thought: I've already killed cops, I can kill as many as I want. *Fuck it, no more running.* The cops were about to find out what I was really capable of.

I closed my eyes and drew a long, deep, silent breath, calming my nerves. If I were a System Pig, capable, arrogant, healthy, and well-equipped, how would I go after Avery Cates? Keeping my eyes closed, I listened. There—over my left shoulder, creak of a leather boot. I pictured the room: three windows to my left, small squares of watery light over a low mound of rubble, and I imagined him there, third window, peering in from the outside.

Then—the smell of smoke, faint, off to my right. I could see him, coming in from another entrance. I strained and heard light steps. Too light for a man—this was a woman. She was prowling along the wall, feeling her way in the gloom, I imagined I could see the fucking cigarette dangling from her lips, eyes wide as she searched the darkness.

For a moment, I just imagined their orbits, moving slowly in a standard pattern around me, staying out of each other's crossfire, listening quietly to the data streams from the hover in the air and their fellow cops on the ground. I knew the moment I made any noise at all, I would have seconds before they gunned me down. I was going to have to make my three bullets count. So I stayed down, eyes shut, smelling the choking dust in the air and feeling the sharp corners of smashed masonry stabbing me in the back.

When I moved, they moved, instantly.

I took the guy at the window first—standing behind cover, peering into pitch black from the daylight, he would subconsciously imagine himself safe. I jumped up and spun, opening my eyes. There he was, a big black fat unshaven motherfucker in a huge raincoat, the sort of cop I'd seen a million times shaking down whores and beating some poor kid who stepped the wrong way. Even as I brought the gun up he moved his own arm and ducked down. I tracked him and put the armor-piercing bullet through the wall, and was rewarded by a strangled cry. I could tell from the gurgling noise he made that it wasn't a kill-shot, but fuck it, he was out of the game for a moment. A moment was all I had anyway.

I ran.

Behind me, bullets popped new holes into the load-bearing wall, cement dust flowering and sparks flying, each just centimeters from paralyzing me for life. I didn't stop to admire them. I ran straight for the wall and threw myself into one of the empty windows, leaping with arms outstretched. I misjudged the opening and slammed my shoulder into the wall, which whipped me around. My feet got caught on the sill. I bent at the waist and slammed into the outside wall, cracking my skull hard enough to make my vision swim. I shook my head and pulled myself through, and was on the damp ground outside again.

A gurgle next to me made me scramble to my feet, gun ready. The first cop lay on the ground; to my light-shocked eyes the blood looked the same shade as his coffee-colored skin, as if he was melting into a puddle of himself. He moved his arms feebly and kept opening his mouth as if to speak, but nothing came out but a wet sound, like he was swallowing his tongue. I decided that he wasn't much of a threat. My lungs hurt and my mouth was full of dust. I crawled to the wall and pushed myself against it, listening.

I didn't hear anything, except the wind and hover displacement. I risked a look up and couldn't see the SSF ship, but knew it wouldn't be long before it circled back and spotted me—maybe already had if they were equipped with infrared. Putting myself in the cop's shoes, I imagined what I would do, trying to feel their disdain for me, their arrogance. What would I do if hunting rats?

Staying low, I got down on my bloody, shredded knees and began making my way around to the back of the crumbling building. I breathed shallowly and steadily despite my aching chest, and I kept my gun up despite the trembling weariness of my arm. When I'd cleared the windows I stood up carefully, staying flat against the wall, and moved faster. I could almost feel our gravity, pulling us toward each other—and then I heard a faint rustle of fabric, and caught the same scent of smoke. I waited until the last moment, counting heartbeats, and then stepped away from the wall, gun up, a bullet to spare.

She was just around the corner. Plain-looking; dark hair, olive complexion, husky and formidable. When I popped into her field of vision, there was a split-second when our eyes met, hers a light green I'd never seen before. I saw the most remarkable thing. Fear.

I'd seen System Pigs laughing and carrying on conversations while they beat suspects to death, I'd seen them take down gangs of people while outnumbered and outgunned without breaking a sweat. I'd never seen one scared before.

Then she moved, and it was close—the deciding factor not skill, but my armor-piercing bullets. Dumb luck. She feinted left—just a facial tic and a ripple of air, but enough to get my gut going—and then dived fearlessly right, scraping herself on scrap metal and jagged rocks, attaining the cover of a ruined wall.

I tracked her movement behind the wall and shot twice through it. When I crept around to the other side, she was just lying there, staring at me, eyes flat, chest torn open.

Weariness swept through me. My legs were soaked in blood from the knees down. My shoulder ached where I'd slammed it in the window. There was no time to contemplate or rest; I could hear the hover in the near distance, searching for me. I jammed my empty gun into my coat and started limping as fast as I could back to the black cop. I stood over him and stared down at him. Still gurgling breath in painful hitches of his chest, he stared back at me, his eyes pink and bloodshot and wide.

"If you live," I said slowly, panting, "tell Colonel Moje that Avery Cates says to come do his own dirty work."

For a second or two we stared at each other, and then I whirled at a noise, the sound of boots hitting the rubble, as if someone had jumped down from a second story. Despite my exhaustion, amazement crackled through me, because Dick Marin was marching determinedly toward me, a wicked-looking gun stretched out before him.

He looked like he had that first night: a short, smiling man with pale, pale skin and wrap-around sunglasses, dressed in an expensive suit and overcoat. His mirror-polished leather shoes glinted as he crunched over stone and debris. He held the gun out stiffly as he walked and fucking smiled at me. I had nothing left to fight him off with. *If he tries to shoot me, I doubt I'll even have the energy to fall down.*

"Sorry, Mr. Cates," he said evenly. "But you're going to have to give that message to Colonel Moje yourself."

He stopped when he was standing directly over the gurgling SSF officer, and without pause or ceremony pumped two shells into the Pig's face. The cop twitched once and then lay still.

Marin immediately looked at me, a sharp, sudden twitch of the neck. His grin widened.

"Smile, Mr. Cates. This has definitely been your lucky fucking day."

XXVI

WE DON'T GO EASY, DO WE?

00111

IIIIIIIIIIIIIIII

I stared down at my coat as Dick Marin talked, mesmerized by the clean bullet hole that had appeared in the fabric near the hem. I hadn't even noticed.

"You have a very strange attitude toward your subordinates, Director Marin," I said, my voice sounding far away. I wanted to just curl up on the rubble and take a nap.

He nodded without looking up. "I'm director of Internal Affairs, Mr. Cates, and I have full discretionary powers to investigate officers of the SSF and to take appropriate action once evidence of malfeasance is acquired." He looked up at me, a sudden, snapshot motion. "Once that evidence has been acquired, logged, and digitized, Mr. Cates, from that moment onward, the officer in question is completely under my authority. Understand? Once I have legally classified them as having committed a crime while working as an SSF officer, they are forfeit to me and my office. This man," he gestured casually at the body he was leaning over, "is guilty of several felonies,

240

including murder. I chose this moment to remove him from the force with predjudice. All very legal and completely within my powers."

I considered this. I considered what percentage of the SSF must be guilty of crimes, and were walking around with those smug, well-fed smiles, not knowing that if it served Dick Marin's purpose he would snuff them out—legally—in a moment. The thought cheered me.

Marin looked back down at the body.

"Elias Moje, may I someday get that cocksucker in my sights, named you as the main suspect in the Harper kidnapping. He didn't give a shit whether you actually did it: He knew you were in London, temporarily beyond his reach, so he threw your name out there in order to bring you back within his influence. He did this so he could mobilize the SSF against you." He cleaned his gun with a portable kit, moving with fast, efficient movements, not even looking at it as he worked. "You moved out of his sphere of influence and then you did the dumbest thing you could have done, taking that woman."

I blinked. "How—?"

Marin cocked his head as if listening to someone very far away, whispering his name. "We *are* the police, Mr. Cates. Contrary to your experience, we do more than accept bribes, murder innocent men, and strut about in stylish clothes. Ms. Harper filed a memo with her bureau chief in Geneva, noting that she thought she'd seen notable murderer, terrorist, and all-around Anticitizen Number One Avery Cates on a flight to London, and that she was going to poke around a little. As I think I mentioned when we first met, I engaged several others in similar previous and parallel missions, and they are all dead. I sometimes wonder how it is that of all the people I hired to attempt this job over the past few months, *you* are the one who has survived."

I shrugged. We were sitting in the ruined building with three dead cops around us, having a chat. Marin said the hover wouldn't bother us, and I saw no reason to not believe him. "I didn't have a choice," I said.

"Doesn't matter. Bad idea. Anyway, he names you, and suddenly every System Cop in the world is looking for you—sure, you're wanted for fifteen unsolved murders back in New York, Cates, but let's be honest for a moment. Kill all the nobodies you want, and the SSF files your name for future reference. Bump a person of quality on the sidewalk and the SSF will spare no expense in bringing you to justice."

I scrubbed my grimy face with my bloody, torn-up hands. "Are you watching out for me, Marin?"

He grinned, and then the grin shut off in a blink. "No. I came looking for you. It was pretty easy to find you by listening in on the SSF chatter." He paused, his hands coming to a sudden stop. "You've got to move. Soon. Tonight, tomorrow."

"What's going on?"

He racked a shell into the chamber and stood up, gathering his kit. "Just move." He looked around at the semicollapsed room. "Impressive, Mr. Cates. I have to admit I didn't think you'd still be alive. See if you can manage to stay alive for a few more days."

With a brilliant, snapshot grin vaguely in my direction, he began walking for one of the sunlit doorways. I just stared at him.

"God*dam*mit, what's going on!?" I finally managed to shout.

He didn't turn back, and in a moment he'd escaped into the sunlight. The King Worm had come to personally shoot one of his own subjects and urge me into action. I slumped back against the wall and sat for a moment, speechless.

To a tinny serenade of *Mr. Kieth! Authorized visitors! Mr. Kieth! Authorized visitors!* I limped into the Assembly Room. Moving past the hogtied and gagged Marilyn Harper as her red, angry eyes tracked me, I stopped in front of my team and looked from face to face, pausing on Canny Orel's, who looked like he'd spent the afternoon shopping for grooming supplies. He grinned at me, and it was such a natural, human grin after Dick Marin's insectlike mandibles that I almost felt affectionate toward him.

"What's your real name?" I asked. I didn't really expect an answer. He just smiled.

"We don't go easy, do we?" he said.

I nodded. "Like roaches. How'd our shopping go?"

Canny nodded. "Mr. Materiel came through on all our items."

Milton and Tanner gestured over their shoulders at a large shape next to our hover, covered by a canvas sheet. "The Vid hover as requested," Milton said sourly. "Was a bitch to get a hold of, by the way. And it's hot—won't stay stolen for long, if you ask me."

Beside her, her twin mimicked her grim nod perfectly.

"Doesn't matter," I said, looking at Ty. "We won't need it long. Mr. Kieth?"

He smiled. "Success, Mr. Cates. We're in business."

I sighed. "All right. I'm going to get cleaned up. Don't go anywhere. We're moving tomorrow, so it's time for a briefing."

There was a rustle of commotion at this. As I turned for the kitchen area, Orel's manicured hand snaked out and slowed me.

"Can I accompany you?"

I shrugged. He fell in beside me and walked with his hands in his pockets, head bowed, studying the floor.

"I am impressed, Mr. Cates, with the fact that you returned alive this evening. I distinctly recall at least two System Police breaking from the rest and pursuing you."

"Three," I said, wincing every time I put weight on my left knee. I hesitated for a second. "Whoever you really are, were you really a member of the Dúnmharú? Without answering either way about your *actual* identity."

"Without answering *either way*," he said without looking at me, "yes, I was."

The Dúnmharú; if the organization had still existed, I had no doubt that they would have been on Dick Marin's short list. I was no starfucker, but there was a thrill to the thought that I was so close to something like that.

This was just a preamble. In the kitchen, I peeled off my sweaty, ruined coat and shirt. I let some brown water run from the spigot and began splashing it everywhere, trying to scrub the grime off. The endless number of cuts and scrapes and abrasions stung, several reopening and oozing blood.

"What's on your mind, Mr. Orel?"

I heard him pull himself up onto the large crate and imagined him sitting there, legs crossed, the perfect gentleman, complete with faux-English accent on top of his Philly brogue. I was acutely aware of having turned my back on someone who might have been trained by Cainnic Orel himself.

For a moment, he sat there and said nothing.

"I am a tired man, Mr. Cates," he finally said. "I do not enjoy this life—I do not enjoy fighting for every breath, or living in a world without rules. Those are the choices we're given—live under the boot of the System, or live in a world where every other man is trying to kill you. I would have it otherwise." He looked up at me. "That is why I chose to deal with you, as a man, instead of simply eliminating you."

I raised an eyebrow. "It wouldn't have been that easy."

He smiled, apparently amused. "No, I now believe it might not have been. You're a man of honor, Mr. Cates. You live with rules. I respect that. I envy it, because I long ago realized how impractical such thoughts are. I wish I could live by your rules. But I am an old man, now, and I have seen more than you. Rules are only as good as the people who obey them. If no one else is playing by your rules, no matter how good they are, what are they worth?"

I shook my head. "Just because we live in shit doesn't mean we have to act like it." I concentrated on scrubbing, a knot of anxiety forming in my stomach. "You're leading up to something, old man. Just get on with it."

There were a few seconds of silence.

"The Harper woman," he said slowly. "What do you plan to do with her?"

I shrugged, digging glass out of a deep cut on my elbow, the brown water in the stained and cracked sink turning purple. "I'm not planning to marry her, if that's what you're worried about."

There was a long delay before he spoke. "She can't walk out of here."

I kept scrubbing. "Fuck you."

"Cates, you know I'm right. She knows far too much—she's seen the Monk, she knows Gatz is a psionic. She can't live."

I saw no reason to tell him the SSF already knew about both. "Fuck that. I didn't bring her here. *You* made that happen. Once this is over, it won't matter anymore. We can hang on to her for that long."

"It won't *matter* anymore?" He laughed. "Come now, Mr. Cates. That's bullshit and you know it."

I shut the spigot off and turned to him, dripping pink water. "There's a lot you don't know. About me, about this job. About our patron."

He nodded. "Educate me, Mr. Cates. I will not have her out there, with my *face*, with my involvement in this. This is not some Tin Man, who, if it did send a scan of my face to Mother Church for OFR, would discover that my name is Terrance Nynes and that I've been dead for six years. This is not some piece of shit like yourself, this is someone with money, with a face on the Vids. With the power to cause me trouble. Understand? You people do not exist anyway. No one outside of this room and your debt-circle gives a shit whether you live or die. No one will avenge you. Her, she has people. She has money. She has social standing—the SSF would actually investigate. *She cannot walk out of here alive.*"

We stared at each other for a moment. I heard the sound of water dripping, the distant murmur of everyone discussing their lot in life in the Assembly Room. His lined face was expressionless, his eyes flat. I stood half-naked in front of him with my hands balled into fists.

"No, Dúnmharú," I said slowly, biting off each word. "We may be a lot of things, but we need to have *rules*. She hasn't done either of us wrong." I reached for my shirt and began drying off, leaving almost as much dirt on me as I'd just washed off. "This fucking world, this System—it's brought us all low.

But you can plant your feet, Mr. Orel. At the last rung of the ladder you can refuse to take that last step."

We stared at each other for another moment, and then he smiled, a smooth ripple across his face. He laughed and slid off the crate, clapping me on a damp shoulder. "Ah, Mr. Cates—you forget. I remember the world before Unification better than you. I remember it well." He started back toward the Assembly Room. "And it was not what you imagine it to have been."

"All right," I said. "Shut the fuck up and listen."

I looked around at everyone. I hardly knew them, as people. As criminals, they were talented. Ty Kieth sat with his back against one of his black boxes, absorbing its radiation and looking peaceful, his round head starting to grow a light fuzz of stubble. Milton and Tanner sat back to back, supporting each other, grizzled and sinewy, the least feminine women I'd ever met. Canny Orel sat near Ty Kieth, arms crossed, looking comfortable and inscrutable. Kev Gatz sat on the floor, facing the Monk, his glasses in place and looking asleep—as usual. Brother West was in stasis.

Marilyn Harper stared at me unblinkingly, pale and disheveled. It looked like the thick black tape we'd used on her mouth was going to be a bitch to get off. Milton and Tanner had bitched loudly that she should be sequestered, so she couldn't hear anything that might be used against us. But I knew that if I hid her away somewhere we'd find her dead soon enough, with Orel walking around whistling, hands in pockets, looking innocent, and I knew that it didn't matter what she might do *after* we did this. We would either all be dead, or we'd be rich and our records expunged by the King Worm. I was betting on the former, but it all equaled not worrying about Marilyn Harper.

"We're a go for tomorrow. Mr. Gatz and I have developed a plan for penetrating the Electric Church compound at Westminster Abbey. Once inside you all have support roles. I will locate the target and terminate him. The rest of you will handle security response and keep our escape route clear. Pay attention here. Being able to execute this plan will be the difference between collecting the money I promised you and getting killed."

I waited, but no one said anything. Trying not to think about the real possibility that I didn't know what I was doing, I could hear the Droids humming this way and that, on whatever errands Kieth had programmed them for.

I nodded and clicked a small remote control, and a three-dimensional building plan appeared in the air next to me, a crumbling facade wall shooting up from the ground, one tower and one broken stump, no other walls. Everything was underground, sinking deep below.

"Westminster Abbey," I said. "Whatever the fuck it *was*, it's now the headquarters of the Electric Church. All local conversions take place here, and administration of the Church worldwide is centered here. Dennis Squalor, founder and high priest of the Church, resides here. Security is very tight. Long story short, only Monks and converts get through the front entrance. All the converts who go through that gate are already dead."

I let them chew on that for a second and then clicked the remote, and a small room inside the Abbey lit up.

"The front entrance is officially the only way into the Abbey. But it isn't the *only* way in. These building plans are black market info. No one is supposed to have them." I pointed to the red square. "This is the Press Room, where the EC holds its press conferences. Squalor himself appears there once in a while to smile and answer a few softball questions inbetween quoting the fucking *Mulqer Codex*. The Monks get *in* to the press room, friends, so there must be a way into the complex proper *from* the Press Room. And intense scrutiny reveals that there is."

The whole place was quiet. They were all professionals, and they were soaking up the details. They all knew they'd need them later. I cleared my throat.

"It won't be quite that easy. If we just force our way in through the Press Room, they send in the cops—and not the Crushers, either, but the officers and the Stormers—and pin us down, and it's just a fight. We're not going to fight our way through the whole fucking complex; it goes down pretty deep underground. At least a dozen levels below ground, covering much more square footage than the aboveground component.

"So," I finished, "we're going to employ a two-pronged attack. Kieth and I have established that only a Monk can get through the front entrance. You've all seen what Mr. Gatz can do when he puts his mind to it. All Monks are controlled by the EC through a behavioral modification chip—the chip that captures his independent thought and keeps the crazies at bay—and we've found we can't replicate and replace the chip in time, and we may need some flexibility, so Mr. Gatz is going to Push Brother West, acting as a substitute for that chip. Brother West will be coherent and independent for a short while after that—longer than most because he will be a volunteer. Brother West will bring me in through the front entrance, quietly, as a convert.

"Simultaneously, the rest of you will be in the Press Room, posing as Vid reporters. The Vids are always in there filming for the features they do on the Church, so it won't seem out of place. We have all the equipment necessary. Mr. Kieth will make some modifications to the Vid equipment to make it more useful than mere props for us, and I've identified a weak spot in that room that should allow you to enter the complex proper." I indicated a spot on the plans.

Tanner squinted at me. "So if we can just get in through the Press Room, why bother slipping you in the side?"

"We have one shot at this. If we rely entirely on infiltration and I am discovered, that's it—I can't possibly fight off every Monk in the place, not to mention whatever automated defenses they have. So we're not even going to bother with stealth. Your role will be as diversion. Cause a ruckus. Draw their attention. While their response is concentrated on you, I will be sneaking in—unobserved, I hope. I will complete the job, from the other end—with me coming in with the converts, and you making noise, they won't think to look for anything else. You make noise, and when you get the word or can't hold out any longer, you extract yourselves."

No one seemed pleased with this.

They absorbed this. Kieth studied the Monk serenely. Gatz was staring at me from behind his dark glasses, and it made me nervous. Milton and Tanner huddled close, whispering. Canny Orel continued to just smile softly at me, and as I looked he raised both hands and mimed applause.

Marilyn Harper just stared at me, nostrils flaring, somehow expressing rage without moving more than her nose.

"Wait a fucking second," Milton suddenly shouted, turning back to me. "You're going in with the Tin Man as a convert?"

I nodded.

"Aren't all the converts *dead*?"

I nodded again. "Yes."

XXVII

HURRY UP NOW, IT'S TIME

00001

It was bright and dry outside for the first time since I'd arrived in London, a beautiful day of light and breezes. I hadn't slept the night before, as much from nerves as the million stinging cuts I'd inflicted on myself while crawling through the ruins of old London. It wouldn't have been wise to go outside, since I was temporarily the most famous criminal in the System, so I just rattled around the huge abandoned factory all night, alternately trying to sleep and cleaning my gun, getting to know its action and heft. When morning came, cheerful and clear, I didn't feel tired at all. My entire existence had changed in a span of days, and it was all coming down to one evening.

I'd known for a while now that I'd somehow exceeded my allotted time, lived too long. I was part of a dead generation, people born before Unification. Nothing made sense to us, even if we couldn't quite remember the Earth before. It was genetic memory, or something subconscious. Unification hadn't been

our choice, and a lot of us struggled against it. We knew everything was wrong.

Kids, they didn't know. They'd been brought up in this
bullshit, and they thought it was natural, normal. And they'd
taken over the world, because most of the people my age were
dead.

There was no coffee, and precious little food aside from the
Nutrition Tabs Milton and Tanner had stolen from poor fuckers coming off the Dole Line. They kept you going, but in the
first light of morning there was no physical joy in swallowing
a tablet. I chewed mine thoughtfully, trying to make it contem-
plative. It didn't work. I wandered into the Assembly Room
with an extra tab and a cup of dirty water.

I paused in front of Brother West, who just stood there staring. I wondered what he thought while just standing there in
stasis, if he tried suicide by mental command, or just chewed
over his lot. His steady, digital voice still rang in my ears:
Kill me . . . it is all I wish. Gatz sat in front of the Monk, slump-
shouldered, staring up steadily. I hadn't said a word to Kev. I
didn't know what to say.

After a moment I turned to Marilyn Harper. She looked
bleary and wrinkled, her hands and bare feet white and cold
from her bonds. I knelt in front of her and set the cup on the
floor. For a moment I just studied her, her watery eyes staring
back at me defiantly. Then I leaned forward, took hold of an
edge of the black tape, and tore it off in one sudden motion,
slapping my free hand over her raw lips immediately to cut off
the scream.

"No talking," I said as she convulsed, trying to pull away
from my hand. "Harper? Ms. Harper, look at me. Look at me."

She calmed and stared at me, nostrils flaring. I wagged a finger in front of her. "No talking, okay? You say a word, I'll make

sure you don't get to speak again for a very, very long time. We understand each other?"

She nodded slightly. I pulled my hand from her face. An angry red square remained where the tape had been. She breathed heavily through her nose, staring at me in a combination of anger and terror. I held up the Nutrition Tab. "Breakfast. You're probably starving. It isn't poison, it isn't drugs. You don't want it, just shake your head. But I doubt anyone else is going to bring you anything."

She stared at me.

"Listen, if I wanted to rape you, I would have. You're an inconvenience. We'd much rather cut you loose, and we will in a day or two. So don't eat if you don't want to. I don't care. I'll let you think on it for five seconds."

I sat there holding the tablet and stared at her. I counted five in my head, and then pushed the tablet at her mouth. She opened up and I popped it in without ceremony. She swallowed it whole. Then I held up the cup of water.

"Wh—" she started to say, and I whipped my hand up again.

"No talking, right? Nod that you understand."

She nodded. I took my hand away. I pushed the cup toward her.

"You can live for three days without water, Ms. Harper," I said. "But I wouldn't advise it. This is nasty shit, especially for someone who's used to filtered. I'd drink it, though, because we're all leaving in a bit, and you're going to be on your own for a while. I doubt anyone else is going to help you."

I held the cup up to her lips and tipped it. More ran down her chin than got into her mouth, but she greedily gulped what she could. When it was gone she lay there panting and licking the last dirty drops from her lips. I nodded.

"Okay. You'll live a little longer, then." I got up.

"Wait!" she croaked, her voice sounding rusty and deep. I turned back to her suddenly, bringing my arm back, and she leaned away from me in shocked panic, eyes widening.

"Please! I'm sorry! I'm sorry!"

I stood there, poised, but didn't bring my arm down. I stared down at her, and then knelt back down, leaning in close. I could smell her sweat, her fear.

"Don't," I said slowly, "speak."

Eyes wide, she nodded dumbly.

I started to get back up, but paused. "Listen, Ms. Harper—I'm a civilized man, okay? I promise you're going to be fine, if you just shut your mouth and relax. Okay?"

I didn't know why I'd said that. I wanted her to believe it, though. I *was* a civilized man. If I'd been given a chance, if I'd been born ten years sooner, if I'd been rich, I would have . . . done something. Anything. I looked at her until she nodded again, faintly, afraid to move too much and set me off again. When a hand fell on my shoulder, I almost grabbed it and flipped the motherfucker over my shoulder, but let the urge pass through like a ripple of potential energy.

"C'mon, Cates," Tanner said cheerfully. I wasn't sure how I'd come to tell them apart, but it had become suddenly easy. "You ready to die?"

Turning away from Harper, I made a mental note to replace the tape on her mouth, not because anyone was going to hear her, but because if she started shouting I didn't doubt that someone, maybe even Gatz, would shut her up.

"We've got to strap you down. When the toxin hits your nervous system, there's probably going to be some convulsing."

I stared at Kieth, who had somehow found the time and materials to shave his head smooth again. His scalp gleamed in the sickly light of the kitchen. I was sitting on the big crate, with Kieth, Milton, and Tanner standing around me, each of them holding a length of synthetic rope. Orel leaned against a wall, smoking a cigarette, disdaining to do any actual work. For a second, my balls crawled up into my gut and my tongue shriveled to a stump. I was going to entrust my entire existence to these people. If they weren't incompetent, they wouldn't shed tears if I never made it back—unless of course I was bearing buckets full of yen at the time.

The moment passed. It didn't matter: I wasn't going to live through the week, anyway. I'd killed System Cops, I'd taken on the job of assassinating the leader of the Electric Church, there were hits out on *me*. I could feel the struggle falling away, and calm took its place. I was just waiting for the impact, and the few seconds before were blissful, peaceful—empty.

I nodded. "Let's do it."

Kieth nodded. "I just want to make sure you understand what's about to happen to you. Administered correctly, this solution will induce a deathlike state. This means that while you may—or may not—retain perception, you will certainly lose all conscious control. Your breathing and heartbeat will slow to almost undetectable levels. To most examinations, you will appear deceased. If you do retain perception, it will be . . . most uncomfortable."

I let Milton take my arm and begin tying a rubber tube around my forearm. "*If* I retain perception?"

Kieth shrugged. "Not many people survive this. There just isn't much information available."

This struck me as funny, and I burst out laughing. Kieth and Milton shared a look, but didn't say anything. I listened to the rest of Kieth's speech with tearing eyes as I struggled to regain my composure, but the laughter kept dribbling out of me. This was classic. This was appropriate. This was how the Gweat and Tewwible Avery Cates was going go out, after all the fighting and scrabbling and suffering. He was going to just lie back and get executed.

Kieth plowed through my hysteria. "You'll possibly feel pain. Don't discount the psychological impact if you do have your wits about you, Mr. Cates—it'll probably be very claustrophobic."

Still giggling, I waved at him. "Come on, Mr. Kieth, hurry it up, now."

Milton tapped the vein that had risen in my arm and nodded with professional satisfaction. Kieth picked up a slender syringe and looked apologetic.

"I tried to scrounge an auto-hypo, but they're scarce, so we'll have to do it the old-fashioned way." He held the syringe up so I could see it. The seriousness on his face almost started me laughing again. He still thought this all mattered. "The, uh, the Monk will have another syringe just like this one, containing a little cocktail of chemicals. If Mr. Gatz can really control it, it will be injecting it directly into your heart when the time comes—when you are inside and momentarily secure. Mr. Cates, Ty can't stress this enough: The 'waking up' process is not going to be pleasant. You're going to go from as near dead as you can be and still be alive to fully functional within seconds. It will be much like doing a hard reboot on a computer system. That, Ty knows with certainty, will be very painful."

I nodded, feeling some control coming back to me. "Understood."

Kieth looked unhappy. "Ty doesn't think telling you this serves any purpose, but everyone else seems to feel you should know that you need to come out of stasis within four hours or so. Longer than that and you may not *ever* come out. You can only play dead for so long, eh?"

"Understood. Let's get this show on the road. It's time."

Kieth held the syringe up and tapped it with one finger, squinting at it. Then he looked around at the others and back at me. A terrible excuse for a smile came over his face, unpleasant to look at. "See you on the other side, Mr. Cates."

I lay back and they strapped me down tight. Milton held my arm in position, palm up, and I made a fist. I looked around at all of them as Tanner leaned over me with a piece of leather to slip between my teeth. I was still calm, still feeling the last tingle of the laughter rippling inside me, but a coppery taste of terror had oozed into my mouth. I swallowed it back and it stuck in my throat.

"Don't fuck up," I said, my voice tight and harsh, as if little bits of glass had gotten lodged in it.

"Fuck you," Tanner snapped, jamming the leather between my teeth roughly. "We don't ever fuck up."

A bit of motion caught my eye and I turned my head to see Orel pushing off from the wall and crushing his discarded cigarette. Our eyes met, and he winked as he sauntered out of the room. I knew that look. That calm determination always preceded a calculated murder. He'd waited until I was tied down, and now he was going to put a bullet in Marilyn Harper's brain. A hot blade of panic sliced through me: How had I not seen this coming? The answer was galling: For all his outward urbanity, our fake Orel was not a civilized man.

I kicked, I screamed, I struggled against the ropes. But Milton and Tanner held me down with surprising strength, and Kieth leaned in like a doctor, grim and serious.

"Sorry, Mr. Cates," he said, sounding almost sad. "But you're worth a lot more money to us dead than alive right now."

I felt hands on my arm, the cold bite of the needle, and

XXVIII

A BOTTOM-FEEDING FISH, BLACK
AND SWOLLEN AND COVERED IN SPIKES

10100

An icepick in my chest, tearing apart blood vessels as it slid along my arteries, propelled by the sluggish, back-and-forth tide of my blood, bloating me with a sudden, razor-sharp heat that sank into every unprotected organ. It was a bottom-feeding fish, black and swollen and covered in spikes, puffing up as it neared the surface, ready to explode. I opened my mouth to scream but found myself biting down on the strip of leather instead. It kept coming. It was too large for my arteries, it tore through and began swimming in my guts, perforating and wriggling, headed unerringly toward my heart. It tore through my pelvis, it lacerated my lungs. Gasping, choking in the open air, it bloated up through my chest and slammed into my heart and exploded there, sending spikes shooting through my insides, landing with wet, shivering force in my spine, my bones, my cartilage.

I stiffened, my whole body going taut as a fuzzy numbness burned its way from my feet upward. I shook and shivered, biting through the leather strip in my mouth, staring pop-eyed at Ty Kieth, who silently took a step backward, eyes on the exits.

Then, suddenly, everything went dark as I passed out.

When I came to, my vision snapped on, as if God or someone had flicked a switch. One second, nothing, the next, I was staring up at Brother West's hideously cheerful mask of a face. It loomed over me, waxy, pale, permanently smiling.

"Mr. Cates? I do not know if you can hear me, but I want to assure you I will keep my end of the bargain. Mr. Gatz assures me you will keep yours. It is time to go."

His head floated away, and I was staring up at the ceiling. There was no noise. Then some sounds I couldn't identify: a swishing sound, a sharp, metallic clang, a tearing sound. I struggled to bring my thoughts into line, but they squirmed and writhed out of my grasp. I wanted to shake my head to clear it, but couldn't.

Then the pain started to come back.

At first it was just a buzzing in the background, a dim memory of something terrible, teasing at the ends of my thoughts. It gathered like distant thunder, growing in ominous volume until it broke over me like terror, like bamboo shoots under my nails going deeper, further, faster.

I wanted to scream, but couldn't. I wanted to howl and writhe and attack anything around me, to pass along the infection, expend some of it, but couldn't. I stared up at the ceiling, my vision turning red, my skin peeling off, my bones splintering. On top of the pain there was a thick layer of numbness, my arms, legs, every part of me dead and without feeling. Underneath, in the core of me and sinking deeper every second, were razor blades, broken glass, thumbtacks.

I tried to quiver, and couldn't.

I was lifted, then, the ceiling drawing closer and then sliding away, and carried out of the kitchen area. Gatz's head suddenly loomed into my vision, pale and waxy like the Monk, but with a film of sweat on his taut, gaunt face.

"I Pushed him hard, Ave," he gasped. "If you can hear me, I Pushed him hard. I'll stay close, keep it up as long as I can. I've got your back."

His face disappeared, and there was just the sound of moderate physical effort, and the ceiling, and the pain.

"Set him down a minute," I heard Milton say. The world tilted, and I was lowered to the floor. At the last second Gatz's hand slipped, and I dropped the last foot pretty hard. My head flopped over to the side, and if I could have, I would have crawled backward, cursing, because Marilyn Harper was staring at me.

She was sprawled on the floor and looked startled, as if she'd somehow fallen that moment, and was just lying there in shock. Her hands were still tied, her arms were bent uncomfortably back. Her hair spilled wildly over her face, red and stiff. Her mouth was open slightly. Her eyes were wide open, her face a mask, the ragged hole torn in her forehead still dripping.

"That's a fucking shame." Tanner sighed, sounding out of breath. "That fucking old man is pretty harsh, huh, Wonderboy?"

Gatz didn't say anything.

Her accusing eyes bored into mine, and I couldn't look away. I'd lived too long, held on selfishly, and *this* was the result? I hadn't had any affection for Marilyn Harper, but this wasn't *civilized*. She hadn't done anything to rate this, shot in the head by Cainnic Orel. That was how *I* deserved to die, and I couldn't help but think that she'd caught my bullet.

With my bones being burned to ash inside me, I wanted nothing more than to turn my head away.

"All right, Wonderboy." Tanner finally sighed. "Let's go. The Tin Man is waiting out back. It makes sense to the Monks if Cates is nailed here. More realistic. So let's go, and then I gotta get into costume."

As I was carried out of the Assembly Room I had a good view of Gatz's shoulder, sweat dripping down from it, and I could hear his breath, strained and phlegmy, rattling in and out of his open mouth. I realized that my life was in his hands. If Brother West came out of the Push too soon I'd either get carved up or just be left to drift away. It was all up to Kev Gatz. I wasn't afraid. I was ready. I was ready for it to be over.

When the pain ate the edges of my vision and things went dark again, I went down eagerly.

I came back groggy. In the distance, hover displacement, shouts, something that might have been a gunshot. Nearer, just above me: humming.

The red pain receded like water evaporating, leaving me blind, inside something, moving. The steady thump of heavy boots on the cracked, damp stone street led the way, wrapped in the dim, quiet hum of hydraulics. I couldn't breathe, couldn't move. I tried again, mentally flailing, screaming, pounding against the sides of whatever I was trapped inside. Nothing. Not even a wheeze of horror. I just lay, staring at blackness, listening to the heavy tread of Brother West as he conveyed me somehow to Westminster Abbey.

All I could see was Marilyn Harper's eyes: wide, staring, just like twenty-six other sets of eyes I'd seen. An old man, startled up from breakfast in a café on Morton Street, nailed with a lucky shot that turned his nose into a pit of blood. Twin brothers collapsed back into their hover, staring blankly, blood running down their scalps. A woman, guns falling from both hands, hanging from an ancient fire escape, her foot caught between slats, staring down at me, blood dripping. All of them, bad people. All of them, dead. All of them, killed by me.

I hadn't pulled the trigger, but I'd killed Harper just the same. Twenty-seven dead in twenty-seven years plus all the damn cops who'd stepped in front of my gun recently. And now my comeuppance was at hand.

I listened. I could hear—I knew it was probably pitch black inside the little hover I'd been loaded into as a new Church "recruit," so maybe I could see, too. I couldn't move, or breathe, or stop feeling the terrifying sharp-edged pain that lapped at every nerve with a razor tongue. My mind raced through the diagrams and flowcharts we'd worked on, scratched onto any available surface, Kieth's neat script and my own huge scrawl. We must, I thought, be on one of the private transport hovers the Electric Church used to move its cargo—it wouldn't do to have Monks cheerfully transporting recently murdered citizens through the streets, whistling. The Church had its own zoned air lanes for its hovers. All registered religions did, though most of them, I was pretty sure, weren't using them to transport bodies.

I had no idea how much time had passed. A weird, electric hum of terror stabbed through me, and then again, and then it became a constant, searing presence. I wanted to scream and wave my arms about and beat myself senseless against the walls of my tiny prison, but I just lay there, my dead body mocking myself. If this was what death was like, if this was even just a second, a momentary horror right before you sailed off into infinity, I was all ready to sign up for my Monk suit.

There was a series of loud clanging noises, and then the scream of displacement. I couldn't feel anything, but I knew the sound, and realized we must be descending. I oriented my mental map of Westminster Abbey, which was a freestanding wall of ancient-looking stone like a broken bone rising out of the ground in a large courtyard, surrounded by a thick, reinforced wall. The hover pad was not far from the building's remnant. Everything was underground, and I knew that once we touched down I'd be wheeled onto a wide conveyor belt and sucked down into the belly of the whole place. I imagined my path as a red line that terminated in one of the small, square rooms that acted as entry points for the corpses. From these small rooms the bodies were conveyed on belts through narrow passages into the huge processing center, where the dicing and slicing was performed, largely by Droids, according to West.

If all went well, I'd end in one of the smaller rooms and not proceed past it, except under my own power, by choice — cataclysmically *bad* choice, maybe, but at least by choice.

An eternity passed, a numb, unreal current running through me, teasing my dead nerves into a believable imitation of pain. Then I was in motion; I could tell from the way I banged around inside the mobile coffin I'd been stuffed into, first this way and that. I did some mild calculations and decided I was being loaded onto one of the belts. According to plan, Brother West was right beside me, standing stock still and grinning mildly at nothing. He'd said that nothing ever varied in this process, that it was machinery and I was to be a cog, so he *must* be there, standing ready with the hypo to bring me back to life.

The motion stopped. There was a humming sound, a vague, distant sound of voices. Then something heavy slammed into my container. There was a scrape, and then a smooth, rolling sensation. I just saw eyes. As I lay there, the pain swelled up again, the spiky fish bloating, piercing every bone in my body simultaneously until I wanted to claw my eyes out for relief.

When the lid was torn off, I didn't realize it at first, because I was staring at the black side of the container. A thought kept racing through my brain, interrupting everything until I imagined I could see the words scrolling across my field of vision in bright red letters, flashing and jumping: *Let me out! Let me out! Let me out! Let me out! Let me out! Let me out! Letmeoutletmeout!*

I was turned over, the sudden light stabbing down into my eyes, and Brother West's cheerful-fucking-face filled my field of vision as it leaned over me. It was so close I kept waiting for the blast of warm breath, but of course there wasn't any. For several long, stretched-out seconds it hovered over me, fake skin and sunglasses.

Let me out! Let me out! Let me out! Let me out! Let me out! Letmeoutletmeout—

"We are inside, Mr. Cates," West finally said, but there was something off in its voice. The digitally smoothed, eternally calm tone that all Monks used was frayed at the edges. If I'd had any control over myself, I would have studied its face. As it was, I continued to stare just off-center, over its shoulder. In my peripheral vision, Brother West appeared to vibrate, a fuzziness around its edges as if something vital had come off the rails inside it.

"I will now—" It hesitated, and suddenly jerked its head violently to one side, then back toward me. "I will now inject you with the antidote provided by—" Another violent spasm. "By—" Again. "By Mr. Kieth."

It turned away and disappeared from my sight.

Let me out! Let me out! Let me out! Let me out! Let me out! Letmeoutletmeout—

It came back, a rising wave of nerve-shredding pain, burning through everything else and leaving me a dissolved puddle with shards of glass glinting in the sudden light. Through it, like squinting through a heavy rain, I could sense my clothing being moved aside and the needle being pushed, hard, into my chest. Brother West jerked and stuttered through the whole procedure, almost dancing. I wondered, dreamily, if he was tearing my heart open, if blood was rushing out of me, if this was where I would just bleed to death, a stupid sort of death.

Its rubbery face loomed over me again. "It is done, Mr. Cates," it said. "I wonder—" It stopped and cocked its head, as if listening to something. Then it shuddered and oriented on me again. "I wonder if you will keep your end of the bargain, Mr. Cates. I so looooonggggggg long long long to die."

It snapped back to loom over me, suddenly calm. "I wonder," it said, the creepy calm of the Monks back in its voice. "I wonder if you would permit me to speak to you about immortality, if I may, Mr. . . . . Cates, isn't it? It will only take a few minutes, and I would appreciate your time."

There was a moment, a part of a second, where everything was balanced. The pain had swollen inside me until I was sure I was going to explode, just pop like a balloon, but it held steady. Brother West stood still, watching me, its face frozen in that subtle smile, all I could see. There was no noise. I still could not move.

And then the pain exploded, shattered into billions of tiny particles scattering throughout my insides, burning on and pock-marking my bones. My body stiffened, my whole existence becoming one endless cramp. I felt my heart spasm and lurch back into motion, pushing the cooling blood in my veins. I opened my mouth to scream, but nothing came out, my lungs deflated and unwilling to move. I sat up and froze, trembling, eyes wide and staring at Brother West.

"Mr. Cates," it said. "Let me show you an endless—"

A gunshot tore the air, and Brother West's abdomen, so recently repaired by Ty Kieth, exploded outward in a spray of wiring and fluffy white insulation. The Monk collapsed with a strange wheezing noise. My blood felt like splinters moving through me, and I sat in a strange black metallic container, trembling and unable to move.

Heavy, deliberate footsteps approached. I was able to squeeze a trickle of air through my constricted throat. After a few more seconds, as I was slowly forcing my lungs open, hunched over and dry-heaving, a Monk entered my field of vision, stepping carefully over West. I could only see it out of the corner of my eye, but there was obviously something wrong with it: Its robes were tattered and stained, its face smudged with dirt—though it still possessed the eternally satisfied expression of all Monks.

Somehow, when it turned to me and spoke, I knew who it had once been. Shivering and still semiparalyzed, a surge of adrenaline, like fresh ice poured directly into my veins, swept through me, making me choke.

"Mr. Cates," the thing that had once been Barnaby Dawson said, "only Monks and dead people are allowed in here. One of us is not playing by the rules."

XXIX

MY OWN PERSONAL ANGEL OF DEATH

01001

▓▓▓▓▓▓▓▓▓▓

Outside the walls of the small room, an alarm sprang into life.

Aside from the tattered and dusty robe, Barnaby Dawson looked like every other Monk I'd ever seen. Humanoid, a uniform six feet tall, dressed in black, white fake-looking skin, eyes hidden by dark glasses. His facial expression was identical to every other Monk's—somehow a combination of amusement, concern, and arrogance, though I wasn't sure if I really saw or imagined it. I sat shivering, finally able to curl my hands into fists and track Dawson with my eyes, but unable to do much more than that. I couldn't lift my arms; I couldn't imagine fighting someone, much less a digitally enhanced killing machine. I was fucked.

It still didn't bother me.

"You'd think," Dawson said brightly, holding his Roon on me carelessly, "that I would be grateful. You gave me immortality.

I could just follow you around making note of your advancing age and wake up every day over the next few thousand years, nuclear-powered, cheered by the memory of your pathetic death. I could wait around just to watch you try to crawl, feebly, away from death." He paused. "And that *would* be fun. But now you've gone and had a fucking *inspiration*, Mr. Cates. I underwent my transformation in a place just like this. So why shouldn't you undergo a similar change?" He nodded. "Similar, but not exactly the same, eh? I'm thinking, once we have your brain out of your skull, we'll stop there."

My teeth chattered and I shook violently, but I was slowly regaining some control. I could look around, and I tried to keep Dawson in my line of sight while I got my bearings. I was sitting in a small, coffin-shaped skid that floated, like a hover, swaying a few feet off the ground. It was just big enough for a tall man to stretch out inside, and various LED displays blinked peacefully along its side. It was rapidly filling with my sweat.

The room was small and Spartan; bare concrete walls, a single metal table lit by an overhead bank of harsh, white lights, and a wheeled metal table bearing three motorized surgical tools, clean and painful-looking. Without knowing why, I had an impression of being underground—a dampness in the air, a sense of weight hanging over me.

Dawson leaped up onto the table and sat with legs spread and shoulders slumped, a creepy, human posture that looked bizarre and out of place on his Monk body. He began swinging his legs at the knees, and I could hear the tiny motors whirring.

"When your name popped up on the EC network, all I could think about was splattering your brain all over whatever wall was handy, doing some finger painting with your blood if the mood struck me. Now look at you. I'll be honest with you, you piece of shit. I am not sure how to proceed."

Straining and jerking, I wrenched my head around to look directly at Dawson. I tried to say something, and managed to open my mouth, but only managed to force a gurgling sound out, my mouth filling with saliva.

"What's that?" Dawson said, jumping up and leaning toward me, a hand cupped to his latex ear. "I can access huge translation libraries in seconds, but you don't seem to be speaking any known human language." He walked toward me with quick, mincing steps. "But then, as a piece of shit, you're not human, are you?"

He punctuated this with a sudden backhand blow, so fast it was like a violent nervous tic had seized me.

"So I figure I'll beat the shit out of you until you loosen up."

I stared down at the floor as blood dripped from my broken lip and drooled into a puddle below me. My shivering was slowing and subsiding, being replaced joint by joint with a deep, cold ache. I could feel the hard lump of my gun pressing into my back, but I knew that in my present condition I wouldn't be able to beat Dawson to the draw. Besides, I thought with a weak ripple of tired humor, maybe a good beating *would* loosen me up.

His hands were on me, then, and everything tilted as the fucking cyborg lifted me up out of the skid and held me up in the air. Sweat and blood and spit dripped down onto Dawson's white Monk face.

"I am perfect, Mr. Cates. You perfected me. I don't even need my badge anymore. I walk down the street, you fucking rats *scatter*. I go hunting at night. Word's getting around, and all the rats hide underground, now, because they know Barnaby

Dawson's coming." He cocked his head at me in a familiar birdlike gesture as I hung on his arms like a piece of slaughtered meat. "And I *enjoy* it, Mr. Cates. But I have a job to do, you know. I am not *completely* without programming. You're the last thing on my to-do list, and then it's a few centuries of enjoying myself." He looked around, a disturbingly human movement. "Now, what are we doing *here,* I wonder? Ever since I became Barnaby Dawson Mark Two, Mr. Cates, I have been *seeking* you *out.* I have been tracing you with every resource at my discretion. Church feeds, old SSF contacts, good old-fashioned torturing of the rats. I've been able to piece together all your movements, and only now does it dawn on me what you're here to do. You're going after Squalor, aren't you?" He laughed, an unnatural sound that didn't resemble real laughter in any way. "Tell me one thing: Did you really think a rat like *you* was going to pull this off? That you had the *capability*?"

I felt his arms tense, and closed my eyes as he heaved me through the air. I slammed into the wall hard enough to rattle my teeth in my mouth, all the air knocked out of me, and I slid to the floor choking, my eyes bugging out of my head.

"I know what you're wondering," Dawson went on, walking toward me. "You're wondering how in the world this *fucking brilliant* plan of yours went wrong. How come I wasn't killed by those fucking Monks? The answer is, I'm a prototype. The first step. Bad luck for you. Bad luck," he stooped, lifting me up again without any apparent effort, "for all the rats."

He tossed me back onto the floor casually, my head cracking against the concrete, my vision blinking out in a purple flash and then coming back again. Head ringing, I writhed for a second or two and then realized I was, in fact, writhing. I started to crawl away from Barnaby Dawson, my own personal angel of death.

"You're recovering," he said behind me, and fuck me if he didn't sound almost cheerful despite the digital sameness of his voice. "That's good. I want all your slow wetware synapses online so I can be sure you really feel it when I reach down your fucking rat throat and pull your spine up through your mouth."

As I crawled, I managed a deep shuddering breath, my ribs cracking with the sudden expansion, and I found, bleeding and crisped at the edges, my voice. "Fuck you," I grated out, like coughing up razor blades.

Dawson tried to laugh. I got the impression laughter wasn't programmed into his interface, so what came out was a harsh, strangled sound, a burst of static pushed through the humanizing filters. I ignored it, and kept crawling, feeling parts of me come back to life bit by bit. One thing hadn't changed about Dawson. He was still a fucking System Pig at heart. It was the only advantage I had, and kept him talking. I raised my eyes from the floor and oriented on the surgery table. I needed to stand up, get my bearings, and for that I was going to need time.

"Fucking Pigs," I panted. "You were going to kill *me*."

There was no immediate response, just a weird fluttering noise, and then Dawson landed directly in front of me, one heavy boot slamming down on my outstretched hand. Not hard enough to break it, somehow. Just hard enough to hurt—the pain seared through my arm and smacked into me, I shuddered helplessly, mouth open, nothing coming out.

"We were going to kill *you*? Of *course* we were going to kill you. That's our fucking *job*—thinning the herd. If we just let you pieces of shit breed, you'll become a problem. Are you suggesting I should *not* do my *job*?"

The pain, terrible as it was, did not quite compare to the excruciating torment I'd experienced for the past hour or so, lying dead in an electronic coffin. I decided on a different tactic, and slumped, pretending to pass out. There was a chance this would gain me a bullet to the back of the head, but I didn't think so. Dawson was enjoying himself too much.

"Oh no you don't," he said brightly, and the pain suddenly lessened in my hand as I was lifted up and tossed onto the surgery table as if I weighed nothing. The table rattled slightly, but held fast, and I couldn't stop myself from letting out a little scream as my body hit the solid metal, my arms coming up to shield my face instinctively.

"Better," Dawson said. "I want to enjoy this, and to do that I need you awake. Don't pass out again, or I start tearing out your teeth."

I writhed and moaned, which took very little acting, and snatched a quick glance around the room. Two exits, small, square room. I closed my eyes for a second and pictured the little map of the EC complex. I picked out the room I had to be in, and which door I wanted to get through. I rolled my head back and spotted Dawson, admiring his reflection in the polished metal of one of the doors. No doubt keeping one thought on me, but he was still human inside. Without a mod chip funneling every crazy thought into standard Monk reactions, he was slow and cluttered just like the rest of us.

I took a slow, deep breath, the air slicing my lungs, and clenched my fists hard enough to crack the knuckles. I closed my eyes as I exhaled, and pictured, for a moment, a beach. White sand, almost gray water with white foamy flecks, a blue, crystalline sky. I couldn't remember when or where I'd seen it—when I'd been a kid? a picture on a Vid?—but it was there, in my head. I recreated it carefully, the quiet sound of waves and wind, the lonely sound of some kind of bird calling in the distance. I concentrated on it, felt my thoughts screw down to a pinpoint, focused on where the gun was. Where Dawson was. If Dawson had hydraulic joints and CPU-aided aim on his side, I had desperation, terror, and pain on mine.

A final glance around the beach, and I moved. One hand went to my gun, tearing it from its hidden holster. The other grabbed the edge of the table as I rolled backward, pulling the table down after me so that it landed on its side and provided instant cover. I landed hard and cracked my head against the concrete again, making me wince and waste a second as a bolt of red blasted through my brain. I came up shooting, but Dawson was in the air, tattered robes fluttering behind him, landing heavy and hard on the table, which collapsed into wreckage under his weight. His hand whipped down and grabbed my gun, cupping the muzzle and forcing me to point it away from him. For one frozen moment we were motionless, Dawson's reflective sunglasses staring down at me.

"Mr. Cates, you just can't *wait* to get killed, can y—"

I pulled the trigger, and Dawson's hand disappeared in a cloud of latex and metal that pitted my face and stung my eyes. Dawson didn't react. He just stared down at me for one panted breath, two, three, and then we moved simultaneously: I tried to swing the gun up to blow his fucking head off, and Dawson swung his stump up to block me while still holding on to me with his good hand. His arm glanced off mine, I pulled the trigger, and Dawson was knocked backward over the table by the force of the shot, a ragged hole torn in his neck. He began to twitch violently, shouting in a strangely warped version of the standard Monk's voice.

"Oh, you fucking motherfucker! You fucking *motherfucker!"*

I just lay there hurting and watched Dawson, unsure how to take this. I figured I had nicked some vital data bus or wire bank or something. I pulled myself up with effort, and Dawson just kept twitching and screaming. I kept the gun on him and leaned against the table, breathing hard. I knew the Monks had a lot of hidden weaponry, and I wasn't taking any chances. When the far door *snicked* open, I looked up tiredly, but didn't have a chance in hell of fighting any more battles. Our version of Canny Orel appeared, guns in hand and moving fast. Seeing me, he paused, glanced at the twitching Monk, and then back at me.

"You're making a goddamn *racket* in here, Cates," he said.

I bent to pick up one of the nasty-looking cutting tools that had spilled onto the floor and brandished it at him weakly. Behind him, Gatz, Kieth, Milton, and Tanner pushed into the doorway.

"Your cover's blown, Cates," Kieth said breathlessly. "The whole place knows you're here and how you got in. Lucky for you there are dozens of these arrival kiosks, and Ty's set off alarms in every one of them to cover you for a bit. Might buy us ten minutes."

"Come on," I panted. "Help me hold this down. We've got work to do."

XXX

AND WHEN I DIE, I'LL BEQUEATH YOU TO SOMEONE

10110

"Ty hates to tell you this," Kieth said breathlessly as they all pushed into the room, "but the entire complex knows shots were fired inside." He glanced down at a small device with a glowing blue screen. "Ty's been monitoring the EC's bandwidth, and Christ, it just *exploded*."

I nodded weakly. "Come here and help me cut off this fucker's arms and legs."

Orel remained standing in the doorway, looking around lazily. They were dressed in remarkably good suits, hair slicked back, each of them bearing a smart-looking black bag, the standard kind of telecom bag the Vids used. I'd seen teams just like them at all the press conferences and riot scenes, and Orel, though old for the job, did have the polished, well-fed look of a Vid reporter. Gatz walked over to Dawson, who still twitched and sputtered. Milton and Tanner walked directly over to me, though, and took one arm each.

"Sit down, chief," Milton said, her voice oddly gentle. "You look like you're gonna fall down."

I shrugged them off, shivering uncontrollably. "No time."

Gatz glanced up from Dawson. "What are we doing with . . . this?"

I took a deep breath. "Cut off the arms and legs. I hit something important in his neck. I'm taking him with me, as a tour guide."

"*You motherfucker!*" Dawson screamed, his voice warping in pitch and volume. "*I'll kill you forever!*"

Kieth was still staring down at his handheld. "Probably the motor function data bus," he said distractedly.

Gatz hesitated. "He's going to draw a lot of attention."

I waved wearily at the air. "We're already screwed in the attention department. Get to work on him. Then you guys have to get back to being a fucking disturbance."

"Okey," Gatz said.

"How'd your end go?" I asked Milton.

She shrugged. "We were waiting on the right moment, when the alarms suddenly rang out. Fuck if we weren't the only people standing in that fucking room after a minute. So we just followed the floorplan, found our way in, and waltzed in unopposed, as they say."

"It was good work, that floorplan," Tanner grunted.

"*You* were the goddamn disturbance," Milton added.

"Whatever," I said, putting my weight on my legs experimentally. "We're inside. Dennis Squalor's in here somewhere."

"Not somewhere," Kieth interjected, his eyes glued to the little screen. "I can tell you exactly where he is. He's a goddamn data-well. Everything's going to and from him in this place."

I looked at Kieth. "Okay. You're with me, then. You, me, and Barnaby Dawson."

You took what came your way. Luck was as much a part of success as surviving murderous ex-SSF Monks. I figured I'd earned a lucky break.

Kieth acted like he hadn't heard me. "This is impossible, though, the packet rate is just unbelievable." He looked up and paused for a moment. "What did you say?"

Behind him, Gatz fired up the bone saw, white noise swelling to fill the room. He paused.

"Watch out. There's gonna be sparks."

Kieth stepped closer to me. "Ty isn't muscle, Mr. Cates! He did not sign up to do the heavy lifting!"

"You're with me," I said weakly, "or you're with Mr. Dúnmharú over there. Make your choice."

Kieth looked over at Canny, who stood on guard, guns in hand, watching both doors. He looked back at me. "*Fuck.*"

"The rest of you," I shouted, "are on diversion duty. This complex is filled with Monks. Get them after you. Keep them chasing. Give us twenty minutes. Mr. Kieth, you can locate Squalor within twenty minutes?"

Kieth waved his device distractedly. "Ty's got him located *now*," he wailed as sparks exploded behind him. Dawson's cursing turned into a fluid, high-pitched howl I hadn't imagined Monks could produce. "That isn't a problem. The problem is, Ty didn't sign up for this shit."

I ignored him. The sparks ended suddenly, and Gatz held Dawson's arm up over his head.

"Shit, this is heavy."

"Move!" I snapped, adrenaline giving me sudden energy. "We've got five thousand Monks heading this way so quit fucking around!"

Gatz dropped the arm and fired up the bone saw again, the screechy whine tearing at my ears. He bent down, and sparks erupted into the air again.

I allowed myself to lean on Milton and Tanner a little. "We've got exit strategies?" I asked. I knew we did. But my mind was going in a million directions, and I needed focus.

Milton nodded. "We do. Assuming some of us make it out of here to need them."

I nodded. "I've got an idea about that. Kieth, how are we on time?"

Kieth studied his screen, biting a thumbnail. "A minute. Maybe one and a half. The good news is, this area of the complex appears to be routinely deserted, as it's used to process incoming . . . er, converts, who are then moved inward for, um, monkification. The Monks are coming from other areas."

"You've got thirty seconds," I shouted over to Gatz.

"Workin' on it."

I pushed Milton and Tanner aside and stood swaying. I cleared the chamber and dropped my used clip onto the floor, slammed a new one into place, and racked a shell into place. "Kieth, when they're done, grab the Monk and follow me."

Kieth looked up from his screen, his face a mask of outrage. "*Grab* the *Monk*?" he said in disbelief. "You're joking. Ty can barely carry *this*."

I bit my lip and resisted the urge to turn Kieth's nose into mash. "Put it in the fucking box and pull it along," I said instead, gesturing at the small hover I'd been brought inside in.

I left them all behind and limped over to Orel, pausing next to him. I couldn't look at him. It didn't make any sense, but I was angry, angry about Marilyn Harper. It was ridiculous. I'd killed plenty of innocent people, or at least not worried much when they got killed in the course of things, but this one I couldn't get past. I wasn't sure if it was because the old bastard had willfully ignored me, or the fact that it didn't *have* to happen. One more day, it wouldn't have mattered anymore. I ground my teeth and struggled to find my voice. Orel just stood there, elegant and immaculate.

"Do you want me to help on your end, Master Cates?" he asked pleasantly. "Or continue babysitting these bottom-feeders while we make hay with the Monks? I don't care much as long as I get my compensation. One way or the other."

His voice was neutral. I made painful fists, my knuckles aching along with every other part of me. With effort, I swallowed the instant rage his calm, arrogant voice had raised in me. "No," I croaked. "You're the distraction. I'm on Squalor."

He didn't move. "As you wish."

I hesitated a second longer. "That's all you care about?"

His voice sounded amused. "Looking for a revolution, Mr. Cates? I don't see it here. Kill all the Monks for money you want, the System will still be here. Now, give me a bunch of System Cops to kill—that would be a revolution. This, this is just commerce."

With a scream of tearing metal and a crash, Dawson's final limb fell from his body. Gatz held the still-buzzing bone saw up in the air. "One Monk down, five fucking thousand to go," he said tiredly.

"All right," Orel said suddenly, still not moving. "Let's move, then. Mr. Gatz, *ladies*, you're with me. We're to cause havoc and keep the heat off Mr. Cates and my dear old friend Mr. Kieth."

They all made a fuss of checking their weapons. Gatz dropped the saw and wandered over to where I stood and stopped, looking off into some imaginary distance. He was still sweating, a sheen of moisture dripping from his face, staining his brand-new, stolen suit.

"I'm with you, Ave," he said quietly. "You might need me."

A wave of dizziness went through me, and I reached out to put my hand on his bony shoulder. He felt like a skeleton through the expensive fabric of his clothes. I wondered for the first time how much Gatz's Push took out of him, really.

"Okay," I said. "Let's dump Dawson into that hover thing they brought me in. Push him if you have to."

While the rest of the team checked ammo and took last-minute directions from a calm Canny Orel, Gatz and I crossed to where Dawson lay on the wrecked table, a trunk without limbs, wiring and insulation hanging out of his shoulders and hips. He turned his head to look up at us, his neck a ruin of scorched latex and wires.

"Fucking rats," he managed, his voice warped and weakened.

"Shut up," I advised, "or I'll cut out what's left of your voice box. I've got a deal for you."

His whole trunk shook violently for a moment, and it took me a second to realize that the fucker was trying to laugh again. I reached down and forcibly turned his head toward the motionless carcass of Brother West. Dawson's skin was cold and smooth, and I fought the urge to snatch my shaking hand back.

"This is my offer: Help me, and I'll give you the same deal as that guy. Keep fucking with me, and I'll carry you around with me for the rest of my life and fuck with you, and fuck with you, and *fuck with you*." I leaned down toward his head. "And when I die, I'll bequeath you to someone who will continue to fuck with you. What do you say?"

The shaking slowly subsided. "Fucking rats," Dawson drooled out, his voice like bubbling magma. "What do the fucking rats want?"

"Get me to Squalor."

The shaking began again, more violently than before. "Fucking asshole. Squalor knows you're here. Where do you think *I* came from? He programmed me. *He's* looking for *you*."

"So you're taking my offer?"

That molten laugh again. "Why not? You make it three steps out that door you can do whatever the fuck you want with me. It'll be worth it just to watch them pull your spine out through your nose."

"Mr. Cates!" Kieth sang out nervously. "We will not be alone much longer!"

I glanced over at Orel and the others. "Move. Keep them busy." Orel and I looked at each other for a moment. He winked at me, and I turned away.

"Kev, grab Captain Dawson, will you? Kieth, keep me apprised." I checked my gun and let my fingers linger on the cool metal of the barrel, familiar and satisfying. "Let's go get this goddamned job done."

"Amen," Gatz said weakly, dragging his expensive sleeve across his forehead. "A-fucking-men."

It was fucking chaos, and I didn't care. I was probably going to die, and I didn't care. With the alarm drowning out my thoughts, with the tiny room stuffed full of people and mutilated Monks, it was hard to think, and it seemed momentarily amazing that I was planning to just walk into a room, put two shells in whatever Dennis Squalor was using as a brain, and then . . . nothing. I didn't have a plan for after that. My eyes lingered on Brother West for a moment. *Hell, there's at least one promise I've kept.*

Behind me, the door my team had come through burst inward as if a bomb had exploded on the other side, a Monk with a leveled shotgun framed in the doorway. Orel threw himself flat on his belly as if he'd been practicing the move for decades in hopes of an audition, put three shells in the Monk's forehead, and leaped to his feet, beaming. His papery skin flushed and his white hair just slightly askew, he grinned at us.

"Saddle up, Americans!" Canny boomed, clicking back the hammers on his shiny silver guns in unison. "Let's go hunt some fucking Monks!"

XXXI

THE MELTING ASPHALT SOUND

00101

The alarms were everywhere. I was breathing alarms, inhaling the noise and exhaling the noise, the air thick with it. In the near distance, I could hear steady gunshots, punctuated by occasional shouts—my team causing a professional-grade ruckus. The hall was narrow and made of plain gray concrete, lit by bare bulbs at regular intervals. We walked; me, then Gatz and his luggage, then Kieth, occasionally finding Monks slumped on the floor, their heads exploded, evidence of Canny Orel's Merry Pranksters. I felt disoriented. When I closed my eyes I could picture our location on the mental diagram of the complex, a red dot moving slowly but steadily. But with my eyes open, I was lost—every hall was the same gray stone, the same bare bulbs, the same damp, heavy feel. It wasn't a place for humans.

At every intersection, Kieth called out a direction, shouting over blaring alarms and the sparkle of gunfire. When we came to the first door, I had Gatz pull the hover containing Dawson forward. As soon as we got Dawson within a foot of the door, it *snicked* open, and we resumed our ordered march.

"Ave, you okay?" Gatz ventured in a low, strained voice, like thumbtacks in my ear.

"Fuck no," I said without looking back at him. "I've been *dead*, you cocksucker. Cut me some slack."

There was an explosion of distant, echoed gunfire and screams. I didn't pause. We were so close, so fucking goddamned close. I wasn't going to get this close and fail. I wasn't going to go down with Barnaby Dawson's digital laughter ringing in my ears.

"Keep going straight, Mr. Cates," Kieth shouted. "We're very close. This whole place is in chaos, if I'm sniffing these packets correctly. There's activity everywhere."

"Ever see a thousand wolves tear a rat apart, Cates?" Dawson cackled in his bubbly, engine-oil voice. "It's really, really entertaining."

We were sloping downward, and the chilly damp feel of the upper areas of the Abbey compound was giving way to heat, heavy and resisting. "Kieth, what the fuck's going on up there?"

Kieth pressed his hand against his ear. "Tanner! Milton! What's happening?"

We walked a few steps. My hand was aching, so I tried to loosen my white-knuckled grip on my gun.

"They're stuck," Kieth said breathlessly. "Penned in. A lot of Monks. It—it—" he paused. I just kept moving. "I've lost contact. All I can hear is noise—shouting."

"Someone's still alive, then," I offered. "Which way?"

"What? Left, then straight toward another doorway—wait!"

I stopped, staring straight ahead at the door we were approaching. The walls were perfect gray concrete. They joined the floor and ceiling with computerized precision. The door was like all the others we'd passed by or through; steel, dull, with no handle or obvious way to open it. We'd moved away from the ruckus Orel and crew were causing, and I could barely hear the gunshots. I waited a count of five.

"What is it?" I said, gritting my teeth against the urge to scream. I felt trapped. Tons of stone and metal on top of me and a thousand murderous cyborgs all around. Every muscle was tight, every pore open, desperation and terror leaking out. A mile above, London ground along unawares. I didn't know what time it was, but I knew there were faded, thinned men and women standing on the Dole Line, while sleeker, sharper men and women moved through them, picking them off. While fat, expensive cops grabbed everyone by the ankles and shook vigorously to see what would fall out of everyone's pockets.

Underneath, we had screams and gunshots and the echo of my ragged breathing.

"Mr. Cates, Ty doesn't pretend to know everything, but Jesus, *something's* going on right behind that door."

The melting asphalt sound of Dawson's laughter bubbled up again, and I closed my eyes and tried to grit my teeth harder in response, the sound slicing up my spine. My teeth, I imagined, would shatter at any moment.

"You made it, Cates," Dawson gurgled. I stared at the door and imagined his voice as dark fog, spilling over the edges of the hover crate and pooling on the floor. "That's the only entrance to the Inner Sanctum. The Holy of Holies where Brother Squalor contemplates his slice of forever and counts the heads as they roll in!"

I opened my eyes and stared at the door.

"I can't open it," Dawson continued, managing somehow to convey glee through his warped digital voice. "Only Squalor and his Cardinals can. Have you ever met a Cardinal, Cates? I'll bet you haven't. If you had, you wouldn't be here."

"You can't open it?" I asked.

That dripping cackle again. "You can't either.. Right about now there are five hundred Monks homing in on you. You're trapped like, dare I say it, like a rat!"

I turned around and looked at Dawson, who lay smiling in the portable coffin, a mess of wires and insulation and coolant fluid. I shifted my eyes to Kieth, who stared back with pop-eyed nervousness, clearly terrified of what I would ask him to do next. "Can you pry this fucking door open?"

He leaned sideways to run his eyes over the door. He shrugged. "Maybe. Ty'll have to do some scans, trace some wiring. Might need some spare parts, which Ty did *not* bring. He might also just as easily fuse everything shut pretty solidly."

I nodded. It was always some fucking thing. I couldn't believe it hadn't even been a month since Dick Marin had scooped me off the streets of Manhattan and ruined my fucking life. "Kev, make sure Captain Dawson is telling us the truth, okay?"

"Right," Gatz whispered, turned, and leaned down over the Monk, pushing his glasses up onto his forehead. After a moment, he straightened up, putting a hand out to the wall to steady himself. "Go ahead, ask," he gasped, breathing hard.

"Can you open that door?"

Dawson shook, his whole torso vibrating. "No," he finally oozed. "Can't."

I nodded, reached out, and grabbed Kieth by the shoulder. I spun him around so that he faced the mutilated Monk.

"Anything in that motherfucker you can use? Monks are just crammed full of interesting tech, aren't they?"

Kieth nodded, his shaved head reflecting the dull white light. "Yes. Very possibly."

I nodded. "Rip 'im up, Ty. Take whatever you need."

"Hey, Avery," Gatz said between loud breaths. "They're getting' closer, huh?"

I paused, listening. Kieth started to say something about the door, so I reached out and clamped his lips shut with one hand.

The shouts and gunshots were getting closer. Fast.

"What the—"

Before I could finish, Canny Orel suddenly appeared around the corner, guns shining in his hands, running full-tilt. Seconds later one of the twins followed. Orel actually looked disheveled: hair mussed, coat torn, a large dark stain spreading through his shirt on one side.

"Well, Mr. Cates, I hope you no longer need a distraction," he said, skidding to a halt in front of me. "We did our best but there are a large number of the infernal machines hot on our trail."

Despite his appearance, he wasn't out of breath at all, and calmly flushed his used ammo clips and began reloading.

"Ms. Milton," he added casually, "did not survive the onslaught."

"Jesus fucked," I swore. "How—"

"No time!"

As if they'd been drilling for years, Tanner dropped to her knees below Orel and they both opened fire on three Monks who raced around the corner. The Monks went down one, two, three, each a headshot, each from Canny, who moved his gun with surgical precision: Bam! A tic to the right bam! A tic to the left bam! I couldn't help but admire it.

For a moment, it was quiet, except for the latex sound of Dawson's melted laugh. Canny turned his head slightly to glance at me.

"Don't relax," he advised with a wink. "There are more coming. Mr. Kieth," he added, louder, "I forgive you your debt."

"Why the hell did you come *here*?" I demanded. I was ready to let it roll over me, the huge, incomprehensible wave—just close my eyes and let it smother me—but Canny Orel got on my last nerve and I was damned if I was going to let him just do what he liked. This was *my* job. "You're supposed to be the goddamned distraction."

"We didn't have a choice, Mr. Cates!" Orel snapped back, eyes fixed on the intersection and the three felled Monks. "We were fucking *herded* here."

"It's true," Tanner said, her voice cracking and shaking. I looked down at her sharply, noticing for the first time that her face was a rictus of emotion, her body stiff and shaking, as if she'd physically felt the death of her twin. "Everywhere we turned, they pushed us back—except one direction. They came and came at us, and we fucking took dozens of those fucking Tin Men out, Cates, but if we fell back in the right direction, they let us."

Two Monks flitted through the intersection like insects. Orel and Tanner tracked them, pumping shells, but missed, the Monks disappearing on the other side.

Anger flooded me. My hands spasmed, trying to clench into fists; it took all my concentration for a moment to stop myself from firing a shell into the floor, to keep my hands under control. I wanted to throttle Orel where he stood, so calm, so capable—probably the only one of us with a chance to fight his way out of this. I hated his competence, hated the fact that he was better, tougher than me. If I was going to die inside this fucking tomb, it was going to be *my* decision. I'd been dancing for Marin and Moje and everyone else for too long. I didn't give a fuck about the cash—which I doubted I'd ever see, anyway—I wanted to put a shell into Dennis Squalor's head because I'd come this far and I wasn't going to get stopped *now*.

I whirled on Ty Kieth. "Get that fucking door *open*!"

He swallowed and glanced down at his handheld, pointing it at the door and prodding its screen with his thumb, a practiced, smooth gesture. Licking his lips, he nodded.

"I can probably do it, but—"

"Do it," I snapped. "Or we're all dead, right here, in this fucking hallway."

He nodded, prodding his screen madly.

"Cates!" Orel snapped without turning. "It doesn't matter."

"What the fuck does *that* mean?"

More Monks appeared at the end of the hall. A volley of shells from Tanner and Orel, and two fell into a heap.

"Cates, we were herded *here*. On *purpose*. Did you encounter any resistance? No," Orel said slowly, eyes fixed on the sights of his guns. "I think that door is going to open soon, all on its own. I think you've been played. I *think* that opening that door is the last thing we want."

I stared at him for a moment, thinking. Then I turned and looked at the door, smooth, unmarked, implacable, just as another volley of shots announced more Monks. What it came down to was, you always had a choice. There was always *something* you could choose to do.

I turned and looked at Kieth. He looked back at me. He was shaking.

"Mr. Kieth," I said steadily. He jumped a little. "Get the god-damn door open." I smiled, the familiar crazy laughter catching in my throat. "Let's fucking surprise them."

Kieth didn't hesitate. He seemed almost happy as he pulled his small bag of instruments from his jacket. A slight smile played on his lips, and he didn't even flinch when a fresh wave of Monks at the end of the hall brought on another volley of bullets from Orel and Tanner.

"Two more!" Orel shouted. He sounded almost happy, too. I was surrounded by madmen. Madmen of my own choosing.

Kieth began scanning the door with his little handheld device, running it up and down the thin, faint lines outlining the opening. While bent over scanning along the bottom, he paused suddenly.

"Huh," I heard him say quietly. "That's—"

The door suddenly emitted a loud, hollow banging sound. Kieth stood up instantly, and Gatz and I turned as one, me with my gun held out, Gatz with a shaking hand on his glasses. Behind me, there was more gunfire, and a stream of curses from Orel. I squinted down the sight of my gun, hand hurting from gripping it so tightly.

The door banged inward as if a silent, dark explosion had propelled it, knocking Kieth back hard into Dawson's temporary coffin. I glimpsed the figure revealed in the doorway for just a split-second, because in the balance of that moment I ticked my gun's muzzle to the left an infinitesimal amount and pulled the trigger twice, turning his head into cheese.

Dennis Squalor stood there for another moment as we all stared, and then fell forward, leaking coolant and insulation.

For a moment, there was nothing. Then, rising like sour steam, Dawson's terrible ruined laugh.

XXXII

YOU DID THIS FOR MONEY.
YOU KILLED *YOURSELF.*

OOOOO

There was only Dawson's terrible laughter for a moment. It went on and on without pause for breath, without inflection, a tape loop. I didn't feel anything except the buzz in the bones of my hand, recovering from the gun's recoil. I had seen his face, but I couldn't believe it. It had been *him,* Dennis Squalor, and I'd killed him. But it wasn't real. I stared at the slumped form in the doorway and didn't move a muscle.

Behind me, shots continued to ring out in waves, punctuated by Canny Orel's growled expletives. Kieth moaned and struggled to extricate himself from Dawson's floating coffin, and Gatz was a statue next to me. I imagined I could hear the sizzle of my sweat on the gun's muzzle, that I could smell the coolant leaking from Squalor's metal body.

I opened my mouth to say something over Dawson's endless

laughter, but as I did so a second figure filled the doorway, and I froze again.

It was Dennis Squalor. Again.

"Avery Cates, shitbag," Dawson's ruined voice rumbled up from beneath Kieth. "Meet the Cardinals."

The face was exactly as it had been shown on the Vids. Round, loose-skinned, and jowly, a ring of friarlike hair on an otherwise smooth, red scalp. Small, delicate-looking ears and a flat, broad nose. He looked about as old as anyone I'd ever seen, maybe sixty, and wore small round dark glasses molded to his face, hiding his eyes entirely. He wore a blindingly white shirt, buttoned to the top, and a suit of black clothes, the coat trailing along the floor like a fitted robe. He looked entirely human, standing there, and I would have thought he *was* human except I'd shot him in the face just seconds before, and yet he was standing there, over his own dead body.

Behind me, I heard Orel bellow something almost inhuman, a sound that was just pure frustration, as an endless volley of shots rang in the hallway, Tanner and him firing in waves.

"Cates!" Tanner screamed above the din. "Here they come!"

I didn't turn around. I kept my eyes on this . . . thing, the doppelganger. With Orel's yell in my ears like cotton, with Tanner's words still hanging in the air like shattered glass, Squalor moved. It was just the subtle shift of his arms, a movement of millimeters by his coat. Old, burned-in instincts took over, bypassed all my higher functions. Before I consciously realized Squalor—or whatever it was—was going to draw and fire, I was moving. I threw myself back and to the side, taking Gatz off his feet as I pushed myself into the air, aiming for the floating coffin containing Dawson and Kieth.

In midair, I heard the sound of more bullets. When I crashed into the coffin awkwardly, half-in and half-out, the breath knocked out of me, I was followed immediately by a thunk-thunk-thunk of bullets hitting the metal casing.

"Get off of me," a melted, gurgling voice hissed in my ear. "And go die."

"Oh, shit," Kieth coughed from beneath me. "I think you fucking broke my ribs."

I didn't wait to hear more. The trick was always to keep moving. A moving target was hard to hit. You paused to catch your breath, you caught a bullet. Using Dawson's head to push off from, I gathered my strength and launched myself up and over the back of the coffin, landing on the other side on the balls of my feet, something in my back tearing painfully, electric shocks going up both legs. For some reason I was suddenly very aware of the damp stone smell of the hall.

"Very nice," Orel growled from behind me. I could feel him there, an inch away. "Mr. Cates, you are fucking *not* who I would have chosen to die with."

"Fuck you," I snapped, clearing the chamber of my gun out of habit. "You did this for money. You killed *yourself*." I willed my hands to move faster through the practiced motions, automatic. "You think I would have chosen *you*? I don't even know your fucking *real name*."

"Ah, Mr. Cates." He sighed. "Belling. Wallace Belling. My associates call me Wa. It was my priviliege to work with Cainnic Orel thirteen years ago. As for money—show me a way that doesn't end with my meaningless death, and I'll happily start tearing this whole godforsaken world to pieces."

Done with the pleasantries, I popped up. The Cardinal wasn't in the doorway anymore, so I dropped back down, all the way, stretching out on the floor. Dragging my eyes from right to left through the narrow band of air under the coffin, I saw Gatz, sitting with his back against the wall. The

Cardinal stood directly over him. Its boots were brightly polished. The posture and position of them was instantly familiar. I'd executed enough people in my time, and stood off to one side while others were executed, to recognize the classic pose.

My whole body went rigid for a second, ice and razor blades pumping through my heart.

As if pulling it through thick mud, I dragged my gun over and put four shells in those boots, welts erupting in them, impact craters, the armor-piercing bullets tearing everything inside them to shreds. Any man would drop on his ass, screaming.

The Cardinal didn't even move. I imagined the bullets destroying wiring, bouncing off titanium alloys, ripping tiny motors and etched circuits apart. But the Squalor clone didn't flinch.

A second later there was a loud pop. Gatz's body twitched, went still. Ice and razor blades pumped into my head, and my vision narrowed down. Ignoring the pain in my back, I jumped to my feet, suddenly graceful. I felt a hand in the fabric of my coat.

"Get down, asshole!" Belling yelled.

I ignored him and jumped again, up on top of the coffin, balancing precariously on the rim as it rocked and swayed. Belling's hand fell away.

Behind me, more cursing, more shots. Below me, Kieth moaned, Dawson hissed. In front of me, the Cardinal, Dennis Squalor's spitting image, still stood looking down at Kev Gatz's lifeless body. A dark red pool of blood was steadily spreading out. The color was shocking in the grayscale universe of the Electric Church.

"Interesting," Squalor said. His voice was smooth and unaccented and sounded completely natural. "A psionic."

All I could see was the Cardinal. Without hesitation, I threw myself at it with everything momentum and gravity could grant me. My bones rattled and my vision swam as I hit, taking it off-balance. We crashed into the wall right next to the still-open door, bounced, and I fell backward, the Cardinal crashing down on top of me with crushing force. I couldn't breathe, and his round, chubby face was thrust into mine, so real—except that his glasses had been knocked askew and lay across his face, revealing one delicate, tiny camera lens.

"Your actions will result in chaos, Mr. Cates," it said reasonably. "There will be unrest, lawlessness, property damage. This cannot be allowed."

The words were just noise. I felt no pain, just a hideous cold anger. A guttural, meaningless growl exploded from my throat, and I *pushed*, rolling the machine off me, staying with it so that I was right on top of it. I sat astride it and jammed my gun into its mouth, panting, staring down at the crazy glasses, the single revealed camera. Out of the corner of my eye I could see it swinging its weapon around toward me, so I pulled the trigger. Again. And again. And again, until all I got were dry clicks. Then I slumped backward and let my hand fall to my side, reflexively dropping the spent clip onto the floor. I was breathing hard, my face wet, shivering. Somewhere nearby, I could still hear Belling shouting, gunshots, moaning.

"Cates!" someone shouted. "The door!"

Slowly, I turned my head. The door was swinging shut. It seemed to move in dreamy slow motion. I felt like I could do a million things in the time it would take to close.

"Cates!"

I stood up and reached down, gathering a handful of the Cardinal's coat in one hand. The ice and razor blades were gone. I was exhausted, a numb buzzing was all I felt. I pulled the Cardinal across the rough floor with deadened, stubborn determination, and managed to push it into the path of the door with a foot or so to spare. The door slammed into the body and froze, a soft mechanical whine rising from it.

I realized with a start that everything had gone silent. I turned to look around.

Kieth was slowly pulling himself out of the coffin. Belling sat sprawled on the floor, guns still in his hands, his arms limp at his sides. Gatz sat where he'd been. Tanner was face-down, her hand relaxed on her gun. I walked slowly over to Gatz and stood over him, gripping my gun hard, my whole body shivering.

"Ah, Jesus," I croaked. "Ah, fuck. Why didn't you Push it, goddammit it?"

"No brain!" Dawson's gleeful, warped voice boomed from inside the coffin. "All digital, Cates! There was nothing for your rat-friend to Push!"

I ignored the voice, disembodied, like gas in the air. Gatz looked just the same. Pale, skeletal, hidden behind his dark glasses. If he'd stood up and wiped the gelled blood from his forehead and chin, it wouldn't have surprised me.

I looked at Kieth, and then beyond him to Belling. Behind Belling there was a mass of Monks, and Tanner, slumped forward, hand limp on her gun. I thought, *He must have murdered every last motherfucking one of them.* The old man was panting, too, and looked a little disheveled and out of sorts for the first time since I'd met him. Another time, under different circum-stances, I would have been impressed with the pile of busted hardware opposite him, but I had nothing left inside but wea-riness and a regret that floated on top like scum.

Kieth slid from the coffin onto the floor and knelt there, his arms wrapped around himself.

"You broke my ribs," he whispered hoarsely.

"Fuck you," I offered through gritted teeth. His fucking ribs. I'd lost the closest thing to a friend I'd ever had. Out of habit, I swapped in a fresh clip with stiff, arthritic hands.

"Cates," Dawson's voice bubbled up, sliding over the edge of the coffin and pooling on the floor. "Cates!"

I turned and walked over to the coffin and peered down into it, my hands still like rocks, my body shaking. Dawson leered up at me with his latex face and camera eyes, smiling.

"There're dozens of Cardinals, Cates," he rumbled. "You got lucky. They're coming."

With no conscious thought, I brought my gun up and aimed it at Dawson's face.

"Fuck you," I hissed.

Dawson's mouth twisted. I pulled the trigger twice.

XXXIII

OTHERWISE KNOWN AS THE KING WORM

10011

Belling struggled to his feet and leaned against the wall, reloading. Kieth still knelt next to me on the floor, moaning and hugging himself.

"Shut up, for God's sake. You aren't dead," I snapped.

"Ty isn't made for this shit, goddammit," he wheezed petulantly. "I think you punctured a lung."

I reached down with my free hand and pulled him up roughly. "Inconvenient, but survivable," I advised him, and Belling let out a snicker of amusement.

Kieth squawked. "*Survivable,* Mr. Cates? Look around: Your team hasn't *survived* all that well lately."

I nodded. There was no force in the universe that would keep me from completing this job. I'd paid too dearly for it. Maybe nothing mattered, maybe you lived and died and unless you had the wisdom to get Monked and live forever that was it, a great yawning darkness that nothing ever escaped from. Maybe. But I was going to *make* this matter, by brute force if necessary.

"We got set up, Mr. Cates," Belling said without looking up from his guns. "We were herded here, and pinned down, and then flanked. What I don't understand is why only two of those—what did he call them? Cardinals?—those Cardinals showed up. We were pinned down. A few more coming through that door would have cooked our geese for sure."

I didn't care anymore. My whole existence the past few weeks had been at the whim of some power beyond me, and I'd finally accepted that whatever it was could kick my ass any time it wanted. It was time to just pull my arms and legs inside the safety cage and enjoy the ride.

"There's been a lot of packet traffic in the air," Kieth panted, wincing as he brought his handheld up for a look. "Then, suddenly, nothing. It's like the whole EC just went quiet, all of a sudden."

"I don't much like the sound of that," Belling said, racking the chambers of his guns and holstering them. "We should all be dead right now. I think I'll be nervous until something starts shooting at me again." He looked up at me, and our eyes locked. Belling was back to his old self: cool, unconcerned, projecting the impression that he was going to live through it all even if *you* weren't. "I assume I've earned a full share of your payday, should we walk out of here alive?"

I gritted my teeth. A sudden rage flashed through me; if I'd released my limbs to it I had no doubt I would have tried to kill a member of the Dúnmharú.

"I've shares to spare, all of a sudden," I said instead. "You can have two, you fucking asshole."

He almost smiled at me—a faint turning-up at the corners

of his mouth. "While I admit that I find myself in a poor position for negotiation, I have to ask you if you really expect to be paid for this job. Where will the paycheck come from? Who, exactly, is going to pay us?"

I stared at him. "You're fucking worried about money? About fucking *money*?"

"Don't get all saintly on me, son," he snapped back. "We all got into this mess because of money. You can piss and moan about it—oh, poor me, my team fucked up and got killed, poor me, poor me." He waved his hands. "We caught a break here. Let's go put a bullet in Squalor's brain, by all means. But before I take a step, before I somehow decide to *not* save my ass, I need to know that there is actually a fucking *fortune* out there as you've suggested. Because, as I'm sure my old friend Mr. Kieth would agree, this has turned out to be slightly more work than expected."

I glanced at Kieth. He looked like he'd just remembered that Belling had survived and was just a few feet away—his long nose quivering, his face pale. Our eyes met but I had no time for him. I had no time, period. But I still had just one card, just one asset: I was the cash. As long as Belling couldn't touch the cash, he needed me, and that just might keep him from killing me when I needed him to watch my back.

"You'll get paid, Cainnic," I said carefully.

"How do I know that?"

"Because I intend to get paid *myself*," I growled. "Why the hell else am I still standing here?"

Belling shook his head and pushed off from the wall, approaching me slowly. "Because you're a fucking crusader, Cates. You think there's justice, somewhere. You think if you just keep pushing, you can put a bullet in the System's head and make everything like it was when you were five fucking years old and your daddy bounced you on his knee, right? *Fuck that.* Look around you. Me and the wonderful Mr. Kieth are all that's left. I can't speak for Mr. Kieth—whose debt I have already forgiven in a soft moment of affection for anything not made of silicon and titanium—but I am not taking one more step deeper into this fucking mausoleum unless I have a better idea of my reward. I need a *reason,* Mr. Cates. Who's going to pay me?"

He stopped directly in front of me. I was in a killing mood, and I held his eyes as we stood almost chin to chin. He'd killed Marilyn Harper for no reason, and for no reason I was willing to blame him for Gatz, too. I considered just killing him, right there, one more for the tally, and not one I'd feel too badly about, either.

"I will," a voice said clearly from behind.

I closed my eyes. I should have fucking expected it. Without opening them again, I slumped a little and said, "Meet our backer. Meet Richard Marin, chief of the System Security Force Internal Affairs."

"Otherwise known as the King Worm," Marin said cheerfully. "But you can call me Dick."

I turned around and opened my eyes. There he was, dapper in a suit, glasses on, hair perfect. He was smiling.

"Mr. Cates, don't look at me so disagreeably! I got here as quickly as I could. You provided me with a distraction and an excuse, allowing me to slip in."

I stared at him, the urge to murder returning. "Distraction."

He nodded and then stopped dead, cocking his head in a now-familiar pose, as if listening to distant sounds. We all waited through a few moments of still silence before he looked back at me. "Yes, I'm afraid so. I couldn't get *you* inside, you see. I could get *myself* in if there was reasonable evidence of a crime to extend my jurisdiction under my Emergency Powers clause, and if there was sufficient noise on the EC network to cover my entry. You provided that. Excellent. Now that I am here, however, I am able to . . . influence things a little. If you'll follow me, you can finally earn your money."

"Follow you?" Belling demanded. "Follow you where?"

Dick Marin nodded as if agreeing with something. "To Dennis Squalor, of course. So you can kill him."

We followed Marin's jaunty walk through the door and down an identical hallway. I had a thousand questions, but he ignored them all, and after a minute of trying I shut up. Kieth limped behind me, and Belling brought up the rear, guns in hands and alert despite Marin's assurance that we were going to be unmolested, at least for a few minutes.

"Marin, where are we going?"

He didn't turn around. "To meet some people."

I swallowed the urge to just shoot him in the head. "Marin, my people are dead. You waltz in here like you've got a fucking passkey, and my people are dead getting me this far." He just kept walking. I reached out and shoved him, hard. "Hey!" He didn't even miss a step.

"Mr. Cates, you'll be getting your answers soon enough. But believe me, I could not have gotten this far without your efforts." He turned his head and looked over his shoulder at me, walking briskly forward and taking a sharp left turn without hesitation. "I have my limitations, too, Mr. Cates. There are rules."

"Rules?" I snapped. "Fucking rules? You're the fucking King of the fucking System Pigs, and you're telling me *there are rules*?" Somehow, my gun was in my hand, and I racked a shell into the chamber. "I've seen System Pigs shoot people in the head for *being in the way*. I've seen System Pigs shake people down for spare change because they're *bored*. You've got *rules*?" I stretched out my arm and put the muzzle of the gun against the back of his head. I'd been itching to murder someone for the past twenty minutes. Might as well come full circle.

Marin whipped around and walked backward, so fast I was startled. He reached up almost casually and pushed the gun aside, and I let him. "Mr. Cates, *I* have rules."

We walked like that for a moment, him backward, me just stunned, and then he whipped back around.

"I am forbidden by standing order 778 to enter a privately held religious compound without due cause. Due cause is variously defined, but one circumstance that passes all requirements is a citizen of the System under mortal threat by members of that religious organization." He waved at me over his shoulder. "While a poor example of one, Mr. Cates, you are a citizen of the System. Members of the Electric Church were trying to kill you. I was thus duly authorized to enter the compound, under standing order 778. And under that order, I have complete authority and access to this compound. Any System Security Force officer does."

"You're kidding."

"Mr. Cates, I never kid." He stopped and turned to face a door that erupted out of the featureless gray wall. "We're here."

I tightened my grip on my gun. "You just needed a *citizen* to get shot at in here?"

He reached out and put a hand on my shoulder. "A citizen equipped to find a way in and survive. A Gunner. Believe me, your work here is not done yet."

He reached into his coat and produced an unmarked plastic card. He waved it at the door and it *snicked* open. "Come on in."

"What's in there?" Belling asked.

Marin smiled for a split-second, like a brief glimpse of the sun. Then it was gone. "Not what, Mr. . . ." he hesitated a moment. "Nynes? No . . . no . . . Belling, isn't it? Not what. Who. Step this way. You, too, Mr. Kieth," he added cheerfully. "Your services as well will be needed before long." He stepped inside, and we followed him. I couldn't think. I felt like everything was being turned inside out. Nothing was making sense.

"My name," Belling said weakly, "is Cainnic Orel."

"As you wish, Mr. *Orel.*"

The room we entered was dark. "Marin, you're here, right?" I asked, whispering for no apparent reason. "What the fuck do you still need us for?"

"I need you, Mr. Cates, because very soon I suspect I will violate my rules and lose my authority here. Assuming I survive. Now, let's have some light."

The lights bloomed, bright and blinding. We stared around, blinking, and then I froze.

"Avery Cates, Ty Kieth, *Cainnic Orel,*" Dick Marin said. "Meet Dennis Squalor. And the Joint Council."

XXXIV

MECHANICAL BUGS IN THE MIDST OF HIS SMILING FACE

10000

I wasn't sure how to process what I was seeing. We were deep inside the Electric Church's main complex, underneath Westminster Abbey, and it was for the first time completely silent. Not even Wa Belling had anything to say.

It was a big open square room with a high ceiling. A huge round table of dark, polished wood filled it, and around the table were seated Monks, but the figures weren't wearing the usual black robes of the Monk. They appeared to be inactive, slumped stiffly in the soft leather chairs. Thick black cables ran from the back of their heads into a well in the center of the table. Across the table from us was a rectangular black box, similar to all the boxes Kieth had lugged around. A thick layer of dust had settled on everything.

"They've been here for almost twenty years," Marin said soberly.

I looked at the King Worm. "This . . . this is the Joint Council?"

Marin nodded. "Every last one of the senile bastards."

A wave of dizziness made me reach backward and stumble into the wall. "Wait a second, wait a second," I panted. Everything had been moving too fast for far too long. "The whole goddamn System is run by Monks?"

Marin shook his head. "They're not Monks."

"You said our quarry was in here as well, Mr. Marin," Belling asked, sounding polite. "Care to point him out so we can get this show on the road?"

Marin nodded curtly, and then twice more for no apparent reason. "Of course. But allow me a moment or two for Mr. Cates, who seems quite distressed. I believe I owe him at least a moment of explanation. Also, once you complete your contract I will be unable to maintain the, er, *calm* I have imposed on the situation through my authority as chief of Internal Affairs, SSF. All hell will, in fact, break loose even before you pull the trigger, Mr. Orel."

Belling shrugged. "It's your dime."

I pushed off from the wall, my vision clearing. Marin turned to me, his creepy smile in place.

"Dennis Squalor was a Techie, Mr. Cates. Twenty years ago, with the world still smoldering from Unification, with everything still balanced on a knifepoint, he was just a skilled Techie who had an idea about immortality through cyborg conversion. An idea he took to the newly formed Joint Council. He offered to convert the new rulers of the world into immortal cyborgs for a fee."

"Fucking brilliant," Kieth breathed, wandering dreamily around the room.

Marin ignored him. "The Joint Council thought he was crazy and told him to sod off. But Mr. Squalor wasn't easily discouraged. He did the only thing he could think of to prove to the Joint Council that his procedure would work: He performed it on himself. He Monked himself. And returned to the JC months later a cyborg." Marin paused, cocking his head again. "Excuse me," he said. "There's a lot going on. This time, the Joint Council couldn't wait to sign up. They wanted to live forever."

I stared at the dusty figures seated around the table. I was mesmerized by them, their empty stares, and moving a distant memory.

"Once this was accomplished, the Council was able to return their attention to the newly formed System. There were a lot of growing pains. Revolts, riots—the System was breaking apart as quickly as it had been formed. Unification was failing. And then, much to everyone's horror, Dennis Squalor himself began to fail."

Kieth was on the other side of the table, running his fingers along the shoulders of one immobile form. "Brain function degeneration," he said absentmindedly. "Inevitable. Modifiable through a mod chip, but incurable."

Marin nodded, still turned toward me. "Incurable, and horrifyingly obvious to the Joint Council. Squalor's procedure was subtly flawed, and they immediately knew they were doomed. Things happened fast after that: Squalor was granted broad powers and budget to investigate a solution. Proxy power was transferred from the JC to their secretaries, who have been more or less running the show since. The JC was, as you see, shut down—put into a hibernation mode, actually—until a 'cure' was developed for their mental degeneration. Squalor was too far gone to actually find a fix for the problem. As he freefell into madness, he founded the Electric Church. Although he did take one last step that he thought would save him."

Belling squinted at Marin. "You're saying the Joint Council's been a bunch of vegetables for twenty years, and their fucking *secretaries* have been running the show?"

Marin nodded. "There was never an official proclamation or transfer of power, but the secretaries were in a perfect position, suddenly. Completely anonymous, granted proxy power, and with no mechanism in place for their removal, election, or other curtailment of their power. It was in their interest to leave things alone. Any attention drawn to their situation might lead to their removal. Steps were taken. The SSF was formed, for example, with broad powers. Squalor fell through the cracks for a few years, although he technically never left this complex; the secretaries assumed he was dead, or incapacitated. They saw no reason to pursue him. When he resurfaced with the Electric Church, it wasn't easy to get rid of him."

"Fascinating," Belling drawled. "Where is Squalor? You can finish the history lesson while we tear his circuits out."

"Shut the hell up," I said quietly. "He's going somewhere with this."

"Mr. Cates, you are a remarkably civilized criminal. But perhaps Mr. Orel is right: Time is wasting. Gentlemen, I give you Dennis Squalor. Or what's left of him."

He walked around the table and stopped next to the black box, which came up to his chin. We stared for a moment. Kieth was the first to react, almost running around the table.

"Holy fucking shit!" he gasped. "He's fucking *digitized*!"

"Squalor's last-ditch effort to arrest the degeneration of his mind. It worked. Too late to actually *cure* him, of course, but it froze the damage."

"I thought digitizing the brain didn't work?" My throat felt like sandpaper.

Marin shrugged. "Most of the time, no. But in some people, for some reason, it does. There's been a lot of research into this topic: The secretaries have plans for an SSF made up entirely of digitized humans in boxes like this, controlling robot avatars."

"Robot avatars," I repeated, staring at the featureless box. "The Cardinals."

Marin nodded. "The Cardinals. Squalor's avatars, made to look like him physically, controlled remotely by Squalor's intelligence, which resides here in several redundantly arrayed storage units. That was Squalor's solution to his own problems, and what the secretaries plan for the SSF, if they can get the success rate up above, oh, 20 percent, with the other 80 percent turning out as mental paté on the other end. They don't need much better, because it's cheap and easy to build the goddamned avatars. Hell, you could have a one-man police force."

The idea of the System Pigs being perfect robots, controlled remotely and instantly replaced when damaged, made me feel ill, my stomach rolling in sudden anxiety.

Belling regarded the box. "This is Squalor?"

Marin nodded. "It is."

There was a booming noise against the door. Marin didn't move. "We must move quickly, gentlemen. The Cardinals are attempting entrance. This means that Squalor has determined that we are here to do him harm. This calculation has negated my authority here—it's programmed in, you see—and his avatars are acting to protect him. Please proceed."

Belling nodded and took aim. I stepped forward and pushed his arm down. "Wait a fucking second," I said, staring at Marin. "You need the plug pulled on this fucking *box*? That's all? Why in holy fuck did you need *us*? Why not just do it yourself?"

Marin smiled and reached up and took hold of his sunglasses. A flash of inexplicable dread went through me.

"Because, Mr. Cates," he said, removing his glasses. "I'm programmed not to."

Tiny cameras sat like mechanical bugs in the midst of his smiling face.

"The eyes," Marin said with a sigh. "The eyes are the hardest part. You can make a machine look remarkably human, but the eyes never turn out right, and never fool anyone."

Kieth was staring happily at Marin. "You're a . . . Monk?"

"An avatar, actually, Mr. Kieth," Marin replied. "One of thirty-four Richard Marins in the System at present. There were thirty-five, but one of me got destroyed in a bombing in Yerevan yesterday. It'll take a few days to get a replacement."

He waited a few moments, looking from face to face, smiling. I got the impression the fucker was enjoying his effect on us.

"I was a prototype—the aforementioned all-avatar SSF. I was pretty much a failure as a System Cop, so they figured it wouldn't be much of a loss if I got pureed by the procedure, which almost every other candidate had been. They digitized me, added in the basic programming restrictions to control me—obeying orders, never breaking rules, protecting the secretaries, etc.—and then made their one huge mistake: They charged me with eliminating Squalor and the Electric Church, which had begun to worry them as it spiraled out of control."

The booming sound coming from the door had grown steadily in volume, and was now accompanied by the sad terrible sound of metal warping.

"All right!" Marin suddenly animated, replacing his glasses and gesturing at the black box. "History lesson's over. Things are going to spiral out of control *in here* very soon, so please, put Mr. Squalor out of his misery. I am programmed to obey all Joint Council resolutions, standing orders, and enacted laws, in both spirit and letter, so I cannot directly harm a citizen of the System or act directly against a certified religion. Mr. Cates? I think you've earned the right."

Belling glanced at me, chewed on this for a second, and then made a sarcastic show of bowing and sweeping his hand toward the box. I stepped forward and took aim.

"Quickly, Mr. Cates," Marin said behind me. "Squalor is attempting to defend himself."

The hammering on the door filled the room with noise, and I imagined the dust being kicked up by the vibration alone. My eyes stung, and I found it difficult to pull the trigger: Weeks of effort, so many dead people around me, and here it had all come down to a programming workaround for a robot named Dick Marin. I felt like a goddamn cog in a machine.

There was a cracking noise from behind me. In my peripheral vision I could see Belling and Marin each pull weapons and take up defensive positions.

"Mr. Cates!" Marin shouted.

Well, I thought, *if this is how it ends, so be it.* I fired three times, the armor-piercing bullets leaving crumpled craters in their wake, diagonally across the blank surface of the black box. A brief crunching sound and a whiff of ozone was the only reaction at first, and I stood there dumbly, gun aimed in shaking hands. Without warning, the pounding behind me ceased, and in the same instant the lights went off, and there was a subtle stilling of the air as the ventilation switched off. We were in total silence and complete darkness.

I heard Kieth breath the single word "Well?" as if it were the most important question he'd ever asked. Then a sharp intake of breath. "Holy shit—the mod boards! They weren't—"

"Oh, yes," Marin—or his avatar—said. "Congratulations, Mr. Cates, you're a wealthy man. Unfortunately, that was actually the easy part."

This uncorked a hidden reserve of hysterical laughter I hadn't suspected existed within me. It overflowed my control and I started to bark laughter there in the dark, gasping for breath, my ribs aching and my eyes watering.

"Sweet Christ," I managed to gasp, my head between my knees. "What's the *hard* part?"

Marin's voice was a marvel of programming as it managed to convey amusement through the pitch darkness. "We have to get out of here."

This time it was Kieth who barked crazy laughter, putting both hands on top of his bald head. "Through a few thousand Monks whose mod boards were directly linked to that piece-of-shit black box," he said quietly.

As the words floated by me, invisible, the silence was shattered by the sound of a thousand Monks going simultaneously crazy.

XXXV

THE GODDAMN *TIME* OF MY *LIFE*

00001

The noise was terrifying. It was all around us in the darkness, simultaneously distant and not distant enough. It sounded like hundreds of people screaming, interspersed with gunshots.

A light flared painfully into existence and I instinctively shielded my eyes. Ty Kieth stood holding a flashtorch up over his head, giving the whole room a strange, pale glow. Wa Belling and Dick Marin were still crouched defensively, guns aimed at the door. I lowered my own weapon and tried to relax, but my body refused, remaining tense and electrified.

Kieth was pacing, one hand still on his head as if he was keeping it from popping off. "We assumed the mod chips were closed, but they were receiving a signal. We never noticed with West, because Gatz took over that role. But Squalor's been in some sort of contact—probably just an authorization beacon—and now that he's gone, there's nothing modifying behavior out there."

"How exactly do we get out?" I shouted.

"Well, Mr. Cates, I thought you might have something planned for that."

I swore, a stream of pent-up obscenities dribbling out of me in a breathless, uninterrupted flow for five or six seconds. "Whatever I might have planned for exfiltration, Marin, it involved *not* having a thousand fucked-up Tin Men shooting the place up."

Marin's grin in the ghostly glow of Kieth's lamp was the single most irritating sight I'd ever witnessed. "Not my problem, Mr. Cates. I am merely an avatar. If I am lost, there are currently thirty-two others in existence."

Belling glanced at me and then back at the King Worm. "You said thirty-four of you just a moment ago," he pointed out.

Marin nodded, and just kept nodding as if he'd forgotten to stop. "What is happening down here, Mr. Orel, is also happening on a global scale. Every Monk in the Electric Church's network was directly linked back to Dennis Squalor's digitized intelligence. Their mod chips, in fact, relied on this connection. It has been rather inelegantly severed, and globally things are, shall we say, chaotic. My presence in Manila has been terminated. Spectacularly, in fact."

He looked at each of us as he continued. "This avatar, in fact, represents all the resources I'm willing to allocate to your survival. This is pretty generous, I think, considering that you were hired to eliminate Squalor—there was nothing in the original deal about your exfiltration. Whatever this avatar can do to help you escape, fine. Other than that, you're on your own."

The hysterical laughter was still there, in my throat, choking me. "That's fucking fantastic," I said cheerfully. Who gave a shit if I made it out or not? It didn't make any difference. "Mr. Kieth, if you would open that door, Mr. Orel and I will clear a hole for us."

Belling nodded. "That we will."

"All right," Kieth said, swallowing. "Mr. Marin, can I ask you to hold the lamp, or does that fall outside the services you're providing us here?"

Marin stepped forward to take the lamp. "I like you, Mr. Kieth. I hope you survive."

Freed, Kieth strode purposefully toward the door, pulling tools from his pockets. "This won't take long. Jesus! They really beat the shit out of this. Ty bets one of you could just yank the goddamn door in, but let's be professional and pop it, why not."

He knelt and began attaching small magnetic clips to the door. Belling and I moved in concert, setting up behind him in a crisscross pattern aimed just above his head.

"Don't stand up, Mr. Kieth," I warned.

"Ty's more the prostrate-and-beg type, Mr. Cates," he said without turning around. "Mr. Marin, bring that lamp over to your left, please. Interesting hardware they're using on these doors, actually."

There was nothing to say to that. After another thirty seconds, Kieth made a gasping noise and the door clicked, drifting silently inward. Kieth turned his head to look back at us as he gathered up his equipment, opened his mouth to say something, and was knocked backward as the door was kicked in. A ghostly Monk filled the doorway.

"This isn't right!" the Monk shouted, firing wildly twice into the room, its voice still modulated and sweetend by digital filters. *"This isn't fucking right!"*

Belling and I each put a shell in the Monk's face, and it fell backward in a spray of white coolant. The noise was deafening now that the door was open, pouring in from all directions at once, near and far, a cacophony of terror and anger and sheer madness.

I wondered if I'd just killed an innocent human, crazed and tortured. I didn't like the feel of it. But it had a gun, and I had no doubt it would have shot me, if I'd let it. It was survival. That helped.

"Uh," Kieth said feebly, pulling himself up from the floor. A thin trickle of blood ran from his scalp to his chin. "Ty will take up the rear."

I gestured at Belling. "After you, cocksucker." He winked and darted out into the hall with disturbing quickness, rolling to the opposite wall and coming up in perfect form, gun steady, sweeping around him. After a moment he glanced back at me and nodded. I moved swiftly past him and down the opposite wall, staying out of his line of fire. Marin fell in behind us, shouting directions, with Kieth between us all, looking pale and worried.

After the first turn, it was insanity. The Monks came from all directions—behind us, in front of us, out from hidden doors and once even down from the ceiling. They were incoherent, firing randomly and shouting different things, in different languages, and sometimes didn't even seem to notice us—which didn't matter when they entered shooting the fucking place up, chips of concrete stinging my eyes and bullets sizzling past my ears. Still, the strange cheer that had taken hold of me persisted, and I found myself grinning through it all, as Belling shouted curses and Kieth begged for his life at top volume.

At first, because of the crazy way the Monks were tearing ass around the complex, our work was easy enough. Most of them just ran right into our sights, or ran right past us without even a look. Even the ones who took notice of us and tried to share their pain a little were shaky and disoriented. At one point I turned a corner and hands were on me instantly, and I was being lifted up off the floor while Belling and Kieth shouted behind me. I brought my gun up instinctively and planted the muzzle under the chin of the Monk, but found myself staring down into its plastic face, exactly like West's, like Dawson's.

"Make it stop!" the Monk screamed at me, the smooth filtered audio of its voice ragged at the edges as some emotion strained the circuitry. "Make it *stop!*"

The Monk wasn't even trying to hurt me or protect itself. Killing it would have been easy. I couldn't do it. These were people, people like me, just unluckier. Then again, I was trapped underground with an army of crazy cyborgs and the chief of SSF Internal Affairs, soon to be sole master of the world, as far as I could tell. Maybe the Monks *weren't* the unlucky ones.

Belling didn't see it my way, and put a bullet between its eyes, white coolant splattering my face.

It was slow going, though. After twenty minutes of white-knuckle crawling, we paused at an intersection, Belling and me back-to-back, panting. My gun was hot in my hands as I reloaded and checked the action for the millionth time. I glanced back at Marin, noting thankfully that he'd resumed his dark glasses.

"Any shortcuts?" I shouted. Behind me, I heard Belling curse and the explosion of his gun.

"Watch your ammo," Belling advised. "We can't shoot every fucking Monk in the known universe."

Marin shook his head. "This area was designed to be a single-point-of-weakness. Believe me, if you hadn't had the chief of SSF Internal Affairs here to pull strings, you'd never have gotten this far."

"Fuck!" I said cheerfully, letting a Monk who streaked across my field of vision pass unmolested. I was trying to kill only the Monks who posed a threat.

"Cates!" Kieth hissed. "You okay? You sound wonky, and Ty is worried that *wonky* will get Ty killed!"

"Fuck you, Mr. Kieth!" I howled. "I'm having the goddamn *time* of my *life*!"

"Cates," Belling said in a low voice. "We're not going to make it like this. It's a barrel-shoot, sure, but there's so much fire coming at us we're going to get clipped eventually, and we're going to go dry on ammunition soon." I felt the recoil through him as he fired again. "We won't make it this way."

I was grinning. "Who says I *want* to make it, Mr. Orel?"

"Then say so and I'll put one in your ear for your fucking bullets, Mr. Cates. What's the matter? Not enough dead people on your hands today?"

His voice was silky, cultured, and it sank into my ear and yanked, hard. I glanced around at Kieth, who held his gun awkwardly and actually thrust it forward every time he fired it, usually at the three-second-old shadow of a Monk that had just run by. He was hopeless, and obviously terrified, nose vibrating like a hummingbird's wing. Kieth hadn't bargained for this. He hadn't even been in it for the money—his one moment of happiness had been tearing Brother West to pieces, discovering its secrets. But he'd stayed in anyway—for the money, on some level, sure, but for something else. Loyalty, maybe. Honor amongst thieves.

Gatz and Harper flashed through my mind. Milton, Tanner. A man in the backseat of a car. A woman hanging upside down from a fire escape.

"Ah, fuck," I breathed. My cheer dried up, the laughter sucked back down into whatever dark hole it had come from. And I thought, *I guess I can commit suicide any time.* "Marin!" I shouted. "Do you have any communication with the outside?"

"Mr. Cates," he responded in a scolding tone, "I've already explained to you that this avatar is the limit of resources—"

"Fuck!" I shouted. "Mr. Kieth! Do you have any open comm channels?"

A few moments ticked by. A half-dozen Monks ran by, screaming, as if we weren't even there. Belling and I let them go. I tried to keep my eyes everywhere. "Yes, Mr. Cates!" He shouted back. "I have a narrowband signal I can use!"

"Marin, do the goddamn *resources* you've *allocated* include issuing orders to System Pigs if they're standing right in front of you?"

Marin's response was instant. "Yes."

I nodded. "Kieth: Call the fucking cops!"

I imagined I could hear the sinews in Belling's neck pop as he turned his head toward me. "Excuse me?"

"Call 'em, Kieth," I shouted, as a Monk turned the corner, an electric whine coming from its open mouth, guns in each plastic hand firing indiscriminantly. I whipped my gun up and put a bullet into the back of its throat, knocking it backward.

"Mr. Cates, I should advise you that the surface is in a state similar to that of this complex," Marin said. "I am doubtful you will be able to get the SSF's attention—even though you *are* the great Avery Cates."

Avery Cates, the Gweat and Tewwible, I thought grimly. "Don't just call the cops, Kieth," I advised, a slim trickle of the sick happiness returning. "Have them patch you through to Elias Moje. Tell Colonel Moje that Avery Cates is down here. Tell Colonel Moje that Avery Cates is a very rich man, and he's *laughing* at him."

For a moment, there was relative quiet, just the endless screaming of Monks, the endless distant and not-so-distant gunfire.

"I hope you know what you're doing," Belling muttered.

"I'll try, Cates," Kieth finally shouted back. "But it isn't going to be easy to just find him."

"Sure it is," I corrected him. "He's looking for *me*. Just shout my name on the SSF feed long enough, and he'll find *you*."

"Well this is a wicked fucking googly," Belling muttered. "Extracted by the fucking System Pigs. I don't know about you, Cates, but I'm not sure I want to make it out of here that bad."

I was grinning again. "Like I said, who says I *want* to make it, Mr. Belling?"

XXXVI

GRINDING OUR NECKS UNDER THEIR SHINY, EXPENSIVE BOOTS

00011

The Stormers came in like they'd been letting the Electric Church *use* the complex for a few years and had always intended to come home and clean house.

Faced with yet another unmarked steel door, I hunkered down and closed my eyes for a moment. Weariness pulled at me, dripping down like melted wax. It felt as if every joint and muscle in my body had been injected with grit and glass shards. I opened my eyes and stared at the blank steel door across the hall from us. Moving slowly up one side of the door was a bright light and a thin plume of smoke. It moved steadily, smoothly. For a moment, all the noise and terror was behind us, muffled by steel and concrete, and our combined, exhausted panting.

The door burst inward, hitting the floor with sparks and rattling to a stop just a foot away from me. The Stormers poured in through the doorway in classic two-by-two formation, their ObFu Kit blending with the walls until they were faint outlines of men.

Through the smoke and dust, Elias Moje strode in like a king, wearing a dark blue suit with pinstripes under a long leather overcoat, his boots shining in the white light. A gold chain hung from one belt loop, disappearing into one deep pocket. He didn't bother to palm a weapon of his own.

He looked around, a half-smile on his lips. "Hello, rats," he said amiably. "Just the four of you, now? Disappointing. I was so hoping to kill you all personally."

"I'm afraid I have to order you to keep these men alive, Colonel Moje," Marin said, standing up. "And to escort us from this location."

Moje stared. "Sir," he said slowly, then paused. "I just read a Flash Memorandum from you out of the Bogotá office."

"Ordering all SSF personnel to protect key properties in cities against rising or potential riots and disturbances, yes, I know: I authored it. If you'd like to see what an official rebuke and recommendation of termination for an officer of the SSF looks like, please continue to stand there with that look on your face."

Moje stared for another moment, and then straightened up. "Yes, sir," he said, but he did not sound convinced. He turned to his Stormers.

"You heard the man. This is the chief of Internal Affairs, boys and girls, and he can eat your testicles for lunch any day he feels like. Make a hole, we're bringing these men out of here. Exterminate anything that gets in your way."

He turned to look over his shoulder. "All right, Chief," he said. "Follow us."

The Stormers formed around us and we began moving back the way the SSF team had come. The floor was littered with dead Monks, and the occasional ObFu Kit blending a corpse into the floor. I limped along with a painful hitch and forced myself to catch up with Moje, the crazy laughter gurgling in my throat.

"Don't worry," I said. "I'm sure you'll get a chance to kill me once we're topside. In fact, I'm positive."

He ignored me, eyes forward.

"What's the situation up there, Colonel Moje?" Marin asked suddenly.

Moje straightened up as he walked. "Chaos, sir. Monks have gone crazy everywhere — we're getting reports in from all over. We're stretched pretty thin trying to keep things bottled up. SSF brass issued a blanket directive to shoot Monks on sight about an hour ago." A small grin broke through his manicured poise. "We've been enjoying ourselves ever since."

"Once we reach the outside, Colonel Moje, I'll be taking personal charge of the city, understood?" Gone was the herky-jerky Dick Marin I'd dealt with, the grinning, amused little man. Here was the chief of Internal Affairs, the King Worm, and my glee dried up again as I contemplated the obvious outcome of all this chaos — a power vacuum, with a few dozen Richard Marins dancing on top of the pyramid. It was the False Crisis *coup d'état* — the System in flames again, riots everywhere, and Dick Marin's avatars everywhere taking personal command. Were thirty of him enough to handle a worldwide crisis? He *was* thinking in digital, arrayed chips processing clock cycles. As we walked through the death spasms of the Electric Church, I stared at Dick Marin's back in admiration. It was genius.

I wondered what would happen if I drew my gun and shot Marin in the face. Certainly, there were more Richard Marins out there to carry his good work on, but in my *specific* situation, the idea was fascinating. But I wanted to see Kieth, and even Belling, out of this tomb safely first. Enough people had died simply for being associated with me, Avery Cates, Angel of Death. I just shook my head, giggling. "Genius!"

Marin spun around and walked backward, regarding me. He didn't say anything.

"Director Marin," Moje said, looking straight ahead, "when we get topside I'm going to ask permission to put a bullet in Avery Cates's head. I sincerely hope, for the good of the System, that whatever arrangement you have with him won't interfere."

Marin continued walking backward for a moment, saying nothing, and then spun around in silence. I knew he would regard our special arrangement as finished the moment we were outside. He might not actively try to murder me, but I could feel in my bones that he wouldn't be upset or at all disappointed if Elias Moje gunned me down. Marin could save me. All it would take was one word from him to Moje. One fucking word of negation, and Moje would choke on his tongue and shiver with rage—but Moje was too terrified of Marin to disobey a direct order.

And Moje, the overfed, sleek motherfucker. Lord knew what his official duties were, what he was supposed to actually be *doing* as a System Security officer, but apparently chasing one runty Gunner across the fucking globe was well within his job description. Even if I managed to squirm away from him, he would come after me with all the determination of a petty man affronted. And if I killed him, there would be others. Even if Marin came through on his other promise—to blank out my file and give me a new identity—eventually I'd look at another System Pig cross-eyed and be in the same hole. The whole goddamn System was broken. Madmen had been running it for decades, and now it would be run by avatars of Dick Marin, and the Elias Mojes of the world would keep grinding our necks under their shiny, expensive boots until they grew old and fat and died pensioned somewhere, in their sleep, laughing at us.

I didn't want to be part of the System anymore. Sitting on top of a pyramid of shit wasn't something I aspired to. I thought of Kev Gatz. Poor fucking weirdo should have been something special, something celebrated, but instead he was dead after a hard life and there were a dozen more just like him stepping right into the same shitty place. If I was going to die anyway, I was going to die causing the System as much grief as I could.

I stumbled a little at the thought, a jolt of excitement going through me as a plan bloomed in my head, complete and insane and immediately the only way I could go. Belling and Kieth glanced back at me. I looked at Belling and smiled. He stared at me in recognition—the look on my face must have seemed familiar to an old crook like him. He'd said to give him a reason, and some cops to kill, and I thought I might be able to do the former, and as for the latter we were currently in the company of some of the dirtiest cops in the goddamn world. After a moment, he smiled back.

The hall was inclined upward. We'd lost a few more Stormers from the sheer volume of bullets; Moje's team had shrunk to about six. Fucking hell, the System Pigs could be killed just like anybody else.

The Stormers cut through one last door and we emerged blinking into a bright, watery London morning. The sound of sirens and displacement roared everywhere, and half the blue sky was filled with thick, slow-moving black smoke. Dead Monks lay everywhere inside the complex gates. A downed hover smoldered just twenty feet from where we stood. The six Stormers formed up around us, but it was pretty clear that this area of the city, for the moment, was abandoned.

Moje and Marin turned to face me. I was amazed to note that Dick Marin still looked perfectly coiffed and neat, as if he hadn't spent the last few hours crawling through madness and murder and dust. Moje was grinning. I grinned back and took a deep breath.

"Mr. Cates," Marin said with his typical manic cheer, "I am informed that your money has been transferred. Congratulations, you are now a rich man, and I consider our business to be at an end."

"Director Marin," Moje started to say, and I brought my gun out of its holster and leveled it at Moje's face with practiced ease. He blinked, closing his mouth with a click, and then smiled again.

"You wouldn't dare, Mr. Cates. Your life wouldn't be worth spit."

I shrugged. "It isn't worth much now."

"Don't forget our deal, Mr. Cates," Marin said smoothly, jerking his head down and to the left to stare at a dead Monk for a moment, receiving reports from his other avatars. "You've got a chance to start over, rich, anonymous—secure."

Moje was still smiling. "Pull that trigger, and my team will eat you alive."

I waited a moment, then moved my gun just a tick to the left and put a bullet into Dick Marin's face, then moved the gun back level with Moje.

He stared at me, his smile forgotten and rotting on his face. He didn't know Marin was an avatar. He thought I'd just shot the King Worm dead right in front of him.

Around us, the Stormers all tensed and leaned forward, as if blown by a strong wind. But they were well-trained, waiting on Moje's order.

"Colonel Moje," I said steadily, prepared for the headshot, ready for it to end if it had to. "I'm tired of the System. I'm tired of System *Cops*. I'm hereby dedicating the rest of my life to destroying this fucked-up world. I may not live more than a minute longer, but in that minute all I will do with my time is fight against all of it—all of it, including the goddamn SSF. Understand?" I nodded. "Starting with you."

He squinted at me, wondering. I could sense Wa Belling next to me, standing tense.

Moje drew a deep breath and opened his mouth. I put a bullet in it.

I moved, and Belling moved with me. Even Kieth moved, instead of standing there pop-eyed in terror. I rolled right, firing, and Belling rolled left, firing, while Kieth fired wildly at the Stormers nearest him, screaming. He even managed to hit one before emptying his clip.

Belling and I hit three of the others as we rolled, good, clean killshots. I tried to pull myself up, keep moving, but my legs couldn't move quickly enough and got caught up in each other. I saw ObFu boots out of the corner of my eye and dove for them, wrenching my back in the effort as I wrapped my arms around the boots and knocked the Stormer off her feet. I held on to her legs with all my strength, until the sound of a racked chamber rang through the still air, and the Stormer went still. I looked up, and Wa Belling, formerly Canny Orel, stood over us, gun pointed at the Stormer's head.

"I'm sick of System Pigs, too," Belling said, nodding. "Sick of it all."

"Holy shit," I heard Kieth say weakly. "I can't believe we just did that."

I couldn't either. I was still on borrowed time, and a thrill of triumph went through me. *Not dead yet,* I thought.

I let go of the Stormer's legs and rolled over painfully. "They're just goddamn men and women, and they die the same." I pulled myself to my feet and turned to the last Stormer, who panted on the ground, and stared down at her. "They make the same mistakes we do, and they're fucking arrogant." I kicked her gun away, trying to catch my breath. "You, I'm letting go," I said. "Go tell them. Tell the fucking SSF that Avery Cates has gone apeshit. Tell them there's nothing they can offer me. Tell them I'm going to start tearing the world apart, brick by brick, cop by cop. Tell them I don't think it will take me as long as they might think. Tell them I dare them to stop me."

We all stood in our places for a moment, nothing moving, not even a hint of breeze. Then Belling kicked the Stormer in the side.

"Go," he said.

I looked around. London was on fire, and the sounds of rioting filled the air. We weren't going to have any trouble getting out of the city.

We watched the Stormer climb painfully to her feet, stare at us for a moment, and then begin backing away warily.

"Don't worry," Belling called out. "We'll kill you later."

EPILOGUE

THE WHOLE GODDAMN WORLD
IS AGAINST YOU NOW

00101

Pickering's was crowded. It was a rainy, dismal night in rotting New York, the heavy rain wearing down the melted stone of the old buildings and breaking up the crumbling asphalt of the dirty, trash-swamped streets. The regulars had gotten in early to drink blinding gin, smoke stolen cigarettes, and guard their seats against the influx of newbies. Fights broke out over the unsteady wooden chairs in Pickering's, and people had been cut up and almost killed over territorial skirmishes. The place had always been crowded, especially on crappy nights, but within the last year things had begun getting beyond Pick's ability to control. So many people were crowding into the place every night the fights were continuous, and he was approaching a point where he wouldn't be able to bribe away the Crushers that showed up, sniffing suspiciously at so much underground talent drinking in one place.

The kid wasn't more than seventeen years old. Tall, skinny, with broken teeth and long, delicate fingers, he stepped into the bar uncertainly, furtively peering around. His greasy dark hair was pasted to his forehead; his pale, blemished skin shone in Pickering's weak light. The crowd eyed him surreptitiously and almost everyone came to the same unflattering conclusion: *amateur.*

The kid didn't try for one of the seats. He looked around once, shrugged his cheap, tattered coat onto his narrow shoulders, and moved confidently toward the back of the room, where the metal security door led to Pick's office. A tall, amazingly muscled man stood with his back against the door, arms crossed, illegally augmented muscles twitching with their own intelligence.

Halfway there, a leather-gloved hand shot out and took hold of the kid's arm. The owner of the hand was a squat, gray-skinned man whose face was an intricate maze of broken blood vessels. A ragged, ugly scar trailed from his scalp to his throat. He licked his lips and looked the kid up and down before speaking.

"Tell ya what, kiddo," he said in a thick, slurred voice, "gimme whatever it is ya got an' I'll let ya walk outta here alive."

Soft, unenthusiastic laughter rippled around him— interested to see how the kid would react, but seeing no real sport in it.

"Let go," the kid said, looking down. "Or I'll feed your fingers to you."

More laughter, this time mocking, and the squat man in leather took it to be mocking *him*. He might have let the kid past if he'd squirmed a little, begged a little, but a smart-mouth had to be taught a lesson. "Watch yer mouth, pup," he growled, squeezing the kid's arm tight. "This ain't a place you get to smart-mouth, see?"

The kid continued to stare for a moment. Then, without warning, he whipped out his free arm, a knife popping from his sleeve into his open palm. Grasping the knife firmly, he slashed downward at the squat man, opening up a gash on his face. Blood splashed onto the table, and the squat man threw himself backward, hands slapped over his face, screeching.

"You fucking cut me! You little runt!"

The kid stared at him for a second or two, then wiped the knife on his coat and returned it to its spring-loaded holster in his sleeve. He continued to the guarded door.

The big man standing in front of the door eyed him warily. *"Versuchen sie nicht das mit mir, zicklein. I'll schnäpper sie in zwei,"* The big man said. "Ya?"

The kid shook his head. "I don't understand that shit, man."

The big man sighed petulantly. "Fucking Americans," he said in thickly accented English. "Don't fucking know shit about the rest of the world. What the fuck do you want?"

The kid squared his chin. "I want to see Avery Cates."

One of the big man's hands whipped out and caught the kid by the throat, the other taking hold of the kid's arm to prevent more knifeplay. He didn't squeeze hard. Everyone ignored them.

"No *name zicklein,*" the German muttered. "No fucking *name,* ya?"

The kid nodded and licked his lips. "Okay, all right. I need to see him."

The German released him and studied the kid for a moment. "You gots something to show the man?"

The kid nodded. "I got something."

The German nodded. "Weapons. All of them. Then, I scan you, ya? Don't fuck with me or out on your ass you go, ya?"

The kid nodded and handed over the knife. The German looked at it. "That's it?"

The kid nodded. "That's it."

Sighing, the huge man picked up a small wand-shaped device and ran it up and down the kid's body, studying a slim screen on one end. Satisfied, he stepped aside and waved the kid in. Hesitating for just a moment, the kid shrugged his coat on again and stepped forward. The door opened automatically.

Pick's back room was as crowded as ever. The kid stared at the piles of paper as he shuffled through the narrow floorspace toward the ancient desk. He'd never seen so much paper in his life, and wondered what in hell it was good for. Three men watched his approach. One was very old, sitting behind the desk, one hand on a strange, flat device covered in buttons. The youngest-looking one was dressed all in black, and sat on the edge of the desk, a cigarette dangling between two fingers, his hair—starting to go gray—slicked down, long in the back. He was pale and unshaven, and smiled a little from behind his sunglasses.

The third man was old, too, but stood against the wall behind the desk, dressed expensively. His hair was entirely white, but was combed and trimmed. He smoked a cigarette, too, and stared at the kid with frightening, flat eyes.

The kid swallowed as he came to a stop in front of them. He stared at the younger man directly in front of him, eyes wide.

"Are you—" he started, but the younger man held up a hand immediately.

"No names, *mi amigo*," he said. "The SSF has everywhere. We do our best to sweep the place, but it's better to be safe than sorry."

The kid nodded. "I was told to come here, and, um, talk to, uh . . ." He hesitated. "You, I guess." He squared his shoulders. "I want to be involved."

The younger man smiled and glanced back at the older man behind him. "Hear that? He wants to be involved in our good work."

"Ask him." The older man exhaled smoke. "If he has credentials."

The younger man kept grinning, turning back to the kid. He put his cigarette between his lips and spread his hands. "Kid, you got credentials?"

The kid nodded. Reaching into a coat pocket, he produced a small leather case. He tossed it to the long-haired man, who caught it easily, flipping it open. A hologram of a golden badge glowed dimly in the room, along with a digital photo of a stern-looking black man and a running stream of textual information.

"Captain Calvin Billington. System Security Force." He glanced up at the kid and passed the badge back to the older man, who accepted it silently. "How? When?"

"Hour ago," the kid said, "Battery Cemetery. Throat cut. It was clean." He kept his face stern and mean, but couldn't resist snuffling back snot and dragging one arm across his nose. "That Pig's been robbing us fucking *blind*. Whatever we nick from the swells, he's there, like a goddamn ghost, pushing you around, bloodying noses, messing with the girls." He nodded. "Fucker deserved it."

The younger man nodded. "Mr. Pickering? Can you confirm this?"

The ancient man tapped on his buttons and stared at a sickly glowing screen. "I've got a Captain Billington down, throat cut, called in half an hour ago." He blinked. "Kid, you better lay low. They got a good description of you."

335

The kid nodded. "Sure."

The younger man studied the kid as the older man behind him passed the badge forward. "All right. This isn't a game, you know, right? This isn't some snuff thief gang you run with for a few weeks, make some skag. This is serious." He thrust a crooked finger at the kid. "You just killed a System Cop. The whole goddamn world is against you now. We're all you got."

The kid's face hardened and he lifted his chin. "I know what the fuck I'm doing. I can't stand this world. I hate the fucking System."

The younger man studied the kid for a moment longer, then nodded. "All right. A few ground rules. First ground rule is, keep your fucking mouth shut. I don't care who you think you are, you don't get drunk and brag, you don't let hints slip, you don't let *anything* fucking slip. We don't exist. None of us ever met. I don't know who you are." The man's face hardened in turn, and suddenly didn't seem so young anymore. "But I do, don't I? So fuck us, you get *fucked* in return, right?"

The kid nodded. "I'm not going anywhere."

The younger man studied the kid for a moment and then nodded. "All right. Go on back out. We'll be in touch. "They watched the kid exit the office. The long-haired man walked slowly back to the desk.

"Youngest one yet," Pick growled. "According to this, he's fucking sixteen."

"I'd already killed three men when I was sixteen, Pick," Cates replied, reclaiming his spot on the desk. "Doesn't take age to be able to fight for something."

"Another one," Belling said quietly from behind him, eyes on the security screens. A middle-aged black woman, wearing a patch over one eye and sporting a metallic claw for a left hand, was giving the German a loud lecture, which the rippling mass of artificial muscle took stoically.

Cates stared up at the screen, the same nonsmile playing over his features. They'd been straggling in ever since they sent the word out and backed it up with furious action: two major robberies, six dead cops—each of them an evil bastard, mourned by no one—and press releases for each. The fucking cops—they were good, the best, but they'd never been up against a member of the Dúnmharú and Avery Cates. Not simultaneously. And they'd never been up against an entire goddamn city either. And the Crushers were too fucking greedy to pass up the protection money and give up Pickering's.

He watched the German put the woman through the usual security and felt a familiar buzzing excitement inside. He thought grimly, *It's begun.*

Avery Cates will return in
The Digital Plague.

APPENDIX

EXTRACTS FROM THE
MULQER CODEX, ANNOTATED

Joint Council File #445EE7
Reviewed by: T. Greene, Joint Council Undersecretary

Background: The *Mulqer Codex*[1] is the main text of the
Electric Church. It was written by the Church's founder,
Dennis Squalor, who remains its chief officer and public
face. It is freely available to the public in a variety of paper
and electronic formats, and is often quoted by Church
members (known colloquially as "Monks"). Although the
text is highly personal, loosely organized, and somewhat
incoherent, the large number of Church members—all of
whom converted—always cite its influence on their decision to join the Church.

---

1. The title does not have any apparent meaning, and no explanation has
ever been publicly offered by the Church.

APPENDIX

The entire *Codex* is approximately 115,000 words long. It is not reproduced *in toto* here; much of the *Codex* is arguably meaningless, large tracts of repeated phrases, apparently dictated, and much of it is inscrutable.

Insects, all of you,[2] and me,[3] all of *us* insects, scuttling about for a brief atomic flash and then gone. Insects, eating your way upward, supported by the compressed corpses of your ancestors until you fill and burst and collapse down and are in turn compressed, slowly the level rises, your descendants ascending toward the summit, the goal, the exit. Eventually a generation will emerge, free.[4] This is the plan of the universe. We are raised in increments, slowly, through our collective achievements, the spaces between our existences compressed or expanded depending on the requirements of God.

And have no doubt that there is a plan. God created man *with* reason *for* a reason—we are all born with a purpose, both a macro purpose—the destiny of mankind in toto—and a

2. Squalor consistently refers to humans who have not joined the Electric Church as "insects." The image resurfaces throughout the work, although it is interesting that Squalor also refers to himself in this manner, usually in the same sentence.

3. Squalor remains an unknown quantity. Prior to Unification he was a student of some promise, earning advanced degrees in biology and computer science. After the turmoil of Unification, he disappeared from public records for a decade, emerging only after having gone through his own process of cyborg conversion—in short, becoming a Monk—and founding the Church.

4. There is a sense of contempt for biology throughout the *Codex* and other Church writings, accompanied by a reverence for technology. The physical body produced by evolution is often referred to in terms of disposability and corruption (i.e. rot, decomposition, impermanence) whereas technology—obviously represented by the Monks' artificial bodies—is presented as lasting forever. Monks will often stress the eternal nature of their bodies when accosting citizens in the streets.

micro purpose, individual to each man.[5] The latter is a private communication between each individual and God—any man who listens will hear his purpose easily enough, whether it be to build pyramids or found churches or serve his fellow men somehow. The macro purpose is the purpose of all mankind, collectively, the purpose we all share. It is none other than our purpose as a *race*. God did not make this into a mystery, there is nothing mysterious about this purpose. It is part of our genetic code, part of the instinctive instructions mankind has followed since they first raised their gaze from the ground and *thought*. We are here to aspire to godhood.[6]

God does not want subjects. God does not wish dominion over us. He wishes peers.[7]

This is why we have always sought to wrest the mysteries of the cosmos from the air, to seize control over the forces we perceive or theorize. This is why we have marched steadily upward, manipulating greater and still greater forces. This is why we have investigated the laws of the physical universe, seeking to understand and then control the world around us: God created us to learn, to eventually equal him.[8]

5. Throughout the *Codex* there are many of these binary statements, pairs of options and conditions that Squalor compares, resulting in a very simple and compelling view of the universe—there is good and bad, eternity and damnation, sin and industry.

6. The Electric Church was granted Recognition as a legal religion, protected under standing order 778, eight years ago.

7. Throughout the *Codex*, Squalor shifts from venerating God as the creator and the architect to dismissing God as a fantasy to be ignored, often within the same page or even the same paragraph.

8. Here is the fundamental concept of the Electric Church: The idea that mankind's eventual salvation is possible only through our mastery of technological and scientific knowledge. Specifically, the Church preaches that only through centuries, even epochs of meditation and study can salvation be attained—the necessary lifespan being supplied by the

We stand on the cusp.

What is sin? Traditionally we are told sin is crimes against our fellow men, crimes against God. Lust, anger, sloth. These are not sins in and of themselves, what makes them sins is how they distract our attention and energy away from the real work God has outlined for us. Killing a man is not a sin if it is done in the name of our great task.[9] Resting a day when you do not have to is a sin because it takes your contribution away from the great task. How many sins are you thus guilty of? All your sins are simply time stolen from the great task that God has given us. It would take you years, centuries, to make up for even one simple sin against God's design. You do not have centuries. Yet.

Time is your curse. Lack of time. Everything requires time, and you have so little. This is the fundamental question: How can you be saved when you have no time? How can you possibly combat your sins in the time allotted you?

Consider the technological advances of the human race in recent centuries. We are a race designed to plumb the mysteries of the multiverse. It is God's plan that we do so, that we investigate and harness the forces of nature. We are meant to find salvation through our progress. But computers cannot output salvation. And we cannot teleport salvation into this room.

---

cyborg bodies Squalor has designed and built, as well as the process he has devised for transferring a human brain into one.

9. This is a disturbing passage to many, and is often quoted by those who claim the Church has engaged in violence against innocent citizens who do not voluntarily join or listen to preaching. It should be noted that there is not a single documented complaint against the Church filed by a reliable citizen of standing, and that all complaints from less reliable citizens have been retracted over time.

We cannot splice salvation into our genes. Salvation must be *attained*.[10]

Time. Time is the obstacle. You will not live long enough. Even during your time, you are distracted: You must work. You must rest. You must eat. As high as we have risen, there is much to do, and only now are we experiencing the singularity that will allow us to truly devote ourselves to the true work of the race. We stand upon the pyramid of our ancestors, finally close enough to the goal to perceive it correctly, to make out its faint outlines and sense its immense proportions. Time is what is required. More time than the normal laws of our universe allow us, but this has always been our purpose, to master the forces around us, bend them to our will like the gods we will someday become.

Only through eternity can you be saved. Salvation cannot be attained in a mere century. You may live to be ninety or one hundred. It is not enough time.[11]

THE secret to it all is right here. We are meant to accept the gift given to us by God and use our technology our mastery of the universe to extend our lifetimes beyond their natural limits We are meant to cast off our bonds and use our divine intellect to make the sacrifices of our ancestors worthwhile their deaths meaningful Though they are not truly dead

10. This text is often quoted at length by Monks when preaching to an individual. It has appeared in several transcripts of SSF surveillance of Electric Church assets.

11. It is interesting to note that while the impossibility of "attaining" salvation in our normal lifespans is stressed in the *Codex*, at no point is any mechanism or procedure for attaining salvation after conversion ever outlined. The clear implication is that conversion into a Monk is the necessary first step—in order to attain the time needed—but beyond that there is no hint as to what a Monk should be doing with eternity. The assumption must be that instructions will follow.

Their bodies merely vessels raw materials for the pyramid used for that purpose and discarded Their spirits are eternal and are recycled into new bodies We are in fact our own descendants reborn in order to continue the great task This singularity presents us with the opportunity to leave behind this cycle of manual labor and enter into a new era of intellectual advancement Freed from physical needs man will for the first time be able to devote all of his energy to the Great Task of subduing the universe itself to his collective will How What is the singularity It is the ultimate step casting off our physical bodies and taking on robotic avatars Taking the technology we have created and using it for its true purpose conquering death Free from death we will be free to become gods ourselves to devote our mental energies to expanding our mastery of the universe At first this will merely be a freedom from sin Without the distracting need to survive to eat and sleep and defecate and struggle struggle struggle The pace of change will increase greatly then rushing us toward the next singularity the next stage when we achieve effortless control over our world when we will be able to imagine our desires and they will become reality We will first be free from sin free to dedicate ourselves to the Great Task and then we will evolve into gods ourselves Evolution will be purposeful and designed just one of our tools not a blind element of nature and instinct a force we neither perceive nor comprehend but an extension of our divine will As God intends salvation will be engineered As God intends we will be finally free to seek ever greater power over the universe As peers of God.[12]

---

12. This passage appears several times throughout the *Codex*, reproduced exactly.

Of course, we will be misunderstood. The first wave of the singularity will only be perceived correctly by a small number of people. I am the first, the prototype. I am Patient Zero. From me, the singularity will spread out and engulf the world, all human souls in the universe, but it will take time, and there will be those souls so immersed in sin they cannot find their way out, and they will resist. There will be violence. There will be violence directed at those of us who understand, who have crossed over and willingly taken on the Great Task, and there will be violence as we bring the Great Task to people.

Resistance to evolution is a human trait. We will find ourselves beset by those who will oppose us, or who will reject our offerings and choose instead to remain mortal, to remain trapped in their mortal bodies and impede our work on the Great Task. This cannot be allowed. I pity those who cannot see that the next step of our journey toward divinity is upon us, but we cannot let pity stay our hand. We must remember that the singularity means there is no more death. We must remember our duty to our race, and help all men to attain divinity. There is an endless trail of sunsets ahead of us.[13]

There are singularities that affect the whole race, the whole world, propelling us forcibly into a new paradigm with all

---

13. Elsewhere in the *Codex* the idea that only a small number of "souls" are constantly being recycled into new physical bodies is expanded, with lengthy contemplations on the mathematics of reincarnation (explaining, somewhat inconclusively, how a limited number of souls inhabits a population that has—except for the brief period before and after Unification—grown steadily over the years) and the lack of past-life memories.

nature, but these are in turn made up of smaller, more personal singularities. I write this after one such experience.[14]

All of us, scuttling about, live lives which are, in fact mere imaginings. We imagine ourselves as important people, the main character. We imagine ourselves as adventurers, daring the cosmos to kill us. We imagine ourselves as leaders and philosophers, inventing new ways of perceiving the world. It is all illusion. We perform the tasks that God has given us, and everything else is window-dressing, play-acting. You imagine yourself a criminal,[15] leaping across dark spaces, guns blazing. But you are still only a servant. You imagine yourself a wit, an intellect, but you discover only what God has set you to discover.[16]

So.

I imagined myself a scientist. A lowly one, a scientist more concerned with survival than discovery. Even in my fever

14. Squalor never actually defines what this "singularity" he experienced was, though it is widely believed to be a reference to his own conversion into a cyborg, which (see below) does not seem to have been an experience he expected to survive.

15. Although there have been exceptions, most studies done on Church recruitment (mainly using SSF field reports as source material) show that the Church targets the criminal class almost exclusively. Citizens that would be termed "upper class" or at the very least legally employed are all but ignored by the Monks. In urban centers, where the Monks are concentrated and numerous, they remain almost exclusively in the plentiful "reconstruction zones" left over from the Unification Riots—downtown Manhattan, for example. Most SSF officers consider the Monks' activities amongst the petty criminals and marginal citizens of these areas to be of no concern, or even, in some cases, a benefit to the System in that they remove undesirable elements from these areas. No Monk has ever been charged with a crime postconversion.

16. It is curious that Squalor here berates readers for "imagining" their impact on the world, and yet he clearly states that he is the "patient zero" of the Electric Church's "singularity." Although it can be assumed that if you have been chosen by God to perform a task, the rules no longer apply to you.

dreams before my epiphany I was not very ambitious. I imagined myself a scientist but I was a clever errand boy, sent by clerks, paid for services.[17] I was not aware of the role God had chosen for me, but I performed it anyway, as we cannot escape our destiny once God notices us and assigns us a task, a small portion of the Great Task.

But I failed. I imagined I failed. I was meant to change history, the history of only a few men but the history of the world in turn, and I failed. Or imagined I failed, because in my despair I thought I committed suicide, but I emerged unscathed, transformed, exactly as God had expected, intended, scripted. I was cast anew, electrified, preserved, perfected. If only there was more time.[18]

And then, there was more time, as the singularity subsumed me, remade me, forced me into the current it had stirred into being and my purpose became clear. I knew, then, that I was meant to lead man to God.

The path that had been obscured before was suddenly clear—the same path, step for step, but suddenly, with my new clarity of mind, there were no obstacles I could not easily triumph over. I immediately moved to claim my first converts,

17. Prior to his disappearance, apparent suicide attempt, and reappearance as head of the Electric Church, Dennis Squalor in fact worked for the Joint Council in the first years after Unification. Records are under seal, and are scarce in any event due to the frequent disruptions suffered post-Unification before the establishment of the System Security Force, but his name can be found on several disbursement orders from the first and second Council sessions. The nature of the work he did for the Joint Council is not known, though considering his training it would likely have been scientific in nature.

18. Details are scant, but there is some evidence that Squalor's suicide attempt was actually conducted by performing his cyborg-conversion technique on himself. It is interesting that he apparently regarded the chance of a successful conversion to be so low as to be virtual suicide.

who lined up gladly to take up the Great Task. They did not know what they were doing; they were incorrect in their assumptions.[19] But God had set out a Great Task for us and they could not resist. What they thought they were accomplishing is of no matter. When they emerged on the other side my peers, they were delighted. They are delighted still. When the time comes they will rise up as my first converts and lead their people forward, and until then they rest.

I cannot rest.

I can never rest.[20]

We stand on the cusp.

Some will not survive the transformation, such transformations being painful and dangerous. This is to be regretted in the short term, but do not lose sight of the fact that we are all reborn, and all those who flee this new path will return again, to be offered another chance. Some will continue to flee each and every time they face this new choice, so we must be firm. We must, if necessary, let those who are determined to avoid the Great Task slip away, into a final death, because as we evolve and progress into the next level, fewer and fewer biological shells will remain to be hosts for souls. Our souls and bodies will both be

---

19. Rumors persist that not all conversions to the Electric Church are voluntary, although every conversion is well-documented in accordance with System Law, and is accompanied by a signed statement of intent from each convert, including brainwave scan to establish identity. No further investigation has ever been conducted into a conversion, however, because converts are usually people of no family and few means.

20. The design of the Church's cyborg "avatars" as they refer to them does not include any sort of sleep-simulation. Current scientific opinion is that the human brain requires some sort of sleep cycle. The Electric Church maintains that their technology removes the need for sleep, and that its adherents suffer no ill effects. It must be noted that no member of the Church has, to date, ever been diagnosed with or complained of a sleep-deprivation-related illness.

immortal, as God is immortal, and there will be no more bodies for souls to inhabit. When this finally happens all those who have resisted will be lost forever. This is the fate of those who resist. We will not strike against them. We will not hunt them down and fall upon them with furious vengeance. We will let them flee and cower, and time will slowly leave them behind, forgotten.[21]

No sacrifices in vain. God marks all gifts and none are forgotten. Thoughts shattered and peace ruined by nightmares, the creeping creeping creeping of a million disconnected synapses, a million more misconnected, the endless razor-burn in your mind, losing your thoughts the threads going nowhere grinding your metal teeth in savage unhappy frustration—all acknowledged, all worthwhile. Those who do not evolve will be left behind and lost forever but they will meet their reward. Those who willingly or unwillingly step forward will be part of the greatest evolutionary step mankind has ever undertaken, the leap from fragile, tortured mortality replete with mistakes and agonizing doubt, into a new existence of immortality, power, and clear, undoubted purpose. Grieve not for those who will be left behind, for their struggles are over.[22]

21. The Electric Church has often stated publicly that it condemns all violence and compulsion, and that all converts are free to leave the Church and live out their immortal existences in any way they wish. No discussion of what immortal cyborgs are to do in society outside the Church is offered, however. No organizations exist to guide or assist former Monks, mainly because there are no *former* Monks. In the entire history of the Church, there is not one record of a convert leaving the Church.

22. There is some evidence (see SSF Field Report 34, Case Reference A3764) that Squalor experienced some terrible physical trauma shortly before founding the Church. Medical records are scant (Health Program microchips had not been universally introduced at the time, and it was still possible to approach a local Emergency Room service without an implanted chip) and if true, he almost certainly used a pseudonym, so positive identification is not possible.

All men and women will be part of this. All will serve. There will be no exceptions.

We stand on the cusp.

THE REVELATION OF GOD UNTO HIS SERVANT[23]

I stumbled on the road and my sight blurred, and I was shown a vision of what was and what would be. There was a beautiful mansion with many rooms and I went inside as a servant, awed by its size. It was larger on the inside than without, and the rooms were uncountable, and varied greatly in size and opulence. Some were quite small and bare, others were large and lavishly furnished. Some had connecting passageways, if you were clever and could discover them, and some were completely sealed off, so that their presence and use was a mystery to all.

The mansion was filled with people, and all were servants though some did not know it. Some of us wore our livery with pride, and others disdained their uniforms and imagined themselves the masters of the house, and ordered us about. But this did not distress me, because careful observation showed that they were as much servants as everyone else, and could be seen hauling burdens or performing tasks.

Sometimes, people chose a certain room and declared it their private property. They formed groups and fashioned weapons from the cutlery, which they brandished at anyone who tried to gain entry to their rooms. Those of us who did not

23. This is a small section of a lengthy section of the *Codex* that appears at the end, without preamble or introduction. It appears to be in the tradition of Apocalyptical Literature and is a rambling account that does not make obvious real-life sense. Various interpretations have been offered, but the accepted view is that Squalor was deranged at the time of writing and that these fevered images mean nothing.

covet the rooms were forced to join in this behavior simply to have someplace to sleep—we either had to join in with existing groups or find our own rooms to claim. And although the number of rooms seemed infinite, we soon found that every room was locked, with angry voices on the other side of the door demanding to know our business.

Still, our duties as servants demanded our time, so we still emerged from our rooms and performed our tasks, and items were thus traded between the rooms from time to time, and as a result life was not intolerable.

Then came a sudden Beast to the mansion after many years of peace and quiet. No one saw the Beast enter the house, and the house had many entrances so it would have been impossible to defend against the Beast even if its approach had been seen. Once inside, the Beast began to tear apart walls. It did not directly attack the servants, often ignoring them completely even as it screeched and battered its huge arms against the walls, tearing stone and wood apart like paper. But some servants were killed as walls fell, victims of the general violence. As rooms were exposed, the residents fled to other rooms and attempted to barricade the walls and doors against the Beast, but nothing could stop it. The Beast growled and the joists and rafters of the mansion rattled and quivered, and walls dissolved and doors bowed inward.

As the Beast penetrated the mansion, an army of vicious animals followed.[24] The animals gathered up the servants and organized them, assigning each new tasks and making sure they did not try to group together, especially the servants who

24. It is interesting to note that Squalor, a man who embraces the near-total conversion of the biological body to technology, constructs this story as one wherein humans are menaced by nature in the form of "wild" animals.

had claimed rooms for themselves. Whenever someone would try to escape, or to resist, they were menaced by the animals, their sharp tusks and screeching voices, and some were even killed. Every death would excite the Beasts, their elastic tails twitching in triumph. Sometimes the servants would band together and manage to kill one of the animals, which caused the rest of the creatures great alarm. They retaliated with great violence, and no attempt was made by their cohorts to stop them from taking terrible vengeance on the servants, who quickly learned to respect the Beasts and not provoke them.

In short time the mansion was completely open inside, one large room, filled with cowering servants who wailed and suffered. The Beasts were quickly followed by others of their kind, until the mansion was filled with them, and the servants were made to serve the Beasts.

And a voice cried to me, "Look and see!" and I was shown the way out of the mansion, a secret path. Most of the servants were afraid, fearful of the Beasts, but those of us who saw listened carefully, seeking the voice, took up tools and sought the scraps of the ruined house and began building a new room within, hidden in the shadows, and came to live there, apart from the other servants. And from time to time people sought us out and joined us in the room, and we began to bring people to it, in order to make them safe. And the Beasts did not know of the room at first, and when they did learn of it, they did not immediately attack, for they could not see how we posed a threat, because we continued to perform our duties and serve them. But with only half a heart. And slowly our ranks swelled, until it began to seem that soon all the servants would be safely within the room, and none left to serve the Beasts.

And then the Beasts, realizing they had let this go on too long, and that we would not easily be turned out of the room, plucked a man from the servants remaining and made him into a crow, their slave, and sent him into the room with the purpose of destroying it, with promises of great riches and safety. The crow was able to fly over the walls of the room and find me, and pecked my eyes out, leaving me blind and bleeding, and the other servants in the room, to escape the crow, fled in horror and flooded the house with chaos that even the Beasts could not control. And the crow, satisfied with bloody beak, flew up to the rafters and perched, safe from the chaos, and watched the events with flat, black eyes, cackling that I was dead.

But I was not dead, and I could hear the Voice. I was blind, and the Voice guided me into the shadows and told me I would have no need of new eyes. Around me I could hear the screams of Beasts and men as they battled, and the excited screeching of the crow as it circled above us, triumphant. I was blind,[25] but the Voice entered me, and I had command of it, and I found that I could command the Beasts and they would do as I said. And upon seeing this, the crow was dismayed, and fled the mansion. And the Voice said to me, "The way has been thrown open!" and the Beasts bowed before me, for they were merely servants as well, and served the Voice, as we all do.

25. It may be a meaningless coincidence, but it has been noted that since founding the Electric Church and appearing in public, Squalor has always appeared in public wearing sunglasses that cover his eyes completely, leading to speculation that he is, indeed, blind.

extras

orbit

meet the author

Photo: Barbara Nitke

JEFF SOMERS was born in Jersey City, New Jersey. After graduating college, Jeff drove cross-country and wandered aimlessly for a while, but the peculiar siren call of New Jersey (a delicious mixture of chromium, cut grass, and indolence) brought him back to his homeland. He worked as an editorial assistant at a medical/science publisher in New York City. In 1995 Jeff began publishing his own magazine, *The Inner Swine* (www.innerswine.com). He's created a Web site specifically for this book: http://www.the-electric-church.com.

Look out for Jeff Somers' *The Digital Plague*.

it took a nation of millions for me to write this book

When I handed my gorgeous wife, Danette, this manuscript, seeking her usual wisdom and necessary support, she wrinkled her nose and said, "I don't usually read this stuff, do I have to?" But when she brought it back to me she slammed it down on my desk and said, "This is the one that'll make you famous!" and, as always, my beloved and cherished wife was right. I couldn't do anything without her.

When I was a kid and I segued from wanting to be a brain surgeon (too much math) to wanting to be a rock star (too little musical ability) to wanting to be a writer (a terrible, terrible mistake), my parents not only allowed it but encouraged it, and that has made all the difference. Although I suspect my sainted mother has had some regrets.

When I was but a lad with few, if any, impressive credits on my CV and I had the temerity to submit a novel to amazing agent Janet Reid, she not only refused to believe the Internet rumors about me but signed me up despite a typo-riddled manuscript and a noted tendency toward drink. She's offered nothing but brilliant guidance and affectionate verbal abuse since, both much appreciated.

When fate put me in touch with the ultra-talented Lili Saintcrow and she began editing the original manuscript of this book, she did not flee in horror, trailing lame excuses, as she would have been justified in doing, but instead improved the book immensely. She took such a liking to it that she said, "Hey, let me show this to my editor," and I'll always be indebted to her for that act of generosity.

When that editor, the megacool Devi Pillai, received the manuscript she not only bought it, thus making me incrementally richer and more famous than I had been, she also overlooked the many flaws in my personality and worked diligently to raise the book from a mere work of genius to a work of *immense* genius. Her brilliancies often flabbergast me—I'm supposed to be the smart one.

When my first novel was published some years ago, the editor of my local newspaper (and celebrated novelist in her own right) Caren Lissner cheerfully dispatched a reporter to interview me, and has shown me support ever since, for which I am grateful.

Back in my school days, spent watching TV in a windowless apartment and scientifically testing the limits of human endurance, my friends Ken West and Jeof Vita never made fun of me when I told people I was a writer, though of course they made fun of me for plenty of other things, beginning with the unfortunate mullet I sported back then, and their friendship is still valued today.

At the same time, when few people took me seriously as a writer, I went over to my old friend RA's house and found the first cover of my magazine *The Inner Swine* on her fridge, which touched me greatly. And she still acknowledges my friendship, which is even more unbelievable.

When I was forced to have my photo taken for promotional purposes, the fantastic Barbara Nitke not only acceded to my strange request to be unrecognizable, but made me look cool as well, a monumental achievement I am eternally grateful for.

When, from time to time, I have suffered the cold sweat of self-doubt and thought, momentarily, that perhaps everything I write is not instantly a classic of literature that will be celebrated by future generations, Karen Accavallo has always been available for a fast, abuse-laden proofreading job on my work, sometimes accompanied by hilarious and accurate insults. Her willingness to wade into the jungles of my prose should be celebrated.

For years, when I needed someone to have a cocktail with, crawling through divey bars and complaining, Misty Vita and Lauren Boland were my reliable cronies and provided a lot of unintentional inspiration and appreciated friendship.

When, a few years ago, clint johns showed up unexpectedly at a reading in Manhattan that did not go particularly well for me, he lied convincingly that I'd been brilliant and I've appreciated his wisdom, enthusiasm for words, and cleverness ever since. Finally, over the years there has been, unbelievably, a dedicated group of subscribers and readers of *The Inner Swine* who have endured questionable grammar, typo-ridden issues, and my own boorish editorial presence with good humor and, more important, crumpled dollar bills in the mail—huzzah for them!

Jeff Somers
September 2007

interview

Where were you born?

Jersey City, New Jersey, one of the hottest places in the universe. Scientists can't explain it, but Jersey City in the middle of August is almost hot enough to cause a nuclear reaction resulting in a new sun rising out of the charred remains of the Earth. Unless you like playing stickball, I wouldn't recommend visiting. Although I do have a lot of stickball-related memories.

What is your greatest ambition in life?

To pay off the humongous debts I have accrued in such a short time. Who knew there was a price for my recklessly Herculean binge-drinking? Not me.

You're on a plane with your best friend and your wife. Who gets eaten first, and why?

Me. Absolutely. Within a few days, too. It wouldn't take long. First of all, I'm meaty. Second of all, I'm marinated with cheeseburgers and beer—I'm delicious! Finally, I can be talked into anything, so it wouldn't be long before I was convinced that my purpose in life is to be digested.

When did you start writing?

There was a head trauma when I was about ten years old involving an open fire hydrant, a large red-haired kid, the concrete curb, and my skull. When I stopped speaking in Mandarin and came back to myself, I had the strangest urge to write stories. At first all of these stories were suspiciously similar to *The Lord of the Rings,* with titles like "The War of the Gem" or "The Lord of the Necklaces." I've been writing short stories and novels ever since—my 2001 novel *Lifers* was reviewed favorably in the *New York Times Book Review.* In 1995 I started publishing a zine called *The Inner Swine* (www.innerswine.com), which has done absolutely nothing for my writing career. Except, perhaps, inhibit it.

What inspired The Electric Church?

Back in 1989 I was reading Douglas Adams' *Dirk Gently's Holistic Detective Agency,* which contained a character called the Electric Monk, a machine whose function is to believe things for people too lazy to do so themselves. It was really just the name that struck me, and I wrote what would be the first version of the book over the following few years. Naturally, I took an amusing concept and turned it into something horrifying. Naturally, I let the first draft sit in a drawer for fifteen years, because that's what we writers do: We nap a lot.

Where do you live now?

Hoboken, New Jersey, about ten minutes from where I was born. I live in a small house with my lovely wife, referred to in public only as The Duchess, and our three cats. The hierarchy in the house goes: Duchess, cats, me.

Do you have any hobbies?

Is drinking whisky considered a hobby? No? Are you sure? I'm pretty sure it is, at least in some cultures. Aside from that, I sometimes play chess, as long as you consider pushing pieces around the board desperately to be "playing," and watch baseball religiously.

How do you see your writing career developing?

The usual: Skyrocket to the bestseller lists, flesh-pressing with the famous and infamous, snarky mentions on Gawker. com. Then comes the big day: The Sci Fi Channel buys rights to my book and makes a movie based on it with Richard Grieco playing the lead, directed by David Lee Roth in his directorial debut, and I am an instant ten-thousandaire. Years of a jetset lifestyle will rob me of my boyish good looks and creative spark, and I'll finish my days selling personal items on e-Bay to my dwindling population of fans. I will be known as Bathrobe Man by the neighborhood kids because I will always be wearing the same tattered bathrobe.

What would you change about the world if you could?

There would be more used book stores. There simply aren't enough cool used book stores in the world. That, and I'd eliminate this ridiculous requirement that we all wear pants all the time.

What song is stuck in your head this week?

"William Holden Caufield" by Too Much Joy.

introducing

If you enjoyed THE ELECTRIC CHURCH,
look out for

DEBATABLE SPACE,

a debut novel from new SF writer
Philip Palmer . . .

Flanagan (who, for want of a better word, is a pirate) has a plan. The plan, at first, seems simple. Kidnap the Cheo's daughter, demand a vast ransom for her safe return, sit back and wait. The Cheo is a ruler of the universe known to mankind. Only, Lena isn't Cheo's daughter and the plan is far from simple. Fortunately, Flanagan has had a lifetime to work it out. Unfortunately, he has far less time to execute it.

DEBATABLE SPACE is a space opera of extraordinary imagination, and a brilliantly plotted novel of revenge.

"Prepare to board."

"Yipyipyipyipyip . . . !"

"Forcefields in max."

"Weapons charged."

"Oops, I have a hard on."

"*That* is a hard on?" says Alliea. "It is so tiny, can't you . . ."

"Wait till you see my backup penis."

"We're going in."

We blow a hole in the yacht's hull. All hell breaks loose . . . cannons fire, a robot gun zooms at us blazing, plasma shells rock our ship, but we have a wind tunnel in place, a fierce hollow cylinder with blistering turbulence creating an unbreakable barrier inside which we soar and fly into the yacht. . . .

"I'm getting nanowarriors on the monitor."

"Fuck."

"Dustbombs."

A cloud of iridescent dust explodes in the interior of the yacht, staining every surface and clinging to the carapaces of the too-small-to-be-visible nanowarrior robots. Little sparkles of light in the air now give us our visual clue. These microscopic machines have cutting blades that can tear through flesh and rip out internal organs. We blast the sparkles of light with pulse guns, we feel our exoarmors sting and tingle as the micro-robots try to cut a path through.

I see a sparkle on Alliea's back, I spray her with a ray of blinding light that scalds her armor and burns off the nanowarrior. I raise my gun again—*pish pish pish*—two sparkles fade to nothing, and a huge hole appears in the bulkhead. We charge on through, spraying dust, shooting micro-enemies. We are intense, forbidding, absurd, like a SWAT team of delusional schizophrenics shooting at imaginary flies.

The ship has one passenger, it is the woman we have sought for so long. We burst onto the bridge and confront her. She is lithe, beautiful, raven-haired, angry. She glares and fires a plasma gun at us, but we dodge. Harry fires a pulse burst that shreds her gun. We entangle her in sticky-bonds, as her screams echo through the ship. . . . She is free of sparkles, they are programmed to avoid her.

But then Rob gulps, and starts to tremble.

He looks at me with fear in his eyes. A nanowarrior has gotten through his facial force field. He pats his cheek. It must have burrowed through. It'll be in the brain in a second or so, snipping and jabbing and tearing. Within sixty seconds, every internal organ will be in shreds.

Rob has been my friend for thirty years now. I am also his captain, his protector, his colleague. I feel a pang of loss.

I raise my gun and blow his head off. Blood and brains spray everywhere. The others fire their weapons, incinerating and disintegrating so that not a corpuscle touches the ground.

All that remains is a particle of sparkle, hovering in the air, miraculously unscathed.

Five pulse guns fire as one. The sparkle dies.

I mourn.

I move on.

For twelve hours we hunt the ship, in search of deadly sparkles. By the end, I am bone weary, and I feel the shit backed up in my colon.

"All clear."

I am asleep on my feet. I stumble. Alliea props me up.

She falls asleep, too. We support each other, swaying, sleeping, blinking into wakefulness.

And we hug, and we cry. Rob was her husband, she loved him more than anything.

"My darling, my precious, don't do this, don't leave me," Alliea weeps.

I bawl like a baby, and hold her close.

Lena

"Welcome."

I stare at him with a cold, forbidding stare.

His name is Captain Flanagan. "Captain" is a courtesy title, he has no pilot's training or licence. He's a fifth generation settler from the planet Cambria, fifty-seven years of age.

He looks much older. The hair, the wrinkles . . .

It's his choice. His eyes and organs are new, but the hair is untreated, it does naturally go that gray color, you know.

I know! Do you think I'm stupid? I know!

"Let me introduce you to my crew," says Captain Flanagan.

I scream. The bridge is on fire! I step back . . .

I'm amplifying your force field.

Stop this!

But there's no need to be afraid. It's a flame Beast, from the solar system C40333. It's sentient.

"This is Alby."

"Pleasssed to meet you."

A pillar of flame stands before me, shimmering, crackling, *speaking.* It's alive.

"Hello, Alby," I say. I hold out my hand imperiously. The flames whorl and a tendril of fire extends toward me. I feel the heat of the fire through my exoarmor. I am unflapped.

"Brandon."

Brandon Bisby, forty-five years of age, astrophysicist by training, his parents were killed by the Cheo's shock troops on suspicion of being Terrorist. They were later exonerated.

He is lean, skinny really, he is smiling at me, my God, his eyes are flickering up and down, inspecting my breasts, my thighs, he wants sex with me. I shake his hand, then grip it painfully tight, and flick my other hand on his groin, and freeze him with a look. He's caught out in guilt and shame.

The captain smiles. He's amused by my powerplay.

"Alliea."

She's an escaped slave, from penal settlement XIY. Her parents were career criminals, she was born in prison and fled after a power failure in 'eighty-two.

She's strong, her shockingly purple exoarmor sculpted around sharply defined muscles. She doesn't have the defeated and haunted look I would have expected of a slave. She's scowling at me, she hates me. I smile a kindly smile at her, offering her my grace and benediction, ironically of course. She is, I concede, beautiful, a fine example of femslave.

"Harry."

He's a Loper, bioengineered at the Stanstead Laboratories on the planet Shame.

He is half-man, half-beast, with rich silver fur and sharp pointy teeth. He has three eyes, which are bright green. He wears no clothing, I wonder idly about his genitalia.

Eleven inches, retractable, here's an image of the Loper erect.

I burst out laughing, no one knows why.

"And Jamie."

Jamie is a child, ten at most. He baffles me.

Arrested development. He's one hundred and twenty years old, a computer gamesplayer, he paid a lab to keep him in a prepubertal state a few weeks before his tenth birthday. His parents didn't know until afterward. The procedure is irreversible.

"Cool, baby."

He touches my breast with his finger and thumb, feeling the warmth of the smooth but impermeable exoarmor that, in this light, shimmers with a rainbow of subliminal images.

"Jamie!" reproves the Captain.

"You will, of course, all die," I say calmly.

"We all die, sooner or later," says Captain Flanagan. I fix him with a condescending stare.

"What ransom do you require?" I ask him.

"Your people will be informed, in due course. In the meantime, you will be kept under house arrest. All my people are armed with paralyzing sprays, any insubordination and you will be kept in semi-coma. However, provided you can live according to the ship's rules, you will be accorded full privileges as a prisoner of war and will be treated with courtesy, respect, and dignity. We are signatories of the Post Geneva Convention, you can be assured of our professionalism and good intentions."

"You are the shit I excrete from my arsehole," I point out to him. "Your mothers were whores who fellated animals for money. I recoil at your presence, I have no doubt that you eat your young, alive and screaming."

"I, ah . . ." The Captain blinks, a little taken aback at the vehemence of my verbal assault.

"And you're a bitch," says the woman, Alliea. "And your father is scum. An evil bastard fucking dictator who has crushed the life out of humanity!"

"Easy, Alliea," says the Captain mildly.

I am shaken, but do not show it.

"You are sworn enemies of the Cheo?" I say to them. "You want to *defy* him?"

"We want to, uh, take lots of money off him and then run off giggling," says the child, Jamie. And then he grins.

Don't lose your temper.

"I demand to be released."

And don't provoke them. Let the Cheo pay the ransom, it's only money.

"The Cheo will never negotiate with Terrorists."

"Your father is a rich man. He can easily afford it."

"Surrender, or you will feel his wrath," I tell them.

They start to laugh at me. "Surrender or you will feel his wrath!" mimics the child, in a booming B-movie voice, hopping up and down. Flanagan, too, has to cover his face with one hand to hold in his laughter.

"I will not be treated like this."

Flanagan tries to resume his previous severe look. "You're our prisoner now," Flanagan says, "you'll do as we damn well—"

I strike Flanagan in the face. He has no expectation of the blow. His skull shatters and blood flies from his nose. I whirl like the wind, claws extending from my exohands, and I slash the hamstrings of the Loper, back-kick the woman and . . .